The next champion in line was about Vykers' age, decked out in armor that must once have been magnificent, but had seen a few too many skirmishes. His grey-blonde hair was pulled back in a topknot, and he sported a long mustache that trailed off either side of his bare chin. The most interesting thing about him, though, were the tattoos of tears that ran from the outer corners of his eyes and down his cheeks to his jaw line. He watched Vykers' approach with an expression of ineffable sadness, a fact the Reaper found more than unsettling, as no one had ever regarded him thusly before. "If you would not fight me, your army must have others who'll take up the challenge," Vykers told the knight. As usual, the Historian translated. Within his aura, however, the other man's words were easily understood. "Alas, it is my duty," he said flatly. "And more, it is my curse." "And I am the Reaper," Vykers said. "So I have been told," the knight responded. Vykers raised his sword. "Let us see whose curse is greater.".

AS FLIES TO WANTON BOYS

IMMORTAL TREACHERY: BOOK 2

By Allan Batchelder

Acknowledgements

The list of Santa's Helpers continues to grow. Much thanks to:

Gillian Avery
Edward Batchelder
Avery Bento
Michael Bento
Kathi Fastnow-Dirske
Bobbi Dreier
Rusty Dreier
Consuelo Gonzalez
James L. Rogers
Rodney Sherwood
For my brother and sisters.

Sartre once wrote, "Hell is other people." Occasionally, though, they can be our salvation, as well

ONE

Vykers, His Sickbed, Lunessfor

Neither men nor beasts thrive in a cage. And when the man in question is something of a beast himself, the situation becomes exponentially worse. And so it was for Tarmun Vykers, the Reaper, who spent three long years confined to the same bed in the same room, eating the same meals at the same time of day, having the same hopeless conversations with the same team of A'Shea. He was sick, of course, and he was sick of *being* sick even more. He'd once been the essence of action; now, he was an invalid, laid low by a sorcerous wound to what had otherwise been an almost indestructible body. At thirty-four (at least, that was his age as near as he could reckon: he had no real memory of a birthday), he had surpassed life expectancy for most men in his profession—if one could accurately describe what that profession was. Soldier? Reaver? Destroyer? Whatever the case, Vykers would just as soon have kept doing it for another twenty years, or until someone bested him. But he had never fully recovered from the injury given him by the so-called End-of-All-Things, which galled him, no end. Yes, he had slaughtered the fiend, even as the other man seemed certain he'd done the same to Vykers. The Reaper took no solace in defeating the End's expectations, though, for as long as he remained a prisoner within this crippled body, within this damnable room, he would never be himself, again. In effect, the End *had* killed him.

Worse than all this, however, was the cloying sympathy—feigned or otherwise—that he received from all who visited him.

The pitying, regretful looks in their eyes made Vykers want to kill them, and he swore more than once that he would. Even the one A'Shea he begrudgingly cared for was too shaken by his illness—and perhaps her inability to help him—to remain at his side any longer. Without so much as a "fare-thee-well," Aoife had abandoned him to the Queen's staff and gone who knew where. Yet, there was one person who still seemed to enjoy Vykers' company and even his plight. Her Majesty made a special point of visiting every Lons Day. At her age, her cynicism made her beyond pretense: she came only to see that the greatest living danger to her throne remained...inert. Perversely, inexplicably, Vykers developed a strange respect for the woman.

Their conversations usually began like this:

"I'd have thought you'd be dead by now," the Queen would say.

"I was thinking the same of you," Vykers would reply.

"What's keeping you alive, do you think?"

"Dunno. Magic?"

"I rather suspect there's more to it than that."

"Might be. And you? What's keeping you alive?"

"Sheer cussedness."

Vykers hated it when she made him laugh; it always hurt like hell. But he figured that was why she did it: the old bitch was a bit of a sadist. Still, she brought news of the world outside his lavish and depressing cell. No gossip, she, the Queen spoke of the things the Reaper found most fascinating: wars, catastrophes and political bids for power. She even taught him a few games of strategy that simulated combat, in one way or another and, naturally, Vykers was a fast learner. But he never beat her Majesty, which was useful information in and of itself.

The Reaper did have one other constant companion in the form of his resident Shaper, Arune. "Resident," because she lived within his body, shared his brain. Most of the time, she watched and listened, like a church mouse standing on the threshold between the safety of her hole and the wider world. Other times, she was alarmingly talkative, jabbering away as if attempting to win some prize for the most words uttered in an hour's time. Often, Vykers let her ramble unopposed. She was a friend, after all, and he hadn't many. And…she was helping to keep him alive.

Another part of that task was shared by his sword, which had changed dramatically since Vykers' battle with the End-of-All-Things. It had devoured and absorbed the other man's magic blade, acquiring some of its properties in the process, making it much, much more unpredictable. Like a cat. But also larger. Whereas the Cat had once been a fairly plain-looking long sword, it was now a monstrous two-handed thing with little spurs and thorns all across the base of the blade and quillons. Sometimes, the sword's laughter woke him in the middle of the night. On other occasions, the blade mewled and groaned. Servants and A'Shea stayed away at such times, so spooked were they.

There was another blade, the cold, invisible thing with which he'd been stabbed. Vykers had no doubt his sword would eat that, as well, given the chance. But the Queen had taken it off somewhere for experimentation and the Reaper hadn't been near it since. He grinned, thinking about it, though. He could just imagine the frustration and rage felt by the End's shade at the knowledge that his secret weapon had failed to kill Vykers.

Such was the daily routine, the life of the greatest warrior the world had ever known: all past, uncertain future. Until the Queen turned up missing.

Every two days, an A'Shea and a team of servants came into change Vykers' sheets and blankets, so the fluids that seeped from his incurable wound did not putrefy or, worse, congeal and glue him in place. The whole process was excruciating. One afternoon a few days shy of Lons, the Queen's Shaper came in and brusquely sent the whole crew away. Vykers didn't know whether to feel grateful that his regularly-scheduled jostling had been halted or concerned that this cryptic fellow had appeared in the first place. He waited.

The old Burner circled the room, whispering to…someone… and touched a number of surfaces, including the door, the windows, and the wall beside Vykers' bed. The Reaper stared at the man. He was tall, gaunt and utterly bald. In fact, if Vykers had to guess, he'd say the man had never had a single hair on his scalp in his entire life. And his appearance hadn't changed one iota since Vykers first laid eyes upon him, the very same moment in which he'd first met the Queen. Though no magician himself, the Reaper had come to understand Shapers better through his long relationship with Arune and very brief but momentous acquaintance with the great Pellas. Thus, despite his obvious vulnerability, he had no fear of his visitor.

"Tarmun Vykers," the Shaper said at last, in a voice surprisingly deep. "The Queen has disappeared."

Arune? Vykers asked his own Shaper.

Listening, came her curt reply.

If Vykers had expected the man to elaborate, he was disappointed. The Queen's Shaper simply stared at him. It was most vexing, and Vykers finally gave up. "And...?" he prompted, none too gently.

The Shaper blinked. "I was gauging your reaction, assessing your..."

Vykers cut him off. "You were looking for any signs of guilt on my part," he said. "And while I'm guilty of a great many things, this ain't one of 'em."

"As I suspected. But one must be thorough." What he said next stunned the Reaper. "Perhaps you can help us find her."

"And how do you expect a dying man to be of service here?" Vykers snorted.

"Perhaps," the man said again, "it is time for you to stop dying and get back to work."

A wild thrill of hope surged through him, and Vykers fought to keep it under control. "You make it sound so simple."

The man hedged for a second, a single, fleeting instant, which told the Reaper they'd had the means to get him back on his feet for some time. Maybe even the entire time he'd been bed-ridden. Now, he was angry. "Ah," he said, "so that's how it is."

"That is how her Majesty wished it to be."

Vykers was shocked by the man's temerity. "And now you want me to help find her?"

"I understand your position," the Shaper countered, "but frankly, what choice have you got?"

Let the lion out of his cage and deal with the damage later, Arune offered, helpfully.

And there will be damage later, Vykers shot back. *I've spent three fuckin' years in this bed. Someone's gonna bleed for it.*

There followed a long, awkward silence in which neither man spoke. Finally, the Shaper continued. "I'll take your lack of argument to mean you agree."

If looks could kill. "As you say, what choice have I got?"

"So. I believe this will be a three-part mission. The first part falls to me and the other Shapers. Our task will be to determine how the Queen was abducted—I'm fairly certain that is what's happened here—and pick up the scent, as it were, of her captors. Your job will be to go after her and bring her back. A third party will have to do some snooping, for want of a better word, into connections between the Eight and Lunessfor's criminal underworld."

"The Eight?" Vykers asked, remembering his Five.

"The eight families jockeying for claim to the throne in the event of the Queen's...demise."

"And you can get me walkin' again?"

The Shaper was caught off guard by the question. "Yes," he replied, after a moment's thought. "Though it will be a test of your legendary strength, I am sure."

"Then what else do I need to know?"

"Unfortunately, this is all I have right now. I'll be back in... two days' time to finalize the details. By then, I should have more to tell you. In the meantime, we are letting it be known the Queen is ill and cannot attend public events."

"I wonder where you got that idea," Vykers mused aloud, his voice dripping with sarcasm.

Long Pete & Family, His Farm

Long Pete had never been so content. After the war, he and Mardine had been able to purchase a small apple orchard with a special dispensation from her Majesty, on the recommendation of Captain Bailis. He missed his old friends, of course— and most especially, those who had passed over: Short Pete and

Esmun Janks—but the simple joys of domesticity, marriage, and fatherhood balanced the scales. Oh, he still carried lingering guilt and sadness for the things he'd done and those he hadn't, but his wife and child had a marvelously soothing effect upon his soul.

And who knew apples were so versatile? When not tending the ripening fruit or picking the ready, he was pressing cider, of which he made both straight and hard varieties. He also helped Mardine in making apple sauce, apple jelly, apple butter, and tarts and pies of every shape and size. One could also make candy from apples, but Long found it too sweet for his taste, though children couldn't get enough of the stuff. All in all, it was humble, honest, productive work. And his neighbors for miles around appreciated him for it, just as he came to appreciate the local cheese maker, the chandler, the butcher, and others. It was amazing, really, how often actual currency was unnecessary in local transactions. Bartering was the dominant practice, and Long rather enjoyed it.

It was springtime, nature's celebration of birth, rebirth and life in general. Long had a bit of last season's harvest stashed away in the form of dried apples and canned goods, but his excitement at seeing the myriad blossoms on his trees was almost unbearable. A gentle breeze wafted their scent across his face, and Long found he could not wait to see this season's bounty. A honeybee landed on his forearm, launching him into fantasies of becoming a beekeeper, on top of everything else. Honey and apples! He'd be the most popular man in the county! Long took a deep and deeply satisfying breath of orchard air… and exhaled immediately, unsettled by the appearance of riders coming down his road.

His eyes weren't what they had once been, so it was difficult to make out the identity of his guests from afar. One thing he did know, though, was that they'd brought an unoccupied horse along with them; nothing about that suggested good news. Long took off in an awkward sprint towards his farmhouse. Whatever was coming, he needed to meet it with Mardine at his side. Once upon a time, he might've shouted something, a greeting, a warning…something. But the End-of-All-Things had taken his voice. Years of attention from various Shapers and A'Shea had given him back some expression: he could croak in a dry, raspy monotone that made him sound much more dangerous than he actually felt. Shouting and singing, however, were lost to him forever, well outside the three or four note range of his voice. Approaching the house, he heard his daughter's laughter, his favorite sound in the world. His wife was murmuring something, as well, but her deep, giant's voice was so low it made words indecipherable at this distance. Allowing himself a moment to catch his breath and calm down, Long paused just outside the door. Esmine was cheerfully babbling something about a mama dolly and a dada dolly. The way she said "dada dolly" over and over almost made Long laugh out loud. With practiced nonchalance, he turned the doorknob and entered.

Esmine and Mardine looked over simultaneously; the toddler broke into the widest, sweetest of smiles. Mardine could tell in an instant something was bothering her husband. "We're going to have company," he crackled, as if that explained everything. With everything they'd been through, perhaps it did. In one massive arm, the giantess scooped up the family cat, which had been sleeping quite comfortably on an old quilt. In the other, she swept up her daughter. "Mama and dada need to talk," she told her daughter. "Be a good little thing and play with kitty in the back room 'til we're done." With that, she deposited kid and cat in Esmine's bedroom and shut the door. When she turned back around, she was not surprised to see her husband had already retrieved his sword. Without a word, she produced a massive meat cleaver from a cupboard near the ceiling.

"What do you figure?" she asked Long.

"No idea. But they've got an extra horse. That ain't good news."

"Isn't," Mardine corrected.

"What?" Long asked, bewildered.

"Isn't good news," she clarified. "Don't want the baby growing up talkin' like a mercenary."

Long Pete studied his wife's face. It was easily as large as a watermelon, with two little dark eyes stuck in it like currents in a massive scone. She had a riot of barely contained auburn and red hair and a wide, generous mouth. Her nose was actually quite normal, considering her size. Long loved that face beyond all sense or reason. If anyone could be truly 'madly in love,' it was he.

Outside, the sound of horses shuffling to a standstill and mounted men landing in the dirt gave proof Long's visitors had arrived. He glanced again at his wife. A knock came at the door.

"Sergeant Major Peter Fendesst?" a familiar voice called out from the other side.

Fuck. Long heaved a sigh of resignation and opened the door. Major Bailis and a second man he didn't recognize stood beyond the threshold. Further out, he spied three other men, all soldiers.

"May we come in?" Bailis asked and proceeded to do so without waiting for a response. "Ah, hello. Mardine, isn't it?" he inquired of the giantess.

"You've a good memory," she replied.

"Well, it's not every day you encounter..." Here, he trailed off. He'd wandered into potentially dangerous waters and wasn't entirely sure how to save himself. "Such a striking woman," he finished with a flourish.

Mardine stared at him, unamused.

Long stared at him, as well. Bailis hadn't changed much—a little more iron in his beard, a touch more weight around his midsection. Long cut to the chase, "I'm guessing you're not here to buy apple products, Captain," he croaked.

Bailis had to lean forward to catch all of it. "It's Colonel, now. They tried to kick me up even higher, but I wasn't having any of it. Nobody really likes a general." Bailis said. "Any chance of a bit of ale or some such? You know how the road gets after a while..."

"It's an apple farm. I got cider and hard cider," Long managed.

"Hard would be most welcome."

"I'm sure," Long grumbled as he went off to fetch it. When he returned with several mugs brimming with cider, he noticed the tension in the room hadn't diminished any. "This's for you and them others," he explained, tilting his jaw towards the door.

"For you and the others," Mardine said. Funny thing about men, the more threatened they felt, the more primitive their language became. Long was infinitely more articulate than the grunt he sometimes pretended to be.

Bailis accepted his mug with effusive praise and took a long, deep pull. "Bloody brilliant!" he declared afterwards, before immediately feeling he might've expressed himself differently.

Long cleared his throat, made his best effort. "Like I said, Colonel: I'm guessing you're not here for apples."

Bailis cast about for somewhere to sit, realized he hadn't been invited and decided he might as well come clean. "Her Majesty requires your services again."

Which explained the extra horse.

"Her Majesty wouldn't know me from a hole in the ground," Long retorted.

"She gave you the gold for this little farm of yours."

"Because you requested it, and I'm grateful. Eternally grateful. But…"

"She needs someone with your experience and skills."

Long laughed at this, startling his daughter in the next room. "What's funny, dada?" He heard her call out. Mardine popped into the back room, leaving Long alone with the two men.

"No offense, Colonel, but that sounds like a load if ever I've heard one."

The Colonel cast a sideways glance at his companion and spoke to Long in a near whisper. "The Queen's gone missing, and we need an experienced man with no connections inside the city to investigate certain…less-than-savory parts of town, to see what kind of information he can turn up."

The Queen, missing? It hardly seemed possible. Long was speechless, so Bailis continued.

"It's likely one or more of the eight families are involved. Sure, we've got spies. But so does everyone else in Lunessfor. That's why our man has to come from outside the city."

Long went and retrieved a small keg and another mug. He refilled Bailis and the soldier's mugs and poured one for himself. "Well, what do you think? She's been kidnapped? Or do you think she might have finally been assassinated."

Bailis downed the rest of his cider and helped himself to seconds. "Our Shapers tell us she's not dead...yet," he added portentously.

Long rubbed at his jaw. "Won't these spies see right through me if I ride into the city at your side?"

"Got any more of those?" the Colonel asked, pointing to the keg.

"Yes..." Long replied, uncertain where this was going.

"So, the boys and I pretend like we traded away our spare horse for some cider. We leave in an hour, you leave tomorrow. Meet your crew at Teshton."

Teshton was a small town a half day's ride from the Capitol. Long wasn't sure he'd heard correctly. "My crew?"

"Certainly. You didn't think I'd toss you into the snake pit without a few allies, did you?"

"Who'd you have in mind?"

"I'm working on gathering some of the fellas from your old unit—the actor, that dense fellow with the odd birthmark, Sergeant Kittins, and that crazy Yendor. I reckon he knows his way around a dive or two."

"What do you mean, you're 'working on'?" Long demanded. "You knew I would say yes, did you?" It was hard to have one's anger taken seriously when one sounded like a sock puppet.

"Look, you're not a self-absorbed ass. You actually care. Lotta men would probably say 'stuff the Queen.' But I know you recognize what's at stake, here."

Mardine chose that moment to creep back into the room. Apparently, their daughter had gone down for her nap. In no time, she sized up the situation and frowned mightily at her husband. Long fumbled to explain himself before Bailis came to his rescue.

"The Queen's missing," he said. "We think Long can help find out how that happened, if not where she's gone."

"Stuff the Queen!" Mardine said, causing her husband to blush furiously. "We've got a life, here, and a good one. We've got a beautiful child that needs her Da."

"Love, the Queen gave us this life, here." Long reminded her.

"You earned it! We earned it."

"And I'm sure her Majesty will be equally if not even more appreciative of your services this time, too," Bailis tossed in.

Mardine began peppering the Colonel with questions. "No combat, then?"

"None. In fact, we'd prefer it that way."

"No extended service?"

"No, this is a one-time circumstance."

"You'll give him whatever he needs for safety's sake?"

"Whatever he needs. This is the Queen we're looking for, after all."

"And he'll be fairly recompensed for his time and the danger?"

"More than so."

"How long will he be gone, do you estimate?"

"I'll not lie to you, Mardine. There's no way to know."

"Tell me everything."

At the end of an hour, Bailis had somehow managed to convince the giantess, a much harder sell than Long.

"So, you've really got the old gang back together?"

Bailis beamed. "Aye."

"But no Shapers, no A'Shea?"

"Hard as it is to believe, you're better off without them. Everyone can smell their magics a mile away. You walk into a strange tavern reeking of arcane energies, you'll raise suspicions in no time."

It made sense, but Long didn't like it. "But the other side will have Shapers."

"Maybe. Probably. And they'll underestimate you as a result."

"That's your plan?" Mardine asked, incredulous. "He's s'posed to succeed by being underestimated?"

Bailis shrugged. "It's worked before."

"I don't like it! And how am I supposed to get by without my husband's help?"

The Colonel extended his right hand, from which a small but heavy-looking purse dangled. "Hire on a couple of stout hands. Those former thralls are always looking for work. And

Long here'll be back before you know it, most likely before harvest!"

Long was a little taken aback by how easily Mardine accepted the money and passed him off into Bailis' hands. At the same time, a small part of him was excited at the prospect of returning to action and seeing his old mates again. Or most of them, anyway. As Mardine and the Colonel continued to work out the details, Long wondered how his old friends had changed over the last three years.

Yendor, a Tavern

"I might have a drinking problem," Yendor Plotz said to himself, upon waking yet again in a pool of his own vomit. "Or, belike it's a vomit problem, 'cause I got no trouble drinking. Contrariwise, I got no trouble barfing, neither." Where was he, he wondered for a long moment. Grainy wooden floor with islands of straw to soak up the likes of...well, what he'd just done. So, he was indoors. In an inn, tavern or pub.

A filthy, wet mop landed on his face—foh! Yendor gagged, coughed and pushed the thing away.

"Awake yet, Princess?" The barman was a merciless son-of-a-bitch. "'Cause you need to be cleaning that mess off the floor, 'fore we open again for business."

Yendor used the mop as a crutch, in order to rise to his feet. "I hear ya, man, I hear ya."

"Hell of a bouncer you are, Plotz! If I'da known what a drunkard you are, I'da never hired ya!"

"I fought in the big one, 'gainst the End-of-All-Things," Yendor whined, defensively.

"Aye, aye, so you say," the bartender quipped.

Yendor fished something out of his collar. "I got this here medal from General Branch!"

The bartender yawned. "I seen it, I seen it a thousand times. But what've ya done since then but drink yourself stupid? Not that ya weren't stupid to begin with..."

Ouch. Yendor took stock: his legs shivered and shook, his stomach rumbled and gurgled most unpleasantly, and his head raged like a demon's forge. In other words, he felt as he normally did, first thing in the morning.

The door banged open and the sound of heavy boots rang out on the floor. "We ain't open, yet!" Yendor heard the bartender say.

"You Yendor Plotz?" a rough voice asked him.

"What's the dumbshit done now?" the bartender yelled.

Yendor struggled to focus his eyes on the stranger, a soldier of some sort. "Aye, I'm Plotz."

"Come with me," the man ordered, taking him by the arm.

"Whoa, whoa, whoa! Who's gonna clean up that puke?" the bartender asked.

The soldier produced a silver royal from somewhere, walked over to the vomit and dropped it in. "You are," he told the bartender. "Let's go," he said to Yendor. "You're done working here."

Spirk, at Home

It had been days since anyone had come by his hovel for help. Must've been that new Shaper on t'other side o' town. Spirk wasn't a Shaper himself, understand, but somehow he'd discovered a trick or two since D'Kem's sacrifice. In truth, he was fairly certain his recent skill with tricks had been the old Shaper's last gift to him—D'Kem's *legacy*, if that was the right word. So it was that he spent day after day, sitting and waiting for folks to come to him with little problems—a knot they couldn't untie, a grain of sand they couldn't dislodge from an eye, an item they'd lost and wished to find again. Always, they'd offer Spirk something in trade. Sometimes it was coin (usually a shim), other times it was food, drink or something else of use.

He did nothing with such rewards in mind, however, but because he truly enjoyed helping, being a helpful person. Time was, he'd fancied himself a soldier of sorts. How wrong he'd been. He hated killing. Doing it, seeing it, being around it. It made him feel so worthless and afraid. He might have gone home, surely. His Da might finally have been proud of his son, the victorious soldier, coming home from war. But Spirk didn't want his Da to be proud of him for killing, even in self-defense. Often, Spirk wished he'd been given the gifts of an A'Shea; whatever he'd gotten from D'Kem didn't seem as useful when his visitor had a broken leg or serious burn. What did it matter if he could start a candle burning, if he could not extinguish the burning in an innocent child's skin? And, just lately, fewer and fewer folk wanted what little he did have to offer.

At last, a knock—a wonderful, beautiful knock!—came on his door. Rising from his cot, Spirk called out "How can I help you?" and unlatched the door. Stepping outside, he stopped in his tracks. Captain Bailis and another man he'd never seen before stood waiting for him.

"Nessno, isn't it? Spurge Nessno?" Bailis asked.

"Spirk." Spirk corrected, as he had a hundred thousand times before.

"Yes, yes, Spirk. Unusual name." Bailis observed. "But then, you're an unusual fellow, so I suppose it's apt."

"Apt? Apt to what?"

Bailis hemmed and hawed a moment before going on. "Young man…" He began.

"Not so young, any more."

The Captain seemed to be getting flustered. "Right. Spirk Nessno, the Queen requires your service."

Were those the most inspiring, delightful, magnificent words Spirk had ever heard? It certainly seemed so, to him. "The Queen? Her Majesty?"

"Uh, yes, her Majesty, the Queen."

Suddenly, Spirk became suspicious. He'd been fooled too often before. "I don't believe you," he exclaimed, petulantly.

Bailis looked at the other soldier, as if seeking advice. "What?" he asked Spirk. "Why?"

"Because," Spirk explained wearily, as if talking to a very small child, "she's never even met me, has she?"

Again, Bailis struggled to find solid ground in this conversation. "I don't…" He stammered. "I mean…how should I know? Has she?"

"Well, I think I'd know if I met the Queen, wouldn't I?"

With a supreme effort at self-control, Bailis tried again.

"Listen, son, the Queen—the legendary Virgin Queen, the mightiest ruler in the land—has need of your services. Will you come willingly, or must we arrest you in her name?"

"Arrest me?" Spirk squeaked at the top of his voice. "Arrest me? All I did was answer me door!"

Bailis smacked him over the head with a small truncheon he'd pulled from his belt, and when Spirk collapsed to the ground, he and his partner hefted him onto their shoulders.

"Thought I'd lose my mind if I let him go on another ten seconds!" Bailis told his companion.

Kittins, Lunessfor

Drafting now-Captain Kittins was a simpler affair, as the man had remained in the Queen's army and continued to work his way up the ranks.

"Captain," Bailis said to him one afternoon, "I've an assignment for you that requires the utmost discretion."

"Me, sir? Discretion?" the big man said. "You know that ain't exactly my strong point, right?"

"In this, I think it will be." Bailis looked around to ensure no one else was within earshot and drew closer. "The Queen's disappeared."

Kittins looked around, himself. "Disappeared? You mean, like, 'wandered off,' or 'kidnapped'?"

"That is part of what we need you and your...teammates... to determine."

The Captain looked askance at his superior upon hearing the word 'teammates.' "Who'm I gonna be stuck with now?" he asked, with more than a hint of irritation in his voice.

"Some old friends, actually." Bailis replied. "Long Pete and some of his gang."

"That's a problem, right there. That Long Pete and me are the same rank now. Who's in charge?"

Bailis paused, long enough for Kittins to take the hint.

"All due respect, sir, I need to step away to do some cursing," Kittins muttered through clenched teeth.

The Colonel nodded, and the Captain walked about fifty

yards away, where he began unleashing a torrent of the most heartfelt, filthy and imaginative profanity Bailis had heard in years. After some time, Kittins returned.

"When and where do we start?" he asked.

Rem, at the Theater

The actor, Remuel Wratch, was equally easy to find, but would like as not be harder to persuade, as, currently, he was starring in a dramatic production of the Vykers/End-of-All-Things clash, a hugely popular work entitled *The Entirely True Account of the Mighty Reaper's Heroic Victory Over the Heinous Tyrant, The-End-of-All-Things*. Bailis hadn't seen the show, but if its length was proportional to its title, he didn't think he could bear to sit through it, no matter how exciting it was alleged to be.

Now, whereas most companies of actors sought out patrons amongst the nobility, Wratch & Company did not, choosing instead to maintain its autonomy and, thus, ability to write about and/or say virtually anything onstage the actors damned-well pleased. Owing their allegiance to none (save her Majesty, of course), they were in some ways the most honest company of actors to be found anywhere. And it was all made possible by Remuel Wratch's completely coincidental presence at the heart of the Vykers/End-of-All-Things conflict, which had rendered him a hero and celebrity of sorts throughout the land.

Which made gaining access to him after a show somewhat challenging, but the pair of soldiers muscled through the crowd of fans and pushed their way into Rem's attention.

"Can I help you, gentlemen?" he asked, looking up from his conversation with an adoring and comely female admirer.

"Yeah. We need you to come with us. Queen's business," the older of the two soldiers said.

If Rem felt even a moment of apprehension, he hid it well, taking full advantage of a situation that might have been damaging to his career and turning it into something that lent him even further gravitas. "The Queen? Of course, of course!" Rem replied in a debonair manner, "I'm always available to help her Majesty in any way possible."

The old soldier was unimpressed. "Actors!" he groaned to

his companion. "What in the Seven Hells was Mahnus thinking when he created them?" To Rem, he said, "Come along, then. Time's a-wasting."

"A moment, please," Rem pleaded. He turned to another of his company and whispered instructions in the man's ear. The other actor, in turn, nodded and hurried away towards the wagons that housed the company's costumes, props, stage and performers.

"I'll see you anon!" Rem called after the fellow. To the soldiers, he said "Lead on!" in his bravest, most resonant voice.

Vykers, His Sickbed

"That's your plan to get me back on my feet?" Vykers asked, disbelief clear in his tone. The Queen's Shaper held a sort of broad girdle, with two gently glowing cones affixed to the inside, roughly where Vykers' wounds would be when worn. "And those...those pointy things are, what, little magic stoppers?"

"Essentially, yes."

"So you're gonna cork me, like a hogshead o' liquor?"

"Yes."

"It'll never work," the Reaper scoffed. "And if it does, it'll still hurt like a bitch!"

The Shaper looked amused. "I was told you had no fear of pain."

"I've been in pain for three years, friend. Whatever you heard don't tell half the truth. But I can't walk much if I'm doubled over in agony."

The other man pursed his lips. "This garment was some time in the making. No expense, no effort was spared to alleviate your pain and contain your wounds."

"But you still can't heal 'em," Vykers said, hoping for contradiction.

"No," the Shaper replied softly, dropping his eyes.

Vykers pulled himself up into a sitting position, to the obvious consternation of the attending A'Shea. "Let's try this fucker out, then."

"You have such a way with words, Reaper," the Shaper said wryly.

"Don't I? I'm a regular poet of profanity."

The Shaper, the A'Shea and Vykers worked together to wrap the girdle around his midriff and carefully place the cones in the proper positions, ever-so-gingerly setting them into the wounds in the Reaper's gut and back. With a sudden yell of defiance, Vykers yanked the girdle taught and cinched it closed.

And then fell over backwards onto his bed, breathing like a battle-weary bull.

"Huh," he said after several seconds had elapsed. "Doesn't hurt half so bad as it should."

"As I said..." the Shaper began.

Vykers interrupted, "I think I can stand on my own, now." Again, he took his time rising to his feet, adjusting his stance, breathing. "I don't see anything dripping out," he said of his now-covered wounds.

"And won't, I expect. But perhaps you should sit in a chair for a while, work your way up to standing and walking."

The Reaper wanted to argue, but he had too much respect for the damned hole that burned through him. If it could be beaten, he would beat it. But it would take time. More time. "Thing is," Vykers said, "aren't we in sort of a hurry, here? For all we know, the Queen's bein' drawn and quartered as we speak, which ain't an entirely unpleasant image, now I think on it."

The mage shook his head. "She's in no imminent danger."

And just how does he know that? Arune prodded.

"And just how do you know that?" Vykers asked.

"Her Majesty and I have had decades to arrange every sort of precaution imaginable. The other Shapers and I have laid spells upon spells. We'd know the second a single drop of her blood was spilled. Indeed, in the event of her death, several of us would be transported to the scene immediately, prepared to dispense justice without hesitation or qualm."

"Damn," the Reaper marveled, "you Shapers sure can talk."

The other man's jaw snapped shut with an audible pop. Apparently, Vykers had offended him.

"The old battle axe has disappeared or been taken, and you can't tell me how it happened or where she's gone, but you are certain she ain't been harmed. That about it?"

The Shaper nodded, a most dour expression on his face.

"So," Vykers said aloud, more to himself than anyone else, "that leaves, what? Ransom? Somebody wants her money but not her throne? That don't make sense. And if this is about the throne," he went on, "why not just kill her and get her out of the way?" Vykers reached out for a goblet of wine, which the A'Shea obligingly put into his hand. "Maybe her captors just want to humiliate her. Get in line!" he said to himself. "But why go to all the trouble of kidnapping her when there's easier ways to embarrass her?" Suddenly, Vykers stared over at the Shaper. "You got answers to any of this?"

"I didn't realize you were speaking to me," the man complained. "And, no, I've got no answers yet. Except…"

Vykers nearly bolted up out of his chair. "Except???"

"She's somewhere southeast of here and moving farther away every hour."

"Shapers," the Reaper hissed, as if that explained everything. "So there is a something of a rush to find her, after all."

"If her captors continue in that direction, they'll reach the southern coast in a week or so."

That's bad, Arune whispered.

Why? Vykers demanded.

Magic can't travel over salt water.

First I've heard of it.

Well, Arune said sheepishly, *it's sort of a secret we like to keep from you non-Shapers.*

I can see why. But wait: I've been a-sea before. Every ship I've been on's had Shapers.

Of course. We can use magic aboard, we just can't…He's watching us.

Vykers looked over and noticed that, yes, in fact he was being scrutinized by the Queen's Shaper.

"We've got scores of spies all up and down the coast," the man said without preamble. "If they board a ship, we'll be following them, even before you get there. We need only ensure you do get there."

Grimacing only slightly, Vykers stood. "I'll get there."

Long & Company, Teshton

Teshton had three inns and two taverns, the cheapest of which, Long reasoned, was the most likely to attract his former colleagues—especially Yendor. At the same time, being cheap, it was also the last place he'd find any of the nobles he was about to investigate. Long sighed. The nature of his new mission would probably drag him through every seedy dive in the realm. It would bring weeks and weeks of sour ale, stale smoke and victuals of questionable origin or substance. He'd gotten himself into decent shape working the apple farm, living off its bounty and basking in the fresh air. That was all about to be tossed on the muck heap, and Mardine would surely scold him until their daughter had grown and moved away.

The cheapest place, according to a passing merchant, was a tavern called "Gangrene & Sons." Long Pete laughed himself into exhaustion upon hearing that name and decided he liked the place already, sight unseen. When, after several minutes of walking, it at last became sight seen, he liked it no less. Gangrene & Co. was a one-storey affair, with a roof that sagged slightly on the western side. A small, feeble stream of smoke groped its way upward from the tavern's chimney. There were shutters in front that might have been opened to the street, but for some reason remained closed. All-in-all, the place looked secretive and dilapidated, not unlike the Shaper D'Kem before the old man had revealed his true identity. Thinking of D'Kem brought a warm smile to Long's face: the man had been so much better, so much greater than Long had given him credit for. It was one of the defining lessons of the Captain's life.

It was a beautiful spring afternoon and Long was loathe to step out of the air into a darkened, claustrophobic room, but distasteful tasks never got any easier through stalling, so in he went.

And was, again, reminded of D'Kem and the lesson he'd learned from the Shaper. Gangrene & Sons was spotless and, behind the obligatory odor of wood smoke, smelled faintly of strawberries. Long glanced about in confusion. There were eight to ten tables, though only three were occupied at the moment. A bar ran the length of the room's eastern end, and behind it stood an enormous brute of a man, obsessively cleaning his mugs, flagons and other drinking vessels.

"Help you?" the colossus called out.

"Uh, yes." Long croaked. He walked over to the bar, so the barkeep could hear him more easily. "Got any cider?"

The giant's doughy face lit up. "Have I got cider?" he repeated, almost laughing. "I've got hard and straight. From three diff'rnt types o' apples and one blend."

"That's quite an inventory for a place like this." Long rasped.

"What do yer mean, 'a place like this'?"

Long had stepped in it again! "No offense, friend. I just meant the...uh...town. Yes, that's a wide enough selection for the whole town."

The dodge worked, and the big man beamed with pride. "That's the point, ain't it?"

"Well," Long confessed, "I'm a little confused. I asked a passing merchant for the...least expensive...drinking establishment, and he sent me here." He was worried he'd dug his own grave, but the barkeep's response again surprised him.

"I don't like to serve rich folk, it's true. Try to scare 'em away, every chance I get."

Long looked at the man as if suddenly turned into a hedgehog. "Really?"

"Rich men destroyed me Da, and his, before that. I'll have no truck with 'em. And if you offer the best you got to the common man, why, he's much more grateful." The huge man swept an arm across the room. "This here's a place for the average fella. A safe haven, if you will."

Delight crept up on Long and surged throughout his body. "Would it be too much trouble," he asked, "for a small sampler of each of your ciders."

The barkeep's big, goofy smile was infectious. "No trouble a 'tall," he said. "In fact, I think I'll join ya!"

In no time, the man set four teacups of hard cider (three single-apple ciders and one blend) and four straight ciders. Long was astonished to discover one came from his own orchard, but he kept that to himself, so as not to endanger the barkeep. His own cider held up well, he thought, though the golden apple cider was magnificent. He wondered if he could find the source and arrange to swap seeds with the farmer responsible. It might be fun to try out a new crop.

Out of nowhere (as was often the case), the barkeep asked "So, what happened to your voice, then?"

Long would have loved to tell the truth: the End-of-All-Things did this to me. What a story it was. Yet, the story marked him in a way, like his cider, that endangered his mission and those about him. "Had the croup for nigh onto a year as a tyke. Never got my full voice back." He hated lying to the man; he liked him already a great deal more than most men he'd met in the past ten years. Thinking this reminded him of his intended reunion, and he stole a quick look around the tavern. Nobody he recognized, thankfully. Long carefully, deliberately placed a noble onto the counter-top. "I ain't rich," he said, dumbing his speech down a bit, "but I do appreciate good service, and I'm mightily impressed so far! Mind if I set by the fire a while?"

"Not a 'tall," the man replied, sweeping the noble into his apron. "Make yourself at home!"

It was an auspicious start to what Long fully expected to be another nerve-wracking and dangerous adventure. Hells, "adventure" wasn't even the right word for it; "Ordeal" was better.

"Look," he said to his new friend, "I'm expecting to meet a few fellows. I'm hoping it's here, but it might be elsewhere. If they show, give me the best you've got, and I'll make it worth your while."

"It'd be my pleasure," the big man answered.

Kittins was first to show. Long had nodded off in his chair, and heard a thump nearby that suggested someone throwing himself into a seat. He sat up and saw the gruff soldier staring at him, his eyes peering out through a mangled face. He'd gotten that damage in the same fight that cost Long his voice.

"Mighta known you'd be first," Long lied. In truth, he'd been expecting Yendor since he walked through the door.

"I like to scout a place before anybody else arrives," Kittins revealed. No surprise, there.

"What'll it be?" the barkeep asked, appearing out of nowhere.

Kittins was impressed. "You're a big fella," he said.

"And you're a brawler. I can tell by the look of ya."

"And?"

"We'll have none o' that, here," the barkeep warned him. "Now, what'd you like?"

"Tankard of ale, any kind o' meat and potatoes."

"Stew work for ya? It's full o' good beef, I'll warrant."

"Sure. Stew sounds good," Kittins said.

"Be right back," the barkeep said.

"I rather like him," Long croaked.

Kittins thought about saying something shitty, mean. Decided to go the easy route. "Do ya, now? Weird kinda name for a place, though, ain't it? Gangrene & Sons?"

Long hadn't expected the man could read. His thoughts must have been clear in his expression, because Kittins awkwardly admitted, "I been taking lessons, these past couple o' years. Always wanted to read about the great battles, and now I can."

Long nodded. Made perfect sense to him.

Spirk arrived before Kittins' meal, looking, as usual, more than a little lost. "Uh...Cap'n?" he asked Long. "Oh, hi Sergeant," he said to Kittins. "Didn't see you at first."

"I'm a Captain now, too," Kittins answered gruffly.

"So..." Spirk ventured, "who should I ask for permission to sit down?"

Kittins' left hand shot out, and he pulled Spirk down onto the nearest chair. "Just sit," he commanded.

The barkeep brought Kittins' ale and stew and asked Spirk "and for you?"

"Well..." Spirk began, "Whadda ya got?"

The barkeep took a deep breath and launched into a lengthy and impressive recitation of options, when Kittins cut him off.

"Just bring him the same's me."

"The same," the barkeep said. "Sounds good." And off he went.

Kittins looked askance at Spirk. "You look diff'rnt somehow."

"I do?" Spirk asked, concerned.

"Older, thinner..." Kittins fumbled for the words.

"Wiser," Long offered, in a crackling whisper.

"You can talk!" Spirk said, amazed.

"After a fashion," Long agreed, "though it ain't easy or fun."

"Makes it easier for me, though," Kittins said belligerently.

Rem and Yendor came through the front door together, both already three sheets to the wind. Surprise, surprise!

"General Long Penis!" Yendor called out at the top of his voice, alarming everyone else in the room.

When they reached the table, Kittins pulled them down into seats even harder and faster than he had Spirk. *Good*, thought Long, *let him be the enforcer. It's not a job I relish, anyway.*

"You all hear how loud I'm talking?" Long asked in his brittle voice, checking to make sure everyone was paying attention. "That's as loud as any o' you need to be for this conversation."

Except for Kittins, the group nodded.

The barkeep approached with Spirk's meal, and Kittins said "I guess it'll be the same all around."

The owner looked to Long for confirmation, and Long countermanded his co-Captain. "Nah," he breathed, "have a little fun with it. I'll pay for the lot, whatever you bring."

"Thought you said you wasn't rich!" the barkeep teased.

"I ain't. But there's no money better spent than on good food and drink."

This was greeted with "hear, hear"s and "aye"s all around, which clearly delighted the barkeep. He seemed lighter of step as he headed off towards his kitchen.

"Now," Long breathed, "We were all given one piece of the same document—a puzzle, like. It's time to put those pieces on the table and see what we've got."

Aoife & Tadpole, an Abandoned Village

Three years, and Tadpole still dogged her every step. "When you gonna teach me some magic?"

Aoife set down the water pail and sighed. "You," she said, touching the tip of his nose with her right index finger, "don't need magic. You're far too tricky as it is." Tadpole frowned.

"And besides," Aoife said, "As I've already explained countless times, it doesn't work that way. We either have the talent for it, or we don't. Even if I taught you the words and gestures, nothing would come of it."

Tadpole, as expected, was having none of it. "So, teach me anyways. For fun, like."

The A'Shea paused, looked about, took stock of her surroundings. The desolate and devastated town she'd stumbled into three years earlier had given rise to a forest—small, but spreading every spring. Buildings sprouted moss, ferns, toadstools and more. Onto the bones of the town's old inn, Shreds and Patches, a new skin of green, lush life had taken root. Streets had been taken over by nameless grasses. Enormous trees filled the spaces between former homes and businesses. It was, Aoife thought, wonderful and strange—and wondrous strange. And like the town, the children who'd survived its destruction at the hands of Aoife's brother had also grown abundantly and wild.

"I hate it when you do that," Tadpole said.

"What?"

"Go away in your head, get all thinky."

Thinky. Aoife smiled despite her best efforts against it. "Don't you ever go away in your head, as you put it? Don't you ever think about things outside of this very moment?"

"Might be," Tadpole allowed, "but when you go away in your head, takin' your body with you ain't far behind."

Aoife put on her most serious expression. "Tadpole," she said, "you know how much I care about you and the others. But I do have a larger calling, at times, that requires me to leave once-in-a..."

They both heard the sound of horse hooves clattering on what remained of the road into town.

"Damn it all!" Tadpole hissed.

"Language!" Aoife scolded him.

"To hells with language. This is just what I said. You wait and see if it ain't!"

Sure enough, around the corner of the nearest house-cum-thicket rode a single A'Shea on a chestnut-colored horse.

Tadpole kicked angrily at a nearby molehill and stomped off, muttering and cursing to himself. When the other A'Shea drew near enough, Aoife recognized her as one of those who tended to Tarmun Vykers, in the Queen's castle. For a moment, her breath caught in her throat and she felt a thrill of panic: Vykers must be dead. Why did the thought bother her so? She wouldn't allow herself to ponder the question, opting instead to meditate until her visitor was close enough to speak. Sixty heartbeats later, the woman arrived.

"Good e'en to you, Sister," she said, dipping her chin in respect.

Aoife straightened, dusted her robes off. "And to you," she replied. "You come with news?"

"I do," the other agreed. "The Queen has not been seen in days and no one can locate her."

How unpredictable was life! That Aoife should feel relief at this potentially devastating news, when she'd been fearing the worst for the Reaper.

"And," the other A'Shea continued, "Tarmun Vykers is back on his feet and preparing to leave the Queen's castle in search of her."

Shapers and A'Shea alike are trained to anticipate and handle the unexpected. These tidings, however, left Aoife gasping for air. The Queen missing and Vykers roused from his sickbed to find her? The situation must be dire, indeed. "But," Aoife protested, "he's not up to that sort of challenge. The man can barely roll over without losing consciousness. Walking or riding a horse could easily kill him!"

"The Queen's Shaper has devised some sort of truss that seems to have helped in this," the other woman said. "I've not been able to examine it, myself, so I can't speak to its nature or effectiveness, but I have seen Vykers limping through the hallways. He is walking again."

Which was impossible, of course. But then, everything about the man was impossible. Why should this be any different? "I need to be...I need to go to him," Aoife said. "I need to make sure he doesn't suffer a setback."

"We thought you might feel that way," the other A'Shea

responded. "I would be honored with your company on the return trip to Lunessfor."

"Thank you. I need but a few moments to gather my necessaries, and I'll join you."

Though Aoife searched and searched, she could not find Tadpole in order to say goodbye and assure him of her eventual return. Sometimes, she reflected, it is better to let folks alone with their anger. Toomt-La was no easier to find, but only because, as the years had gone by, his natural camouflage had gotten more and more extreme. Now, he was virtually indistinguishable from foliage, unless he wished to seen and noticed by humans.

When he spoke, his voice was like the creaking of trees and the rustling of leaves. "And so," he said, before she could even open her mouth, "another ordeal beckons. Go, go, tend to your Reaper. Again, so much depends upon his every action."

Aoife wanted to question him further, but Toomt-La drifted into silence and, she assumed, sleep, a sleep such as humans have never known.

Vykers, the Queen's Castle

"What's your name, anyway, Burn?" Vykers finally asked the Queen's Shaper.

"Cindor," the man said.

"Cinder?" Said Vykers. "That some kind of Burner joke?"

"Not 'Cinder'; Cindor."

The Reaper stared at the fellow blankly.

"It's spelled differently," Cindor explained.

"The fuck difference does that make?" Vykers asked, irritably.

"The difference," Cindor explained, struggling to contain his annoyance, "is that one is the name for a person, and the other is the name for a thing."

"Yeah, well, I think I'll just call you Cinder." They'd been walking down a side corridor towards the outdoors—promised sunshine and relatively fresh air. Vykers took a moment to lean on the wall and gather his strength for the next hundred steps. "But I'da thought a big Shaper like you'd have a whole string o' fancy names," he managed.

"You'd have been mistaken. I have been Cindor since I can remember."

Vykers switched topics. "Tell me something, Mr. Cindor..."

"No 'mister'; just Cindor."

"Right," Vykers responded. "I was wondering how and when you first met her Majesty."

"That is too long a tale to share at the moment," Cindor answered smugly.

The Reaper pushed himself up and off the wall, resumed walking. "Alrighty, then: have you ever worked with Pellas?"

The question seemed to let some air out of Cindor, and the Shaper's haughty demeanor changed completely. "He was a friend," Cindor said so softly Vykers could barely hear him. "His death was a loss we may not endure."

Vykers lost all desire to goad the man. After a respectful silence, he changed topics again. "So, what's our plan?"

"You're leaving tomorrow, first light. I've created a special saddle for your horse that will enhance and support the enchantments on your girdle. You won't have the mobility you're accustomed to, but you'll be able to ride considerably longer than would otherwise be possible."

"I'm not going alone..." Vykers said, in a tone that sat somewhere between question and statement.

"Of course not. You'll be joined by an old friend, and I understand there's a certain A'Shea who absolutely insists on joining you."

Aoife, Arune thought, irritably.

Aoife? Vykers thought back.

Don't pretend you're not pleased.

Clearly you are not, Vykers retorted.

You're damned right. Her presence will just...weaken you.

I think she means to strengthen me.

Physically, perhaps, Arune snorted. *Emotionally?*

I am not some woman, to weep over the fall of a flower petal!

Arune kicked him in the jewels. Or, that's what it felt like, anyway. Vykers doubled over in pain.

Cindor looked sincerely alarmed. "Has your wound worsened?"

"Nah, nah," Vykers groaned. "Just having a lovers' spat with my resident spook."

"Ah," Cindor nodded, "Arune. I thought she was on your side."

"Only because she's on my *in*side. There's times I think she'd happily kill me if she had a body of her own."

That's a lie! Arune protested.

Vykers chuckled, which made him wince. *Is it?* To Cindor, he said "Just the three of us, then? Me, the A'Shea, and this mysterious old friend?"

"We thought a larger party would draw undue attention."

"I'm the Reaper. 'Undue Attention' is my middle name."

Long & Co., Teshton

Each fragment of the document, each puzzle piece, was blank, but no one was aware of this, or would admit the blankness of his own piece to his companions. When all the pieces were fitted together, however, an elaborate and lengthy message faded into view.

"Magic," Kittins spat, contemptuously.

"Magic!" Spirk agreed, with much greater enthusiasm.

"Keep it down, lad," Long warned the younger man. "Captain?" he asked, looking at Kittins, "You wanna do the honors?"

If this was a test, Kittins was up for it. First, though, he looked around the tavern's main room, to make sure no one was listening or looking their way. Then, he began to speak in a quiet rumble. "Greetings. As you all now know, her Majesty has gone missing—kidnapped, we believe. Finding her, rescuing her (if possible) or punishing her killers (in the worst case), are tasks we have assigned elsewhere." Kittins looked up. Everyone stared at the letter in his hands with rapt attention. "Your job is to infiltrate Lunessfor's Eight Great Families, to determine what, if anything, they had to do with our Queen's disappearance. We suggest beginning at The Fretful Porpentine, in Lunessfor.

And, look you, any rumors or gossip could prove most useful. Be vigilant, be wary, be careful. Danger lurks in unexpected places; allies may appear in the most unlikely forms."

"What's that mean?" Spirk interrupted. "Like...furniture? Or barnyard animals?"

Yendor wisely clamped a sweaty hand over Spirk's mouth.

Kittins continued. "This tavern, Gangrene & Sons, is the only place you can safely discuss what you've learned. Mark it. Remember it. The barkeep will have something for you as you leave." The instant Kittins finished reading the letter, it crumbled to dust in his hands and blew away on a breeze that had no business being there.

For a long moment, no one spoke—largely because Yendor still had his hand over Spirk's mouth. Finally, it was Yendor himself who broke the silence.

"A job that starts in a bar? If that don't prove Mahnus exists, I don't know what will."

"Huh," Kittins said to Yendor. "I never understood why you were invited along, but now I get it. You offer a certain...what's the word?...verisimilitude."

Everyone gaped at him.

"A what?" Long asked.

"Verisimilitude. It means, like, he looks and acts right...for a wastrel."

"Well, my big, beefy friend," Long responded, "You have far too much time on your hands if you can pull words like that outta your ass."

Kittins thought about belting him, but flashed a huge, toothy grin, instead. "Do I scare ya, little man?"

"Let's say you won the pissing match, shall we?" Rem interjected. "We've more important things to do than squabble amongst ourselves."

"Right," Long agreed. "I don't see much point in puttin' this off. Let's collect whatever the barkeep has for us and be off. The sooner begun, the sooner done, as the missus likes to say."

At the bar, the barkeep actually winked—winked!—at Long and his companions before tossing a purse in Rem's direction.

"Money?" Rem asked.

The huge man winked again.

"'S not often you leave a tavern *with* money," Yendor observed. "Another proof of Mahnus' existence!"

Vykers, Lunessfor

The sky was still dark when Cindor led Vykers down yet another corridor and out into a little-used courtyard, in the middle of which waited four horses and a couple of cloaked figures the Reaper did not immediately recognize. The smell of bread baking wafted down from...somewhere, a comforting, welcome aroma in direct juxtaposition to the seriousness of the coming journey. Drawing nearer the two strangers, Vykers suddenly recognized the taller of the two.

"Three!" he said, jubilantly. The chimera smiled, as well, or it did whatever passed for a smile on its exceptionally weird face. "Guess they figured you survived workin' with me last time, so you'd probably survive another go, huh?"

Three chuffed and chuckled. Or at least that's what it sounded like.

Vykers looked over at the other figure, a short, older man in patchwork motley. "Alheria's tits! What are you supposed to be?"

"I am Hoosh Bindy, the Queen's Fool."

Vykers cast a disapproving eye in Cindor's direction. Turning back to Hoosh, he said, "Well, if this is your idea o' funny, you must be a fuckin' failure in your job. This here's a life-and-death kinda situation. We don't have time for concerned hangers-on. Everyone on this trip pulls his own weight and then some." The Reaper paused, scowling at the Fool. "What've you got to offer?"

"That remains to be seen," the man said, pulling a crudely made cap down over his wispy white hair.

"Like hell," Vykers retorted. "I ain't takin' this one," he shouted at Cindor (and felt his wound throb in the process). "I won't have time to bury his corpse."

"No one alive knows her Majesty better," the Shaper replied calmly.

"Like I said, unless he's got more to offer than the occasional jape or two—o' which I've heard exactly none—he may not be alive much longer. We can expect fighting, ambushes, all manner o' bullshit."

Vykers, Arune interrupted. *He's got some talent.*

What kind o' talent? Morris dancing? He gonna play his pipes and tabor 'til the enemy throws himself at our feet, beggin' for mercy?

He's got a talent for magic. What it is, how it manifests itself, I don't yet know.

Vykers stepped into the little man's face. "What've you got to say for yourself?"

"Tis true, I am milady's fool, though it seems you covet my coxcomb."

"So," Vykers growled, "it's riddles now, is it?"

"I've a dry wit, you lack wit!" Hoosh said, capering around in a circle. "I'm a dry fool for..."

Vykers grabbed him by the front of his jerkin and violently heaved him headfirst into a nearby rain barrel. "Now, you're a wet fool and suddenly I can't help laughing!"

"That's enough, Vykers!" Cindor called over. "Like him or not, he's the Queen's closest friend and he goes."

The Reaper stepped away, and Hoosh extracted himself from the barrel, sputtering, gagging and gasping for breath. "I like a good joke," he coughed, "and so, I'll warrant, did your folks."

Let him have his moment, Arune told Vykers. *You're twice his size and ten times as dangerous.*

But ten?

You know what I mean.

"Fine." Vykers said. "I'll take the clown. It'll amuse me to see how he fares in the wild."

"Tarmun," a voice called from the doorway.

Vykers felt Arune's irritation surge in the back of his mind. What in Mahnus' name was her problem? "I didn't expect to see you here," he said as the A'Shea walked towards him.

Didn't expect it, but hoped desperately, Arune grumbled.

"You shouldn't be out of bed," Aoife complained. "But I suppose there's no helping it, under the circumstances."

"I'll be all right."

"You will if I have anything to say about it," Aoife said. "Is your wound giving you much trouble? Are you feeling weak?"

Vykers laughed with studied insouciance. "I'm the Reaper, remember?"

"Yes," Aoife frowned with equally studied disapproval, "I remember."

"Time is short," Cindor cut in. "The sun is rising. This is your party, these are your horses. Go."

"Just like that, eh?"

"Take the southern gate and continue south. I'll be in touch with your Shaper constantly," Cindor said. "Go."

Without another moment's delay, Three, Hoosh and Aoife mounted their horses, then turned to watch Vykers, waiting to see if he could make the climb or whether he'd need help. Gritting his teeth, he pulled himself up into the unusual saddle Cindor had designed for him. It was high in front, higher in back and awkward as hell to sit in. But somehow its magics stabilized the Reaper and made him feel more at ease.

"Let's go, then," he urged his companions. "Mustn't keep trouble waiting…"

TWO

As agreed, Yendor was the first to enter The Fretful Porpentine, a full two days ahead of his colleagues. His was a role best-suited to his special talents: he was to pose as a drunk, making himself at home in the inn's main room and, if need be, on its floors, the ever-annoying barfly that could not, would not be shooed away through persistence or force. Paid handsomely to drink and pass out? Yendor crept ever closer towards faith.

The first day, of course, he drew many sideways glances— some furtive, others aggressive—but even those petered out by the middle of his second day. He was, indeed, a very convincing inebriate, and the authentic and powerful stench he gave off compelled the inn's other patrons to give him a wide birth, in serendipitous accordance with his private wishes. This made it a little more difficult to secure future drinks, as none of the barmaids would come anywhere near him, but even a man like Yendor had ways of getting what he wanted when he wanted it badly enough. And he always wanted drink badly enough. Yet, what was the point in brow-beating himself? He was as Mahnus had made him. Or maybe he was as the End-of-All-Things had made him, and he'd never recovered. It was all one, to him.

Operatives or functionaries of three of Lunessfor's Great Eight regularly appeared in The Fretful Porpentine, so it seemed to Yendor as excellent a starting point as advertised. He had only to keep his ears open (even if he could not reliably do the same with his eyes), and vital, valuable information would surely be his.

The problem was that he kept nodding off. Drink did that. Sometimes, he'd find himself immersed in the middle of someone else's conversation, only to awaken and see a whole new group of customers spread about the room. A thought came to him, something he feared even to entertain, lest it become reality, but perhaps...perhaps he should drink a bit less. Heresy! Heresy, surely. And yet...he needed to piece together the frayed threads of conversation and gossip he'd heard—or thought he'd heard— over the past two days. It simply wouldn't do to have nothing to share with Long when he arrived. Sometimes, it was all he could do to remember the names of the Great Eight: Radcliffe, Hawsey, Thornton, Blackbyrne, Amberly, D'Escurzy, Gault and Hawsey. No, that weren't right: he'd named Hawsey twice and forgotten one. Amberly, Gault...? He fell asleep.

"Fyne, you old bastard!" someone yelled jovially across the inn. "'S been a while since you've been by!"

Yendor fought through the haze besieging his brain. Fyne! That was it. That was the eighth family. He peered over at this Fyne with eyes set at two in the morning. The man seemed a fop, decked out in the latest fashion and frippery. A festive fop, festooned with frippery, Yendor thought, and giggled to himself. I'm a poet! He passed out again.

Later, someone banged loudly into a chair not two feet from Yendor's head. It took all the man's strength and willpower to raise his eyes to identify his latest assailant, who turned out to be none other than Long Pete.

"Can somebody move this corpse away from my table?" Long growled in his damaged voice. "'S enough to make a man retch!"

Corpse, Yendor thought. I smell like a corpse? I'm a better actor than Rem, that's certain! He figured Long was just piling on the cover, making out like he and Yendor had never met. Good move. Next to Long, Yendor noticed, sat Spirk, absently fiddling with a piece of knotted rope. Yendor battled his way into a sitting position.

"Buy a man a drink?" he asked Long.

The old Captain scrunched up his face as if struggling to avoid inhaling. "I'll stand ya to a bath, i' faith. You take a bath, we c'n talk about a drink."

Long was overplaying his part, clearly. A bath? It weren't even Midsummer's, yet. Still, his friend didn't appear ready to back down, so Yendor agreed. "A bath it is, then." He stood and accepted the handful of shims Long extended his way.

"Not in my inn," the innkeeper warned from a distance. "You c'n use the tub outback, the one we use for our horses and such."

Surprisingly, Yendor found this a better, more appealing notion than bathing indoors in hot, clean water. "If it's good enough for the ponies, it's good enough for Maltos Stack," he proclaimed, pulling an assumed name out of thin air. Or out of his ass, as Long would later assert.

Twenty minutes later and sixty percent cleaner—as much as a man could gauge these things—Maltos Stack returned to the alleged stranger who'd insisted he bathe. "And now, that drink you promised."

"Seems like you've had more'n enough already," Long said.

"More than enough!" Spirk added, not wanting to be left out. Fact was, Spirk was here because none of the others wanted to take on the added burden. Kittins and Rem had been given separate missions, and neither felt comfortable with Spirk in tow.

"Oh, no," Yendor warned, "you're not going to back out on Maltos Stack! A deal's a deal!"

Long muttered something under his breath—or perhaps he said it aloud, it was hard to tell anymore—and motioned for Yendor to sit. "No need to get all hot-headed; I'll buy yer damned drink. Innkeeper!" he called out. "A round o' your best ale for this table. Ah, hells," he added, "it's only coin: a round for the house!"

And so Long, Yendor and Spirk established themselves as more or less welcome regulars at The Fretful Porpentine in a mere three days' time. Such is the power of money and public drunkenness.

Vykers & Co., On the Road

He'd been excited to leave his sickbed, excited to leave his room, excited to leave the castle and excited to leave the city. With all of that behind him, his excitement naturally waned, allowing the pain he lived with constantly to return to the forefront of his thoughts. Certainly, Aoife and Cindor had achieved miracles in lessening the intensity of his pain, but they hadn't dispelled it completely. He doubted anyone in the world had such power, which left him irritable and despondent much of the time. Too much of the time.

And travelling with her Majesty's windbag didn't help. The Fool jabbered incessantly, often in the most inane and incomprehensible manner. Vykers couldn't believe there was anyone, anywhere, who found that kind of prattle amusing. Perhaps he'd overestimated the old bitch. Or perhaps she'd begun to go senile at last. Either way, Hoosh, or Bindy, or whatever he called himself was a secondary kind of pain the Reaper could barely tolerate. He spent hours upon hours fantasizing about different ways to kill the fellow. Whenever he found himself close to acting on those ideas, however, Arune would inevitably intrude and attempt to disarm or distract him.

I still can't work out how her Majesty was taken from her chambers without setting off the countless spell traps surrounding her.

Maybe they shrunk her down to the size of a bedbug's turd and she flew out the window on the breeze, Vykers replied, sardonically.

They? Why do you say 'they'?

No reason. You think it mighta been just one person?

We don't even know if her abductor is human, Arune replied.

This gave Vykers an idea. "Say, healer…" (He had a hard time addressing Aoife by name). "What's the chance yer fey folk had a hand in this?"

She pulled up, stared at him. "None whatsoever. What makes you think otherwise?"

Arune loved it when Vykers antagonized Aoife. She couldn't say why; that was simply the way of things.

"Just tryin' to figure if her captors were human or… something else."

"Trust me," the A'Shea said, "there's nothing alive more treacherous than humans."

"Belike it's something dead took her Majesty, then," Hoosh interjected.

That shut everyone up for a good while. Something dead? The End-of-All-Things again, or something worse? What could possibly be worse?

"Master," Three began, before an arrow whooshed out of the roadside trees and took the Fool right out of his saddle and into the dirt.

Arune! Vykers roared in his mind.

Sorry! She roared back. *I was preoccupied with that last comment.*

"We are beset!" Three yelled, as if anyone was still unaware of that fact.

Out of the trees on either side of the Queen's Highway rode more than twenty raiders, laden with weapons of every sort and expressions of pure hostility.

"Finally!" Vykers exulted. "Some fuckin' action!"

The raiders sneered at his approach, until some of them recognized his face. Arrogance was quickly replaced with desperate humility. They would never have moved against him had they known, they mumbled. Vykers didn't give two shits for their excuses; they'd given him the chance to do what he enjoyed most in the world: killing. Yet, these men were not cowards. As Vykers charged into their midst, his sword singing from its scabbard, the raiders encircled him, hoping to land an easy blow from whatever direction he wasn't facing. Arcane energies shot from the Reaper's chest, dazing anyone within ten feet. On the far side of the throng, Vykers heard the familiar sound of his chimera friend tearing into one or more of his enemies. It was good to be back in a brawl again!

This was the first time the Reaper had used his sword since the battle with the End-of-All-Things, the first time since it had somehow absorbed or merged with the other man's weapon. It had once appeared to be a rather mundane long sword. Now, it was an ugly and menacing thing nearly five feet in length, studded up and down its hilt and the base of its blade with odd thorn-like spurs. Vykers swung it two-handed, but that was more out of habit than need; in combat, it seemed to weigh nothing and, indeed, leapt with a will of its own towards the nearest target.

Vykers cut through the raiders with addictive ease, almost as if he were fighting paper dolls instead of men. Then, too, they faced the problem of Vykers' preternatural battle sense, his ability to predict when and where their blows would come and put himself somewhere else altogether. In the end, it was a short-lived conflict, with the raiders dying to a man, whilst Vykers and his chimera friend sustained not a scratch.

Gradually, the world intruded upon the Reaper's consciousness again, and his pain returned. Huh. If fighting was the only antidote, he'd have to do more of it. Gradually, too, Vykers became aware of Aoife's voice, as she conversed softly with someone off to his left. Hoosh must not be dead, after all. Aoife had saved the Fool, the fool. Nervous horses lingered throughout the area. They were well-trained, and Vykers supposed they could use extra horses. The rest they could sell somewhere or…He searched the area for Three and found him standing a few feet away, cleaning himself.

"You…want…one of these horses?" He asked. "I mean for, uh…"

Three nodded, guiltily.

The Reaper returned the nod. "You'll have to go off a bit," he said. "I'm not sure the A'Shea's ready for your eatin' habits." He then dismounted and searched the remains of his adversaries. From the odds and ends he found, he determined this group to have been a mix of former thralls and mercenaries. They'd found no welcome in the midlands and been forced to choose between long travel to uncertain destinations or staying put and eking out an existence as highwaymen. And now they were carrion, as they perhaps ought to have been three winters past. Wiping the blood off his face as best he could, Vykers turned and walked over to the A'Shea and her patient.

"He gonna live?" he asked Aoife, more than half hoping she'd say no.

"You can't kill good Master Merriment!" Hoosh piped up.

"More's the pity," Vykers grumbled, just under his breath.

Aoife looked up from her position at Hoosh's side. "Who were they?"

"The dregs of the End's army. Men without a home or a cause."

"Was it necessary to kill them all?" the A'Shea asked.

That got Vykers' dander up. "The Fool wearing off on you, milady? Those men attacked us in full daylight on the Queen's Highway. They couldn't a' been more brazen or desperate. Dogs like that need to be put down."

Aoife could not hold Vykers' glare and looked away, helping the Fool to his feet.

"I think I broke me arse!" the man cried. "Look," he said, dropping his pantaloons and baring his backside, "there's a big crack in it!"

At last, Vykers laughed, but only because Aoife flushed with embarrassment and averted her eyes as quickly as possible.

Oh, of course! Arune protested. *You'd think she'd never seen a man's ass before.*

Now, now, Vykers chided. *She is an A'Shea, after all. They're s'posed to be more, uh, virtuous or some such.*

More virtuous doesn't mean better, Arune retorted.

Vykers was curious. "How come that arrow didn't kill him?" He asked, tilting his jaw in Hoosh's direction.

Aoife sighed. "I'm...uncertain. It hit him, but he seems to have...recovered."

Will I never see anyone normal again? The Reaper lamented to himself.

Never one to pass up a dig at Vykers' expense, Arune said, *Would you even recognize him if you did?*

Kittins, House Gault

Kittins lifted a big, mailed fist and smashed it into the door: thunk, thunk, thunk! It was a sound not unlike that made by a battering ram. He waited. Counted to thirty-something, lost interest and pounded again. Thunk, thunk, thunk! This time, he could hear deadbolts being thrown aside with urgency. The left-hand door swung open a foot or two, and a sword appeared at Kittins' throat. He chuckled and slapped it aside. Another appeared at his midriff.

"What's your business?" a voice asked gruffly.

"Looking for steady work," Kittins replied in grim monotone. The door swung open further and two heavily armed guards stepped into the gap. Both were near Kittins in age, but smaller in stature. The bolder of the two spoke up, "That a fact? And who says we're hiring?"

With impressive speed, Kittins grabbed both men by the front of their collars and smashed them into each other as violently as possible. In the brief moment both men were stunned, Kittins slammed them into the thick oaken doors and booted them out into the street. Without rushing, he pushed the door closed behind them and threw the deadbolts.

As expected, a new voice commented from the shadows. "Of course we're always looking for men of talent, and you're a definite upgrade over those two cretins."

Kittins waited, and the new man stepped into the sunlight. He was tall and sinewy, a bit older than Kittins, but still boasted a thick shock of black hair atop his head and equally bushy eyebrows. Cold blue eyes sparkled on either side of his hooked nose, underneath which was a very well-kept mustache. A powerful jaw completed the image of a man both sardonic and imperious, but above all dangerously competent.

"You've demonstrated your skill, to a degree. But what sort of references can you provide. What is your history?" the man inquired.

"I've been wandering since our man Vykers took down the End-of-All-Things."

"Have you?" The man's eyes blazed with curiosity. "And upon whose side did you fight?"

"Her Majesty's o' course," Kittins replied almost contemptuously. He didn't want to seem too eager, too ready to please.

"Of course," the stranger said cynically. "And whom did you serve in that battle, if I may be so bold?"

"Captain Grundig, and the Darwood Auxiliary."

The stranger tilted his head skeptically. "Indeed. Which conveniently makes you the only survivor..."

"Ain't nothing convenient about it. You weren't there; you wouldn't know," Kittins growled ominously. "And if you ain't got work for me, just say so. I'll be on my way to one o' the other Eight."

"That won't be necessary," the other man said hastily. In response to a timid knocking on the door, he added, "Just get rid those two buffoons and meet me inside the main hall hard by. You'll have your work."

"Yes, sir," Kittins nodded. "Thank you, sir." Shame to further abuse the two fools outside, but if he wanted to keep his cover, well…He yanked the deadbolts back again and shoved the door into the two hapless guards as hard as he could, sending them tumbling across the cobblestones. Before they could even climb to their knees, Kittins kicked one in the face and the second in the gut. "Go away and don't ever come back or I'll carve you both up like suckling pigs."

When they were able, the former guards slunk away.

Rem, House-Hunting

Rem had a hard time convincing his company members that it was suddenly acceptable to pursue patronage, particularly since their previous refusal to do so was the one thing that made them unique amongst the realm's myriad acting troupes. The men (and boys) of Wratch & Company were concerned they'd be accused of selling out, of pandering to the rich and powerful. And more than a few were worried that serving any of Lunessfor's Great Eight would mean new limits and restraints on what the company could and could not perform, that inevitably they'd lose creative control of their own work to the ignorant and fickle impositions of their new masters.

"Lads," Rem told them, "lads, it's on a trial-basis only. We'll sign for, say, one year. At the end of a twelve-month, if it please not every last man jack of you, we'll off into the world again, freemen each and every one." There was no way to explain the power Rem had over his company mates. It wasn't through words alone, or simple charisma. But somehow, when he took it upon himself to motivate and inspire his troupe, he invariably did so with marvelous aplomb. And they were powerless to resist.

"Which of the Eight were you thinking?" one of the other players asked.

"I'm told Hawsey sets a fine table and possesses an even better wine cellar," Rem replied, mischievously. "And," he admitted, "they've already approached us with an offer of patronage, so we don't risk rejection."

A second actor, the troupe's 'old man', cut in. "Just the one year, though, right? You won't ink us to a longer term without our say-so..."

"Of course not!" Rem assured the man. "We're a company!"

Vykers, In Pursuit

Something should be said of Vykers' pain. It is true that as a warrior he'd experienced far fewer injuries than could reasonably be expected for someone in his profession—particularly someone who'd lived through as many battles as he had—but Vykers had known pain nonetheless. Indeed, he had suffered both emotional and physical agonies that would leave most men groveling for death, beginning with the loss of his only beloved and continuing through the once-upon-a-time removal of his hands and feet, right up to the malevolent, never-healing hole through his abdomen. The Reaper thought on the fiend who had given it to him, now less than worm-shit. He thought, too, of the mysterious, invisible weapon the fiend had used. For whom was it originally designed? What had been its original purpose? Vykers' wound throbbed, bringing him back to the present.

He was bitter, almost always angry. He'd saved the world, so they said. And what had been his reward? He never knew a moment's reprieve from the pain that bedeviled him, even in his sleep. Oh, he regularly dreamt of being pain-free, but even his unconscious mind could not convince him it was so. Sleeping or awake, his pain was with him. Certainly the Shaper's girdle helped to some degree, as did Aoife's constant ministrations. Yet, Vykers would gladly have conquered the world in exchange for a day, an hour, a mere five minutes' time without pain. The grand scope of earlier ambitions had been reduced to that: anything, everything for a moment's peace.

"You're hurting again," the A'Shea said behind his back. It was weird how she could tell without speaking with him, looking him in the eye.

"Again?" Vykers asked. "Still. Always."

Aoife spurred her pony alongside the Reaper's. "Yes, yes. But it's worse at the moment." She fished around in the pockets of her robe and brought forth a handful of hard, waxy yellow berries. "Chew on these," she said. "They'll help a bit."

For the briefest of moments, Vykers thought of slapping her hand away, sending her offering flying off into the scrub at road's edge. But he didn't understand the impulse, nor the countering impulse to cooperate. "You know what'd really help, Sister?" he grumbled. "Not havin' a ghastly fuckin' hole through my gut."

Aoife bowed her head, scolded or embarrassed. Vykers couldn't tell. Her right hand fiddled with her pony's mane while her left continued to hold the berries.

"Oh, for Mahnus' sake…" Vykers blurted out, "give 'em here. I'll give 'em a try. This point, I'll try anything." When the A'Shea looked up and made eye contact, the Reaper felt surprisingly self-conscious. Her eyes were so big, so blue.

Speaking of Mahnus, Arune cut in, as she always did when Vykers began really thinking about Aoife, *what in his name are you getting yourself into with this A'Shea? You know they've got no use for men, and least of all men like you. Don't give her another moment's thought.*

But that was like saying "don't think of a jack rabbit." Soon as you hear that, it's all you can think about. Still, Vykers had to agree he'd been thinking of the A'Shea entirely too much of late. He was afraid his constant pain was dulling his wits and reflexes. Thinking of women could only exacerbate the problem. Hastily, he grabbed the proffered berries, tossed them into his mouth and urged his horse forward without so much as a nod of thanks. He needed to get out in front of his companions, get a little fresh air, some breathing room. Mostly, he just needed to be left alone.

Well done! Arune said.

Alone? Fat chance. He'd never be alone with the damned Shaper stuck in his head.

Not two minutes later, Number 3 rode up on Vykers' right. "Do you smell that?" the chimera inquired, squinting into the late afternoon breeze. Vykers' nose was full of the berries' floral aroma. "No. What'm I s'posed to be smelling?" "Something...familiar. I just can't put a name to it at the moment." The Reaper hardly heard him: the berries were actually working. "Dip me in tallow and set me ablaze," he breathed to himself. "Master?" Number 3 asked. Vykers snapped out of it. "Huh? Oh, sorry, my friend. Got a little distracted for a moment, there. What were you sayin' about some odor?"

"There's a scent on the wind I've smelled before, but I can't remember where. In truth, I've been smelling it on and off for a couple of days now." "Some kinda threat?" "Might be. I am uncertain." "Well," Vykers said, "we'll be ready for it, just the same." Just then, the Fool started singing, "Olario meedle, O, pransical kay, I'll foop with your deedle And diddle all day..." Vykers leaned into Number 3 and whispered, "Can you do me a favor, 3? Can you shut that clown up for a while?" The chimera offered a furtive grin and pulled up, allowing Vykers' horse to resume the lead and Aoife and Hoosh's ponies to catch up. The Reaper never looked back, but it got quiet in a hurry. Must've been subtle, too, because even the A'Shea didn't object.

The little party continued south into the evening, and the Reaper experienced no more interruptions until it was time to make camp.

It was a dark night; the sky was overcast, offering not a hint of moon or stars. The firelight seemed boxed in by the clouds, confined to the circle of travelers huddled around its warmth. Vykers felt disinclined to speak, as if every word was secret that needs must be kept. And so, as close as they were to one another 'round the campfire, the companions may as well have been thousands of miles apart, isolated and alone. The Reaper sat bundled in blankets between the A'Shea and the chimera, staring into the fire's embers in order to avoid looking at the Fool, who sat directly opposite. Pensively, he picked at his teeth with a small sliver of bone left over from the evening's meal, worrying a piece of gristle caught between his molars.

"Master," Number Three whispered quietly in his direction. "We are being watched."

Vykers' eyes flickered over to Aoife, across to Hoosh, and then back to the chimera. "A moment," he murmured. *Burn?* He probed. *You hear that?*

Mmmm, she replied, almost sleepily. *It's a boy.*

Thanks, Vykers responded, absentmindedly.

Still, Arune thought to herself, from Vykers, any thanks is great thanks.

Vykers leaned towards Number Three. "It's a boy."

"Yes," Three said. He'd already worked that much out on his own. "Shall I go and...retrieve him?"

The Reaper's nod was almost imperceptible, so lost was he in other thoughts. The chimera disappeared in the space between heartbeats, and the darkness seemed to creep in to the spot he'd occupied and settle down in his place, an unwelcome usurper. Suddenly, there was a startled yelp beyond the firelight, and Aoife reached over in alarm and put a hand on Vykers' left arm, whereupon Arune zapped her with a spark of static electricity. The A'Shea pulled her hand back, uncertain what had just occurred. She hadn't been aware of electricity in the air and yet, with Tarmun Vykers, who could say? A new face loomed into view at the light's extremity. Behind it, Number Three's odd visage faded into view. Vykers leaned forward.

"Whadda you got there?" he asked the chimera.

It was Aoife who answered, though. "Tadpole!" she blurted out, alarm evident in her voice.

"Mighty big tadpole, you ask me," Vykers said.

Number Three chuffed and pushed the boy forward into the fire circle. He was ragged and filthy, with perhaps ten summers behind him and a defiant look in his eye. Not afraid: defiant. Aoife was on her feet and by his side in seconds. Nervously, she shot a glance Vykers' way.

"I'll...I'll see him back to the capital," she said hastily, as if fearing the Reaper's wrath and trying to preempt it.

Languidly, Vykers rose to his feet, felt a stitch in his side, did his best to hide it. "No," he said, "you won't."

The A'Shea wrapped her arms around the boy, shielding him from the warrior. "I will. You'll not lay a finger on him, Tarmun Vykers."

Oh, now the boy looked afraid.

The Reaper sauntered over to Aoife and her charge until he was within kissing distance. He squinted down at the boy. The A'Shea braced herself for the worst. "What's your name?" he demanded.

"T-Tadpole," the boy stammered.

Vykers grinned. "Not anymore," he said. "From now on, you're The Frog." He turned to Aoife. "And The Frog stays."

"That's ridiculous!" she objected.

"Is it? The Frog here crossed countless miles of open land—on foot, no less—without gettin' killed by bears or bandits, all so's he could be with you. You don't turn your back on such loyalty, such bravery."

The color rose in Aoife's cheeks. Even in the play of light and shadows from the flickering firelight, it was obvious she was upset. "I'll not allow him to stay, Tarmun Vykers. He'll get killed in your company."

"He might do. On the other hand, he's safer with me than travelling back to Lunessfor in your company." Aoife fumed. "'Sides," Vykers added, "I won't be without you, either." Aoife blushed.

Oh, you're a smooth one, Vykers, Arune said sarcastically.

Man does what he has to, he replied.

Has to? That's a laugh. You're smitten and you know it.

Vykers knew when to ignore the Shaper and did so now. "The Frog stays," he told the A'Shea with finality. "Now find him something to eat and let 'im bed down for the night."

The Frog glanced from the A'Shea to the Reaper and then over to the frightening chimera and the Fool. What in the world had he gotten himself into this time?

Kittins, House Gault

"So," the man said.

"So?" Kittins asked, straightening up from his bowl of soup.

"I see you found the kitchen."

"The man can't find a kitchen ain't a man," Kittins growled.

The nobleman seemed to consider this a moment, and then spoke. "I am Lord Darley, of House Gault," he said. He pointed his chin at Kittins' ravaged face. "You get that in the war, then?"

If he was trying to catch the Captain off guard, he'd have to do better than that. The truth was so close to the lie he'd already offered, the two stories were nearly one and the same. "Gang o' thralls tried to eat my head while I was still wearin' it."

"I'm relieved to see they failed," Darley said wryly.

"Well, it ain't exactly been a boon for my love life, if you take my meaning. But, yes, I made 'em pay for it."

Again, Darley examined Kittins with an appraising eye. "'Round here, a man of good service has no difficulty finding female companionship...or whatever other kind of... recreation...suits his tastes."

"Huh," Kittins grunted. He didn't know what else to say, and daren't say too much.

"You'll get two Merchants a week—not exorbitant pay, but more than enough when you factor in room and board. And your pay will go up as you demonstrate your worth to House Gault."

On top of the money he already had stashed away, it was, indeed, more than enough. "Sounds fair," Kittins replied.

"I think we'll start you on guard duty, and you'll bunk in the barracks. From time-to-time, odd jobs will need doing, and that's when you'll have your best chance to prove yourself." Darley paused. "You'll need to see Cieriste, he's the household chief of staff." Apparently, Kittins looked somewhat confused, because Darley felt the need to clarify, "He's sort of the household Captain and Quartermaster in one. You'll want to stay on his good side."

"Will do."

"One thing more," Darley added. "You'll address me as 'your lordship', 'milord', or 'Lord Darley.' Do not forget that: around here, station is everything."

Kittins rose hastily and affected an almost graceful bow from the waist. "Yes, milord. As you say."

Darley smiled, and Kittins knew he was in.

Rem, House Hawsey

Patronage from House Hawsey meant guaranteed salaries and access to special performance venues and opportunities. But it also meant sleeping in an old, somewhat neglected barracks off to the side of the estate. It was true that with the extra money they brought in, the men of Wratch & Company could easily have paid for much more comfortable accommodations in any of the city's better inns, but they'd be less likely to overhear house gossip, which was, after all, their whole reason—or Rem's, anyway—for accepting Hawsey's patronage in the first place.

As the actors' first official performance wasn't due for another week at the least, they busied themselves mending props, practicing stage combat or tormenting the housemaids. Rem watched and listened to everything. He possessed tremendous attention to detail and could memorize an amazing amount of information in almost no time. And so, he did some of his best "work," merely sitting and whiling away the time, feeling absolutely no pressure or even desire to perfect his Morris dancing, his juggling or his rather famous death throes.

It was during one of these moments of quiet observation that he was at last approached by the Lord of House Hawsey. Henton Hawsey was all of five feet tall and nearly the same in width. The jaw line obesity had stolen from him, he had regained with a crisp and neatly trimmed beard, dyed one shade beyond convincing. Upon his head sat "the wig that must not be mentioned," which was a helpful title, indeed, because the damned thing was so heinous, it was hard not to laugh outright. Whether its hairs had once belonged to a human or an animal was a topic of much debate...at the other Houses. No one in House Hawsey ever spoke of it, for fear of banishment. For his part, Rem wasn't entirely sure where to look when speaking to His Lordship. As if the rest wasn't bad enough, the fellow was slightly cross-eyed and had a fairly dramatic overbite. After much internal struggle, Rem settled on the end of the man's nose—which was mercifully mundane—as his focal point in this and all future conversations. Certainly, every city, town and village in the land had its share of misshapen, misbegotten unfortunates, but never had Rem seen anyone so ludicrously ill-fashioned as the lord of House Hawsey. The man looked like he'd been assembled from cast-offs by a blind, drunken godling with chronic palsy.

"Ah! Remuel! I withed to thpeak with you!" His Lordship began.

Although he was an actor of some note, Rem never gave a better performance than he did in that moment, pretending that his spontaneous and uncontrollable laughing fit was, instead, the result of having swallowed a fly. He harnessed all of his willpower, all of his mental energies and forced himself to stare only at Lord Henton's nose.

"I would like to hear my opthions for entertainment on my beloved's birthday, thome fortnight henth."

How about articulation exercises? Rem thought to himself. "Of course, of course!" he said aloud. "We have a number of plays, as you know, including the saga of Tarmun Vykers' defeat of the End-of-All-Things. That's quite popular. And we have a number of dances, masques, dumb shows and the like as well. Sooth to say, we have entertainment for every taste and occasion."

"Oh," His Lordship said with a disturbingly ribald giggle, "I thintherely doubt that! But let's have your tale of Tarmun Vykers, all the thame. I'm told you were prethent at the final engagement. Now, tell me," Henton asked, "Can you inthert any thord thwallowers? Effiny loves her thord thwallowers, no end. And who can blame her, eh, my friend? 'Tizth a poorly kept thecret that I've got quite the thord mythelf..."

Insert random sword swallowers into his masterpiece? The indignities true artists were made to endure were beyond reason or reckoning. "Er, yes," Rem muttered awkwardly, "I think we've got thome thord thwallowers about." Damn it all, Lord Henton's speech was infectious!

Vykers, In Pursuit

The stars were out. Were out? Were *all*. Vykers couldn't remember ever having seen so many. He'd been unable to sleep, so he passed the time marveling at their numbers, wondering about their purpose. Eventually, he grew bored.

Arune?

Vykers.

You don't sleep in there, huh?

Wish I could. You've no idea what it's like being alone with your thoughts, day in and day out, with no body of your own to distract you.

Sometimes, the Shaper was a keg too easily tapped, and once she started flowing, it was hard to stop her again.

What news from her Majesty's Shaper?

Cindor? The same: the Queen and her captors continue to travel southeast, towards the coast.

That makes no sense, Vykers complained. *The way you Burners blink in and out, she oughta be wherever-it -is they're takin' her by now.*

Yes, that occurred to me, too.

Then, what's going on here, really? They using her as bait to catch me?

Arune laughed. *It's always about you, isn't it?*

Vykers rolled onto his side, looked into the fire's embers. *And what's your problem with the A'Shea, anyway?* He asked, in retaliation.

Problems, plural, she corrected. *In the first place, she's a little too self-important. She's only an A'Shea, after all...*

Oh, Vykers scoffed, *so it's like that, is it?*

Yes, Arune confirmed, *it is 'like that,' as you say. A'Shea are less powerful, less versatile and far more pretentious than we Shapers. Before Vykers could get a word in edgewise, she hurried on. Secondly, I don't want you two getting too close. That's a distraction we don't need, a distraction that could get you both killed. Third, she's the reason that boy's here. We don't need another liability.*

Who says he's a liability?

He's a boy! Arune shouted. *What else could he be?*

Anybody called me a liability when I was his age, I'd've killed the bastard.

This boy's not you. There's only one Tarmun Vykers.

I thought it wasn't all about me! Vykers laughed.

As expected, Arune went away to pout. Or at least, that's how Vykers always viewed it. Abruptly, she returned.

Trouble.

The Reaper sat up, felt an agonizing twinge in his gut, and immediately regretted it. *What kind o' trouble?*

Why don't you ask your pet...whatever he is?

For once, Number Three was fast asleep.

"I'll be damned," Vykers said out loud.

And, just like that, Three woke up. "Is there a...Oh! Yes, yes, there is."

"Little feet, little feet!" Hoosh said, cheerfully, despite his bleary eyes and rumpled demeanor.

"The fuck's that supposed to..."

The ground under Vykers' bedroll began vibrating rapidly, or, rather, say a rapid vibration faded into existence and grew in intensity as the seconds passed. The Reaper stood. "What is that?" he asked, of no one in particular. It was too shallow, too high in pitch to be an elk stampede. "Three?"

"The ground is moving across the entire western horizon. And there's a stench..."

"If it's Svarren, I shoulda seen 'em by now."

It's not Svarren.

"Well, what the hell is it?" Vykers snapped.

Aoife and the Frog awoke, struggling to make sense of the situation.

Out at the edge of human vision, a dark wave surged towards the camp. Vykers thought he could make out thousands—millions—of tiny arms and legs, heads, weapons. And when he saw them, their owners saw him. A strange chittering sound erupted throughout the approaching wave. Vykers drew his sword. "This oughta be interesting," he muttered. He glanced over at the A'Shea, thought he'd find her shielding the boy in a protective embrace. To his surprise, the Frog planted his legs wide and pulled a large knife from his trousers. Vykers could tell Aoife didn't approve, but hadn't the time to argue. "Interesting, indeed," the warrior told himself.

The chittering rose to almost unbearable levels. It was a noise like all the birds in the world shrieking in unison. And it was made by...little grey men, or something man-like. As soon as they set eyes on Vykers and his companions, they charged. Perhaps he hadn't been their initial target, but he certainly was now.

Good, Vykers thought. *Killin' makes the pain go away.*

A bright flare burst from his chest and exploded amongst the enemy. Arune had struck first. Squeals of terror, rage and confusion shattered the night. The little man-things pushed closer, and Vykers could clearly see they were not human, nor any offshoot of humanity. About knee height, the creatures seemed almost to be made from clay, from mud and loam. Their features were but half-finished, though the malice in their eyes was very real, very complete. Each wielded a weapon of some sort, proving they had both the ability to use tools and to fabricate them. And there were millions of them. When they arrived within ten feet of Vykers, some leapt at him. Others lowered their shoulders and ran towards his legs. The Reaper felt a familiar rush of adrenaline and euphoria; his sword sang in excitement. In moments, it scythed through the little grey men, cutting them down by the hundreds, like wheat for the harvest.

A curious shimmer of sparks appeared here and there in the enemy's ranks and the little men fell to the ground, giggling in frightening hysteria. Vykers had no time to wonder at this, though. Nearby, Aoife was shocking, burning and freezing as

many of the creatures as her humble magics allowed, whilst the
Frog was an absolute fiend with his knife, slashing to and fro, up
and down and virtually every other direction humanly possible.
Meanwhile, Number Three did what he did best, launching
himself into the fray with deadly effect and becoming a bloody
blur of destruction. There were so many of the damned things,
even Vykers couldn't keep them all at bay. He felt a constant
stinging on his legs and lower arms as one or another of the little
bastards (as he came to think of them) snuck past his attention
and landed whatever little blow he could. Soon, a great bulwark
of the dead ringed the little encampment, and the attackers had
to climb to nearly chest height to leap over and resume their
efforts. Which of course was all the worse for them, making
it so much easier for Vykers, the Frog, Number Three and the
others to take off their heads with every blow. Throughout this
action, Arune continued her arcane assaults and had somehow
contrived to make the group's mounts invisible to the creatures,
perhaps the smartest move anyone had made thus far.

Sometime later, Vykers noticed the sky was brightening,
and the little bastards were running wide of his camp on either
side. Eventually, they stopped attacking altogether and just
ran past, desperate to get wherever they were going before the
sun climbed too much farther into the sky. Vykers thought of
giving chase (and Three did), but realized he could never kill
all of the things, even had he wanted to. It was like trying to
kill all the gnats in the world: a worthy idea, but impractical.
Finally, he lowered his sword and turned to his companions,
to assess the damage. To his relief, they all stood, staring back
at him with equal measures of fatigue and bewilderment. His
adrenaline gone, the pain came rushing back and robbed his
legs of strength. Carefully, with as much dignity as he could
muster, Vykers sank to the ground. His old wound raged like
wildfire.

"That was something, eh?" Vykers asked, as blithely as
possible. "Never seen anything like it." The fallen creatures
were piled chest high, by the hundreds if not thousands, in a
large semi-circle in front of the party.

"Really?" the Frog asked. "But you're the…"

Vykers chuffed. A real laugh would've been too painful. "'S a big world. You'll never see it all, boy, no matter how hard you try, or how badly you want to."

Aoife looked at him reproachfully, as if to say he should keep his distance from the boy, in word and deed.

"What's eatin' you?" Vykers asked.

Instead of answering, she pulled the Frog aside and made sure he had no pressing injuries.

She's just bursting with admiration, isn't she? Arune quipped.

Yeah, Vykers replied, distractedly. Casually, he reached over and picked up one of the dead. It was a little under two feet in height, with a bulbous head that sported equally bulbous eyes, pointing in different directions. It had only the barest suggestion of a nose, over a wide slit of a mouth, full of needle-sharp teeth. A sickly yellow ichor oozed from a wound in the creature's neck, where, the Reaper surmised, he'd been stabbed by the Frog. Vykers was amazed he'd never heard or seen one of these before, given the numbers he'd just witnessed and fought.

They're called 'Grebbers,' Arune offered.

So, you have heard o' these?

Heard of them, yes. These are the first I've ever seen.

Where do they come from? What were they after?

They live underground, generally. Leastways, that's what the stories say. As for what they were after, I've no idea. They weren't after us, or they'd have focused their full force on us.

Vykers nodded. Makes sense. Grebbers. Still, you'd think they'd avoid the Queen's Highway, even this far out. A snoring noise interrupted his thoughts, and he turned to see the Fool asleep on the ground, using several dead grebbers as pillows. "I've half a mind to leave him here," Vykers said in Aoife's direction.

"You'll do no such thing, Tarmun Vykers!" she scolded. "That was an exhausting and unexpected battle. I'm not surprised he's asleep."

The Frog stepped forward. "Well, I think it's kinda weird, sleepin' on dead things like that."

Vykers winked at the boy. "Ya see, milady? The lad agrees with me!"

Again, Aoife flushed. "Don't call me that, and don't pander to the boy. The last thing he needs is to follow in your footsteps!"

"Oh ho!" Vykers responded. "So that's it, is it? Don't want him growin' up like nasty old Vykers, eh?" Aoife said nothing. "In case you haven't noticed, that 'boy' is quite the demon with that little knife o' his! And what's wrong with growing up like me, anyway? They say I saved the world a while back!" Vykers realized he was nearly shouting, and the sounds of the retreating grebbers no longer masked his excessive volume. He fell silent a moment and then said "We'll wait for Three to get back and then continue on our journey." He looked over at the horses and ponies. Like Hoosh, they were all somehow asleep. *That your doing, Burn?*

None but, she answered proudly.

Vykers was too irritated to thank her. Huh was all he could manage and nothing less than she'd expected.

The Fretful Porpentine

Long Pete and Yendor had the look of hard, desperate men, hanging around the Fretful Porpentine because they were either looking for work or had nowhere else to go. As for Spirk, well, when anyone noticed him at all, he seemed like the other men's lackey, which, given how eager he was to please, was not far from the truth. Miraculously, Yendor had both sobered and cleaned up considerably, to the point where he seemed almost plausibly human. Between the three men, they'd picked up enough gossip to learn that low level functionaries of Houses Radcliffe, Thornton, Fyne, Gault and sometimes even D'Escurzy dropped in on occasion, to sniff one another's hind quarters and determine who was top dog in a given week. Of course, their betters would never be caught dead in such a place, lest they be caught dead in such a place, literally or metaphorically. So, with Kittins off spying on House Gault and Rem and his mates working for House Hawsey, there remained only Blackbyrne and Amberly unaccounted for.

"Have to do something about that," Long said Yendor's way in a gravelly whisper.

"Aye. Too many Houses, not enough men," his friend replied.
"I can help!" Spirk offered cheerfully.
What in the hells had Bailis been thinking, sending Spirk
along? "That you can," Long croaked. "By staying close 'til a
need presents itself."
The young man was clearly disappointed. It seemed
everyone had a job, except for him: Long was in charge, Yendor
drank, Kittins was off spying, Rem was putting on a play
somewheres, leaving naught for Spirk to do. "I can magic my
way into to one o' them other two Houses."
Long shook his head no.
"But I can. Just like I done with my magic stone!"
"Which," Yendor chimed in, "You ain't got anymore."
Spirk shrugged. "Might be as I don't need it now. Might be
Pellas' legacy's enough."
"Pellas' what, now? What are you on about?" Long rumbled.
"Pellas' legacy. When he disappeared in that burst o' stars,
he left me some o' his magics."
Yendor was grinning like the village idiot on Wildside
mushrooms. "Did he, now?" He asked. "Then I suppose you'll
have no trouble witchin' me up some more ale in my mug..."
Spirk dropped his head, planting his chin right onto his
chest. "Can't do that," he admitted.
"How about you just move my mug, then?"
"Can't do that, neither."
"Oh, it's that kind o' magic, eh?" Yendor asked, rolling his
eyes at Long.
"I...I don't know what kind o' magic it is!" Spirk protested.
"I only know I didn't used ta have it, and now I do!" With that,
he pushed his chair back from the table, stood up and stalked
off towards the privy.
"There's no call to mock the fellow," Long admonished his
friend. "He can't help what he is. Or isn't. But you, now."
Yendor pretended offense. "Me? I'm better'n I was, that's
certain, and as good as any man here."
"You're bored, is what you are. So'm I. Spirk gets back, we'll
settle on one o' these targets," he indicated a few minor nobles
across the room, "and follow him for a while. See where he

goes. Maybe stand him to a few drinks in some other part o' town. Get 'im drunk, see what he has to say when he's away from his mates."

At least, that's what Long said as far as Yendor could make out. The Captain's voice was a nightmare of noises that set a man's teeth on edge. "Well," he sighed, "man's gotta do more with his mouth than talkin' and drinkin'. How about you bust open that bulging purse and get us some dinner?"

"Another dinner?" Long winced.

"What d'ya mean, 'another dinner'?"

"Can't be an hour since we ate that cheese."

Yendor scowled dismissively. "Cheese ain't a dinner. Meat's a dinner. Cheese is…I dunno. But it ain't dinner."

"Fine," Long relented. He raised an arm and summoned a passing barmaid. Once he got her attention, he looked Yendor's way, so his friend could do the talking.

"A goodly plate o' meat, miss, and whatever goes with it."

"Aye," the woman replied demurely. Long imagined that boosted her tips, but the woman was well past demure in years. It was sad, really, that she felt she needed to act that way, which thought carried him home to Mardine. Now there was a woman!

Halfway through the meal, Long realized Spirk had not returned to the table. "The kid's not back," he growled (although Spirk was clearly no longer a boy).

Yendor shrugged. So?

"Go check the jakes."

"Me?" Yendor whined. "Why don't you?"

"Because I outrank you."

"And you send me to the jakes when another man's using 'em, I'll be far more rank than your rank, which means I'll outrank you."

"Clever," Long smirked. "Now, go find the kid."

But he could not find the kid; there was no Nessno anywhere on the premises.

"You don't think…?" Yendor trailed off.

Long laced his fingers behind his head, spread his elbows, put his feet up on the table and closed his eyes. "Yes," he breathed. "Yes, I do: he's gone to infiltrate one o' the other Houses."

Vykers, In Pursuit

Vykers would like to have been first up, mornings, but he could never beat Number Three to it. Good thing the chimera was on his side. As he got to his feet and shook off the last of his sleep, though, he felt a brief moment of alarm: the Frog was missing. Vykers paced over to Aoife's side, where the boy usually slept, and noticed an odd pattern to the grass, almost as if...

The Frog rolled over and sat up, surprised to find the Reaper standing over him and even more surprised when Vykers suddenly laughed out loud. Aoife bolted upright, clearly disoriented and whispered a few quiet words to calm herself.

"What's going on?" she asked with more than a trace of irritation in her voice.

Vykers looked her way, smiled what he thought his most appealing smile, and said "Your boy's got a few tricks up his sleeve, I see."

Aoife digested this for a few seconds and finally understood. "He lives amongst the children of Nar. He has...learned a few things, yes."

"No wonder he was able to reach us without getting eaten, then: kid blends right into the grass."

"Or anything else!" the Frog added. "Anything natural, that is."

"I'd like to learn that trick, myself," Vykers said.

Aoife objected. "You're too dangerous as it is, Tarmun Vykers. I'd fear for the world if you adopted the ways of the children of Nar."

Mercurial thing that he was, Vykers' good humor was gone. "Fear for it now," he said, and walked back to his things, ready to start packing up and moving out.

The A'Shea despaired of ever understanding the man. Or her feelings for him. About him. She couldn't accept that she had feelings for him. And then there was the Shaper who shared his body. Oh yes, it was supposed to be Vykers' big secret. In Aoife's mind, it was the smallest of his secrets, dwarfed by questions of his origins, his intent, his absolute isolation. What was he, really? What did he want? Why had he set himself—or been set by forces unknown and unseen—so far apart from the rest of humanity?

"We got anything to eat?" the Frog wondered aloud.

Aoife smiled a small, tight smile. Even she was now thinking of him as 'the Frog.' Vykers' influence was pervasive...and undoubtedly unhealthy for young Tadpole.

"There is meat," Number Three offered, helpfully.

"Mead?" Hoosh cried merrily, leaping up from his bedroll. "Did someone say mead?"

"There's no mead," Vykers answered, more forcefully than necessary. He was gratified, however, to see the Fool plop back down onto his ass dejectedly.

Shaper, Vykers thought, I'm tired of this. *How much further to the coast?*

A week, perhaps.

Perhaps?

Assuming we don't run across any more highwaymen, Grebbers, Oursine, Svarren or other threats.

Actually, I'd welcome a few more threats.

I'm sure you would, Arune snorted. *But I suspect your companions don't share your enthusiasm for conflict. Except for Number Three, that is.*

And you?

I admit to getting bored on occasion. But it might be better for everyone if we kept the boy, the A'Shea and the Fool out of harm's way.

You're joking, right? They might as well rename the Queen's Highway 'Harm's Way' for all the safety you'll find here. I—

More company.

Vykers scanned the horizon in each direction. I don't...

"Master," Number Three said, "something approaches."

"Trouble? More o' them grubbers?"

Grebbers. And no. Not more of them. Something else.

The Reaper pulled his sword and planted it, point down, in the grass between his legs. His rested his forearms on its quillons. Gradually, he became aware of something moving along the ground in the distance. "What in Mahnus' name's this, then?" he said to no one in particular. "A host of angry mice?"

"Entoo-Rii-ii," the A'Shea said.

She was the last person Vykers would have picked to identify the oncoming threat. "The what?"

She searched his face, her blue eyes, arresting. "They are of faerie."

Vykers exhaled aggressively. "Great. Fuckin' great. What next? A mob o' rutting will-o-wisps?"

The A'Shea cocked her head at him, quizzically. "Will-o-wisps don't...mate...like that."

"Don't they?" Vykers responded, unimpressed.

In minutes, the blur of moment resolved itself into a group of creatures even smaller in stature than the Grebbers and much fewer in number.

"You won't need that sword," Aoife told Vykers. "Or any other weapon," she hastily added to the Frog. "They're not here to fight."

"Think I'll decide that for myself," Vykers replied. Looking around, he noted that Number Three and the Fool (he couldn't call the man by name. It was too ridiculous to be counted a name) were both on their feet and facing the approaching whatever-they-were. And although Aoife had a restraining arm on the Frog, the boy seemed braced for all eventualities, as well. When at last the Entoo-rii-ii came into view, the Frog visibly relaxed.

"Oh," he said, as casually as you please.

Vykers looked askance at the boy. "Oh? That's it?"

The Entoo-rii-ii came to a stop a good twenty paces away, or further than Vykers or his chimera friend could leap. They were but half as tall as the Grebbers and in appearance reminded the Reaper of the A'Shea's former companion, Toomt'-La—not in any particular, but in their overall aspect, as if they'd sprouted from the ground rather than having been born from a womb. Their leader was a curious being of indeterminate age and gender who bowed in Aoife's direction when he (?) had come near enough. The A'Shea returned his bow without saying a word to alleviate Vykers' confusion.

The woman's got secrets, Arune observed.

The Reaper couldn't help chuckling softly to himself. That was funny, coming from the Shaper.

The fairy leader turned to Vykers and appraised him before speaking. "Hedeshai testori i m'derrial oo tsa noomin."

Vykers could hear the Fool, off to his left, struggling to stifle the giggles. For once, he and the Fool were in agreement. "Look," he began, "I got no..."

"He wishes to thank you for weakening the Grebbers, "Aoife said.

"You can speak his language?"

"No," Aoife admitted, "but somehow...I understand what he says."

The little being continued. "Hedesh-o, sestura a mahni fendri o o. Hedesh-ha choo tansy. Tzuri i a a? Vestoo am qui am."

"He says the Grebbers had been massing to attack for days and days, and we broke the back of their host."

"I'm the Reaper," Vykers said. "That's what I do."

"Hesheshai im woonata, hedeshai a a biscooli. Fantra a oo hinsi."

"In payment of this debt, he tells you to beware. All is not as it seems."

Vykers wondered what the fairy words for "no shit" were. Since when was anything ever as it seemed? Some payment. "Well," Vykers told Aoife, "tell him thank you and...uh...thank you. That's all, I guess." The warrior was just turning to head back to his belongings when the fairy leader held forth a small, amber orb, about the size of a pea.

"He wants you to take it," Aoife explained.

The Reaper turned back to the fairy leader, knelt down, and accepted the orb. Maybe this was the actual gift and not the self-evident advice. He made an effort to make eye contact with the leader and all of his retinue. They gazed back impassively, with eyes that seemed a thousand years old. "Thank you, again," he told the leader.

"You're meant to eat that, but wait until the king and his subjects have departed," Aoife warned.

"King?" Vykers asked, unsure he'd heard correctly.

"Yes," Aoife responded, waving gently to the Entoo-rii-ii as they departed. "Leaders come in all shapes and sizes."

When the fairies were at last out of sight, Vykers popped the golden orb into his mouth. "It's honey," he said, to his own surprise. Aoife offered a smile so bright and so fleeting, Vykers thought he'd imagined it. He shook his head. Honey.

Kittins, House Gault

The other men in the barracks liked to think of themselves as a hard bunch—ruthless, cruel and without fear. They were forced to rethink those beliefs the first time Kittins came through their door. The man was big. Bigger'n big. And his battle-ruined face was a nightmare. It was obvious he knew all about pain—givin' and takin'—and cared not one whit for surface appearances or considerations. He was the new man, but the second he walked into the room, he was *the* man. No one wanted to fuck with him.

This much and more the Lord of House Gault observed when dropping in to spy on his newest recruit. The big brute was almost too perfect, which immediately raised Darley's hackles. Fortunately, there was one fail-proof test of a man's utility and loyalty, and His Lordship would propose it the first time he found himself alone with the new man. If the fellow passed, well, there was no end to the jobs Lord Darley could find for him. If he passed. Darley continued on his business, leaving Kittins to his own.

The big warrior swept his gaze across the room. A handful of men were engaged in a game of cards, a couple more slept in their beds. One fellow picked at his toenails, and another sat in a chair, reading, with his legs propped up on his bed.

"Anybody wanna give up his watch?" Kittins asked. "I gotta get out o' this room or I'm like to hurt someone doesn't need hurtin'."

The toe-picker looked up, fella named Wrensl Deda. "I'm up next. Y'can 'ave my watch, if you like. I was s'posed to man the kitchen gate, but I think that old cook's taken a shine to me, and I'd just as soon avoid her."

Kittins smirked. He'd seen the old cook. Despite her lack of height, she went twice the weight of a man at the very least and maybe thrice. Her skin had a permanent greasy sheen to it, almost as if she'd been dipped in oil, and she smelled, faintly but persistently, of old cheese. Kittins could see why the man wished to avoid her. "Yeah," he said, "I'll take that watch. What are you going to do, instead?"

Normally, Deda—or any of the others—wouldn't have answered such a question from a new recruit. But, again, Kittins' frightening visage and fierce demeanor made the other men more pliable. "Thought I'd go down to the basement. Watch 'em torture the prisoners and what-not."

He hadn't gone yet, himself, but Kittins wondered if there wasn't more occurring down there than Deda was letting on. A quick glance at the furtive looks of the other men confirmed this suspicion. Could it be that House Gault had her Majesty in its dungeons? It didn't seem likely, but he supposed he'd have to investigate…after this next watch. As Kittins turned to go, he believed he could actually feel the other guards making faces at him and each other behind his back. He figured he'd have to kill one, as publically and painfully as possible, make an example of him, in order to keep the rest in line.

Long Pete, House-Hunting

It was a simple plan, but the best they could do on such short notice: Long and Yendor would separately pose as mercs looking for work. They would visit each of the Houses they hadn't covered in their previous plans and discussions, believing those to be Spirk's most likely targets. Once there, Long or Yendor would claim to be waiting for a fellow-in-arms and inquire as to whether or not anyone matching Spirk's description had been seen of late. Yes, yes: it was true that even folks who saw Spirk rarely noticed him. But his two companions could think of no other way to approach the problem.

Long had had no luck at the first of the great Houses, and as he made for the next, rehearsing everything he planned to say, he turned a corner without looking and ran smack into…

Esmun Janks.

Flustered as he was from the unexpected collision, Long first thought he was imagining things. As he put his hands out to steady and reassure the other man, however, he became quite certain of it. Except that Janks was dead, killed by Long's own hands. Except that Janks didn't seem to recognize his old friend. Of course, Janks hadn't recognized him the last time they met, either, but Long was under no spell this time. At least not so far as he knew.

"Janks?" he asked the man in his raspy voice.

"Might want to pay more attention where you're walking, mate," Janks said.

This was too uncanny a moment for Long to process in a mere ten seconds. "I...I'm sorry," he stammered. "I was in a bit of a rush, it's true. But, now we're stopped, you look a mite familiar. Have we met before? Isn't your name Esmun Janks?"

"Whoozit Janks? No," the man stated emphatically, almost wincing at Long's voice. "Never heard o' him. Now, if you'll be so kind as to get out o' my way, I have business to attend to."

Long needed more time, couldn't let the man go. "Look, at least let me stand you to a drink or two, eh? Little peace offering for nearly running you over?"

"I'm sorry, no," Janks replied. "I've lost too much time already." With that, he bustled past Long and rushed off in the opposite direction.

Long leaned into the wall of the nearest building, slid down it and sat, utterly and absolutely confounded. The man was Janks' twin. But Janks had never mentioned a brother, and Long felt certain he would have. If he'd liked him, Janks would have boasted of his brother's qualities incessantly; if he'd hated him, Janks would have complained about his shortcomings to the same degree. Was it possible Long hadn't killed his old friend, that Janks had somehow survived and harbored a grudge? But that made no sense, either. The real Janks would've punched Long in the mouth for such an injury. Long Pete felt a familiar, prickly sensation up and down his arms and legs: Goosebumps. He stumbled back up to his feet, torn. On the one hand, he was supposed to be looking for Spirk, needed to find him, in fact, before the young man got himself—or the whole gang—into trouble. On the other hand, Long had just seen a ghost and wanted to follow the apparition to learn the truth of things. When he looked again, Janks had rounded another corner— Long wasn't sure which—and disappeared. Well, Long thought, he would go after Spirk. He could always come back here later with the rest of the boys and see if Janks came by again.

A half mile and several minutes later, however, time worked its usual magic, and Long began to think he'd imagined the whole encounter, or at least been so shaken by the unexpected impact that he'd misidentified the other fellow. Yes, that was it. Janks was dead, had been so for three years. Maybe Long was so homesick for Mardine and Esmine that he'd made himself see something, someone, that wasn't there.

After stopping to ask directions twice, the old soldier finally found his way to the gates of House Fyne. Like House D'Escurzy, from which he'd come, House Fyne was located in a part of town well beyond Long's means—had he any interest in living there. North Hill, as the district was called, was actually built on a series of hills. The highest of these were entirely taken over by the opulent estates of Houses Fyne, Radcliffe, and Thornton, along with the less magnificent mansions of several lesser Houses. The whole place was immaculate, as if the address was even too dear for fallen leaves, litter and dirt. As Long drew near the gate, one of the four—four!—men standing guard out front snarled at him.

"Shove off!"

Though taken aback, Long struggled to remain calm and professional. "Was just checkin' to see if your fair House needed any more swordhands…"

Two of the guards traded disbelieving looks, and the rude one spoke up again. "You ain't speakin' of yourself, I hope, old man."

"Me and a friend," Long crackled. "Younger fella with a port wine birthmark on his face. He ain't been by, has he?"

Rude didn't even glance over at his cohorts before answering. "No, he ain't, old crow. Now, like I said, you'd best shove off, 'fore I give you a beating."

"You sure you ain't seen…"

That was too much. Rude yanked his sword out of his scabbard and swaggered over to Long. "Thought you said you was a swordhand, but you seem more like a stupid bastard to me. That what you are, old man? A stupid bastard?"

Slowly, Long grimaced, grabbed at his chest and doubled over, letting out a low groan. When the other man drew nearer to inspect or perhaps mock him further, Long straightened out in an instant, driving the top of his head into the other man's chin and knocking him backwards onto his ass. Before Rude could even rise to a sitting position, Long's sword was at his throat. Seeing this, the other guards stood down.

"If I'm a stupid bastard, what's that make you?" he asked the man at his feet. Eyes filled with fury and embarrassment glared back at him. "All I did's walk into your little square, offer my services and ask if you'd seen my friend. There's no call to get nasty." Oh, he wanted to say more, to unload on the young thug. You think you're the cock of the walk, do you? I've stood nose-to-nose with the End-of-All-Things, had him screaming threats in my face that would've shriveled your testicles up like raisins. Well, I'm still here, and the End ain't! But Long said none of that. Keeping the point of sword on Rude's neck, he surveyed the square again, made eye contact with each of the guards. No, they hadn't seen Spirk. Carefully, Long lowered his sword and backed away.

Rude crab-walked backwards another three or four feet and then lurched upright. "I ever see you again," he said, "I'll kill ya. Whether you see me first or not."

Long continued to back away. "Something tells me you ain't gonna live that long," he retorted in his most gravelly voice. A moment later, he had backed out of range of any kind of charge, so he turned and walked as calmly as possible back in the direction he had come, listening with bated breath for any signs of movement behind him.

"Yah, you'd best keep walkin', old man!" Rude shouted from a safe distance.

Long chuckled to himself, but it was sound advice, really. There was no way he could have defended himself if all four guards had attacked in unison. He wondered why they had not.

THREE

Rem, House Hawsey

As a reasonably handsome, dashing young actor, a war hero (according to his own plays) and, frankly, a new face on an estate too focused on all things Henton, Rem found himself in almost constant demand in House Hawsey. All in all, things were going quite *swimmingly*, Rem thought, as he lounged in a large bath with not one, not two, but three naked and wonderfully shameless chambermaids. Rem supposed there were those who might find three to be rather a lot of naked women for one man to handle, but, for himself, he didn't feel there was any number too large. He was *up* for the job, in every sense of the word.

And then he heard a familiar voice. He was about to panic, when His Lordship laid his fears to rest.

"Oh, don't trouble yourthelf!" Henton crooned. "I've done the thame, many a time and oft."

Sure you have, Rem thought.

"With those thame three girls, as like as not!" His Lordship added.

Suddenly, the ladies seemed rather unsavory to Rem, as if rather than becoming clean in the bath, they were instead befouling it. He was no longer up, in any sense of the word.

His Lordship loomed over the lip of the bath. "Ah, I thee the worm hath wilted."

Rem didn't know what was worse, the fact Lord Hawsey was ogling his business or the mixed metaphor of a wilted worm. He looked up and noticed the chambermaids acting demure under

His Lordship's gaze, but they were not good actors. Nothing like. Rem let his torso sink deeper into the soapy water and went on the offensive.

"How may I help your most esteemed Lordship?"

"I'd like to thuggest you continue your revelries, as I'm thure they'd make a motht interethting dithplay. Thadly, I haven't the time to enjoy them right now. I with to thpeak to you in private about an acting-related opportunity I have in mind for you."

Speech coaching, Rem didn't doubt.

Well versed in the subtleties of their Lord's conversation and moods, the chambermaids helped one another out of the bath, bundled each other up and capered off, giggling, into the next room. His mood having soured considerably, Rem sank still deeper into the bath, 'til the bubbles rose to his chin.

His Lordship made a big show of peering left and right before speaking again. "Ath you are an actor," he began, "I athume you're adept at playing other people..."

"Of course, my Lord. It is what I do." Rem managed to say this with such nuance that it was deeply condescending without being perceived as such by his employer.

"Indeed, indeed." Henton mused. "I wonder if you would be interethted in taking on another contract, thith time athuming the role of a thervant, in order to thpy upon a rival."

Rem sat up straighter at this and watched as His Lordship's eyes followed his progress. "It might be...arranged." Rem said carefully.

"But tell me, my friend, can you dithguise yourthelf, thuch that none would recognithze you? You are famouth, after all."

"I can so change myself that my own mother wouldn't know me!"

Lord Hawsey smiled. Or rather, he thmiled. "Then, in brief, here is the thituathion: no one hathz theen her Majethty in many dayth. We're told theeth thick. I would like to thee for mythelf, but no one can penetrate her inner thecurity. No one, exthept, perhapth, Lord Radcliffe. I with you to gain entranth to his ethtate and thnoop around. Thee if you can't disthcover any newth."

Rem dipped his head to wash off the spittle shower he'd just received, courtesy of His Lordship. "Surely you must have other spies in House Radcliffe."

"Thertainly. But I can never be thure they haven't been compromithzed. One can't have too many ironth in the fire!"

"As you say," Rem agreed. "When shall I start?"

"Immediately. Your performanthe at my ethtate ithn't due for a week yet, so that givth us plenty of time. And bethides," Henton said with a lascivious leer, "I can't have you dethpoiling all my pretty chickenth, eh?"

Kittins, House Gault

He'd been living and working at House Gault for several days and hadn't come close to making anything that remotely resembled a friend. Ironically, that is precisely why Lord Darley trusted him. Darley couldn't stand the glad-handing type, the hail fellow well-mets who always seemed to have a secret agenda behind their twinkling eyes. Kittins, on the other hand, was as grim and quiet as the grave. Hells, he even looked like he might've just climbed out of one. Darley liked him, liked him well. He found the big merc eating alone, on a balcony off one of the more obscure wings of the house.

"Ah, soldier," he began, suddenly remembering he'd never asked the big man's name. "Enjoying a bit of night air?"

Kittins looked up, only the war-ravaged half of his face visible in the moonlight. "Enjoying some solitude's more like. Not from your lordship," he hastened to add. "It's just, them boys in the barracks can try a man's nerves at times."

"Oh ho, yes!" Darley agreed. "So they can. And it wouldn't do to have you killing the rest of the guards in your first week." He paused, studied Kittins with his piercing blue eyes. "How are you enjoying House Gault, by the by?"

Kittins set his platter aside, dusted the crumbs off his hands. "It's nice enough, I suppose."

Darley's eyebrows shot up.

"But a little quiet." Kittins explained. "I'm used to more… killin'."

The more he spoke, the more Darley liked him. "I neglected

to ask your name when we met," he confessed.

"Esmun. Esmun Janks," Kittins said without a second's pause.

Darley tested the name, as if tasting its veracity. "Janks. Janks." Then a small grin came to his lips. "Listen, Janks: I've a good feeling about you. You do right by me and House Gault, and you could end up richer and more powerful than you ever dreamed."

Kittins stood. It seemed the thing to do. "That so?"

"Absolutely." Darley replied. "Does that sound appealing to you?"

"I ain't a man to spit on 'rich and powerful'."

"Good, good." Darley looked around, made sure they were alone. "Of course, you must pass a test first, to demonstrate your…loyalty."

Somebody needed killing, was what Kittins figured.

"You won't be surprised to hear I have a mistress." Darley said. "In fact, I have several. Great men have great appetites. One of them has given birth to a girl. I don't mind leaving a few bastards behind, but I've no use for illegitimate daughters." His Lordship ceased speaking for a moment, as if allowing suspense to build. "I need you to kill the child and bring me its corpse."

Baby killers were the worst kind 'o scum, forever damned. "I'll do it," Kittins answered, more to reassure his new employer than out of any real interest in the job. He'd have to think on this, certainly. "Can I have a day to scout the target?"

"Of course," Darley said, with the darkest of smiles. "I'd expect no less." With that, he proceeded to tell Kittins everything he needed to know.

Aoife, Vykers & Co.

She was as flustered, as rattled, as she had ever been. She'd just awoken from a lengthy and uncomfortably detailed sex dream about Vykers and didn't immediately know how to flush the images from her mind, or the excitement from her body. At length, she incanted a brief spell and felt her pulse slow, her muscles relax. She took in a deep breath through her nose, let it out through her mouth. In through her nose, out through her mouth. The very same mouth she'd just...Oh, bother!

She stole a quick peek in Vykers' direction. Even sprawled out on the ground asleep, he possessed a powerful animal magnetism. Then, she remembered those claws, those canines, and how they'd...

She had a problem.

Aoife looked down at Frog. Frog? He was a boy, still her little Tadpole, no matter what that beast, that big, delicious beast of a man...

She got up, walked over and kicked Vykers' foot. He lurched into an upright position, growling at the pain from his wound.

"What?" he demanded, bleary-eyed but improving rapidly.

"You were snoring," the A'Shea lied. "I thought it might attract predators."

Vykers fell back, stretched out, languidly. "You sure you're not the one attracted?" he asked with a wolfish grin.

"Ha!" Aoife snorted. Inwardly, she was terrified. It was as if he could see right through her. Or perhaps it was wishful thinking on his part, but it coincided with her own, treacherous thoughts. In desperation, she turned and headed for the nearby creek.

"Little too close to the bone?" the Reaper called at her back.

She decided to throw herself into icy waters with all her clothes on. The creek was too shallow to drown in, and she had no desire to do so, anyway. But spending the next few hours in cold, sodden clothing should keep her mind off...well, things it shouldn't be entertaining.

Vykers heard a loud splash and came running. Or nearly so. "You fall in, A'Shea?" he asked from some distance away.

"I'm washing my clothing!" Aoife shouted back, defiantly.

"While you're still in 'em?" Vykers asked, disbelieving. He pulled up when he reached the creek's far shore. "Seems a little, uh, crazy to me."

Aoife sat on the creek bottom, her robes billowing up around her like a great flower. "That," she retorted, "is because you know nothing of the A'Shea."

She's crazy, all right. Out of her mind! Arune offered.

Vykers shrugged. That s'posed to scare me away? 'Cause it don't. "Can I help you outta there?" The Reaper asked aloud. "No, thank you," Aoife responded. "I'm fine where I am. Why don't you and your...friend...go and find us some breakfast?" With one last, lingering gaze, Vykers turned and headed back to camp. "I know what you want!" he sang out over his shoulder. "And you know I know!"

The last thing Aoife heard was the man's laughter as he vanished around a stand of trees. "Alheria," she whispered, "where are you when I need you most?"

Why won't you listen to me? Arune nagged. *I know where this is going, and it's not good.*

Look, Burner, I know you think you're smarter 'n me. Might be you are. But I wanna remind you, when we first met you were dead. I was in bad shape, too, but I was gettin' by. I think I can survive the A'Shea.

That was, for Vykers, what amounted to a monologue. Clearly, Arune thought, he'd been pondering this for some time. And that was alarming in and of itself.

And, Vykers continued, *if this goes where I think it might, I don't want you interfering like you did that one time.*

Once upon a time, he'd intended to visit a few of Lunessfor's working women, but Arune had enspelled him, making him temporarily unable to perform.

We might be sharing this body, the Reaper continued, *but in the end, it's my body. Always was, always will be. You don't like it, you know what you can do about it.*

Arune fumed. There was no point in reminding him that he'd die if she left him now, while his wound remained unhealed. And there seemed no way to prevent her host—her friend—from making a right mess of everything. *And if it does go your way, what am I supposed to do while you're, uhhhh...?* She asked, letting the question trail off before she had to get any more specific.

I don't care. Whatever you like. You can even watch, if that's your sort of thing...

Arune shrieked.

Vykers laughed.

The A'Shea was in an odd mood, the Shaper was in a foul mood, and Vykers was in a good mood, for the moment, despite his pain. It had turned out to be a beautiful spring afternoon. The whispering of the breeze as it swept across the rolling grasslands, combined with the scents of earth and air brought the Reaper a sense of peace he hadn't known in some time. Butterflies floated amongst the wildflowers that grew here and there. A rabbit even appeared off to Vykers' left, and before Three could race off and catch it, the Reaper waved him off: one less soul on his conscience. True, it was but a rabbit's soul, but he'd known men with less in their breasts.

Vykers considered the boy, Frog, who rode alongside the A'Shea and stole convert glances at the Reaper whenever he thought the warrior wasn't looking. Aoife was likely correct in thinking he'd get the boy killed, much as he hated to admit it for any number of reasons. At the same time, there seemed no practical way of seeing the boy to safety without losing vital time in pursuit of the Queen's abductors—if that's what they were. Too, Vykers might be able to teach the lad a few things, toughen him up, prepare him for whatever destiny had in store.

Ah, nonsense. Vykers was a self-absorbed force of nature, and he knew it. The only teaching he ever did was with a sword, the only lessons, lessons of blood, pain and death. Maybe the A'Shea was right: best to keep the boy as far away from him as possible.

Vykers moved on to the Fool, Hoosh. He'd never had a real conversation with the fellow. Hoosh seemed incapable of saying anything that wasn't childish gibberish. Even now, he could just hear the Fool mumbling some sing-song melody to himself, something reminiscent of a child's nursery rhyme. For the life of him, Vykers couldn't understand how that was meant to be amusing. Surely the Queen, that aged, world-weary and eternally sardonic creature, didn't enjoy the Fool's japes—if that's what they were. Perhaps Hoosh was more of a lapdog, with limited speech. It didn't matter what he said, the fact a lapdog was speaking at all was the miracle.

No, that made no sense. There was something else at work,

here, if only the Reaper could put his finger on it. For instance, what had the Fool been doing during the group's battle with the grebbers? Nothing? Something. He'd seen inexplicable things. He'd have to ask Arune was she was in a better mood.

Ahead of him, Three had pulled up and was again sniffing the air in every direction. He turned and looked directly into Vykers' eyes, a sure sign he had something to say. Vykers couldn't smell anything unusual, but he rode up next to his friend and leaned close.

"What've you got?"

"It's that odor, again."

Vykers shrugged. It was a positively lovely afternoon. "I don't smell it, and I don't see anything out there, either."

"Yet, it is there. Something alive."

The A'Shea, Frog and the Fool were still a ways back, bringing the extra horses in tow. "You worried?"

"Vexed, my friend. I know this odor, but I cannot recall where or how."

"Well," the Reaper sighed, "less you wanna go chasin' after it, there's not much we can do 'til we can actually see the source."

Three nodded. "You are right. It will either reveal itself in time...or it will not." He fell silent a moment and then changed the subject. "Does your...does Arune tell you how much farther it is to the coast? One thing I do not yet smell is this ocean I've heard of."

"Last time I asked, it was a week away. Should be only a few days, now."

Three leaned back in his saddle, inhaled deeply and smiled. "I am excited to see this ocean. I hear it is the mightiest thing in the world." The chimera caught Vykers' frown and immediately amended his statement, "The second mightiest, that is."

The Reaper shook his head and chuckled. If Three was teasing him now, they must be friends indeed.

The Fretful Porpentine

Yendor hadn't had any luck in finding Spirk, either, which resulted in perhaps the only time in his life in which he entered an inn in a bad mood. In two seconds, his eyes adjusted to the gloomy interior and he spied Long already seated at their usual table. Yendor raised his eyebrows inquisitively; Long shook his head 'no' in reply.

"This could fuck the whole mission," Yendor said when he drew near enough.

"Yup," his friend answered.

Yendor noticed Long was drinking something other than ale, something stronger. "What's that, then?" he asked.

"Apricot brandy. Used to have a thing for it back when."

"And now?"

"I just wanna get shit-faced."

"Ah," Yendor smiled, "you've come to the right man, then."

"Actually, you're the one came in. I was already here," Long pointed out.

"Fair point, my friend. But then, I'm a high priest of shit-facery, whilst you are but an initiate."

"Huh," Long grunted, before tilting his cup up and draining it. He then slammed the cup down and raised his arm in the air, waving at a passing barmaid. "More o' the same," he rasped. "A whole bottle, if you've got it."

"I'd no idea the boy meant so much to you," Yendor said, impressed by Long's determination to drink.

"It ain't just that," his friend croaked. "I nearly got killed at House Fyne, and before that, even, I ran into..." His voice faded out, as if he'd decided against speaking any further.

"Who?" Yendor urged. "Who'd you run into?"

Long fixed his increasingly blurry eyes on his friend, began to speak and again stopped short.

Yendor took a guess. "The missus?"

The barmaid arrived with the requested bottle and even poured some of its contents into Long's cup. Without having to be asked or told, she produced a second cup, placed it before Yendor...and walked away without filling his cup.

"Swear to Mahnus, they can smell who's got the money and who don't," Yendor muttered. "Anyway..." he continued, cueing his pal.

"Weren't the missus," Long grumbled. "Ya think I'd be in

this mood if I'd seen my Mardine?" Before allowing Yendor to respond, he continued, "No. No, the person I ran into was..."

Yendor was like to scream if the man didn't spit it out. "Who?" he said as loudly as he dared.

"Janks."

Yendor said nothing, waited for the punch line he felt sure was coming. But Long's focus had turned to his brandy, and he said nothing further. After a good, long pause, Yendor said "Janks. You think you saw Janks?"

Long downed his second cup, grimaced ever so slightly, and looked over at Yendor. "I thought I did, yeah. Then I wasn't sure. Now...?"

"Well, I'm sure you didn't. Look, the man's dead. He's dead. I know that's a right sore spot for you. I understand that. But whoever you saw today ain't Janks." Yendor poured himself a cup of brandy, took a sip. "Alheria's thorny undergrowth, that's some good stuff!" He exclaimed. "Much better'n Skent."

The captain actually giggled. "Skent," he said, reminiscing. "I'd almost forgot about that." Shortly, he grew somber again. "I say tomorrow, we switch Houses and do the same thing. We go out again today, they might get suspicious. We go tomorrow, they oughta have different guards on duty. I'll go to your Houses; you go to mine."

Yendor nodded. It sounded like a plan to him. Suddenly, he remembered something. "You said you almost got killed! What's the story there?"

Long grinned drunkenly. "Ain't gonna tell you. Wanna see if you're smart enough to avoid making the same mistake."

Spirk, House D'Escurzy

Pellas' Legacy was powerful magic indeed. Almost as powerful as Spirk's magic stone. Or maybe more powerful. It was hard to tell. Nevertheless, Spirk had walked right into House D'Escurzy on the heels of a poulterer, and no one had seen fit to challenge him—not even the poulterer. And certainly not the poulterer's birds, which were, in any event, dead. Spirk might have taken a moment to mourn them, but, in truth, he hadn't really been acquainted with them, and such unasked for sympathy seemed a touch presumptuous to him. He felt reasonably sure the chickens would say the same, if dead chickens could speak. And happened to speak the Queen's tongue. Of course, if that had been the case, the poulterer probably wouldn't have killed them, Spirk reflected, choosing, instead, to sell them to a circus or, perhaps, make a gift of them to her Majesty, herself. If she weren't missing.

"You there!" the poulterer suddenly said to him, "Where's the blighted kitchens in this place?"

Spirk looked about and noticed that he and the poulterer stood in a large foyer, with hallways running off in three directions: left, right, and straight-on. Not wanting to appear completely unhelpful, Spirk selected a direction at random. "That way," he said at last, pointing to the right.

With a demonstrative harrumph, the poulterer hitched up his birds and set off.

"And I'm sorry about your chickens!" Spirk called out, feeling he should say something after all.

The poulterer looked back at him with an expression of utter contempt. "They's ducks!" He spat, and stomped off down the corridor.

Not wanting to run afoul—or even a fowl—of the angry poulterer again, Spirk chose the opposite hallway, to his left. He passed a number of doors that were locked and a number of others that were guarded. He noticed the guards never looked at him, which seemed further proof of Pellas' Legacy at work. Eventually, the hallway took several turns, to the left and right before opening into a vast room with animal heads hung all over the walls. Atop various tables, shelves and bookcases were smaller animals in their entireties. Spirk was momentarily frightened to discover a positively ferocious looking skunk perched on a bookcase not two feet from his face. It was amazing, really, how lifelike they'd managed to make the thing. Its eyes were particularly well done, in Spirk's opinion. Once he was certain the skunk posed no threat, Spirk took a brief tour of the room, studying all the animals, many of which he was familiar with, but others, as well, that remained completely unknown to him. He stopped to examine one especially odd creature and received yet another fright when a voice from behind addressed him unexpectedly.

"The lot could use a good dusting," the voice wheezed.

Spirk turned. In a chair he hadn't seen earlier because it was located behind a rampant bear sat a wizened old man. Or at least Spirk thought he was a man. The creature was but half the size of a normal man and might have been fashioned of bone and aged leather. The hair on his head looked as if it were made of cobwebs, of gossamer, and floated in a diaphanous haze around his skull. Draped in dark, heavy satins of a most somber hue, he looked more like an imperious but poorly made puppet than a man.

"Well?" the puppet breathed impatiently.

"Yeah?" Spirk asked, somewhat taken aback.

"I say the lot could use a good dusting. And I don't like to repeat myself."

Epiphany! "Oh!" Spirk exclaimed, "You want me to..."

"Of course I want you, addle pate! Who else is there?" the puppet replied.

"Um...I, uh..."

"Oh, for Mahnus' sake. Another imbecile!" the puppet said. "I do hope we're not paying you much." At this moment, he was seized with a racking cough that sounded at once painful and phlegm-y. After he calmed down somewhat, he paused, looked Spirk up and down and said, "Your first day, is it?"

At last, something Spirk could answer truthfully. "Yes, sir. My first day."

"Sir? I am 'Your Lordship'. Or, if needs must, 'Titus D'Escurzy'. Address me incorrectly again, and I'll make you smart for it!"

Knowing he wasn't bright, Spirk responded, "Oh, can you? I'd very much like to be smart."

Titus rolled his eyes. "I'll be sorry to hear we're paying a single shim for such foolery. Tell me, dolt, can you handle a feather duster without injuring yourself?"

"I hope so, sir, your Lordship."

His Lordship pulled his robes tighter across his chest and

hawked some mucus into an enormous handkerchief. "I hope so, too. There's a false panel behind that stag over there," he pointed. "Behind it, you'll find cleaning equipment, a small ladder and more. When you're done dusting you can stoke the fire in yon fireplace."

"Stoke the fire, yes, your Lordship." Spirk said eagerly. "Anything else sir, your Lordship?"

But His Lordship had fallen asleep. Or perhaps he had died. Oh, let him not be dead! Spirk thought to himself as he set about fetching the tools for dusting. I'd hate to have lost my new employer in the first few minutes!

After successfully dusting every head in the room, including His Lordship's, Spirk put a couple of logs on the pitiful fire in the room's oversized fireplace and returned to Titus D'Escurzy's side, awaiting further instructions. It was a long wait, for while the man was not, in fact, dead, he could nap with the best of 'em. The sun had set and the room had gotten dark by the time His Lordship awoke. He seemed almost depressed to see Spirk again.

"Still here, eh?" he asked irritably.

"Yes, your Lordship, I am."

"I didn't mean you, dolt. I was referring to myself."

Spirk was himself, which is to say bewildered. "You don't wanna be here, your Lordship? Can I take you somewhere else?"

Titus groaned in exasperation. "Idiot!" he yelled. And then, "Yes, wheel me to my room before any of my wretched children come looking for me."

It was at this moment that Spirk noticed that the chair His Lordship sat in had wheels attached to its legs. He'd never seen such a thing before and was quite delighted with the chance to experiment. "As you say, your Lordship," he replied. Placing his hands on the chair back, he spun it around, pulled it closer and began pushing towards the door, to a constant monologue of "Easy! Slow down! Left, left, left!" from His Lordship. They collided with several objects on the way out of the room, but only managed to topple one, which Spirk thought was quite an accomplishment. His Lordship did not agree.

"Are you blind and stupid? Is this how my family thinks to

serve me? With cripples and imbeciles?" Lord Titus complained. Spirk had been called worse (by his own father, no less) and so took it in stride. "I'm sorry, Your Lordship," he said. "Won't happen again."

"Ha!" Titus cackled, before launching into another coughing fit.

An eternity later, they reached Lord Titus' bed chambers, which were as dark and cavernous as a cave. Even the clutter of overstuffed furniture did nothing to diminish the excessively empty feel of the place. Spirk thought to beg off, but his new master would have none of it.

"You stay!" he commanded, as Spirk backed towards the door. "I think I'll make you my personal valet. Can't be betrayed by an idiot, after all."

Spirk looked at the old man. "Wh...what happened to your last valet?" he asked.

"I had him killed," his replied, flashing a picket fence of a smile.

For a moment, Spirk stopped breathing.

"What is your name, anyway, dolt?"

Not having planned this part very well, Spirk blurted out the first false name he could think of, "Long Pete."

His Lordship eyed Spirk skeptically. "Long Pete, is it? Are you certain it's not 'Thick Pete', or 'Slow Pete'? How about 'Dumb-as-a-Goat's Arsehole Pete'?"

"No, sir, your Lordship. It's just, uh, just Long Pete."

Thus, quite by accident, Long Pete had successfully infiltrated the D'Escurzy estate.

Kittins, House Gault

It was a genuine dilemma and no two ways about it: if Kittins wanted to earn Lord Darley's trust, he needed to make the man's bastard daughter disappear somehow. He had also to come up with a child's corpse that would fool His Lordship into thinking Kittins had done his bidding. Or...he could actually kill the child. But no, he was no Tarmun Vykers, that innocence meant so little to him. Back to the first plan, then: hide the daughter and substitute some other child's body. Where to find one, though? After more than a day of wracking his brains, Kittins hit on an idea.

There were certain districts in Lunessfor where the streets featuring the fronts of buildings were entirely respectable, but those on the same buildings' backsides were anything but. Travelers was such a district, with long, wide and relatively clean avenues in front, and filthy, urine-drenched alleys in back. Kittins stalked up just such an alley in search of a door he'd heard tell of, the door to a 'business' where a working woman or somebody's mistress could unburden herself of infants who looked nothing like their husbands, were born with various deformities or might otherwise be in the way of a profitable career. The thought that such places existed filled Kittins with rage and disgust. Unfortunately, on this occasion, he found himself complicit in their crimes. He needed one of these discarded babes. Yet, he swore he'd return some time later and burn the place to the ground, but it made him feel none the better for all that.

He passed a few urchins asleep in the refuse along the way, as well as one or two drunkards with no safer place to sleep. There were stray dogs, cats and rats in evidence, too, but Kittins paid them little attention. The door he sought was in surprisingly good condition, with a new coat of paint and a polished wooden knocker (brass being of too great value to thieves). Knockers of whatever sort were not Kittins' style, however, and he simply pounded on the door with his fist.

At length, rattling could be heard, and the door crept open the tiniest crack.

"What is it?" a voice demanded in an unexpectedly upper class accent.

"I need something that you need to dispose of," the big man growled in reply.

"What's that to me?" the voice asked. "We burn our garbage."

"Not always," Kittins said. "For a price, I'm told you'll sell the live ones."

There was a pause, and then the voice said, "You don't look as if you can afford a live one."

"I'm not looking for a live one."

"But I thought you just said..."

"I hear you sell live ones. So, I'm guessing you'll have no problem selling me a dead one for less."

"Hmph. You don't look like...the type for that, either."

Kittins grew impatient. "I'm not. This is a one-time thing. Have you got something for sale or not?"

"One noble."

More than a week's wages. Without warning, Kittins threw himself against the door and shoved it open, knocking the man behind it onto the floor, on his back. He was a thin, frail fellow with watery eyes and an overlarge nose. "I'll give you a merchant, and I'll let you live. How's that?"

"Fine," the man said immediately. "There's no need for violence."

"When can I have it?"

"That depends on how particular you are about its gender, health and appearance."

"I want one's been mangled. The worse off, the better."

The man climbed to his feet, dusted himself off and looked askance at Kittins. "I can't imagine what you..."

"Don't," Kittins cut in. "Don't imagine. Don't wonder."

The man nodded, as if acknowledging the wisdom of this. "After dark. That's the busiest time. Closer to midnight."

Kittins nodded in return. "Good," he said. "I'll be back then."

He turned and moved off down the alley, hating himself, feeling vile. Still, it was better 'n killing a babe himself. Had to be. His next stop was the home of his intended victim. At war with himself as he was, it seemed to take Kittins no time to reach his destination. He was almost surprised when he looked up from the cobblestones and found himself in the proper neighborhood. It was a working-class place, but still nicer than he'd ever known. The apartment Darley had directed him to was on the third floor of a tall, narrow building. The stairwell and hallways smelled faintly of incense, but the place was clean, cleaner than just about anywhere else he'd been in the past several years. That was a woman's touch, Kittins thought. Men were not so particular, leastways, not the kinda men he knew.

He found the door he was looking for at the end of the third floor hallway. Good. Nice and private. Uncharacteristically, he tapped softly. From within, he heard a woman's voice murmur something and then, "Who is it?"

"Friend of His Lordship," he answered, trying his best not to sound threatening.

"Lord Darley?" the voice asked.

"None else," Kittins replied.

For the second time in the past half hour, a door inched open without giving Kittins a view inside. He hadn't known people in Lunessfor were so paranoid. On the other hand, seeing him on the stoop couldn't be good for anyone's nerves. He heard a slight gasp.

"I am sorry, I...I do not know you," the woman said, before shutting the door in Kittins' face.

Nor want to, the big man thought. He sighed, stepped back and looked at the door. No, it wouldn't do to bash it in. He was here to save the woman, not terrify her. He knelt and studied the base of the door. Yes, there was a space just large enough for...Taking a Noble out of his purse, he forced it under the door. It was a tight fit, but he made it work with a little pounding.

"Am I being...let go?" the woman asked through the door.

This was silly, of course, but Kittins lay down on his stomach and spoke through the crack. "Would that you were," he said. "It's worse than that."

"Worse?" He could hear the rising anxiety in her voice.

"You don't wanna know. Just...take the money, the child and whatever else you've got and leave town as fast as ever you can."

"The child?" She knew.

Kittins shoved another Noble—his last—under the door. "Look," he said, "that's all I got, all I can afford. Now, you'd best be gone in five minutes. Three, if you can manage it. Leave Lunessfor and don't come back." He saw a flicker of movement through the crack and the sliver of a very fair face, resting itself against the floor.

"I knew this day might come," she said. "Damn him."

"This place have a back door?"

"Yes."

"Use it."

The face was still a moment, and then the woman said, "Bless you, stranger" and disappeared.

"Bless me? Fuck me." Kittins said to himself.

What he brought back to Lord Darley had required a bucket for transportation. Kittins was not the sort to be unsettled by gore—Mahnus knew he'd created enough in his time—but even he was shocked by what he'd been given for his money. The man who'd sold it him assured Kittins the child had never been born and like as not would never have survived long if it had. It changed little for Kittins: he would come back, burn the place down, and kill the man standing before him. Yet...he was complicit. How could he not be? He needed the contents of this bucket in order to save an already living child. The horrendous condition of the thing he held, Kittins hoped, was its proof against detection. Surely even Darley was not so inhuman as to root around in this stew, to scrutinize it too closely.

But when he handed it to Darley, that is precisely what His Lordship did. "This is too much, man!" he complained, poking at the bucket with a knife. "I wanted a good look at the child, to put my mind at ease."

At ease? At ease? "That's her, milord." Kittins went on to describe the building, the doorway, and as many other details as he could add without ever having seen Darley's mistress. "That's her."

Darley paced, his hands clasped behind his back. "Yes, but why so much violence?" He asked, frustrated.

Kittins caught his eye. "Beggin' your pardon, milord, but you wanted killin' done, and I'm a killer."

"Yes, yes," His Lordship said, more to himself than to Kittins. "If you send a wolf to kill a lamb, you can't be surprised when he eats it, I suppose." He put a hand on the captain's shoulder. "Next time, though, try a touch less...enthusiasm, eh?" With that, Darley turned to leave.

"And what of this?" Kittins interjected, holding the bucket out at arm's length.

Darley chuckled, shrugged. "Damned if I know. Throw it in down the sewer?"

Kittins watched His Lordship walk away and exhaled slowly: his ruse had worked, but he felt none the better for it. After following His Lordship's advice and tossing the remains into the city sewer, the captain wandered into the first tavern he could find and began to drink, heavily, in an effort to cleanse his mind of the mess in the bucket. As is often the way with such things, drink only made him feel worse and brood more. When he'd gotten himself nearly blind drunk, Kittins staggered out into the night and made for the baby butcher's home, or shop, or whatever in Mahnus' name it was. He had a hard go of it, in his inebriated state, couldn't remember if he was meant to take a right or a left at such and such a street, and the burning oil from the city's lamps made him more than a little queasy. Finally, he found the place, almost by accident. This time he didn't bother to knock or even bash on the door, but threw his whole weight into it, blasting it off its hinges and several feet into the small foyer beyond. From somewhere down the darkened hallway in front of him, Kittins heard murmurs of alarm and the sound of a metal weapon scraping on stone. Well, he figured there'd be a body guard of some sort. The baby butcher hadn't seemed like the type who could handle anyone his own size. Or bigger. In seconds, a dark shape appeared at the end of the hall, backlit by candle light or perhaps a small fire in the room behind him.

"What's this, then?" a rough, belligerent voice demanded.

What a stupid fuckin' question. Kittins just laughed.

"Ya won't be laughin' when I shove this sword up yer ass!" the other man growled before charging.

While it was still hard to see much of his opponent, the man's blade flickered in the firelight, allowing Kittins to slap it aside at the last second and smash his fist into the fellow's face, breaking his nose and, Kittins suspected, a few of his teeth as well. That kind of damage, though not fatal, almost always caused a brief moment of panic in the recipient. Kittins waded into that panic and put the man down with another blow to the head. Once he hit the floor, the captain stomped on the back of his neck, snapping it like well-cured kindling.

A noise in the room beyond told Kittins his quarry had fled up an unseen staircase. Good. He might've run out another ground-level floor and into the city beyond. Instead, he had hemmed himself in.

Stepping over the guard's body, Kittins proceeded less than carefully into the next room, which turned out to be some sort of workshop, complete with a bench, several basins and countless tools. Oh, Kittins understood the place, he just chose not to dwell on it. He'd erase the entire mess soon enough. There was a door straight ahead and another to his left, but neither had been opened. To his right, a narrow stair spiraled up out of sight. He listened, might have heard a few faint, furtive sounds. He stomped slowly, heavily up the stairs. What did he care? The baby butcher knew he was coming and had to know why, too. This wouldn't be no sneaky, underhanded death. This was coming straight at its intended victim like a forest fire. He could see it coming, but would be unable to avoid it.

On the top step, Kittins paused, listened again. Nothing. The landing atop the stairs was poorly lit by a single candle and barely large enough for a man his size. As below, he found a door directly in front of him and another to his left. This second door was slightly ajar. Sensing a ruse, Kittins threw a mighty kick at the door in front, sending it crashing open into blackness. The big man grabbed the landing's candle from its wall sconce and stepped into the room, a rather spartan bed chamber. There were a cot, a small table and a battered chest in the corner with an open hasp. Without a moment's thought, Kittins strode to the chest and flung open the lid. Before he was even able to see inside, a terrified sobbing from within told him he'd found his prey. Extending the candle over the chest, Kittins saw that, yes, the baby butcher had folded himself inside and now cowered and shook with fear. There was an odor of fresh urine about the man, too.

"Please," he cried, "I gave you what you asked for. I'll gladly return your money..."

Kittins slammed the lid, fastened the hasp. The man inside the chest grew silent briefly before beginning to pound on its sides and top. Kittins turned to the nearby cot and dripped wax over its blankets. Finally, he tossed the still-burning candle onto them and stood, watching, until he was certain the fire would catch. When the bed was fully ablaze, he headed back downstairs, accompanied by the increasingly desperate and alarmed ravings of the man in the chest upstairs. In the workshop, Kittins used other candles and lamps to ignite the baby butcher's various papers and books, which, in turn, set fire to the surrounding surfaces. Overhead, the sounds of wooden walls cracking and the chest bouncing about the floor above were as nothing to the frantic pitch and frequency of the man's screaming. Kittins turned in a complete circle, taking everything in. The room was well and truly burning. Satisfied—or as satisfied as he was ever like to be—he turned and walked out the way he'd come in.

Five minutes later, he watched the inferno from the mouth of an alley down the street. Members of the city watch and scores of neighbors raced to evacuate the buildings on either side of the conflagration, and a bucket brigade was quickly formed. Inevitably, a Shaper would show up and contain the fire. The only question was how much damage it would do before he or she appeared.

As Kittins was about to stagger off towards House Gault, he was brought back 'round by an unexpected, horrifying sound: a baby's wail could clearly be heard rising above the smoke and flames. The butcher had had one alive in there. Instinctively, Kittins sprinted towards the building, only to see it crumble and collapse in on itself. The baby's cry had gone silent.

Kittins was damned.

Vykers, In Pursuit

He was pissing in a stand of trees when Arune spoke up.

There's something watching us. It's…oh!

Vykers finished up. 'Oh?' What's that *mean*?

Before she could answer, he heard a muffled grunt and turned in the direction from which it came. There was a momentary scuffle in some nearby bushes and then, through a part in the branches, out walked what could only have been a new chimera, albeit a smaller and frailer looking one than

Vykers was accustomed to seeing. Gripping it by the scruff of its neck and its left arm was Three, wearing an expression that was at once bemused and triumphant.

"Caught him at last!" Three beamed.

"Him, who?" the Reaper asked.

"One of my brothers, I'd say. I knew I recognized the odor." Vykers guessed the new chimera was male, though it was a good third smaller than the other five he had known. Pale and emaciated, this new creature had a pained, weary look on its face—at least as far as the Reaper could read such things—and an overall affect of someone defeated and waiting for execution. As Three forced it closer, Vykers made out a musky, cinnamon-y scent.

Well? The Reaper prodded Arune.

Hush. I'm studying him.

"Can you speak?"

The creature lowered its head deferentially but lifted a melancholy eye in Vykers' direction. "I can."

"You've obviously been following us for some time. What is it you want?"

"I thought myself the last, believed I'd never see another of...my kind," the chimera said quietly, as if to himself. "When your party travelled past my den and I spied a brother amongst your number..."

"You reckoned you'd have to get a closer look, maybe make contact," Vykers concluded. "And then?"

He's no threat, Arune offered. At the moment. I'm surprised he's even able to stand under his own power.

"I...do not know," the chimera confessed.

"What do you want to do with him?" Vykers asked Three.

The bigger chimera pointed towards camp with his chin. "Take him back to the fire. Feed him something. Question him, certainly. I don't believe he will choose to battle the group of us."

Vykers nodded his agreement, but placed a hand on his sword just in case and was reassured when the new chimera noticed the gesture. Good. Now we know where we stand.

When three figures came out of the woods where only one

had gone in, Aoife became instantly wary. There was Vykers, of course, and his odd companion, Number Three, whom Aoife hadn't seen slip away. But who or what was this new arrival? She glanced over at the Frog, who was learning a trick or two about slight-of-hand from Hoosh, but as yet the boy remained immersed in his current business. Without so much as a "how do you do," Vykers made straight for the fire and sat in his accustomed spot. Three glanced at Aoife as he ushered the new creature to another spot near the flames, but offered no explanation, either. At last, the Frog and the Fool looked over, whereupon their faces lit up with surprise and, in the Frog's case, a bit of trepidation.

"The circus grows!" Hoosh declared.

"Perhaps," Vykers sneered back. He directed his gaze to the newcomer. "So. You've found us. What have you learned?"

The chimera glanced around the circle before speaking. "Of you? That you are a fierce warrior, that your companions are dangerous, as well, that you are headed to the sea. Beyond that? Nothing. Of myself? That I am not the last of my kind and certainly not the biggest or most fearsome, that my fate depends upon your good will."

"Then you are doomed; I have none," Vykers responded.

"And yet, master," Three said, "I would know more of my brother, here. And, for that to happen, he must live."

A long silence fell over the campsite as Vykers pondered his chimera's words, staring into the flames all the while. Finally, he said, "As you wish, my friend." Immediately, he stood up and surveyed their surroundings. "The day wears on. Let's get back on the road."

There was no room for debate. There was never any room for debate with the Reaper, Aoife observed. He spoke and everyone else did as he commanded. No wonder her Majesty had placed him in control of her armies against the End-of-All-Things. Still, Vykers' way wasn't necessarily always the best way for their little party. The A'Shea promised herself she'd speak to him about this when occasion permitted. For now, she began gathering her things and those of the Frog and making ready to depart.

"Will we never reach the bloody coast?" Aoife overheard Vykers muttering to himself.

He was in a foul mood. As ever. Aoife kept her distance and minded her own affairs.

Long & Mardine's Farm

Purebred children were more docile, Mardine knew, than her spirited and overly inquisitive daughter. That was the human side of her. Without Long around to help, Mardine found running the orchard and raising Esmine rather more taxing than she'd expected. Ultimately, she could think of no alternative to hiring extra help, and there certainly was no shortage of folks looking for work. The "Hire a Thrall" campaign that had been pushed by the crown almost endlessly over the past three years was intended to give some of these displaced and desperate people the funds and purpose they needed to recover their lost lives. At the same time, former thralls encountered overwhelming prejudice nearly everywhere they turned. Many people resented them for their role in the last war, whether or not they'd been willing and cognizant participants. Yet, Mardine possessed a good and an honest heart; she knew the same fate might have befallen her husband if things had gone differently. With that thought in mind, she decided to take on one of these unlucky, hopeless souls—a young woman, to help her around the cottage and to watch the child when Mardine had to work in the orchard.

Nelby was a gaunt thing, with white blond hair and eyebrows, over blue-grey eyes and a small, turned-up nose. Her skin was impossibly pale, except for the occasional outbreaks of acne that spread pinkish blotches across her face. She was a quiet but nervous girl who bit her nails to the quick and always smelled vaguely and inexplicably of potato skins. But she was obedient, grateful to have work and eager to please. Nevertheless, Mardine was slow to trust her alone with Esmine, taking close to a fortnight to adjust to the young woman's presence in her home and accept that she earnestly meant to help however she could.

The orchard's apple trees had long since blossomed; the current challenge was in ensuring the trees did not become infested with caterpillars, which might eat the nascent fruit before it developed. This turned out to be a painstaking process that involved visually inspecting every branch of every tree, every single day, or as near to it as one giantess could manage. Caterpillar season was vexingly long.

And there was no question of asking Nelby to search for caterpillars; Mardine's height made her a natural for the job, whereas the smaller, frailer former thrall would have been hard-pressed to search even half the orchard in one day. Thus, inevitably and with great reluctance, Mardine asked Nelby to look after her daughter and home each day while she worked amongst the trees.

But Esmine did not take to her new nanny with her customary enthusiasm, which both alarmed and embarrassed Mardine. She would have liked to think the open-mindedness she had modeled in hiring Nelby had made some kind of impression on her daughter; she was disappointed. Whenever Nelby was out of earshot—fetching firewood from the shed, milk from the cows or other suchlike duties—Esmine complained of the woman's appearance, her manner and, above all, her odor.

For her part, Nelby was never anything but unfailingly polite. Any and every request was met with a "yes, mum," an "of course, mum," or an "I'd be happy to." Ah, if only Esmine had such manners. Mardine wondered if she and Long hadn't spoiled the child. Perhaps she needed to interact with other children more. This was problematic, though, because, at a shade under four feet in height, she dwarfed other three-year-olds and would undoubtedly be tested and bullied by older children. And so, for the nonce, Esmine would have to learn to adapt and accept her new nanny. Mardine had too much work to do elsewhere. If only Long would return!

Rem, House Radcliffe

Rem fancied himself a good actor—excellent, even—but he

was smart enough to suspect that acting ability alone would not guarantee swift and smooth passage through House Radcliffe's security. One person there was, though, whom no one ever questioned, a person so essential yet low in station and loathsome in nature that everyone avoided him whenever possible: the Mucker, the man who cleaned the jakes. Rem had no trouble locating the tools of the trade. And being a good actor, he understood the importance of olfactory verisimilitude and had a good—or a bad—soak in a back-alley cesspool before reporting to the servants' gate of House Radcliffe. Oh, there was every probability Rem would get quite, quite sick from this action, but he had more than enough coin in reserve to afford the most talented A'Sheas, whose services were acquired by means of charitable donations to various causes. Rem could be staggeringly generous, if need be.

He was surprised, upon arriving at House Radcliffe, to find two women "manning" the gate. Both were of average height, with dark brown hair and eyes to match. Sisters, then. The older-looking of the two addressed Rem.

"Where in Mahnus' name have you been, Mucker? The privy's nigh unapproachable!"

"Sfljj," Rem mumbled.

"Wonderful. An imbecile!" the other sister exclaimed irritably. "Well, I suppose that's fitting."

The first sister sighed, equally annoyed. "You'd best get to work, then. And, mind you, don't touch anything outside the jakes. You'll never be heard from again if you do!"

With that dire warning ringing in his ears, the actor was ushered into House Radcliffe. He'd no idea how the other members of Long's team were faring, but he very much doubted a single one of them had managed to gain entrance to two of the Eight Houses. Then, he remembered how dangerous a place this was and eschewed any sense of pride in being there.

Just inside the door, an old man sat behind a miniscule desk, lit by a lone candle on the verge of guttering out. He looked up from the ledger in which he'd been writing and squinted at Rem inquiringly. "And you are?" A moment, and then he caught the scent. "Oh, yes. Never mind. I can bloody well smell who y're. The first-floor jakes are straight on, first hallway on your left. Go to the end, hard right, you're there. Come back when you've finished, I'll direct ye to the next."

"Mmllrp," Rem replied.

Advancing further into the mansion, Rem quickly realized he had not merely come in the servants' gate but was, indeed, in the bowels, so to speak, of the servants' wing. There was little to indicate power or wealth here; the floor and walls were plain and unadorned. There weren't even any windows to look out. Rem came to a standstill, gathered his thoughts. Wandering around the servants' wing dressed as a turd was hardly going to give him access to the kind of gossip he needed if he was going to satisfy either Henton or Captain Long. Well, the old man at the door had promised to direct him to the next privy as soon as he'd finished cleaning the first. Nothing to be done, really, but muck it out.

Had it not been for his experience in battle, Rem would never have had the stomach for it. But he had seen and done things in combat that made even plunging the jakes seem wholesome. Still, he suspected it would be some time before he felt the desire to eat anything. Finished with his task at last, he returned to the old man by the door.

"Gods, I could smell ye comin' 'fore I saw ye." The old man remarked. "Well, then," he said, "next one's up a flight. Go back down yon hallway, pass two doors on your right, take the third. Go up the stairs, down the new hallway. It's the second door on your left. And don't wander nor poke you nose where it don't belong. Have ye got alla that?"

"Amerpg." Rem was rather enjoying this mumbling business. His regular line of work placed such emphasis on diction and articulation that he never got to fully explore or enjoy the vagaries of incoherence. What freedom! What boundless possibilities were contained in the indecipherable response! He felt like some cryptic oracle of yore: his utterances might be taken to mean virtually anything!

"Huh," the man grunted. "Well, off with you, afore I 'gin to gag."

This time, Rem took a couple of wrong turns—on purpose,

naturally—before he found the specified location. Ah, yes, this shit was of a much higher caliber, to be sure. If only he were a real Mucker. Stashing his tools near an open toilet, the actor wandered back down the hallway and revisited the second room he'd popped his head into moments earlier. It was a drawing room of some sort, richly appointed in dark wood paneling and equally dark, seductive velour in tasteful curtains and wall-hangings. Even the upholstery was fitted with matching fabric. It was the two doors beyond, however, that most interested Rem, as potentially leading to someone's private quarters.

Walking carefully along the perimeter of the room so as not to track footprints in the most obvious line of sight, Rem proceeded to the door at the right rear. Pressing his ear against it, he was disappointed to hear snoring: an occupied room was a useless room, even if the occupant was asleep. Cautiously, he crept to the second door, in the opposite corner. This time, he heard nothing from the room beyond. Placing his hand gently, carefully upon the handle, he tested it and found the door unlocked. With patience he hadn't known he possessed, he opened it slowly, by degrees, to avoid making the slightest sound. Now he was aware of it, he could still hear the unknown snorer laboring away in the other room. Excellent. Let the man be his warning bell: if the snoring stopped, it would be time to leave with all haste. To Rem's surprise, however, the snoring got louder as he worked the door open wider, which suggested the two rooms were connected somehow, perhaps by a third, unseen doorway. At last, he pushed his own door wide enough to offer a view of the room on the other side. Predictably, it was dark, but not completely so. Like a tortoise, he extended his neck into the space and waited for his eyes to adjust.

It was a dressing room, presumably that of the next room's resident. But more than that, it was a possible source of alternate clothing, a new disguise, if only Rem could locate something sufficiently subdued as to seem commonplace. It wouldn't do to appear in the sleeper's custom made, courtly attire. Quickly, Rem slipped into the room and pulled the door nearly closed behind him, allowing just enough light to seep through that he could navigate without mishap.

As he suspected, there was another door to the back of this room, slightly ajar. He left it that way. The room also contained an ornate dressing table and mirror, a chair, several chests and a large wardrobe. First sight of the sleeper's clothing revealed him to be a man. Rem might've guessed that from the snoring, but he'd been wrong about such things before. After several minutes of pawing through the man's clothing in semi-darkness, Rem chose a sleeping gown and night cap. What the sleeper was wearing at present didn't bear thinking on. Why the fellow was still abed so late into the morning, however, did pique his interest. Perhaps he was one of the indolent rich, who had nothing better to do than lounge around whilst others did all the work. Or maybe he was sleeping one off. It occurred to Rem the man might be sick, and just as the actor began to frighten himself with the possibility of contagion, he remembered he, himself, was covered in shit. In a flash, he restored the room's contents as best he could, grabbed the garments in question and snuck back through the door into the drawing room. On a table near the hall, he found a pitcher full of water, which he picked up with his unburdened hand and carried with him back to the jakes.

His tools and the cell's overwhelming stench were exactly as he left them. Using the water he'd just found, Rem cleaned himself up as much as possible and then shoved his Mucker's outfit down the shithole before gingerly stepping into the purloined sleeping robe. Last of all, he pulled the night cap onto his head and low over his brow, to conceal his features from casual glances. He'd never fool anyone close up, of course, but then he didn't intend to meet anyone close up.

Sometimes, however, life couldn't care less what we intend. Just as Rem opened the door to step back in the hallway, he spied someone approaching and hastily slammed it shut again, frantically wondering what to do next.

"Still got the runs, have you, March?" a man's voice asked him. "Serves you right, you old fool. You shouldn't be out of bed, anyway."

March? March Radcliffe? Rem had never heard of him. Perhaps he was a guest? He did hear the door to the stall next to him open, followed by the unmistakable sound of urination. "That was a devil of a feast, though, wasn't it?" the unknown man continued.

"Gnrrphlx," Rem replied. Why ruin a good thing?

"That's as may be," the man responded, "But I still think Her Ladyship lays a good table...and a goodly number of her squires, from what I hear." Although he had seemingly finished his task, the man next door continued to ramble. "Wouldn't mind seein' a piece o' that action, myself, truth to tell."

Rem felt vexed, to say the least. Who socializes in the privy?

"What do you think, eh, March? Think you could handle Her Ladyship?"

The man expected a response? Gods! The longer this fellow engaged him, the more likely Rem was to be caught. "Zrrrmmnnttppt," he mumbled.

"I'm sorry, old fellow; I don't believe I caught that last..."

Rem made the loudest, most liquid farting noise he could simulate. There was a prolonged silence from the next stall, and then...

"Really! Really, March. I know you're not feeling well, but that's..."

Rem let loose with another louder and longer one.

"Good gods, man!" the other man exclaimed. "You're really not well, are you?"

And again, the biggest, longest, foulest noise the city's best actor could muster. The man next door bolted from the privy, slamming the door behind himself and stomping off down the hall. After waiting a good two minutes to ensure his visitor did not return, Rem cracked his own door and peered into the hallway. Seeing he was indeed alone, he stepped out into the comparatively fresh air and noticed a book on the floor, obviously dropped by the talkative tinkler on his flight to freedom.

A book? No, a diary. A lavishly decorated, heavily scented

and surprisingly thick diary, filled with the flamboyant script of a man who thought himself immensely important. Suddenly, Rem got nervous, realizing exactly where he was and how ill-prepared to deal with exposure or, Mahnus forbid, capture. He regretted disposing of his Mucker costume, as he wanted nothing more than to leave with this new treasure immediately. With great reluctance and a sudden case of the shakes, Rem began his search for a place to hide until nightfall.

FOUR

Vykers, In Pursuit

There were villages, towns and cities along the Queen's Highway, to be sure, and Vykers avoided them all, along with the unwanted attention he and his band would have received, were he to set foot in the smallest of them. But he was able to send Aoife or Hoosh into various towns along their journey, whenever staples ran low or he wanted to sample the latest rumors.

On one such occasion, the Fool returned with a coin he could not stop chuckling over. With the exception of the Frog, no one else seemed to care or notice. Yet, Hoosh got under Vykers' skin like no one else in the party.

"What are you cackling at, fool?" Vykers said that last word like an insult, but Hoosh never took it that way.

"A coin I've not seen before," the Fool grinned. He held out his palm, inviting Vykers to take a closer look. "Behold, 'the Hero'."

Faster than Hoosh thought possible, the Reaper snatched the coin from his hand and held it up before his face. Pretending to look at it, Vykers stole a glance at the Fool's face and was gratified to see the fellow's façade crack. Good: he'd made him uneasy. Vykers' satisfaction was short-lived, however, once he turned his focus to the coin, for there, in cold, finely stamped silver, was his own likeness. "Fuck is this?" he asked, alarmed.

"As I said," the Fool responded smugly, "it's a new coin, a new denomination, if you will. I'm told it fits right between the Noble and the Royal.

"It's worth that much?" Vykers was impressed.

"Not to me," the Fool countered.

Vykers sneered back. "Still, I don't reckon I like seein' my face on a coin."

"Can I see?" the Frog asked from his place by the fire.

With a loud 'ping,' the Reaper flicked the coin in the boy's direction. The kid grabbed it, right out of the air.

"I think it's meant to be a compliment," Aoife said, as she leaned over the Frog's shoulder to get a closer look.

Only the two chimeras remained unmoved.

"That's as may be," Vykers said, "But I don't want the people's...admiration. Makes it harder to..."

"What? Betray them when the time comes?"

There were a lot of ways the warrior might have responded. He might, for instance, have lashed out and broken the Fool's nose. Or his neck. He might have shoved him into the fire. What he chose instead was to merely answer "Yes" and walk away. *Let* the *Fool chew on* that *for a while*, Vykers thought.

Am I imagining things, or are you developing self-restraint? Arune asked.

Gods, Vykers groaned. *It never rains, but it pours. And what do you want?*

Your welfare.

Vykers snorted. *O' course you do.*

Of course I do, Arune assured him. *The Fool is testing you. What I can't figure is why.*

'Cause he's stupid? The Reaper offered unhelpfully.

He's not stupid.

Then maybe he's just suicidal. One o' these days, I'll grant his wish and plant him. Let him laugh at that.

Humans do not have the most sensitive of noses, and yet there are certain scents that never fail to engage their imaginations: wood smoke, snow, baking bread. And the sea. When Vykers caught his first whiff, he inhaled mightily, almost in spite of himself. The sea, at last. How long had it been since he'd seen it? Too, too long. Perhaps if he ever became king, he'd establish his capitol on the shore. And then again, perhaps not. There were, after all, things that came from the sea that did not always smell so pleasant. Still, he looked forward to the sounds of surf, the sight of massive breakers crashing onto the beach, the brisk breeze on his face. He looked forward, too, to a change in diet, however brief. In her Majesty's castle, he'd been stuffed on poultry and rich sauces. On the road, Three had supplied him with endless game. A bit of fish would make a nice change. Maybe some crab. Fresh chowder with bacon.

His thoughts were drawn back to her Majesty. Finding her, rescuing her, was his real priority, although he didn't entirely understand his own thinking on the matter. What was she to him? So what if she died?

He felt Three approaching before he saw him.

"So, this is your ocean I smell?"

"My ocean?" Vykers grinned. "Aye. What do you think of it?"

"Smells big," Three replied.

Vykers laughed. "Oh, it's big. You got no idea!" Three looked a touch nervous, which only made Vykers laugh louder. "Nothin' to worry about, though. It can't come ashore and eat you."

Three relaxed. "That's good to hear."

"Actually, that ain't true, neither. It does come ashore sometimes, carrying homes and people away with it, never to be seen again...but not very often." The chimera looked positively sick, and now Vykers struggled to stifle his laughter. Eventually, he changed the subject. "What's the story with your new brother?"

Three opened his mouth slightly, in the manner of a cat that smells something unpleasant or unwelcome. He glanced over at the new chimera, who was warming himself by the last of the fire. Cautiously, Three took Vykers by the elbow and encouraged him to put a few more yards between them and the fire. "He seems confused" the chimera said in a low voice.

"Seems," Vykers answered.

"Yes."

"But?"

Three nodded. It was good Vykers could read him so well. "It's been over three years since my brothers and I escaped from that fell compound. We found no survivors..."

"Which don't mean he hadn't escaped already."

"Possibly," Three admitted. "But what's he been doing all this time? Where has he been, and why does he show up now?"

Vykers flashed a grim smile. "You don't trust him." Statement.

"No. I trust no one." A second later, realizing he might have offended his former master, Three added, "Except for you."

"Except no one, old friend. Not even me."

Three frowned, but it was a frown of agreement. It was sage advice, after all.

Vykers spoke again, "So, in a scrape..."

"I'll keep my eyes on him," Three replied quickly. "And I will kill him if he does anything untoward."

The Reaper looked directly into the chimera's eyes. "I know you will," he said.

Kittins, House Gault

There was a thud against the side of his bunk, and Kittins opened bleary eyes to find His Lordship staring down at him.

"Haven't seen you in days, man. Are you ill?"

"Yeah," Kittins said. And it wasn't entirely a lie. He'd become sick of himself, of his own careless violence.

Darley eyed him skeptically. "Have you seen the A'Shea?" he asked. "I won't have you spreading anything catching."

Kittins forced himself into a sitting position. "I ain't contagious, and I'm past the worst of it."

"Glad to hear it. I thought, perhaps, that last job had affected your conscience."

"If I had one, I'm sure it mighta," Kittins rumbled. "But it died years ago. This here's naught but a flu or some such. Nearly gone, as I said."

His Lordship relaxed visibly. "Good, good. Hope I'll see you on your feet soon, then. There's quite a lot going on and much to be done."

"I'll be in the kitchen within the hour," the big captain said. "You can find me there, your lordship, if I can be of service." For some strange reason, His Lordship seemed to like Kittins, to value his opinion and proximity. It wasn't like the captain had made any special effort to flatter or please the fellow. Hells, he wouldn't have known how had he wanted to. Maybe Kittins was the kind of man—hard, strong and frightening—that Darley had wished himself to be, might in fact have been if things had turned out differently. Whatever the case, in no time at all, Kittins had somehow become His Lordship's right-hand man. There was something in that that bothered the big man, but he couldn't puzzle it out at the moment. And certainly not on an empty stomach.

For the first time, Kittins noticed the other bunks were empty. He wondered what time it was. Then he wondered what day it was. Then he realized it didn't matter. One day in hell's the same as another. But about those empty bunks... everyone else must be at dinner. He could join them, but he preferred not to. Besides, he'd already told His Lordship he could be found in the kitchen, so that was where he'd be.

A half hour later, the big man had discovered his appetite and was making short work of a sizeable hunk of beef and an equally large loaf of bread. In between bites, he drank from a pitcher of milk, as if it were an enormous flagon. He rarely drank milk—hadn't had any, in fact, in years—but for some reason he found himself craving and thoroughly enjoying it.

"You're feeling better, I see." Lord Darley stood in the doorway and watched Kittins eat.

The captain grunted in affirmation. The cook, who had been puttering around near the oven, had conveniently disappeared.

Darley eyed Kittins speculatively. "How would you like a room of your own? You don't seem to care for the other men—and I can't say I blame you—and a little more privacy would make it easier for us to do business."

Kittins wipe his mouth with the back of his arm and stood. "Sounds good, your lordship. I'd like that."

"Finish eating. There's no rush."

Kittins grinned. "Truth is, this is my third helping. I've prob'ly had enough."

Darley arched his eyebrows. "Ah! Yes, must stay in fighting trim, eh?" After a pause, he continued. "Have you ever been down to the cellars?"

"Can't say as I have," Kittins replied.

"Well, then, let's take a little tour, shall we?"

For a moment, Kittins wondered if this new, private room wouldn't be found on the upcoming tour, a cell in the family dungeon. Reflecting on his actions of the past week, he realized he wouldn't care if it did. Maybe a prolonged period of solitary confinement was what he needed, or at least what he deserved. Nah. Few get what they deserve. His Lordship had something else in store for Kittins.

The route to the cellars was impressively labyrinthine. They could almost assuredly not be found by accident, and there was a series of minor security measures along the way that, collectively, made such a prospect virtually unthinkable. Kittins marveled at the ever-unfolding size of the Gault estate. The horizontal, above-ground spread of it, alone, was considerable, but when one took the subterranean, vertical reach of House Gault into account as well, it was staggering, mind-boggling.

"Musta taken your folk hundreds o' years to build this," he told His Lordship, when he stopped to unlock a door.

"Hundreds and hundreds, I'd say."

"The estate's that old, is it?"

"You've no idea. No one has. By virtue of mere longevity, Gault's got a better claim to the throne than any of the other eight, and perhaps even Her Majesty."

Kittins sniggered. "She's not going anywhere."

Darley looked over at him. "Isn't she?" he asked pointedly. "Rumor has it, she may have already gone."

A greener, less experienced man might've pressed the issue— this was, after all, the very topic of Kittins' investigation—but the captain kept his cool, feigned indifference. Darley was more likely to confide in him if he felt Kittins wasn't overly interested in everything he had to say.

After a time, the two men arrived at an immense chamber, fashioned out of the very bedrock. Pillars separated the space into a number of smaller rooms, but did nothing to diminish the emotional impact of its overall size.

His Lordship smiled proudly and said "Welcome to the grotto. It's a sort of informal men's club beneath House Gault."

Kittins was too flabbergasted to speak.

His Lordship continued, "Here, you'll find drink, games of chance, sparring partners and women to suit your every taste and purpose. But if you don't fancy women, why..."

"I like women just fine," Kittins said quickly. A breath or two later, he added, "But I was expecting to find a dungeon, cells, prisoners, when you led me down here."

"Naturally. And we have those, as well, just off to the left there," Darley pointed. "Past the fire pit." At Kittins' bewildered expression he went on. "All the big houses have their dungeons. It's where we keep our hostages." He looked Kittins directly in the eyes. "And our traitors. Conventional wisdom has it that solitary confinement is what breaks a man. I disagree. I say what breaks him is listening to others enjoy themselves and knowing he'll never experience that again for himself. Thus, the grotto— an endless orgy of every vice you'd care to indulge. And it keeps the guards happy and loyal."

"No doubt," Kittins replied.

Darley nodded. "Have a look around, make yourself at home. I've a little business to attend to but I'll find you again later."

"No doubt," Kittins repeated quietly, as His Lordship headed off into the room about his affairs.

Stepping fully into the chamber, the big man took his time surveying the scene before him. Just a few feet away was an apparently makeshift bar that had clearly become more permanent than originally intended. It was only large enough to accommodate two or three patrons, but Kittins noticed the barkeep was handing out entire bottles to any and everyone who approached. One of the men at the bar was Kittins' barracks mate, Wrensl Deda. When the man saw him coming, he straightened up on his stool and put on his best glad-handing expression.

"Ah, there you are, Janks!" he called out cheerfully.

Funny, the cheer in his voice was not in evidence on his face.

"I was startin' to think you lived only for work."

"Huh," Kittins grunted. "What're you drinkin'?"

Deda stared at this bottle as if seeing it for the first time. "Dunno, really. Some sort of wine. Red wine, must be. It's good, though. Old Darley knows how to keep his men happy."

"So I've heard," Kittins observed wryly.

"Stand you to a bottle or two?" Deda asked.

"Why not?"

Deda laughed. It was a weird sound, completely devoid of mirth. "Yeah, why not? Why the hells not? Barkeep!" he yelled, "a bottle o' yer best for my friend Janks, here!"

"What else you fancy down here? What's good?"

The other man took a long pull from his bottle and leered at Kittins. "Well, the ladies is good, 'o course...always assumin' you like the ladies..."

"I like the ladies!" Kittins came back a good deal louder than he'd meant.

Deda leaned away from him. "Alright, okay. You like the ladies. There's some don't, is all I'm saying. There's some prefer other..."

Kittins cut in, "I get it. But apart from the ladies and the drink, what's to do? You got a favorite past time, Deda?"

"Well," Wrensl began, "there's some like to fight. You might enjoy that. Me, I'd rather gamble. And then there's the freak show."

"The what?"

"Freak show. Old Darley's got a bunch o' Svarren down here, keeps 'em in cages to frighten the prisoners, I guess. But sometimes, they bring 'em out and parade 'em through the grotto. It's kinda fun to hurl insults at 'em. Or bottles. For the right price, you can even try bedding the females...if that's your thing."

Kittins felt that black anger rising inside himself again, the anger that had led him to burn the baby butcher alive...and a baby along with him. He tamped it down, took the proffered bottle of wine and drank deeply. Deda, he saw, did the same.

"Show me this freak show," he commanded.

Vykers, at the Coast

They'd reached the coast at last, and not a moment too soon, to Vykers' way of thinking. In his weakened state, he'd grown weary of the chase and no longer found interest or intrigue in the mystery of the Queen's disappearance. He just wanted to find her, bring her home, and be done with it. He did experience a brief instant of amusement when Number 3 saw the sea for the first time. The chimera's expression was almost that of a small boy, frightened by a thunderstorm, funny to see in one so otherwise unshakeable. Then Vykers remembered there was, in fact, a small boy in their company. Yes, the Frog was no less astounded.

"This the edge o' the world?" he asked the group.

"It certainly is, from the fishes point o' view!" Hoosh cackled.

"Think of it as a large lake," Aoife instructed.

Vykers stole a look in her direction. The wind had blown her hood back, and even now it danced in her luxuriant red locks and brought a blush to her cheeks. She caught Vykers' eye and immediately looked away.

Figures, he thought.

What figures? Arune asked coyly.

He wasn't in the mood. *The Queen's Shaper promise us a boat or some such?*

Should be just down the coast. Now we're here, I can probably get them to meet us halfway.

Do that. I wanna get outta this saddle as soon as possible.

As you say, Master.

Master? Vykers said. *I like that.*

The sun was setting when at last they spied their ship—a single-masted cog, bobbing at anchor more than an arrow shot offshore—so Vykers opted to make camp on the beach. "Could be our last time on solid ground for a while," he said. The truth was, he wanted to give the Frog and Number 3 a little more time to get used to the idea of leaving said ground and consigning themselves to the sea.

Three sprinted off into the surrounding hills on his regular evening hunt. The best he could manage, however, was a pile of seabirds, albeit a staggeringly large pile. He might have done better if the other chimera had helped hunt, but it seemed that was not amongst his talents.

Vykers moved to stand over him. "You don't hunt?"

"I'm a poor hunter, I'm afraid."

"And yet you've survived in the wilderness for more 'n three years."

"I was hardly thriving when you found me."

"You mean, when you found us."

The chimera lowered his gaze. "Just so."

Vykers scowled at him. "I got my hands full with these others," he said, indicating the boy and the Fool. "I don't need any more dead weight."

The Frog was about to object, but Aoife put a restraining hand on his shoulder. This was between the Reaper and the newcomer.

The chimera's body language became even more subservient, like that of a whipped dog. "I will find some way to be of service, Tarmun Vykers. I give you my word."

"Your word, is it?" Clearly, Vykers was unimpressed. "What do we call you then? What's your number?"

"I am Forty-Seven," the creature said, extending his hand to show the sigil burned onto its back.

Vykers whistled. "Forty-Seven? Gods, how many o' you fellas did they make, anyway?"

"I believe I was one of the last."

"You believe." The Reaper wasn't buying it. "You know how many men I've killed, Forty-Seven?"

The chimera was silent while he weighed his answer. "A number beyond counting."

As there was no hint of irony or sarcasm in the comment, Vykers let it stand. "Remember that," he warned, and turned back towards the others. "Tomorrow," he said, "we take to the sea, and from there, only Mahnus knows how or when we'll return. Any of you wanna part ways, this is the time to do it."

Nobody spoke, not even the Fool. Vykers sighed. He was sort of hoping Hoosh would give up.

"Alright then," he said in a tone that suggested they'd all had their chance, "let's finish these birds and get some sleep. Three," he asked the chimera, "you take first watch?"

"I will."

In the end, they had to let the horses go, as Vykers had suspected they might. While the hold of the cog was undoubtedly large enough to accommodate them all, there was no way of knowing how long they'd be at sea, and the Reaper wasn't sure they could keep the beasts healthy and alive for the duration. Too, the longboat dispatched by the ship to pick them up wasn't designed for such large animals, and they'd have had to make a separate trip ashore for each horse. Vykers wanted to board, set sail and resume the chase. He had precious little patience in the best of times; his wound made him even more restive.

Once aboard, he endured another less than welcome surprise.

"Ah, Reaper," a familiar voice called out, "it is good to see you again."

"Historian," Vykers rumbled. "I didn't think you folks ever left Ahklat. What's your stake in this?"

"Direct as ever, I see. Like a sword thrust," the pale man replied. He cast his black eyes over the rest of Vykers' companions and continued, "Perhaps we should discuss this in private, in the Captain's quarters..."

"I'd rather do it in my cabin."

"The Captain's quarters are your cabin, Reaper."

"And the Captain?"

The Historian showed the barest hint of a smile. "He's bunking with the cook, I'm told. He was afraid you'd take his quarters anyway, so he abandoned them voluntarily."

Vykers looked about the deck, frowned. "I'da been good with a simple hammock. I'm a warrior, not a thief."

"Nevertheless. Shall I show you the way?"

Again Vykers scanned the deck. Most of his party was still boarding, whilst the deck was alive with sailors preparing to raise the anchor, hoist the sails and depart.

"Lead on," he answered.

The Captain's quarters did not disappoint. They boasted the most floor space, the biggest bed and the largest windows on the ship. There was also an excellent selection of alcohol, although it was obvious from placement of the bottles that one of their number was missing. Ah, well, Captain's prerogative.

The Historian gestured to a table at the back of the room—the stern, Vykers was certain. "Shall we sit?"

The Reaper shook his head. "I'm good. What's this all about?"

"Her Majesty the Queen is almost certainly the most powerful person on the continent. On this continent," the Historian clarified. "When her well-being is threatened, it threatens everyone's well-being. Even that of my fellow Ahklatians."

Vykers stepped over to the Captain's collection of bottles, picked one up, uncorked it, sniffed and grinned. "Uh-huh," he said. "So, you didn't intervene when the End was threatening Her Majesty, but now…"

"Threatening to attack Lunessfor and actually taking it are two entirely different things, as I'm sure you know," the Ahklatian responded dryly. "Stealing the Queen from her elaborately warded bed chambers in the middle of the night, however…that is significantly more difficult. The person or people responsible for that are profoundly dangerous."

Vykers sat down on the bed and took a long swig from the bottle. "And you know this because…"

"I laid some of those spell wards myself, ages ago. Their secrets, their provenance were beyond the ken of most mortals."

"Most?" Swig.

"I do not presume to know everything, only a great deal more than most. There may be mortals of sufficient power across the southern sea. There may also be something worse. At any rate, I've done little but study in my long life; I know more of what lies ahead than anyone else in our land."

Vykers had fallen asleep.

He felt a hand on his forehead and, without even opening his eyes, shot a hand out and grabbed a fistful of fabric, pulling his unseen visitor closer. Of course, it was Aoife. By the time he actually looked at her, her face was a mere twelve inches from his own. His actions and proximity rattled her, and she stammered in explaining herself.

"I was...I mean, you...it's still early..." Finally, she regained her equilibrium. "It's not mid-day and you were sleeping. I was worried you'd taken a turn for the worse." As Vykers said nothing in response, Aoife continued. "I'd appreciate it if you'd unhand me now."

Instead, he pulled her slowly but firmly closer.

"What are you...Vykers. Tarmun, this isn't..."

Closer, two inches from his face. She could smell alcohol on his breath and wood smoke in his hair.

"Tarmun, I am A'Shea. You cannot..."

I wouldn't do this if I were you, Arune warned.

You ain't me, Vykers retorted.

And kissed Aoife.

Alheria's tits! Arune cursed in the back of his mind. Vykers shut her out.

For the briefest of moments, Aoife resisted, then returned the kiss. His mouth tasted of rum. His beard stubble scratched not unpleasantly across her chin and cheeks. She realized her heart was pounding, and she was breathing more heavily. She had never felt such exhilaration, such an odd combination of fear mingled with jubilation in her life. She was dimly aware of things happening down below for the both of them and so pushed away so forcefully that she almost fell over backwards. She stared at Vykers in shock and noticed an almost hungry gleam in his eyes.

"Never do that again, Tarmun Vykers!" she yelled.

He sat up, wincing. "Never's a long time, Aoife." He rarely used her name; now, it seemed too intimate.

"Yes, exactly!" she countered. She felt it important to stand her ground; backing away would seem too weak. Vykers needed to know she meant what she'd said, that she had the force of will to resist and even fight back if necessary. "I am here as your healer, nothing more."

Vykers stood, approached her.

Aoife felt her resolve wavering. She glanced at the door, wondering whether she ought to make a run for it. She did not.

The Reaper returned to within a foot of her and stood, unmoving, letting her senses take him in. His right hand reached up, and his fingers gently traced the outline of her face, as a blind man might do. He towered over her, and she found she could not maintain eye contact. For some reason, she could not even find the will to move. Vykers' hand wandered into her hair, slowly, reverently.

In a quiet voice, he said "I don't know why, I can't say how, but you are the most magnificent woman I have ever..." He stopped himself. "You are magnificent," he concluded.

And you are drunk, Aoife nearly said in return. But of course, she could not. Her whole being was seized with miniature tremors of nervousness, fear, excitement...desire. She was a wreck, and it frightened her, no end.

Hoosh ambled into the room and had to pretend he was unaware of what been transpiring. "Rumor has it, there's drink to be had hereabouts!"

Aoife took advantage of this distraction to step away from the Reaper and rearrange her hair.

"I've half a mind to put you in the drink," Vykers told the man.

"You're half right, anyhow."

"How's that?" Vykers asked belligerently.

"You've half a mind."

"I'm only keeping..."

Aoife bolted from the room.

Vykers looked at Hoosh with a cold fury. "You're looking at your death, old man," he told the Fool. "Think on that. Live with it. Sooner or later, I will kill you." With that, he headed out onto the deck.

Spirk, House D'Escurzy

Spirk lived a strange existence on the D'Escurzy estate, a life of echoes and shadows, of cavernous, drafty rooms and old men snoring. It was rare that he saw anyone other than His Lordship, and he often wondered if Mahnus had created House D'Escurzy as a world all its own and abandoned the two of them in it. Spirk's routine consisted of little more than keeping His Lordship warm, wheeling him to and fro, lifting him in and out of his bed and/or ringing the peculiar silent service bells that nevertheless always caused meals, fresh clothing and whatever else to appear nearby as if by magic. But it was not magic. Spirk knew a thing or two about magic, and though it was only a thing or two, he recognized it when he saw it. Or didn't see it. No, these items were delivered by servants so stealthy and quick as to be virtually invisible. Servants...or boblins. He was thinking of goblins, of course, but he'd called them boblins his entire life and had no plans to change now. Especially not for cowardly boblins who refused to show themselves when he sought them out...

"Cretin!" Titus rasped. "I've done with my bedpan. Take it away this instant!"

Spirk snapped to attention; he'd been day-dreaming again—hard to avoid in an atmosphere so dreamlike—but His Lordship was not accustomed to waiting for anything, and Spirk knew he had precious little tolerance for dawdlers. Moving as quickly as he dared, the young man fetched the offending container and made for the nearest jakes. It wouldn't do to be gone too long; he worried how His Lordship might fare alone with the boblins. Upon his return, he found his master as cheerful as ever.

"Clodpoll!" the man wheezed. "Carry me to my chair."

Without hesitation, Spirk complied. He rushed to Titus' bedside and lifted the gnomish fellow into his arms. His Lordship weighed so little that Spirk worried constantly for his health. At first, he'd worried mostly for himself and what might befall him should Titus die in his care. Gradually, though, he came to feel for the man, isolated from his own kin by their fear of him, by their greed for his power and possessions.

"Endless hells," Titus sighed, "I am too old for this shit."

As usual, Spirk's stupidity served him well. "Beggin' your pardon, your Lordship, but you don't seem so old to me."

"Bullshit, lad. Don't speak bullshit to me."

"Well," Spirk hedged, "you can't be as old as Her Majesty."

"And what o' that? That bitch isn't human!"

"She's not?"

"Of course she is," Titus spat irritably. "She just doesn't seem to be." And then, a bit of luck: "I do hear her health's failing at last, though." Titus grinned. "Maybe I'll outlive her after all."

There it was: Lord Titus himself seemed convinced the Queen was ill, and his conviction sounded genuine enough. If something had befallen Her Majesty, it had not been at Titus' behest. This did not mean, however, that the rest of his family was innocent...

Rem, House Hawsey

Unable to come up with a plan to escape the Radcliffe estate, Rem had been forced to hide under the sleeping man's bed in order to avoid discovery. Providence intervened, however (on the actor's side, anyhow), when the sleeper was found dead by his nephew. Between the time the monks were summoned to take the man's body to temple and the time the same monks actually arrived, Rem managed to hide the corpse in a nearby armoire and substitute himself in its place. The monks, being somewhat credulous to begin with, bought Rem's performance lock, stock and barrel. It was only when he wrestled free of their grasp some half mile from House Radcliffe and ran off into the morning's crush that they began to suspect something was amiss.

Back in the safety of the barracks at House Hawsey—and after a lengthy bath—Rem spent a good hour perusing the diary he'd found. The handwriting within was both ornate and miniscule, making the pages vexingly hard to read. On the positive side, smaller writing meant more room; more room meant more words, and more words meant more information. In the brief time he'd examined the diary, Rem learned of insanity, infanticide, incest, intemperance, incontinence, and impotence in abundance at House Radcliffe. But nothing of the Queen's whereabouts. Yet. He was certain when he did discover something, it would undoubtedly start with the letter "i." Before he could prove his theory, His Lordship arrived to welcome him home.

Now, Rem had a difficult time referring to Henton Hawsey as "Your Lordship." If he were casting a play about various midlands nobles, Henton would be the last person he'd consider for such a role. There is casting-against-type after all, and there is casting-against-reason. Nonetheless, Rem somehow marshaled his acting talents and strove to maintain the façade of respect that was so necessary under his present circumstances.

"Ah, Your Lordship!" he sang out, "I was just coming to see you after I finished my bath."

Henton looked as if he understood completely. "I underthtand completely," he replied, to underscore the point. "I wouldn't want filthy dutht from Houth Radcliffe on my thkin, either. He paused. "But what have you learned?"

Truth be told, Rem was loath to surrender the diary now that he'd finally begun reading it, but if it would please His Lordship, curry favor and buy a few days of peace from His Lordship's attentions, he supposed it was worth the trade. "I found this," he said, holding the diary in the light so His Lordship could see it better.

Henton reached out and snatched it in a most lascivious manner. "It-th a diary!" he exclaimed. "But whooth?"

"Someone named Gelter," Rem offered helpfully.

His Lordship's eyebrows shot up in surprise and his mouth formed a perfect 'o.' "Gelter Radcliffe?" He giggled. "Gelter Radcliffe?" He giggled more—longer, louder and harder. "Oh, very well done Mathter Wratch, very well done indeed!"

"You'll forgive me, Your Lordship, but I am not as familiar with the, er, Radcliffe family tree as perhaps I ought to be. I'm not sure who this Gelter…"

"Oh, he'th a fop!" Henton cut in, scornfully. "A fop and a dandy. One that thtyles himthelf the young bravo, but quailth at hith own thyadow. One that hath all the wordth i' the world, but none o' the acthionth. Would that I could meet thith good Thir Codpiethe in a duel; I'd thyow him the Hawthey 'High and Low'!"

That speech was a fruitcake, so packed with delectable absurdities that Rem wished he could slow it down, have it all over again and better attend its every sweet surprise. Henton calling another man 'fop?' Questioning another man's courage? Accusing another man of being long on words, but short on action? For an instant, Rem wondered whether a meeting between these two peacocks might be arranged and, further, whether there was any betting action to be had on either side. Before he could work out the details—alas!—His Lordship interrupted.

"But! But! But! But! Now, we have hith diary. Thith fallth out better than I'd hoped. If thith ith a thample of your work, Mathter Wratch, you may make Lord yourthelf ere long!" And, in a whirl of lilac scented...something or other...His Lordship was off to pour over his ill-gotten gains.

Rem watched him go. He searched his thoughts for a metaphor, a simile that might adequately describe Lord Hawsey's quality, in the event he ever decided to write the man into a play. Lord Hawsey was like...stumbling out of bed with one's breeches half-on and then tumbling headlong down a flight of stairs. He was like sneezing in the face of a beautiful woman. He was accidentally sitting on a bee hive whilst eating honey-glazed almonds.

And he was the head of one of Lunessfor's most powerful families and a suspect in the disappearance of the Queen. However precious, however outlandish the man might seem, there had to be more to him than he let on. Rem resolved to redouble his efforts to investigate His Lordship. And he knew just where to start.

Yendor, House Fyne

Sometimes, one person succeeds where another has failed simply because he's a different person—in bearing, tone of voice or overall demeanor. Such was the case for Yendor, who had little difficulty gaining entrance to House Fyne for an interview after flashing the medal he'd once been awarded by General Branch.

"So, you fought the End, eh?" the Captain of the House Guard asked him.

Yendor nodded. "That's a fact."

The other man worked his lower jaw side to side, squinted at Yendor. "You don't look in fightin' trim to me, though."

"Ah, but you know it ain't always about muscles or speed. It's about guile!" Yendor boasted enthusiastically. "Guile and experience!"

The Captain didn't seem convinced. "Well," he confessed, "I dunno. But you caught me at a good time. One o' my guards got beaten up pretty bad by the other fellers for bein' a dick at the front gate. He's in the infirmary now, and I don't see him gettin' back on his feet for a spell. Guess I could give you a shot."

"Thank you, sir," Yendor replied.

"But you heard that, right? We run a tight outfit. 'Round here, there's no tolerance for stupidity or incompetence. You screw up, I'll never have to kick your ass, 'cause the rest o' the boys'll do it for me."

Yendor nodded. "I hear you."

The Captain was not warming to him. "Right," he said with palpable skepticism. "Let me show you to the bunk house."

Arune

She'd almost forgotten Brouton's Bind, and now it roared back at her with a vengeance. The horrifying, unacceptable, but somehow darkly thrilling fact of the matter was that Arune had enjoyed that kiss almost more than Vykers—and she'd felt some evidence that he liked it very much, indeed. Oh, this was beyond mere quandary; this was a near-lethal dose of frustration and aggravation beyond anything Arune had known in ages. She had despised the prissy, self-righteous Mender, and now she lusted after the woman. The obvious solution was to keep Vykers away from Aoife—by force, if necessary. But the more she thought on it, the more she wanted the A'Shea. It was maddening. Ultimately, she'd withdrawn from Vykers' surface consciousness; she knew he'd assume she'd gone off to sulk. In fact, she'd retreated in shock and confusion, desire consuming her energies like wildfire.

Arune was in peril.

Spirk, House D'Escurzy

Spirk Nessno was in peril, as well, but he did not know it. Improbably, he grew closer and closer to his hard, diminutive master, making the man's life imperceptibly easier through the careful use of Pellas' legacy—expelling the dust and the chill from Titus' chambers, eradicating the bedbugs from his mattress, compelling the candles to burn longer and brighter than they ought. But these acts of kindness did not go unnoticed by His Lordship's next of kin. Though none of them could remember Spirk's face when he wasn't around, they certainly remembered his impact on the patriarch, and they did not appreciate it in the least. To their minds, Spirk—or, as they knew him, Long Pete—was prolonging the old geezer's life unnecessarily and providing him comfort they would just as soon he did not receive. Thus, amongst themselves, they had quietly decided that Spirk must die.

One afternoon, whilst Titus was regaling Spirk with tales of his youth—an act which bore an uncanny resemblance to telling the young man to go fuck himself—one of His Lordship's relatives was finally bold enough to enter his presence and inquire after his health.

"Faenia," His Lordship said flatly as she glided into his chambers.

"Uncle," she replied, in a smooth, silky alto. "I haven't seen you at supper in ages."

"Nor missed me, I'll warrant."

Faenia swept her big, expressive eyes over Spirk. Was she smiling at him? Her small, tight mouth made it hard to tell. "You have a new servant, I see."

"Your grasp of the obvious is truly astounding. What do you want?" Titus spat.

"Really, uncle, we haven't seen each other in so long. Must you be so combative? I merely came to visit, to…bring you comfort, if I might."

Titus laughed his hacking laugh. "You? Comfort? When a dagger in the gut is comfort, I'm sure that will be true."

"I'm told your servant's name is Long Pete," Faenia said. "What an odd name that is!" She followed up with a giggle that was meant to sound delighted; Spirk heard no mirth in it. Before he knew it, she was upon him, inches from his face. "Why long?" she breathed. "How long are you?"

Spirk had no idea what she was getting at, but he suddenly felt horribly uncomfortable in his own skin. "Dunno, mistress. It's just a nickname, an' it please you."

Faenia got closer, still. Her night-black hair was pulled back behind her head, save for a meticulously staged lock that tumbled across her left eye. This had some meaning, Spirk knew, but it was lost on him. "You might please me, I'm sure, if indeed you are long," Faenia whispered.

Spirk shrugged. "Well, I am," was all he could say in his defense.

From his chair, Titus cackled again. "Ah, Faenia, you're pathetic! Trying to seduce my simpleton? Are you really so desperate to undermine me?"

Faenia stepped back from Spirk as if she'd been slapped across the face. "I was only being sociable!" she protested. "There's no call for such accusations, uncle."

"You have scouted my new attendant. You may now leave. I'm sure the rest of your...pack...will be delighted to know I yet live."

"Oh!" the woman responded, taking umbrage at her uncle's dismissal. "You are impossible." She spun on her heel and stalked, rather noisily this time, from Titus' chambers.

His Lordship beckoned Spirk to his side. "Listen to me, cretin: do not let that woman within ten feet of you—further, if you can manage it. She and all of her kin are not to be trusted in anything but evil intent. You've been marked, now. Make one mistake, and that bitch'll kill you." Titus paused, drew in a deep, ragged breath. "Now fetch me some soup and be quick about it."

All the way to His Lordship's private kitchen and all the way back, Spirk fretted about this new threat, this Faenia, and wondered what he'd done to her that she wanted him dead. By the time he returned to His Lordship's room, the man was asleep in his chair. For an ordinary person, this might present a conundrum: whether to wake him while his soup was still warm and risk punishment for disturbing him, or to let him sleep and risk punishment for letting his soup cool. Spirk, however, had never been ordinary and especially not since he'd received Pellas' legacy, which made it possible for him to keep Titus' soup warm virtually indefinitely. With a few meaningless gestures but some very real energy, he did just that. Now, he had some time on his hands and so decided to continue his ongoing battle with dust.

Moving to a remote corner of Titus' room to which he had never previously ventured, Spirk began chasing the dust along the walls and floor towards the room's fireplace. From there, it was his practice to shoot it all up the chimney and from thence who-knew-where. The point, as Spirk saw it, was that it was no longer around to trouble His Lordship's breathing or redden his already rheumy eyes. In the process of chasing this dust, however, Spirk happened upon a slightly sunken panel in the wall, just beneath the stuffed and mounted head of a large oursine. In the permanent gloom of the master's chambers, such an imperfection might go unnoticed for, well, a very, very long time. But Spirk possessed—or rather believed he possessed—heightened senses, again as a result of Pellas' legacy, and so it was no trouble at all for him to spot the depression. As gently as he could, Spirk ran his fingers around the perimeter of the panel. He sensed nothing, other than the fact that the wall needed a good cleaning. Carefully, he pressed on the area; nothing happened. He pressed more forcefully with the same result. At last, he brushed it lightly with his arcane senses and found it was, as he suspected, a door. Yet, the absence of a handle or knob of any kind baffled him. Not wanting to admit defeat, he pulled a chair over and set it where he could watch both the door and his sleeping master and had a seat. It wasn't long before he fell asleep, himself.

And was subsequently awakened by Titus' bellowing. "Idiot! Where are you? Come here this instant or I'll make you smart for it!"

Spirk fairly flew out of his chair and into His Lordship's line of sight. "Apologies, milord. I was just inspecting...That is... Well..."

"Spit it out, addle-pated git!"

"It seems there's a secret door over by the stuffed animal head."

Titus smirked. "Of course there's a secret door!" he snapped. "We're a sneaky, skulking, treacherous folk, we D'Escurzys." After a moment's breath, he continued, "However...that particular one is news to me."

"You mean there's others?" Spirk asked, aghast.

"Did I not just admit as much? Alheria's tits, man! What are you using for brains?"

So focused was he on the issue at hand that Spirk was completely unfazed by his master's abusive manner. "Why would somebody wanna sneak in here?" he wondered aloud.

Titus heaved his most melodramatic sigh. "To kill me, of course!"

"I'm confused," Spirk admitted.

"Do tell," His Lordship retorted.

"You say Faenia wants to kill me and somebody else wants to kill you. Why's all this killin' necessary?"

"Because my worthless children and their children and their cousins want the title to this estate, along with all my money and the various seats I hold on numerous councils and committees around the city. Oh, they can't wait to get their hands on it all."

Spirk looked about to cry. "That's terrible," he said.

Titus' beady little eyes opened a touch wider at that and his face relaxed a moment. "Yes," he agreed. "'Tis that. Time was, I thought I'd raise my children to be better people than I'd been." He glanced wistfully around his room, as if his children could be found stationed nearby, attentive and adoring. "I failed. As you can see."

"Why?" Spirk asked, not knowing any better.

His Lordship reflected he might have had anyone else killed for such bluntness. In his idiotic companion, however, it was almost charming. "Might be I over indulged them, didn't say 'no' often enough. Might be I was kind to them, but they saw me being cruel to outsiders, and that's all they learned from me. Whatever the case, they're bastards now, each and every one. Even the women."

A single tear ran down Spirk's left cheek, and before he could wipe it away, His Lordship reached out and stayed his hand. "You really are dumber than a stump, aren't you lad?" he asked, not unlovingly. "Go and fetch some more firewood now. I'm feeling a chill in my bones, something awful."

Even Spirk understood His Lordship had saved him the embarrassment of open sobbing for an old man he hardly knew. He was grateful for the chance to distract himself in the pursuit of firewood.

Long, House Thornton

He was at a complete loss. He hadn't seen Yendor in over a day and Spirk in longer than that. Who knew how Rem and Kittins were faring? In short, his entire team was off somewhere, carrying out the mission (he hoped), and he hadn't been able to get past the front gate at any of Lunessfor's great Eight. Clearly, Bailis had been mistaken to place such trust in him. And unable to get anything of consequence done, Long Pete was sorely tempted to just chuck the whole hopeless exercise and run home to his wife and kid. Hells, even Spirk had gotten further than he. Unless he was dead.

Long pulled his feet off the table and dropped the front two legs of his chair back onto the floor. If he accomplished nothing else, he had to make sure the young fool hadn't gotten himself killed. Where to start, though? How to start? Spirk had always seemed easily distracted to Long, so it made sense to begin the search in Market Square. Lunessfor, being an enormous city, had several markets and market squares. There was only one Market Square, though, and Long judged it the best place to begin looking for his missing companion.

It always appeared to take longer to get there than he'd expected. The market was so enormous, so sprawling, it seemed it should be mere minutes away from anywhere else in town. But it was a goodly stretch o' the leg from the Fretful Porpentine, and Long found he was eager for a loaf of fresh bread, a hunk of cheese or perhaps a bit of grilled meat. He could find all that and more in the market. He still wondered whether any of that "more" would be Spirk.

After three hours of fruitless searching, Long had all but given up and given in to despair. *Who the fuck am I kidding?* He asked himself. *I'm an apple farmer. Sort of.* He was just about to pack it in for the day when someone yelled at him.

"You there!" a nearby merchant called. "Help a fella out?"

Long spun in a circle in attempt to see if the man was speaking to someone behind him and saw nobody within ten paces. *Me?* He motioned to himself.

The merchant nodded. "Yes! Yes, you!"

Long looked left and right again, just to be certain this wasn't some kind of set up. "Yes?" he finally croaked.

If the merchant was put off by Long's voice, he showed no sign of it. "I'm in a fix. My delivery boy's disappeared, and I need this crate delivered by sundown or I'm screwed."

"That so?" Long asked, still uncertain what to make of the situation. "What's in it?"

"Goose liver paste," the man responded. "If I don't get it to its destination on time, I may lose my sale and the customer's business."

"The market must be full of errand boys, though..." Long hedged.

"That crate's thirty pounds, easy. Besides," the merchant added, "most o' these boys are like to try and steal it."

"And what makes you think I won't?"

"You don't remember me, do you, sir?"

What in the hells was going on? Long blinked stupidly. "No, I, er..."

"I worked in the Officer's Mess, when Vykers fought the End. I musta served you and your friends for three days after the battle was done." The man had an amazing memory, and Long was embarrassed by his own. "You're a Queen's man; that's why I trust you."

"I'll do it," the captain said at last.

"I thought you might. Look, come back when you're done,

and there's a Merchant in it for you. You know I'm good for it."

Long nodded. "Where's it going?"

"House Thornton."

He'd been already, but maybe this goose liver was just important enough to whomever to get him past the guards this time. He had nothing to lose, when it came down to it. With a bob of his head, Long shouldered the crate and moved off into the city. It was funny what life on a farm did for a man. Three years ago, he couldn't have carried his burden for five minutes, to say nothing of the half hour it would take him to reach House Thornton; now, the weight of the thing was little more than a mild irritant.

Luck was with him when he reached his destination, because the guards he'd spoken with before had been replaced by two men he'd never seen before. When he reached them, he set the crate down, arched and back and tried to be sociable.

"Nice evening to be out-o'-doors, eh? This House Thornton?" He decided to pretend ignorance, in hope of looking less suspicious.

"It is," answered the guard to his left, in a voice so deep it hardly seemed human.

"Whatcha got there?" the other guard asked, pointing his lengthy nose at the crate.

Long laid it on. "Fifty pounds o' goose liver. Have fun carryin' that into the master kitchen." He turned to go, and, as he'd hoped, long-nose stopped him.

"Whoa, there! We ain't carryin' no fifty pound box o' nothing, nowheres! We's guards, Trank 'n me. We can't be leavin' our posts, can we, Trank?"

Trank said nothing, which long-nose took as agreement. "Y'see? Now, why'nt you carry that into the kitchen?"

"Me?" Long cried. "I'm just paid to deliver it to House Thornton, I..."

"Well, it don't look delivered to me!" Long-nose countered. "Behind me's House Thornton; where you're standing's outside House Thornton."

Trank pointed a mace at the crate. "Pick it up," he told Long. "Take it in."

Long complied. As he passed through the gates, he heard long-nose congratulating his associate on their fine work.

"That's tellin' 'im, old boy! You let them common laborers push you 'round, there's no knowin' what'll come of it!"

But Long had finally gotten himself inside one of the Great Eight. He would either find Spirk or the information Bailis had requested. He might even do both! First, he had to find the kitchen.

Out of nowhere the House Steward came upon him and immediately upbraided him.

"What are you doing at this end of the house?" he barked. "All deliveries come in the servants' gate!"

"Beggin' your pardon, sir. I'm a fill-in for the man was meant to bring this."

The Steward groaned in such a way that he was able to convey irritation, weariness and contempt all at once. Long looked at the man. He had a high forehead over carefully sculpted eyebrows, which in turn were perched over light brown eyes. His small mouth seemed permanently fixed in a pursed position and was framed by an ornate though tiny mustache and beard.

"And what is this, pray tell?" the man demanded.

"Goose liver."

"Goose liver? At last! You're late. Almost unforgivably so."

"Well, as I said, I'm a fill-in for…"

"Excuses are unacceptable."

"Right," Long replied. He could feign weariness as well as the next man. "Where's this servants' gate, then?"

"Pshaw! There's not time for that now. You'll have to go through the house."

As Long had intended all along.

"Follow me," the man said.

Well, you can't have everything. Long followed, as ordered. He'd expected a series of dark, winding hallways, but House Thornton was light and airy, with brightly colored artwork and floral arrangements throughout—hardly the shadowy, brooding warren he'd expected. And the master kitchen amazed him further. The place was as spacious and active as an outdoor bazaar, though admittedly it smelled a thousand times better. Armies of cooks raced back and forth from cupboards to counter tops to sinks and to ovens. Long would never have known who was in charge if not for the house Steward, who knifed right through the crowd and arrived at the person in question, a willowy raven-haired woman who looked as if she were made of cobwebs.

"The goose liver," the Steward announced, "has arrived at last."

The cook squinted at Long and barked "put it over there and then leave. There's no room for gawkers nor folks lookin' for scraps. We're busier 'n a rooster in a hen house."

Long deposited the crate on the specified counter and looked back to the Steward, only to find he'd gone. Perfect. Long approached the cook again.

"Now I'm here, anything else you need done? Crates broken down? Garbage hauled? Dishes washed? Can't have too much help!"

The cook turned and was clearly surprised to find him still standing before her. "What's wrong with your voice?" Of course: the question was mandatory. "You one o' them thralls?"

"Not a thrall, no. Just a former soldier down on his luck."

"Uh-huh," the cook answered. "Y'ever shuck on oyster?"

Long lied. "Course I have. Who ain't?"

"There's a barrel by that back winder over there. Grab yourself a knife and get shucking."

He didn't have to be told twice. Without another moment's delay, the old captain made his way to the oyster barrel and surveyed the task assigned him. He smiled. How hard could it be?

Very, very hard, as it turned out. At first, he broke more shells than he opened. Then, he stabbed himself in the palm a number of times. Once or twice, he pried a shell open, only to inadvertently flip the innards onto the floor with his knife. He looked around in embarrassment, but everyone else was too busy to pay him any mind, thank Mahnus. After some fifty oysters or so, he finally got into something of a rhythm. Indeed, he became so engrossed in getting it right that he temporarily forgot his actual purpose inside House Thornton. And there was some pleasure in doing a simple thing well, over and over. As he worked, he was able to bask in the myriad aromas— familiar and exotic—that were called into existence by the cooks swarming around him. He found he was hungry and more than so: his mouth was watering as if he hadn't eaten in days. How anyone avoided obesity in such an environment was beyond Long.

After some time, he realized he had to flee the kitchen and get about his business or be driven mad by the culinary delights surrounding but denied him. Looking up, he saw no one was paying him the slightest attention, so he wiped his hands on a nearby towel and sauntered into a side hallway, from which he'd seen various porters come and go. He passed several cooks or cooks' assistants bustling about their affairs as he walked; Long's luck held, as none showed any interest in him. At the end of the hallway, he came to a tee, with the option of going either left or right. He felt a slight breeze to his right and guessed that led, eventually, outside. Having no desire to leave, he turned left. He continued to be amazed at the variety and sheer volume of artwork on display everywhere he looked—some of it even appealed to him. Long had never owned any and wondered what Mardine would say if he dropped a Noble or two on a painting and carried it home with him when he returned. He was genuinely unable to imagine her response, which was one of the characteristics her found so charming in her.

Before Long knew it, he was lost. He'd wandered into a room full of books—a library, he believed it was called—and couldn't remember how he'd gotten there, which alarmed him no end. He couldn't afford to lose focus for even a second—

He felt the cold, hard and sharp blade of a knife against his neck. He froze.

"There's an artery just there. If I so much as nick it, you're a dead man."

Long recognized the voice as that of the Steward. He found himself unable to think of a response.

"What?" the man asked, "No excuses? No pretense of looking for the privy?"

Previous experience had taught Long the best thing to do was keep his trap shut.

"Who are you really, Mr. Deliveryman? What are you looking for?"

Long felt a trickle of blood down his neck. Just a trickle, mercifully. Then his skull blazed with pain, he saw stars and passed out.

FIVE

It was raining like all hells, so everyone fled below decks and huddled together in semi-social clumps. Aoife had her own tiny cabin, but the Frog preferred to spend his time around the ship's crew, listening to their far-fetched tales of life at sea, regularly interspersed with songs, jokes and general jabber from Hoosh. Of Vykers and his chimeras, there was no sign, for which the A'Shea was grateful and beyond grateful. She still hadn't recovered from Vykers' assault.

Well, that wasn't entirely accurate. She'd kissed him back, was what she'd done. What in Alheria's name had she been thinking? Had she been thinking? Or was some other part of her body in control? She yearned for her old satyr friend Toomt'-La's counsel and genteel xenophobia. Vykers was poison—a necessary poison in many instances, but as the poet once wrote, "they love not poison that do poison need." Nothing good could ever come of letting the man have his way with her. And, really, it wasn't fair to him, either. She could never love him. Not truly. He was a beast—he even had fangs of a sort! Better to rebuff him and let him find satisfaction somewhere else. And that was all it was, she was sure: satisfaction. He merely desired to sate his lust upon her and then she'd be cast aside, forgotten as all women were with such men. She'd have no part of that.

And yet…there were spells all A'Shea used to dampen such feelings within themselves, and Aoife had inexplicably chosen not to employ them. She knew she should, even thought she wanted to. But she could not bring herself to do it. And see how much time she'd wasted pondering the matter! Vykers had infected her thoughts like a disease. A poisonous disease. Aoife laughed ruefully to herself. *I am losing my mind!*

After the rains came the doldrums. Although there was of course no breeze above decks, the passengers and crew came up anyway, to escape the stuffy, close air below. Aoife poked her head outside and decided she'd risk a possible encounter with the Reaper for a bit of fresh air. It seemed everyone aboard was of her mind, for the deck was packed with sailors and passengers alike, some working, some mingling, all enjoying the fine spring sunshine and a good taste of air that did not savor of sweat, tobacco smoke and mildew. She located Vykers in the bow, chatting in quiet tones with the Historian and the ship's captain, a fellow who, in any other company, would have been accounted muscular. Not far away was the Frog, pretending fascination with some of the ship's rigging while he quite obviously eavesdropped. Aoife signaled to him and was relieved when he smiled back, stood up and walked in her direction.

"So?" she asked.

"They're talkin' 'bout the Queen."

Aoife smiled indulgently. "I gathered. Have they any idea where she's gone?"

"They're sayin' not upcoast or down, but across the sea," the Frog breathed excitedly.

Across the sea. That was frightening. She was sure it made no difference to Vykers, but to Aoife the fabled lands across the sea were a mystery she felt thoroughly unprepared to handle. Would Alheria even respond to her prayers? Her training said yes, but her heart was not so sure.

A scream fractured the calm, and Aoife and everyone else frantically searched for its source. Along the starboard rail, a sailor struggled with an enormous, dog-sized squid that had somehow attached itself to his face. Miniature lightning crackled across the creature's body and from thence, across the sailor's. A shape flew across Aoife's vision and landed on one of the other sailors.

"Storm squid!" the captain roared. "We are beset."

Aoife pulled the Frog close and ducked back into the stairwell. Now, scores of the impossible sea creatures flew across the ship, issuing high-pitched shrieks and attacking anyone foolish enough to remain on deck. The A'Shea had no time to wonder how such a thing was possible, so busy was she in searching out the wounded or dying.

"Mahnus' balls!" she heard the Frog say. Following his gaze, she saw the Reaper had gone into action, whirling his blade through the clouds of flying squid, like a windmill beating back flocks of crows. He was surrounded by a nimbus of flames that engulfed any creatures his blade failed to dissect. At the same time, the Historian cast spells of his own, instantly freezing his attackers in thick crusts of ice, which subsequently sent them tumbling to the deck, where they shattered like so much crystal. The A'Shea felt movement behind her and looked back to see the Fool, crouching in shadows just downstairs of her. A body raced past, followed more slowly by another, and Aoife realized the chimeras had joined the fray. A few of the ship's crew flung nets at the squid and, once successful in snaring them, beat them to jelly with belaying pins. The whole action smacked of routine, and Aoife felt certain this ship had known many such encounters. At her side, the Frog pulled his dirk and prepared to enter the fight, compelling the A'Shea to enspell him, calming the boy immediately. He would resent her for it, she knew, when the spell wore off, but that was better than seeing him carried overboard to his death.

For a fleeting moment, it seemed as if the squid were winning the melee. But the combined efforts of Vykers' party and the crew proved too much for them, and they sank back into the sea, having managed to steal only one man.

"That there's Dobbins, sir," one of the sailors told the captain.

"He was a good 'un," the captain replied, panting heavily. "Now, let's get this shit cleared off my decks."

"Cookie'll be happy with the fresh catch," another man said.

"And so'll them squid!" the first sailor shot back angrily.

In no time, the sailors had piled a number of the squid into a single net and begun hauling it off towards the galley. The rest of the creatures, those deemed too damaged, small or otherwise inedible, were swept off the deck and back into the sea.

"Say 'ello to the sharks for me, you tentacled bastards!" the second sailor yelled after them.

Aoife continued to survey the scene, checking for injuries. Two or three sailors had sustained electrical damage; it would have been far worse for them if the squid had succeeded in mobbing them. They'd have been fried in their own skins or dragged overboard like Dobbins. Vykers was down on one knee, wincing at the pain in his side. Aoife resisted the urge to rush to him, though as an A'Shea she felt ashamed for doing so. Whatever their personal issues, it was her duty to help him. The Historian, she saw, glanced her way and then bent to help the Reaper, himself. Too late now. Aoife had lost her chance.

"What'd you do to me?" the Frog asked behind her.

Aoife was in no mood. "Saved your life. You're welcome."

"You don't know as you saved me life!" the Frog protested.

The A'Shea turned to him. "You're still here and unhurt. That's all that matters. Do you disagree?"

He was a boy; he could not refute her logic, so he dodged: "I mighta helped! I coulda maybe saved that sailor!"

"And you," Aoife countered, "do not know that!"

Frustrated, the Frog kicked the step above his own and headed back below decks.

While her attention was focused on the boy, the Reaper snuck up behind her (although it was rather unlikely he 'snuck'). "Looks like it's chowder tonight," he said.

"Are you hurt?" Aoife asked. Stupid question! Of course, he's hurt! She turned to look at him, and he stared directly into her eyes.

"I'll live," he answered flatly and squeezed past her so closely that she felt his breath on her neck, eliciting spontaneous butterflies in her stomach. *Yes*, she thought, *I'm sure you will. But will I?*

Chowder it was, as Vykers had predicted, and not an especially appealing one, at that. Oh, the Reaper had eaten worse in his time. It was just that he'd expected more of a ship's cook, particularly one who'd recently been ashore and restocked his larder. This stuff could've done with a bit of bacon, a trace of onion, something. Vykers was no chef, but, during his time in the Queen's castle, he'd learned there was more to a good bowl of chowder than milk and root vegetables. To be fair, the generous chunks o' squid weren't half bad...but they weren't half good, neither. Somehow or other, cookie had managed to produce plenty of bread, though. If the whole meal was bland, it was filling. There'd been times when the Reaper would've conquered the kingdom for an old rind of cheese.

The Historian sat nearby, eating something of his own creation. Vykers understood it was Ahklatian ritual to eat unpleasant meals as penance for crimes past. He wondered what the strange man would make of the chowder.

"So," the Historian said, continuing an earlier conversation, "If her Majesty had made landfall anywhere on the continent, we might have found and joined her in a heartbeat. That we did not leaves only two possibilities: one, her captors are attempting to lose us in the vastness of the ocean and will return to land, somewhere, when we've abandoned hope, or two, they are, as we've surmised, leading us across the sea to the lands beyond, where they assuredly have an advantage."

Vykers belched. "What advantage is that?"

"I don't speak of a specific advantage. We can infer they know the territory better. It's also possible they're leading us into a trap."

"Everything's a trap."

The Ahklatian looked at Vykers with his black eyes, his expression unreadable. "I'll not argue the point."

"Arune says it'll be harder to track her Majesty in this other land."

"That is true."

"Because?"

"We know our own lands fairly well; we know almost nothing of what lies across the sea."

"Seems like we've had plenty o' time since the Awakening."

"Aye. But being unable to cross the seas by arcane means has forced us to explore in the more conventional, slower manner. And, almost to a man, those we've sent have not returned."

Vykers regarded the Historian quizzically. "Almost to a man?"

The Ahklatian beamed back at him. "Almost."

"Alheria's tits, man, why do you take so long to get to the marrow of it?"

"Time is all I have, Tarmun Vykers," the Historian responded, with more than a hint of sadness in his voice.

"You've been to these lands," Vykers grumbled.

"Not all of them. But I have been across this sea, yes."

"Looks like you'll be of some use, after all."

Kittins, House Gault

They kept Long Teeth—Svarren—in cages, just off the main chamber in the Grotto. This was the so-called "freak show." The "full freak show" involved bringing the creatures out in chains and parading them around the Grotto, to be poked, prodded and pelted with stones or refuse by guardsmen of House Gault. Sometimes, the men would pull an especially ugly specimen aside and get the hapless thing drunk, after which they'd dress him up in woman's clothing and taunt him nearly to death. It was pure, unadulterated and unrelenting sadism. And it disgusted Kittins. Worse, some of the men had a penchant for sexually assaulting the female Svarren and killing them if they tried to resist. Kittins hated Long Teeth, but he hated bullies worse. If he had his way, he'd castrate the lot of 'em and toss 'em into a bear-baiting pit. But...The nature of his mission compelled him to play along. Drunken, rowdy guards were happy guards and more likely to spill the House secrets

One night, however, they brought in a few new Svarren to replace those they'd killed, and Kittins saw something he'd never seen before: an attractive female. Oh, she was no great beauty, but she was tall and graceful and boasted an unusual sloe-eyed look that made her appear perpetually wistful and sympathetic. The instant he spotted her, Kittins knew her future in the Grotto held nothing but misery and abuse. He wondered how much he could tolerate before he was forced to act, to intervene on this strange Svarra's behalf. The question unsettled him so much that he downed half a bottle of wine brooding on it. And, hells, he was drinking far too much lately. As had become his habit of late, Wrensl Deda came into the Grotto and immediately sought Kittins out. He was under the misapprehension that he and Kittins were now friends. Kittins would happily have broken his neck. Too, ever since he'd begun reading in earnest, he found it more and more difficult to indulge in the commoner's cant that Deda and the other guards spoke. There were some, certainly, who could adapt their speech to any occasion, but more and more, Kittins was not of their number. Secretly, he worried this would prove his undoing, yet he simply could not dumb his language down enough to fit in everywhere he went. And he was not sure he wanted to, anyhow. He didn't want to come off like a Mahnus-cursed Shaper, but neither did he care to sound like a knuckle-dragging grunt.

"I hear they got some fresh Long Teats!" Wrensl cracked.

Kittins took a monstrous swig of wine and wondered whether it might not be more fun to choke the smaller man to death.

"You seen 'em?" Wrensl asked, looking around.

"I've seen them," Kittins admitted. "Same old, same-old."

"Hey, new meat's never old." Such a philosopher, he was.

Kittins held out a massive paw to the barkeep, who placed a fresh bottle of wine in it, which the captain plunked down in front of his companion. "Svarren are boring. Drink. Tell me what in all hells in going on upstairs."

Wrensl gladly accepted the bottle and took several audible gulps. "How d'ya mean?"

"I don't know," Kittins hedged. "Just if this is the most interesting place in House Gault, we're all fucked."

"Yeah, well, there's always some kinda political shit goin' on, you can count on that," Wrensl said, dragging the palm of his right hand across his mouth.

Kittins looked away, pretended boredom. "That right? Like what?"

"Oh, you know, who's a cuckold, who's a spy, who's a thief, who's anglin' for power."

"Right!" Kittins laughed, as if the very idea was beneath

consideration. "Like anyone cares about that 'round here."

"You'd be surprised, my friend, you'd be surprised."

"Bet I wouldn't."

Wrensl's ruddy face lit up. "You bet, do ya? Fine, then: what's the bet?"

Kittins set his bottle down, flexed his fingers, appeared to think about it. "Coin or Courage?"

"Shit!" Wrensl scoffed, "You ain't got no money, you're a guard! Let's go with Courage."

"Courage it is."

A sly, cunning look came into Wrensl's eyes. "Right: I come up with a little tidbit surprises you, you gotta...get friendly with one o' them Svarren. And you know what I mean by 'friendly,' right?"

"You're a sick bastard, you know that, Deda?"

Wrensl cackled with glee. "So, you got the courage?"

Kittins nodded, took another prodigious gulp of wine. "I've got it. What's the tidbit?"

"Them two guards bunk on either side o' me? They're doing it."

"That's nothing. I've seen that kind of thing in the army."

Wrensl's eyes grew wide. "Truth?"

"Truth. I won't say it was an everyday thing, but I've seen a lot of it. What else have you got?"

The other man swiveled his head to and fro, making sure no one he couldn't see was listening. His voice got quiet. "They say Darley killed one o' his mistresses and her babe a while back."

Kittins yawned. "So I've heard."

"Where?" Wrensl demanded, sounding offended.

"I swore I wouldn't say."

Wrensl looked crestfallen.

"That the best you've got, then?" Kittins asked.

"You got any better?" the other man asked, somewhat belligerently.

"Might be I do." Kittins considered his surroundings, felt a sudden urge to hurt someone. He scanned the Grotto, picked a random target. "You see that fellow over at the card table? Man going bald on top?"

"Who, Buke?"

"That his name? Buke?"

Wrensl nodded. "That's the balding fella."

"Right, well, I saw that bastard commanding a squad on the other side of the line," Kittins lied. There was no question what line Kittins was referring to; virtually everyone knew it to be the line between the End-of-All-Things' horde and the Queen's army.

"Son of a whore!" Wrensl said. "I knew there was somethin' dodgy about that jackanapes."

"Don't let on I recognized him," Kittins warned. "I need time to figure what I'm going to do about it."

Wresnl beamed and slapped his companion on the shoulder. "Janks, old pal, I'd be happy to take care o' this for you."

It was amazing how quickly Deda had taken the bait, how eager he'd been to accept and act upon the lie. Kittins shook his head. "No, this is something I've got to do myself. I appreciate the offer, though."

"Hey, what are friends for?" the other man exclaimed.

"Think I'll go get some sleep before my next watch," Kittins said as he stood up.

"In your new room, eh?" Wrensl asked, a touch of envy evident in his voice.

"I had to move," Kittins explained, "The smell of your feet was killing me!"

He moved off towards the entrance to the Grotto, with Deda's laughter ringing in his ears. If he was right about the man, Deda would obsess about this Buke fellow until he couldn't restrain himself any longer, at which point, there'd be blood. Kittins reckoned Deda could hold his tongue for three days, maybe five, before enlisting a few buddies to help him teach Buke a lesson. So, that was how long Kittins had to come up with some way to exonerate himself in the event it all came back to his doorstep.

He was both uneasy and excited with anticipation. He'd set something in motion tonight, and there was no telling where it would go from here.

Rem, House Hawsey

The Entirely True Account of the Mighty Reaper's Heroic Victory Over the Heinous Tyrant, The-End-of-All-Things was a huge success, if the private audience's reaction was any gauge. Curiously, though, each time Rem caught a glimpse of Henton is his private box, the man seemed to be frowning. Whether in concentration, consternation or constipation, Rem couldn't begin to guess. With Lord Hawsey, any or all of those options might be in play. Still, it was not a good sign, and Rem was a believer in signs. While Henton's guests mingled with his actors in the rush of excitement after a successful performance, Rem pulled one of his oldest, most trusted mates aside.

"Keez," he whispered, "Meet me backstage, if you would—and be discrete as possible."

Two minutes later, both men reconvened in the appointed spot.

"Keez, old friend, did you mark His Lordship during our performance?"

"I'm an actor. How could I fail to notice our patron's demeanor?"

"And what did you make of it?"

"Something displeased or displeases him."

Rem bobbed his head in agreement. "That was my impression, as well. This does not bode well for continued stay at House Hawsey."

"It may not bode well for our continued stay in the world, either."

That was further than Rem was willing to go, but he could not discount it, either. "As quietly as you can, secure our most valuable properties and prepare for a precipitous departure. It may not come to that, but…"

"I'll make ready," Keez answered and walked off without another word.

Rem sauntered back onstage and grabbed a cup of wine from a nearby server. Best to play innocent. In seconds, he was surrounded by members of the Hawsey family and household and their invited guests. Notable for his absence was His Lordship. Rem decided to stick to one cup of wine, in order to keep his thoughts clear, in the event his fears—nebulous though they were—became reality. Patiently, Rem greeted everyone who pushed forward to congratulate, or, in some cases, fawn upon him. At last, a stern-looking messenger approached. And Rem gracefully detached himself from his fans.

"His Lordship would like to speak with you in the Blue Room, as soon as possible, by which he means now," the messenger said.

Under other circumstances, Rem might've chuckled at the strange pronouncement. He found he could not this time. "I'm on my way," he said at the back of the already-departed messenger. With a deep sigh, he set down his cup, tugged on his doublet to remove any wrinkles and headed off to the Blue Room.

Which, of course, was not blue, but rust-colored. In the course of his stay at House Hawsey, he'd learned the room had once been blue, and the name had stuck, even after the décor had changed. Strange, how set folks could be in their ways. Upon arriving, he found His Lordship pacing back and forth. Out of the corner of his eye, Rem saw that guards had materialized at the far door and the one he'd just entered.

"Ah, you're here," Henton said flatly.

"Of course," Rem replied, putting on his best smile. "I am your servant."

Henton pursed his lips at this and pinned his chin to his chest. "I hope you are," he said.

"Have I given you any cause to doubt me, your Lordship?"

Henton's response, when it came, was utterly bewildering. "How much of Gelter Radcliffe'thz diary did you read?"

There was no point in pretending ignorance, Rem decided. "I was only able to read the first few pages, before you appeared and I handed it over."

"Only a few?" Henton asked gravely.

"Five or six, at the utmost, your Lordship. That handwriting was so small and crabbed, you know."

For several seconds, Rem heard nothing at all, save the

ticking of an unseen clock he dared not search for at the moment. Instead, he did his best to keep an open and honest expression on his face as he continued to maintain eye contact with His Lordship. After what seemed an eternity, Henton finally spoke.

"Allth well, then," he said in a manner that suggested it wasn't.

"Yes, indeed. Happy I could be of service," Rem replied.

Henton seemed to relax just the tiniest amount. "You may go," he said.

That their relationship had changed, Rem saw clearly. What he did not know was the extent of the damage or whether it might be reversed. Just as he was about to leave, he turned back to Lord Hawsey and asked, "what did you think of the play, your Lordship?"

"The play?" Henton repeated, as if he'd never heard the word before. "It wath fine. Good, even. And, you weren't half-bad, either. Your dicthion could yooth a little more work, but otherwithz it wath quite thatithfactory."

His diction? *His* diction? Satisfactory? Rem smiled wanly, bowed, and left the room before he decided to smash something of irreplaceable value.

"What's the plan?" Keez wanted to know when he saw Rem again.

"We're staying. For the nonce. Can you find Aadie for me?"

"The props master? I expect he's locking up the props."

"Yes," Rem agreed. "Well, help him finish up and send him along, will you? I'll be in my room."

"As you say," Keez answered.

Rem spent the walk to his room plotting and scheming. Obviously, there was something in Gelter's diary that reflected poorly on Lord Hawsey, something His Lordship could not simply laugh off or attribute to the mean-spiritedness of a rival. And this mysterious something might be the very information he'd been sent by Colonel Bailis to find, and, if not, it might have monetary or political value to someone else. There were so many possibilities that Rem gave up even trying to imagine what had so sobered His Lordship. Back in the Blue Room,

Rem had unexpectedly arrived at the precipice of disaster. His apparent ignorance had saved him, but, going forward, he felt certain knowledge would serve him better.

Rem's room was actually a suite, large and spacious, offering many hiding places for things he didn't want found. As he retrieved a special dagger he had secreted in one of these locations, he realized His Lordship's staff might likewise have hidden things from him within his chambers, and he felt a surge of paranoia coming on, the like of which he'd never before experienced. His room, he determined, was no place for a private conversation with the prop master. Slipping his dagger into his doublet, he stepped outside the door and waited for his friend to arrive. He didn't have long to wait.

"Good show tonight!" Aadie called out.

"Seemed a bit slow in the last two acts, but perhaps that's just a reflection of my eagerness to get to the banquet," Rem replied. In fact, he'd completely forgotten the banquet.

"So," the prop master said.

"So...let's take a stroll, shall we?"

Aadie was no rube; he knew something was afoot from the second he'd been summoned. "Where d'you fancy?"

"Safest place of all: through the banquet room."

Made sense to the prop master. Rem and he could play drunken celebrants about as well as any, especially if they were drunken celebrants.

Entering the banquet room, Rem was hailed by a number of folks who were already well into their cups. The actor offered a wave in return and began talking to Aadie in a voice intended to be overheard.

"Vykers' sword needs to be, how shall I say it, more magnificent. After so many performances, it's looking rather pathetic, I'm afraid."

Aadie played his part. "Pathetic? I keep my props in the best working order. The problem's not my props, it's your actors. They don't know how to take care of anything!"

The two men went back and forth like this long enough to down several cups of wine and a capon leg or three. When at last the rest of the chamber's revelers seemed to lose interest in their presence, Rem lowered his voice somewhat and continued. "I need you to teach me how to make a book."

"Teach you? Why don't I just make it for you?"

"But Keez is one of our best actors!" Rem burst out, before quickly fading his voice back to normal. "Because it's going to be the twin of another book only two people on this estate have ever seen. I cannot describe it in sufficient detail to ensure the copy's perfection; therefore, I must make it myself.

Aadie looked perplexed. "But how can I instruct you in this without drawing suspicion?"

"A codpiece?" Rem blurted out. And then, more silently, "We'll insert our conversation into a rehearsal of The Milkmaid's Tragedy. His Lordship's spies will be none the wiser."

Oh, he was clever, that Remuel Wratch. The question was whether he was clever enough.

Long & Mardine's Farm

The girl was a decent enough cook, Mardine allowed, which was especially surprising, given the ordeal she'd been through with the End-of-All-Things. And Esmine seemed to like her well enough. Still, the giantess had her doubts. It was hard to trust anyone else with her daughter, much less a former thrall. Mardine looked up from her work on the orchard's accounts and peeked over at Nelby, who was busy tending an iron pot over the fire.

"Smells good," Mardine said. "What is it?"

"It's an old family recipe," Nelby answered shyly. "A stew of pork, apples, raisins and other things."

"Apples, eh? You're using some o' last season's dried, then?"

"I am, yes. You'll see, though, they'll go well with the meat."

"I'm sure," Mardine replied. "Ask you a question, Nelby?"

"Yes, mum."

"Your family still alive somewhere?"

Nelby looked down into the pot, stirred it. "I...I don't rightly know." And then she began to weep. She made a heroic effort to hide her tears from Mardine, but the giant saw them anyhow.

"Oh, oh, I'm sorry, Nelby," Mardine offered. "I didn't mean

to cause you distress. I was only wondering..."

"As am I," the thrall girl replied. "Only, I wouldn't even know where to begin to look. I...I can't recall...where I came from."

"You can't recall?"

"No, mum. My memories are as mixed up as, well, this here stew. Sometimes things are as clear as daylight; others, well..." And again she wept.

As quietly as she could, Mardine closed her book and crossed over to Nelby's side. She put an arm around the girl and held her for a good while.

A fine, welcome drizzle fell on the orchard. Long had never complained about spring rains, and Mardine shared his view: what was good for the trees was good for the family, no matter that her clothes were soaked through by the time she'd finished her daily inspections. The blossoms on each branch had long since turned into tiny apples—not much to look at now, but promising a magnificent bounty when they ripened to full size in a few month's time.

The giantess stepped away from the branch she'd been examining, took a deep breath. Of a sudden, she felt lightheaded. She must not have eaten enough for breakfast, she assumed. But as she returned her attention to the tree, her dizziness grew. Must be the onset of a flu or some such, she mused unhappily. Nelby would have to watch Esmine at night, too, if...The orchard spun around Mardine, and she became afraid. Something was wrong, terribly wrong. She looked through the trees towards her cottage, thought briefly of yelling for help.

And hit the ground with a tremendous thud.

It was the cold and damp that brought her back around. She had a skull-splitting headache and was shivering violently when she opened her eyes and discovered night had fallen. In fact, as she climbed to her feet, she could see the barest glimmer of light in the eastern sky. Night had not only fallen, it seemed, but almost passed. Without warning, Mardine vomited onto the grass. And vomited onto the grass again. Carefully, she sat back down and rolled over onto her side. What in the infinite hells was happening to her?

She heard a knocking sound; someone was at the door and would not be deterred by her refusal to answer. Mardine opened her eyes. She was outside. Gradually, her head cleared enough for her to recall what had happened to her. This time, she took a long moment to consider her condition before attempting to rise. The knocking sound came again. A woodpecker worked away on a nearby tree. Let him alone long enough, and that tree would die. Mardine cast about for a stone, located one, and tossed it at the bird. Her throw went wide of the mark, but its ensuing impact on a neighboring tree was enough to chase the woodpecker away. Mardine did not bask in her victory long, however, as the odor of something foul came to her, and she realized she'd fallen asleep near the puddle of sick she'd created during the night. Still too weak to stand, she crawled away to fresher—and sunnier—surroundings. Between the rows of trees, mid-afternoon sun lanced down and warmed the grass most pleasantly. The giantess was terribly tempted to lie down again and sleep off whatever it was that ailed her, but she knew she'd left Esmine and Nelby without company or attention all night. Surely, they were as worried about her as she was about them.

Mardine continued crawling. She felt feeble and foolish, but she knew she'd feel better as soon as she got inside. Coming over the last rise between her position and her home, Mardine was stunned to see the front door standing wide open and all the lights off inside. Adrenaline did what willpower alone could not, yanking the big woman to her feet in an instant. And now she was running, albeit awkwardly, towards the cottage, calling out to her daughter and the child's nanny. "Esmine! Esmine! Nelby!"

No one answered.

Without regard for her own safety, Mardine barreled into the cottage's front room, still yelling her daughter's name. In a rising panic, she raced through the other rooms and then checked them a second time. Esmine and Nelby were undeniably gone. Mardine wanted to run screaming into the orchard. Instead, she forced herself to sit down, calm her nerves and think things through. Hysteria, she knew, would get her nowhere.

I must've been poisoned, the giantess thought. Nelby poisoned me and waited until I was unconscious, then she ran off with my daughter. On the heels of that, she thought I should never have taken on that thrall. Oh, they warned me. Did they ever. But stupid old me, I wanted to see the good in such folks...

Struck by a thought, Mardine got up and went into Esmine's room. It had not been ransacked; there was not the slightest trace of a struggle. Next, she poked her head into the loft she and Long had given Nelby. It, too, was as neat as you please... if bare of the woman's belongings. Yes, this abduction had been carefully planned and executed. Perhaps from the moment Nelby had first laid eyes on Esmine.

But why? There were plenty of reasons, if Mardine was honest: to the best of anyone's knowledge, Esmine was unique in the world—at least, that was so locally. The giantess dared not even allow herself to explore and enumerate the uses a cold world might find for such a child, as if merely thinking such thoughts made them facts. But these fears did galvanize her: she had to go find her child, before it was too late. And she might be gone for days, or even weeks. With Long unavailable to her, Mardine had no choice but to appeal to her neighbors for help. Pulling the door shut behind her, she headed off to nearest farm. It was still early, but, if she remembered rightly, Old Cargon had cows to milk and chickens to feed.

Halfway across the apple orchard, Mardine saw lights in the windows of Cargon's cottage and knew he and his wife were awake and at work. Mardine worried about dealing with Cargon—he was a cantankerous and tight-fisted fellow at the best of times—but his farm was also the closest, and he'd have a much easier time watching her orchard than just about anyone else hereabouts. It was also possible that he and his wife had seen something the night before. Mardine was reluctant to hope, but the heart sometimes does what it will, reality be damned.

Before she'd come within twenty-five paces of Cargon's door, his wife peeked her little, white-haired head out and asked, "Mornin', Mardine. Is somethin' the matter, dearie?"

The giantess nearly burst into tears at the sound of the old woman's sweet, sympathetic voice. "The help's stolen my babe in the night!"

Cargon's wife, whose name was Leetsa, threw wide the door and rushed out to take Mardine's hands? "How's that? Your baby's been ta'en?" she cried. Old Cargon himself stepped into doorway his wife had only just vacated and stared suspiciously at the two women, though it was hard to tell what if anything he saw from through his monstrously overgrown eyebrows.

"Nelby's made off with Esmine!" Mardine said again, adding the names for clarity.

"And where's that war hee-ro man o' yourn?" Cargon snapped.

Mardine struggled to maintain her composure. "Still away on business."

"Oh, dearie," Leetsa said, attempting to take Mardine's massive head onto her shoulder. "We'll have to run fetch the constable."

"There's no time for that," Mardine said. "I've got to go after them."

"Well," Cargon exclaimed, "Best o' luck to you!" and started to shut his door, with his wife and Mardine still standing together in the yard.

"You mind your manners!" Leetsa scolded him. "A baby's in danger here, and…"

Cargon snorted. "Some baby! She's near up to me chin."

"Don't be a beast, now," Leetsa replied. "The girl's still a babe, no matter her size. And we're bound as good neighbors to help."

"Bound are we?" Cargon asked. "And what is it you're wanting of us, giant?"

"Her name's Mardine," Leetsa said.

"I need someone to tend the orchard while I'm gone."

Cargon laughed long and loudly. "Oh, I'm sure!" he said at last. "I'm sure you do."

"I'll make it worth you while," Mardine responded.

To Mardine, Leetsa said, "Don't let the old skinflint steal you blind!" To Cargon, she chided, "'Tis a sin to take advantage of a woman in distress, Cargon!"

"And an equal sin for a man 'o business to let his wife talk him out of his profit!" The farmer looked up at his massive neighbor and continued. "What's yer proposal?"

Mardine had no time to waste bartering with the fellow, so she made the best offer she had. "You take care of my apple trees, for as long as it takes, and I'll give you one hundred percent of our take this year."

Leetsa's mouth fell open in shock.

Her husband made a brief show of pretending to consider the offer; in the end, it was too generous to pass up. Even if Cargon had to hire extra hands to help, he'd still make more money than he'd made in many and many a year.

"But you'll watch my cottage, into the bargain!" Mardine tossed in.

Incredibly, it seemed the old farmer was about to object, when Leetsa came to the rescue. "I'll do it, dearie. 'Least I can do for you and yourn. But how'll you make do if you give us the proceeds from this season?"

"If I don't find my daughter," Mardine answered gravely, "there'll be no point in even trying to make do; we'll be done."

The comment resonated with Cargon somehow, as his aspect quickly softened, grew more sympathetic. "Don't you worry none," he said. "You'll get her back, and we'll keep your place safe 'til you return."

The giantess nearly choked up with gratitude. With a nod, she headed back to her cottage to pack the few things she might need to begin and sustain her search.

Yendor, House Fyne

It seemed to take forever for Yendor to earn his first day off, and he couldn't remember having been so sober in his life. He burst into the Fretful Porpentine, hoping to drink himself stupid and catch up with his buddy Long and perhaps even Spirk, but neither was present. Frankly, the place felt kinda weird without 'em. Might be Long had finally infiltrated one o' the other Houses. His absence was no reason to forego a hard won drink or five, though, so Yendor plunked himself down in the nearest chair and signaled the barkeep to send someone over.

He did his best, as he drank, to play 'Hail fellow, well met,' and he learned that the man he was looking for (the other patrons knew Long by sight only) hadn't been 'round in a few days. And nobody had seen the invisible idiot. Nobody ever saw him.

With unexpected time on his hands and a bit more money in his purse than he'd been accustomed to, Yendor fancied a bit of the old slap-and-tickle before he was too inebriated to act upon his desires. And if a man had the coin, sexual companionship was not hard to find in a place like the Fretful Porpentine. In addition, Long had already paid several weeks' worth of rent on a room upstairs, thus, completing the necessary troublemaker's triumvirate of time, money and a room.

Yendor couldn't remember the last time he'd gone pearl diving, but he was fairly certain it was the sort of thing one remembered rather easily once the festivities got underway. And if the wench was good and sauced as well, he might be forgiven any awkwardness in the attempt.

Somehow or other, he awoke on the floor, whilst a pair—a pair!—of plump, sweaty doxies slept off their stupor in the bed. Being well acquainted with the floor as a general concept, Yendor took no especial umbrage at the sleeping arrangements. He was heartened, in fact, by an appropriate soreness in all the expected areas, which led him to believe he'd been quite the lady killer. Too bad he couldn't remember the least detail. It seemed a pity, really: half the fun in experiencing pleasure, he felt, was in being able to recall it later. For all Yendor knew, in his drunken state, he'd gotten intimate with the nightstand, while the ladies went on without him. Alarmed by the notion, he turned his back to the bed and checked himself for splinters. Finding none, he spun again towards his sleeping companions. Or non-companions. He'd intended to say something at parting, but it hardly seemed important now. And he didn't want to be late in returning to work.

Not that work was particularly enthralling. At House Fyne, Yendor had been assigned to guard the garbage. At first, he'd found the situation preposterous. Then he got a look at the garbage and understood: the Fyne cast-offs were fine, indeed. In an enormous open-aired 'room' at the back of the estate, a huge pile, twice the height of a man contained fruit and vegetables that had barely perceptible or even imagined imperfections, along with clothing, dishes and flatware that had become unfashionable, books that had been read once, furniture made of rare materials that had been accidentally scratched or cracked by obese relatives and more, so much more than Yendor could even begin to describe or inventory. Once every few days, a large wagon drawn by a team of oxen came to haul much of the garbage away; much, but not all. The last foot-and-a-half to two feet of the pile never quite made it off the premises, congealing, instead, into a fetid stew, the mere odor of which had caused Yendor to lose his appetite often enough for the man to drop ten pounds. One of the other guards had assured him he'd grow used to the smell. He had not and did not foresee ever doing so. Still, there were many things near the top of the pile that seemed perfectly good to Yendor, things that might sustain a working family for days or weeks, and he saw no reason to throw such items away, save that some Fyne or other had deemed them garbage, and that, apparently, could not be gainsaid by anyone else in the House. Yet, the Fyne folk knew the value of their discards, else they would not have posted guards to keep watch over it. Yendor was not a man to get angry, in general, but this infuriated him. Why commit to the city dump or the river things that might keep others alive? He felt powerless to change things, so he forced himself to think of other things.

He had learned nothing, for instance, of House Fyne's possible involvement in the Queen's disappearance. Nor had he seen or heard anything of his missing comrade, Spirk, which made him reasonably confident the young man hadn't come 'round the estate. Yendor wondered which of the Houses Long might have infiltrated, but that was a fruitless exercise: he would only learn when Long told him.

The next day off was mercifully quicker in coming than

the last. Once again, Yendor dropped by the Fretful Porpentine to see if Long and/or Spirk were around. Once again, he was disappointed. His disappointment only grew when the two whores he'd hired last time appeared to have no recollection of ever having met him, much less…well, who could say what had transpired? Certainly not Yendor.

There was still time, if he hurried, to make it to Teshton and inquire after his companions at Gangrene & Sons. Heading out to the Fretful Porpentine's stables, Yendor was enraged to discover his horse—for which he'd paid a good month's boarding—had been fed to the inn's clientele the week previous. Yendor stormed back inside and raged at the innkeeper.

"What in Mahnus' name d'you think you're doin', eatin' me horse?"

"You didn't read the customer's contract, then?" the innkeeper responded.

"What customer's contract?"

"Why, the one behind the bar!"

Yendor craned his neck over the bar. There, tacked to the rear wall, was a scrap of paper no bigger across than an apricot. "What—that?" he asked in disbelief.

The innkeeper nodded. "The same."

"I'd have to have the eyes of an eagle to see that thing from the common room, much less read it!"

"Oh," the innkeeper said, "You can read, then?"

"Not much," Yendor admitted.

"Then what's the difference?"

Yendor was beside himself. "The difference? The difference is, I'da never boarded me horse wi' you an' I'd known you was gonna eat her!"

The innkeeper spread his hands wide. "Ah, but we're all eaten eventually, ain't we?"

"I demand—what's the word—restimation!"

There was no such word, of course, but the innkeeper seemed to understand, nonetheless. "I can let you borrow one o' them others," he suggested.

"But," Yendor protested, "Don't those belong to the other patrons?"

"For now," the other man agreed.

"I'll take one."

"How long'll you be needing it?" the innkeeper asked.

"Dunno. 'Til tonight, maybe. Why?"

"Oh, just in case the butcher don't come 'round with our regular delivery o' beef…"

And no one had come by Gangrene & Son's since the original meeting, with the exception of Rem, who'd been by "several days ago," by the giant barkeep's estimation. The whole thing had become an exercise in frustration and impotence—not that Yendor knew anything about impotence, of course. But…what to do? House Fyne seemed a dead end, as devoid of gossip as a graveyard at midnight. Could he, should he give the Fynes the slip and attempt to join one of the other Houses, in hopes of locating Long or Spirk? Or would he be better off staying where he was, hoping his patience was rewarded? Normally when Yendor had no direction, he drank himself into oblivion, until something presented itself. At the moment, however, he felt too much depended upon his remaining conscious. Unhappily, he rode back to the Fretful Porpentine, returned the nag they'd lent him, and made his way back to House Fyne.

He hadn't been back five minutes when the captain of the guard cornered him in the barracks.

"What's of interest in Teshton?"

Ah. They'd had Yendor followed. Of course. Fortunately, he was an accomplished liar and missed not a beat in responding. "Best cider in the Queen's realm."

The captain drew his dagger, began tossing it into the air and catching it. "We got plenty o' cider in Lunessfor."

"That's as may be," Yendor countered. "But the fella in Teshton's devoted to the stuff. He's got a c'llection you wouldn't believe."

The captain smirked at him. "Has he, now? Still, that's a mighty long trip for a few mugs 'o cider."

"That it would be, if that were all my interest in it. Truth is, I was thinkin' o' getting into the apple-growing business one day."

"That a fact?" the captain said flatly.

"Oh, 'tis that. Y'see, with a couple of acres o' land, man can grow more 'n one variety of apples—and that's good proof against yer mildews, yer cankerblossoms, yer chaffing burr weevils. Why, time was..." He looked up and saw that the captain had departed. The speech had had the same effect on him as it had on Yendor, when Long first delivered it, though Long's version had presumably been more rooted in reality.

So, Yendor's rather boring tenure at House Fyne had suddenly taken a turn for the worse, which was, to his way of thinking, paradoxically a turn for the better. If they were spying on him, it meant the Fynes suspecting him of spying; if they were worried about spies, they must have something to hide; if they had something to hide, it could be found.

Unless they killed him first.

Vykers, at Sea

Some men drank, some whored, some gambled. Vykers killed, people and things. And if he wasn't killing, he was daydreaming about it. Killing was how he imposed his will on an otherwise indifferent world, how he made his mark, how he defined himself. When he wasn't engaged in slaughter, he felt lost and confused, as if his mind could entertain no other thoughts and his limbs knew no other function. And yet, for too long now, he *had* been lost—lying and dying in a bed, sitting on a horse, lounging in a ship's cabin. Supposedly, he was chasing the Queen's captors. But that was not what he'd been made for, he was certain, nor the best use of his talents.

Vykers glanced over at the Captain's collection of liquor bottles. There was no salvation or even escape to be found there. His mind wandered to the A'Shea—a little too willingly, he felt. She, she could provide distraction. Some might even have said comfort, but he was not a man to ask or accept such a thing, wouldn't know how to wear it in any case. Not like he wore his constant pain.

The Reaper smashed a fist down onto his bedside table. He was too much alone with his thoughts, or saddled with appetites he was currently unable to satiate. For the hundredth—thousandth?—time, he lurched up from his bed, grabbed his sword and staggered out onto the deck, hoping to find... something. Anything to alleviate his boredom and frustration. Sadly, the looked-for sea monsters were otherwise engaged, and the raging sea was not raging. He was not alone, though. A few of the crew could be seen in the rigging. The Fool was regaling the Captain, aft, and the Historian and the Frog were in close counsel in the cog's primitive forecastle. And where was Aoife? Mahnus-be-damned for making him wonder.

Gradually, the conversation between the Historian and the Frog caught his ear.

"But 'ow can there be anything 'cross the sea?" the boy asked the Ahklatian.

As he drew near, Vykers saw the Historian look up, catch his eye, and look away again sheepishly. To be seen merely speaking with the boy made the older man uncomfortable. So, the old ancient guilt remained. Vykers let him stew in it for a moment, curious how the Ahklatian would proceed.

"Vast as the ocean is," the Historian said, while seeming to study his hands, "it is not the end of the world, simply a desert of sorts between far-flung lands. Though it might take a man three months or more to cross our own land on horseback—and thrice that, riding north to south—it is still only a small part of a larger world. Our friend, here, Tarmun Vykers," the older man said as he directed the boy's attention to the Reaper's presence, "is a legend in our land, but unknown across the sea, for all his might."

But a moment earlier, Vykers had watched with interest as the Ahklatian struggled silently with his inner demons. Now, in a bit of clever turnabout, the Historian had invoked one of Vykers'—the notion that, in spite of everything, the Reaper might be insignificant in the grand scheme of things, unknown and unimportant outside his homeland.

"Not for long," Vykers said.

The Frog smiled at this, as if he'd been told there'd be pie with dinner.

Be careful with that one.

So, you're still with me.

You're alive, aren't you? Arune quipped.

"I've noticed you carry an oddly-fashioned club with your pack," the Historian said to Vykers. "If you don't mind sharing, where did you happen to come by it?

"Morden's Cairn," Vykers answered. "It's something called a 'Ntambi war club'."

"You're well informed."

Of course.

"Would you believe the men who carry such weapons are of skin so dark they cannot be seen at night, but for the whites of their eyes?"

Vykers grunted. "I've heard such things. Time was, I'da called 'em fairy tales. But I used to say the same of magic swords." He hefted his own. "Not anymore."

The Frog was much more impressed. "You sure they're men?"

The Historian offered a wan smile. "As much as we."

*If a nine hundred year old cannibal counts as a man...*Arune muttered.

"Good," Vykers exclaimed. "Men can be killed, if they won't cooperate."

"Will they attack us when we land?" the Frog asked, his tone a mixture of fear and excitement.

"No," the Historian replied. "Their realm is far, far to the south, a land as hot as a blast furnace, excepting the two month rainstorm they call winter."

"And yet," Vykers observed, "at least one of their number died in Morden's Cairn, a world away from home."

"I, too, have wondered about that," the Ahklatian said.

"Any idea when we'll make landfall?" the Reaper inquired. "I'm getting damned sick o' this boat."

"Sick of it? I love it!" the Frog declared. And it was true, Vykers had seen him chasing—and being chased by—the sailors, up and down the rigging on more occasions than he could count. The boy looked as if he'd been born to it.

Vykers shrugged indifferently. "Well, you c'n have it." He realized, too late, that he might've hurt the lad's feelings, but that was probably just as well. Couldn't have the kid getting too attached, after all. Vykers was nobody's hero, and the sooner the Frog figured that out, the better chance he'd have of seeing adulthood. Abruptly, he turned and walked back down to his cabin.

Burner, he thought.

Yes?

You know anything else about these dark men livin' in a blast furnace?

She sighed. *I do not. Just the same rumors, folktales and myths we're all privy to. The Historian has a bit more...life experience... under his belt. You're not worried, are you, Reaper?*

Vykers didn't reply. Instead, he retrieved his pack, untied the knots securing the Ntambi club, and walked back to his bed. He laid his sword down on the mattress' far side and carefully reclined next to it, with the club held up before his eyes.

He did not hate these strange, dark men. But, oh, how he wanted to fight them.

Kittins, House Gault

What was happening to him? Lord Darley had sent him out to intimidate an unappreciative merchant and Kittins had gotten carried away and beaten the man almost to death. He'd paid one of Lunessfor's ubiquitous street urchins to inform the nearest A'Shea and made his escape before she arrived. Now, once again, he sought understanding in the bottom of a bottle of cheap wine in the Grotto. Which was exactly the wrong thing to do, he knew. Spirits never made anything better, although they sometimes provided fleeting moments of obliviousness. There was no denying it, though: ever since he'd come into Lord Darley's service, he'd become more prone to bleak moods, mindless aggression and subsequent self-loathing. He told himself for the millionth time he was not like Tarmun Vykers, not a man who reveled in carnage for its own sake. But he was finding it increasingly difficult to convince himself.

It was usually around this time of an evening that Deda

slithered into the Grotto and made his way to the bar and Kittins' side. Then the captain remembered: he'd set Deda up and hadn't seen him since.

"Barkeep," Kittins called to the man serving drinks, "Have you seen my friend this evening?"

The bartender, a sleepy-eyed lug with protruding teeth, thought about it and then said "Heard he got stabbed in a fight. Heard he's in the infirmary."

Whilst the other man had been speaking, Kittins had been drinking. Now, he almost sneezed wine out his nose in an effort to stifle surprised laughter. "Stabbed, you say?"

"'S what I heard. Word is, he and a friend jumped one o' the other guards, but their target was a mite too strong for 'em. Dunno what happened to the second man."

Kittins set his bottle down, wondered if there'd be an investigation and whether his name would come up. He'd had time to plan for such a contingency, but had been rather preoccupied with his latest assignment. "Thanks," he told the barkeep and slapped a few extra shims on the counter. He had the funds to tip more generously, but most of the guards were notoriously cheap bastards and Kittins had a disguise to maintain.

Drunk, his mind a maelstrom of conflicting concerns, Kittins wandered the Grotto, only peripherally observing the various activities on offer, until he arrived—quite without forethought—at the side corridor that housed the Svarren cages. Several men were gathered around the open door to one of the cages and whooping and hollering at whatever was transpiring within. Kittins thought he knew and pushed his way through the small mob of men in order to see for himself. Sure enough, a couple of half-naked guards were doing unspeakable things to the lone attractive Svarra and beating her if she resisted.

Kittins erupted, his anger getting the best of him once again. He crashed past the last few guards blocking his path and thundered into the cell. At first, the two men inside thought perhaps Kittins had come to join in their fun, but there was no mistaking the look on the big man's ravaged face: he'd come to kill them. The first man made the mistake of bending over to pull up his breeches before defending himself. Kittins palmed his face like a cantaloupe and smashed it into the nearby wall. He'd only intended to knock the man unconscious, but his rage was in complete control of him now, and he reduced the fellow's head to a bloody, broken pulp instead. Outside the cell, the men who'd been watching stood dumbstruck, uncertain what it was they were witnessing or even what should be done about it. Kittins moved on the second man, who'd thrown the Svarren female to the floor and stepped back into a fighting stance—with his trousers still down around his ankles.

"Helluva way to die," Kittins growled, "with your pecker hanging out." He bull -rushed the man without another thought and drove him into the back wall. This man was stronger than the first and sustained little or no damage after Kittins' initial charge. In fact, he bashed his forehead into Kittins' face once the captain's momentum had carried him fully into the second guard. Kittins didn't feel it. The only thought, the only impulse in his brain was to obliterate his opponent, to annihilate him completely. While his rival sought to push him away and perhaps clear some room for a series of blows, Kittins forced his hands up around the man's throat and began tightening his grip like a vise. The other man quickly understood that he needed to break this grip or lose consciousness, so he pounded away at Kittins' midsection with fists, elbows and knees. He might as well have assaulted a stone column. Next, he brought his fingers up to Kittins' face, hoping to gouge at his eyes or tear at his lips. Having had half his face ripped off by thralls, Kittins laughed at the man's efforts, with a bestial, snarling sound that further unmanned his opponent. Suddenly, there was a warm, wet sensation down Kittins' legs, and he realized the man had pissed on him. With a last, monstrous wrench, Kittins crushed the guard's windpipe and retreated a step to watch him die. All was quiet in the cell doorway. Too quiet. The other guards had fled, or gone to fetch reinforcements. It mattered little to Kittins. He looked over at the Svarra, who sat cowering in the corner.

"You're coming with me," he told her. Even if she understood not a word of the Queen's tongue, she understood Kittins' tone.

He walked over to the Svarra and extended his hand. When

she failed to take it, he grabbed her wrist—not roughly, but firmly—and pulled her out of the cell in his wake.

The women of the household staff scattered like chickens when they saw him come into the baths, dragging the Svarren creature behind him. "Stay!" he yelled at the two closest women. "Clean her up!"

It was a near thing, in their minds, which was worse: risking the wrath of this fearsome guard or complying with his wishes and attempting to bathe the savage thing he'd brought with him. In the end, they feared Kittins more.

"Stay calm," he said to the Svarra. "No one's going to hurt you. Stay calm."

The sloe-eyed creature looked askance at her surroundings, as well as the women approaching her, but showed no sign of intent either to fight or to flee.

"You there," Kittins called to the younger of the two women, "what's your name?"

"Mopsa, an' it please you," the woman said, bowing her head a bit in deference. Kittins' station in the household was no higher than her own, but he was a man—a big, horribly scarred man—who fought and killed for a living. Just about everyone short of His Lordship would defer to him when his ire was up.

"And you?" he asked the older woman.

"Dorcas, sir." Less deference, but deference nonetheless.

"Well, ladies, you clean up my new friend, here, and make her presentable, and I'll give you each a merchant for your troubles."

Seeing the big guard would not simply impose his will upon them, but was actually offering recompense relaxed both women considerably. With utmost care, they approached the Svarra and gingerly laid their hands upon her forearms, exerting the slightest pressure in the direction of the nearest bath.

Kittins nodded at the Svarra to indicate his approval and said "I'll be back in an hour's time," to the ladies holding her.

He sat, alone, in another bath in a different part of the estate. It had taken a good fifteen minutes in the bath's scalding hot water for Kittins' fury to subside and a measure of his sobriety to return. He was just beginning to ponder what he should do about the men he'd killed when the room's only door slowly creaked open and His Lordship stepped through, carrying a loaded crossbow.

Before Kittins had a chance to react, Darley spoke. "You're not an easy man to find."

Kittins could think of nothing appropriate to say, so he remained silent.

"I'm seeing a pattern with you," Darley said. "You're dangerously short-tempered and given to overreact. You execute orders in the most literal way." He stared down at Kittins in his usual, probing manner. "I suppose I ought to let you go. Indeed, an intelligent man would probably have you killed. The irony there, of course, is that you're the very man I'd ask to handle such a job."

Here it comes, Kittins thought.

"Almost everyone is frightened of you, excepting myself, naturally. And so I think instead of killing you, I'm going to promote you."

Even Kittins' inner-monologue was speechless.

"From now on, you're Captain of the Guard and in charge of the Grotto, as well. It's high time the guards, servants and lower family members took things a bit more seriously, and you're the man to make them do so."

This time, Kittins was able to cough out a response. "Your Lordship is most generous.'

"Yes, yes," the other man returned blithely. Just as he was about to leave, he turned back and said "Do let me know how you find that Svarren wench when you're done with her. A man does get curious, once in a while." With that, he stepped back into the hall and was gone, closing the door behind himself.

Captain of the Guard. It was madness, certainly, but Kittins was beginning to like it.

Spirk, House D'Escurzy

Lord Titus had not been disposed to leave his bed for days,

despite Spirk's best efforts to motivate him. Was he ailing? Spirk couldn't tell. The little man had always been frail. Now, though, he was alternately hot or cold to the touch, seemingly never anywhere in between. Oh, he remained as impervious—*was that the word?*—and insulting as ever, but Spirk didn't mind. His own father had been impervious and insulting, so, in a way, His Lordship's chambers felt like home.

One afternoon while Titus slept, Faenia reappeared. Or rather, her perfume wafted into the room and Spirk knew she was not far behind. He considered waking His Lordship, but imagined the old man would not be pleased. No, this was one terror Spirk had to face by himself.

Faenia tread lightly as she walked into view, too lightly, in Spirk's view. She was like a cat—sleek, dark and unknowable. "Oh," she sighed, in almost convincing disappointment. "Is my uncle asleep then? Poor fellow. I hate to see him so tired all the time."

Suddenly, Spirk became uncomfortably aware of Faenia's dramatically heaving bosom and felt somehow enspelled by the woman's cleavage, as if powerful but unseen magics emanated from thence. He struggled to look elsewhere.

"So...Long Pete," Faenia breathed in a low, husky voice, "what is it exactly that you do for Lord Titus?"

"Oh, uh," he stammered, "a little o' this and some o' t'other." The breasts were getting too close. Spirk stared at his feet, hoping somehow he'd find salvation in them.

"I'd've thought a big, strong man like you capable of a good deal more than that, Long," Faenia purred.

Spirk could avert his eyes, but what could he do about his nose? Faenia's perfume hung thick in his nostrils, making him feel almost drunk with...something. And now he could feel the heat of her breath near his neck. He hoped to Mahnus he was imperious to her charms, but he feared this might be Mahnus' will.

She put her hand on his chest.

Spirk wanted to scream, to shriek like the Miller's girl on Spirits Night. If only he could, he was sure he'd awaken His Lordship. But he had no breath left to shriek with. To his

horror, Faenia's hand began to slide down his chest towards...
towards...In that fleeting infinity of time, that eternal instant,
Spirk understood that what really frightened him was that he
had no idea what to do with a woman and, worse still, what she
might do to him.

The blood rushed to his head and his vision went black.
Just as he was about to lose consciousness, Faenia pulled away
from him and toppled onto the floor, herself. Was she mocking
him? No, she had well and truly passed out. A wheezing sound
he'd come to recognize as Titus' laughter assailed him from the
depths of the enormous bed.

"Nice trick, that. I hope you killed her."

Spirk looked over at his master in shock. "Killed her? Me?
No, no. I dint do nothing. Anything."

Titus' 'laughter' intensified until it overwhelmed the
little man, dissolved into an uncontrollable hacking cough.
Forgetting about the lovely young thing asleep on the floor, his
manservant rushed to his side and gently elevated his head and
torso so that he might spit up or swallow whatever it was that
was troubling his lungs. After several long, terrifying (for Spirk)
moments, His Lordship's breathing eased.

"Would have been a fine way to go out, laughing."

Spirk frowned. "Don't say such things, milord."

"Long," said Titus irritably, "I never know whether to smack
you or laugh at you." This was quite a speech for His Lordship,
and required several deep breaths before continuing. "There's
none here cares for me. And none anywhere cares you for, I
don't doubt." At Spirk's dismayed expression, Titus add, "But
you make my passing easier, and I...thank you for it."

Now, it was applause coming from the other side of the
room that caught Spirk off guard. Before he could look over, His
Lordship grabbed his ear and pulled him closer. "Don't. Even.
Acknowledge. Her," he wheezed.

"A touching, touching performance!" Faenia called out.
She must have awakened during her uncle's coughing fit
and climbed to her feet in the commotion. "But, sadly, only a
performance. You've never known gratitude a day in your life,
uncle!"

Titus hadn't the strength or the breath to respond.

"And you!" Faenia called over to Spirk. "What sort of a trick was that to play upon a lady? Or do you dislike women, eh?"

"Watch your tongue, wench!" said Titus at last. "Or my Shaper here will fry your innards!"

It was a ludicrous gambit, of course. Spirk, a Shaper?

Faenia bought it, or seemed to. Something had caused her to collapse, after all, and just when she'd been about to pounce. She stared warily at Spirk. "There's never been a Shaper yet who could withstand a knife in the back."

"Or a harlot!" Titus parried.

Faenia made a sour expression with her mouth, sneered at both men a final time, and spun on her heel, headed out of the room much more noisily than she'd entered.

"Clodpoll," His Lordship whispered in Spirk's direction, "send for my notary."

"Your what?"

Titus rolled his eyes and sighed. "My notary. Look, cockscomb, do you know who the House Steward is?"

Spirk nodded.

"Progress! Find out the Steward and tell him to send the notary to my chambers forthwith. And you'd better ask for the Captain of my guard, as well."

"Is there trouble?" asked Spirk.

"Oh," the ancient little man smiled, "there's always trouble."

SIX

Long, House Thornton

It was as authentic a dungeon cell as could be imagined, if only Long had merely imagined it. The wall at his back was every bit as cold and dank as common mythology made such walls out to be; the chains attaching him to said wall were as heavy, rusted and unforgiving, and even the floor on which he sat was as damp and filthy. The air was both chilly and putrescent, a sickening miasma of sweat, urine, feces, lime, calcite and other, less identifiable odors. If Long had had anything in his stomach, he might have vomited, save that fear of adding to the general stench discouraged such behavior. If all of this weren't bad enough, there was the darkness, such darkness as Long had never experienced. His eyes had never adjusted to it, and he could see nothing at any distance. He even punched himself in the mouth once accidentally, waving his hands about in attempt to spot them in the blackness. Here, again, was the despair he'd forgotten when the End-of-All-Things was destroyed.

How long had he been here? Long couldn't begin to guess. It felt like days, at the very least. It might have been weeks. He remembered being struck across the back of his head. And then he'd woken up in blackness—cold, stiff, sore and hungry. Once in a while, he heard a faint babbling from the cell next door, which made him wonder if there wasn't a hole or crack in the wall between his own cell and its neighbor. He would have liked to find it, were he not chained in place, so that he might listen more closely to his unseen companion in misery.

And he thought of Mardine and little—relatively

little—Esmine. Long had been in worse scrapes. Or closer to death, anyway. Since he couldn't see a way out of his current predicament, he was perhaps as good as dead. What in Mahnus' name had possessed him to take this cursed assignment? And why-oh-why had he attempted to sneak off into the mansion by himself? He'd stolen the life meant for Short Pete, he figured, and Short Pete had stolen Long's death. At all events, he'd probably never see his beloved wife and daughter again.

Long sagged in his chains, allowed his thoughts to wander to things less painful. Although his prison was precise in every detail, it lacked rats, so far as he'd been able to tell. That was an oversight on his captors' part, surely. Or it might have been that the rats of House Thornton were of a better sort, too refined for skulking about in such undignified surroundings. Long envied them.

The Babbler started up again, and Long Pete called out to him, at least as well as his ruined voice would allow.

"Hello!" he croaked.

The babbling continued without pause.

"You there, neighbor!" Long yelled. It was a horrific sound, like that of a table being dragged across a rough stone floor.

The babbling stopped. Before Long could muster another call, the babbling resumed.

Finally, Long rattled his chains and roared incoherently. The babbling and the Babbler stopped.

"Eh?" someone ventured from beyond the wall. So, there was a hole somewhere.

"Have you got a name, friend?" Long asked of the darkness.

"Name?" Lunatic laughter. "My name's a shame, my claim to fame. I'm not to blame if you touch the flame. You'll come up lame, all the same."

Ugh. A madman. Still, Long supposed, in his desperate situation, a madman's company had to be better than no company at all. "A poet, are you? You got a name, poet?"

"My name's a shame," the Babbler said again. "They call me 'Peppers,' a name I wouldn't give to lepers. 'Peppers,' they call me, spicy and hot, it says what I am, but it hides what I'm not."

"Peppers," Long echoed. "Peppers."

"Peppers, Peppers, that's how I'm known, a spicy name is all I own. You can bitch, and I can moan, but it's still the same: my name's a shame."

With little else to do, Long indulged the man. "How a shame?"

"How a shame? It's just the frame, it's not the painting. It's says what I am, but not what I ainting. Nobody knows the man I was, nobody does, and that's because that man I am is just a sham."

Long debated the wisdom in continuing the conversation. In the end, he pressed on. "Why did they put you in here, Peppers?" he rasped.

"In the huggermugger was I taken, to make me know I was mistaken, I played my game, I sullied their name, they took it amiss and this and this, down into the black, alas, alack! Will no one ever fetch me back?"

If there was method in this madness, Long could not see it. But then, he could see nothing else, either. He grew both frustrated and bored trying to decipher Pepper's strange jabbering, and it was not long before he fell asleep from the effort.

Sometime later, he drifted awake and miraculously understood at least a small part of Pepper's riddling: the fellow had insulted House Thornton and they'd imprisoned him for it. Or maybe they'd just imprisoned him for his bad poetry. Long could hardly blame them. It was a strange kind of verse, really. Less about lyrics than rhythm, it pounded its way into one's mind like a drum beat. Before he knew what he was doing, Long found himself repeated some of the phrases.

"I sullied their name, they took it amiss and this and this..." He ought to have known he'd rouse the poet.

"I coulda stayed out, I coulda been free, not here in the dark, in the damp, in the dank with thee. But I spoke my piece, I said what I must, now I'm down in the dark, in the damp, in the dust."

"Peppers!" Long yelled (as best he was able).

Silence.

"Can you speak to me, man-to-man, without all that rhyming?"

A pause.

"No."

And Peppers said nothing else. Minutes went by, perhaps even an hour, and Long decided to let the matter drop for the time being.

There was a rattling in what Long took to be the lock of the cell's door, followed by a painful screeching from its hinges, and then light, lantern light, leapt into the cell, temporarily dazing the prisoner. The shapes of two men stomped heavily in his direction; the lantern swung round 'til it was right in his face. He winced and turned his head away.

"Still alive, then? Good." Said the man whose voice Long recognized as belonging to the Steward. To his companion, the Steward said "Unlock the wall chain, but leave the manacles. Sometimes, these bastards get stupid and we have to kill them."

Oh, Long heard that. He was in no condition to put up a fight, anyway.

"We'll take him to Master Dorrick's study," the Steward continued.

From the next cell, "Master Dorrick, worthless prick, perfect Fyne, asinine."

"You want me to piss in your water, Peppers, I will!" the Steward yelled back.

"Again?" Peppers cackled. "What men, what men! They piss in my drink, they spit on my bread, they shit on my spirit, I'm still not dead!"

The Steward's companion violently yanked Long to his feet. He barely noticed. He was thinking of Peppers. Madman he may be, but he was also undeniably quick. Long supposed it a natural consequence of living in rhyme. What purpose did this serve? That was harder to reason out.

An exhausting series of passageways and then hallways flew by as Long was roughly hustled through the dungeons and ultimately into a large, well-lit, sparsely furnished chamber that must have been on the other side of the world from his cell. A sturdy, solitary chair stood in the middle of the room, and Long understood its purpose immediately.

"So," he gasped, "it's torture, is it?"

The Steward slapped him across the face, whilst the other man secured his chains to the chair and floor. "No torture today, we're too far behind schedule. But I wanted to make sure you tasted a little pain, so you wouldn't be disappointed."

None of which made the least bit of sense to Long.

"Watch him," the Steward told his companion. "I'll be right back with Master Dorrick." Long listened to the sound of the Steward's footsteps on the stone floor, reckoned the door was some fourteen paces away. The door opened and closed and silence followed. The second man stood nearby, smelling of fish oil.

Long tried again. "You're behind schedule, then?"

The other man punched him in the stomach so hard, he would have vomited, had he eaten recently. Long had to admire the man's choice of targets: a blow to the face or head was usually the popular option, but those left marks that sometimes frustrated higher ranking sadists, who invariably preferred a pristine canvas on which to work. Long wondered if he could goad the fellow into breaking his nose and thus bring punishment upon himself when the Steward returned. He decided he liked his nose more than he hated his nameless persecutor, so he said nothing further.

In time, the door opened and two sets of footsteps made their way over to the chair.

"Is this the spy?" a voice asked. But it was not just any voice.

"That's what we're here to determine," replied the Steward.

"They're always spies," Janks answered, "in my experience."

Mardine, in the Village

Everyone knew Mardine, of course. How could they not? She was the only giant hereabouts and one of the few red-heads, to boot. She was also one of the friendliest folk you'd ever care to meet. But not today. Today, she came into town like a winter storm—cold, powerful and bent on damage. Those who called out to her in expectation of a warm greeting were mystified when she ignored them as she thundered past. Trouble was coming. Trouble was here. The only question was, was it wiser to secure the shutters and hide under the bed, or follow in the giantess' wake and see where help was needed most? Another question occurred to a number of townsfolk: which of them had been stupid enough to anger Mardine?

When the giantess reached the heart of the village, she grabbed the nearest thrall by the throat and lifted him high into the air. The rest of the villagers stared from a safe distance.

"Where's Nelby got to?"

The thrall could hardly speak.

Mardine loosened her grip. "Where's Nelby?"

"Nelby?" the man whined.

Mardine snapped his neck and tossed him aside, fire in her eyes. She spotted a 'Hire a Thrall' poster on the side of the town grocery and tore it down. "Where is Nelby?" she roared. The only response she heard was the sound—a chorus—of doors slamming, windows shutting, bolts being thrown.

Mardine kicked in the door of the grocery and squeezed into the shop. Several people were hiding behind the counter at the room's far end.

"N-now, M-Mardine, that's my d-door you just busted. 'S g-gonna c-cost me a few shims to f-fix that, I'll w-warrant."

"I'm right sorry, Myx," said Mardine, "But I haven't got time for nonsense. Nelby's ta'en my girl, and I mean to get her back before…before…" She couldn't finish the sentence.

In no time, Myx found his way to her side, completely unconcerned for his own welfare. "Nelby's got Esmine, you say? Why ever would she do that?"

"I've no idea, Myx. But I mean to find out."

"How can I help?"

Mardine looked into the man's kind, eternally rosy face. "Can you help? I need to know where the thralls go when they're not working."

"Thought everyone knew that," he said. "They're down by the river, most days."

The river? Sweet Alheria, not the river. If Nelby boarded a barge, Mardine wasn't like to find her again in this lifetime.

Myx put a hand on Mardine's forearm. "C'mon, Em, I'll

show you," he said. The giantess suspected he was really just trying to lead her away from his shop, but she could hardly refuse a little guidance at this point.

Outside the shop, the Constable pointed his sword at Mardine and Myx.

"Can't have you killin' the thralls, Mardine. No matter what you think they done."

"They took my Esmine, Rannidge."

"You know for a fact it was this one?" he asked, indicated the corpse across the road.

"I don't. And I don't care, either. One of 'em did it, and they're all going to pay."

"Don't make me arrest you," the little constable warned.

"Go ahead and try, Rannidge. I'm in no mood."

Myx said nothing.

Rannidge shrugged. "Gotta enforce the law."

"And what about the mother's law?" Mardine bellowed in his face. "What about a mother's obligation to her child? I swear, Constable, you get in my way, it'll be the last thing you do in this life."

The Constable lowered his weapon, stared at his feet. "They'll have my job for this," he said, more to himself than the giantess. "They might even put me behind bars."

"Mahnus'll look out for you, Ran. I'm sure o' that." Mardine nodded to Myx, who began walking towards River road. With a final glance at Rannidge, Mardine followed.

Ten minutes later, the pair arrived at the boat landing, trailed by some twenty or twenty-five curious villagers who wanted to see what happened next. And what happened next was, Mardine went crazy. With a quick burst of speed, she closed on the nearest bunch of thralls—who had somehow failed to mark her arrival—and grabbed three of them in her enormous hands. She had two by their shirts in her right hand and one by the hair in her left. All, she lifted into the air. If the other thralls spent even a moment considering some sort of resistance, it wasn't obvious to anyone watching. Instead, they jumped into bushes, dove into the river, or ran up or downstream along its banks. Thralls were used to being treated with suspicion or contempt;

they were accustomed to being abused by the Free Folk, as they called the natives. And so, when Mardine charged into action, they fled.

In Mardine's mind, however, this was evidence of their complicity in Esmine's disappearance, and it only made her angrier.

"Where is Nelby?" she screamed at her dangling captives.

"Don't be killin' 'em, Em!" the Constable called at her back. "Ask your questions and let 'em go."

The giantess growled in frustration and slammed the three thralls to the ground, stunning them. Before they recovered, she stood on their feet. The pain brought 'em 'round right quick.

"Ahhhhgggh!" they all cried in unison, like a chorus of the damned.

"I won't ask again," said Mardine, through clenched teeth. "Where. Is. Nelby?"

"Ain't seen 'er," groaned the oldest of her captives, a grey-haired ghost of a man.

"I'm dyin'! I'm dyin'!" moaned the younger man.

"Dunno," the third captive, a woman, managed. "I dunno nothin', I swear."

"She and her man rode out by the north road," came a fourth voice.

Mardine looked up. A slightly plump woman with dirty blond hair and bare feet looked back at her, face set in a permanent frown. By now, two of her three captives were not-so-quietly sobbing in their fear and misery. The old man just endured.

"And you know this how?" Mardine asked the other woman.

"'Cause her man used ta be mine," the woman admitted. She scanned the crowd defiantly. "I been spyin' on 'em for a couple 'o weeks now."

The giantess stepped off and away from her prisoners, eliciting a final cry from each. "And how do I know you're not lying to me in order to throw me off the scent?"

The thrall had a ready answer. "You can take me with you. You find out I'm lyin', you do what you gotta do."

Ah. The woman scorned, looking for a little revenge.

Mardine had never experienced such feelings herself, but she'd seen them often enough to recognize their dark power. "Come along, then," said she. "I'm after them right now."

The crowd parted, allowing the thrall woman and Mardine to make their way back up River road and into the village.

Trailing along behind her, Myx said "You need any supplies, Em?"

Without looking back, Mardine answered, "I'm fine, thanks. Could probably use a pony for this one, here. Otherwise, I'm fine."

"I got one as you can borrow," one of the other townsfolk called out. "Long Pete's been mighty helpful to me and mine. Figure I owe you at least that much."

It didn't stop with the pony, though. In half an hour's time, Mardine's neighbors and friends had outfitted her and the thrall woman like royalty on tour. The giantess nearly wept at the townsfolk's generosity; the watchful eye of her companion stopped her. In short order, Mardine and the thrall were back on the road, escorted along by a chorus of farewells. She hadn't realized how much she loved the little village and its outlying farms. She wondered when or if she'd see them again.

"You have a name?" Mardine asked the thrall as they plodded along.

"Tresa," the woman said.

"And this man o' yours?"

"He ain't mine no more."

"Right. This man travelling with Nelby...what's his name?"

"Jaddo."

Mardine tried the name on her tongue. "Jaddo. Jaddo." She paused. "I don't recognize it."

Tresa laughed a short, bitter laugh. "He's kinda like termites in your walls; you don't know he's about unless ye go lookin' for 'im."

"You figure he's the one took my daughter, or was it Nelby and he's just along for the company?"

Tresa screwed up her face. "I'm guessing Jaddo. Nelby ain't never seemed too smart to me."

Mardine bristled at this. "You think it was smart to take my Esmine?"

The thrall wasn't cowed in the least. "I mean, it sounds like one o' Jaddo's schemes."

"This is why you people have such a hard time getting back on your feet," Mardine said irritably.

"Oh!" said Tresa, her voice dripping with sarcasm, "Is that why? I thought it was the lack o' work."

"Seems to me there ought to be plenty 'o work, back where you came from. Not to mention folks who miss you."

Tresa stopped in her tracks and shot Mardine a look of such contempt it unnerved the giantess. "And how're we supposed to get back there, eh? That's a journey of months, and none of us has so much as two shims to rub together. How're we supposed to buy supplies, horses and all o' that? Oh, the crown said they'd help us after the war, but all they done is dump us into everybody else's laps. Nobody's got enough work for all of us. Nobody's got enough food, nor shelter. What we are is just a bunch o' hangers-on, and nobody likes that."

Clearly, this was a speech Tresa had heard or delivered on many occasions, and Mardine was under prepared to debate the logic of it. "But…stealing and kidnapping don't make you any more welcome…"

"Say somebody gives you a mangy old hound. For a while, you feed 'im and care for 'im. Time goes by and you get bored or tired o' feedin' and caring for im. But the hound's gotta live, no? So, he starts sneaking food when you're not lookin'. It's nothing 'gainst you, but he's gotta eat. That make 'im a bad dog, or you a bad master?"

"But we never asked to be your masters!" Mardine countered.

"Then you shouldn't-a never taken us in!" Tresa yelled back. "You shoulda said 'sorry, but we cain't help you' from the get-go. Woulda been a lot more merciful!"

"None o' that excuses stealing my little one. None of it. And if she's not right when we find her again, there'll be two fewer thralls looking for food and shelter."

Early summer meant longer days; longer days meant more miles travelled before camping each night. For the first few days, Mardine and Tresa were so exhausted by the time they made camp that they barely had time to start a fire and eat something before falling asleep where they sat. Often, Mardine would get up in the middle of the night and drape a blanket over the thrall woman—not out of kindness or pity, but because she didn't want the woman dying on her before they found Nelby, Jaddo and, most importantly, Esmine.

During these mid-night periods, Mardine inevitably began worrying about things, anything, everything. What would they do when they came to a fork in the road? Sooner or later, they'd have to choose a direction. What if they chose wrong? And then there was the issue of bandits. Or worse. There were things in the wilderness between towns that had no love of men...or giants. Mardine was confident she could handle up to five men, maybe even seven or eight if they were sick or doing poorly. More than that, though, she hoped she'd never see. She worried, too, about what she could expect from Tresa in a fight. For all she knew, the woman would turn on her when she was otherwise engaged and stick a knife in the giant's back. Not that a single knife would do much damage, but it certainly wouldn't help.

More than anything, she worried about her daughter. Were her captors treating her well or had they abused her? Surely they'd want her in good health if they meant to sell her into service or slavery, wouldn't they? Even if they weren't beating and starving Esmine, Mardine feared the experience alone could traumatize the child for years to come, break her spirit and change her essential nature forever.

The irony of the situation was not lost on Mardine. Oh no, far from it. Her husband's departure to investigate the kidnapping of the Queen had directly created the circumstances under which Esmine could likewise be kidnapped. Hang her for treason—if you could find a rope stout enough—but Mardine would save her daughter's life over the Queen's any and every time. Besides, the old hag had lived her span and then some, whereas Esmine—sweet natured, beautiful Esmine...

Mardine hoped the Queen was suffering, wherever she was. Then she regretted such thoughts. Then she feared she'd jinxed herself and her daughter. Then she cursed Mahnus and Alheria. Then she repented. Then she started all over again.

Mornings, Mardine questioned Tresa over and over again about what she'd heard, seen or suspected. The giantess understood she'd run off half-blind, but what else could she do?

"You're positive you heard this Jaddo planning to head north?" she'd say for the hundredth time.

"Dead certain," Tresa answered, time and again.

"It makes no sense, though," Mardine complained. "On the river, he could have made much better time in either direction than travelling over land. And it's much easier to follow him now, too."

"Might be he figured you'd take to the river and his escape to the north would be that much easier."

Mardine shook her head, frustrated. "And what's to the north but more small towns? He won't reach a bigger one for a week or more."

"Unless he ain't aiming for a city."

Disturbing thought, that.

"You don't trust my word, we can always head back, find a boat and search the river..." Tresa offered, knowing full well Mardine would decline.

"We'll press on," said the giantess, her face a mask of grim determination.

Aoife, at Sea

Aoife had never been so indolent. There was really nowhere to go on the little ship and nothing to do once you got there. Anyhow, that's what she'd been trying to tell herself for weeks now. The truth was, despite all her prayers and meditation, she hadn't found a solution to the problem of Tarmun Vykers and his damnable...*charisma*, for want of a better word. She wished she had Toomt'-La's counsel, though she could well guess what he might say. He had little use for humans at the best of times and no use for their warriors. So, Toomt'-La would tease her, nimbly walking a fine line between gentle humor and biting cynicism. One moment, he'd have the A'Shea laughing, the next, she'd feel tempted to vex him with agues. But if anyone could keep her away from the Reaper, it was he.

Without warning, there was a thunderous noise, and the whole ship shook so violently for an instant that Aoife cried out, certain the end of the world had arrived. From the alarmed shouts of the crew, she was not alone in this fear. To her surprise, however, and before her heart had even returned to its normal rhythm, the same crew could be heard cheering and then outright roaring with laughter. What in Mahnus' name was going on? Well, she had to know, even if it meant running into Vykers. Resigned, Aoife climbed out of her bunk and made her way into the narrow hallway that ran to the stairs. She passed the tiny cabin the Frog shared with Hoosh and the Historian and noticed that all three were out. A party on deck? And she hadn't been invited.

When at last she arrived on deck, she discovered the entire ship's population at the port railing, staring out to sea and raining laughter and curses in the same direction. Had they run aground? Spotted land? Pushing her way through the crowd, she, too, stared out to sea and was shaken by what she saw. A bowshot away, a serpentine creature of unimaginable proportions raged and thrashed in frothy waves of its own making, bleeding profusely from an area Aoife took to be its head. In its agony, the beast knew no particular direction, but writhed and spasmed in a chaotic and unpredictable manner.

"What in the countless hells it that thing?" she breathed.

"That," the Captain beamed, "is the reason nobody's ever returned from a voyage across this ocean. Don't rightly know what it's called, but he's a big bastard, ain't he?"

Big? Aoife had seen pictures of whales as an initiate to the Sisterhood. This thing could have swallowed a school of whales and not even noticed.

"And it rammed us?" the A'Shea asked. "How is it we're not dead?"

The Captain gave her his best, toothy grin. "'Cause I knew there was something like him out here. I seen too much wreckage washed up on shore, too many broken hulls. I fitted my lady here with six foot spikes all over her bottom. And I

painted those spikes with poisoned pitch, to boot!" He pointed
to the monster, still boiling away in the distance. "Our lad here
came along and thought to sink us, but came away with a brain
full o' steel instead."

Aoife would have liked to feel shock or revulsion. All she
felt was relief. She had no trouble believing the creature had
ruined entire fleets of explorers and merchants. And he was
but one of his species. Surely there were others. The monster
began to scream and wail, and Aoife observed that its bleeding
increased. Suddenly, the water around it was alive with sharks
and other, less identifiable predators. The leviathan's death
struggle soon became too vicious, too brutal for the A'Shea, and
she turned to leave, only to run smack into Vykers' chest. She
reached out a hand to ensure she didn't collide with him and
inadvertently placed it on the upper left side of his chest. It was
like touching a stone. At first, anyway. It shortly became a much
more pleasant and therefore unpleasant experience.

"Feelin' the merchandise before you buy, are you?" Vykers
grinned.

Aoife pulled her hand away and looked down. She hoped
no one else was watching. "I'm not buying," she said.

"Then mayhap you're selling?"

"You know I am not."

Vykers took her chin in his hand, gently but firmly, made
sure she looked into his eyes. "D'you think we'll live forever?
That we've got forever?"

"I don't know what you're talking about."

He traced the surface of her lips with his thumb. "I'll not lie
to you: as a boy, I took what I wanted from women and had no
regrets. That's how it was in the army. But I've learned a thing's
worth less if you have to steal it than if it's given outright."

"It will never be given."

The Reaper cupped her face in both his hands, drew her
close. In a whisper, he said "Words are not actions, my lady.
Remember that."

"Land!" A voice yelled from the rigging. "Land off the
Starboard side!"

Vykers withdrew from Aoife so quickly there was almost a

vacuum in his absence. The warrior jumped for the nearest rope and climbed up into the rigging himself, anxious to see this land with his own eyes. "True enough!" he called down. "We've crossed this Mahnus-cursed sea at last!"

This latest near-kiss was perhaps harder on Arune than on Aoife and Vykers combined. While the Reaper possessed an impressive ability to put the A'Shea out of his mind when necessary, Arune was shockingly weak in that area. The feel of Aoife's skin in Vykers' hands had been tantalizing, whetting Arune's appetite for a "more" that never came. If it was possible for a ghost to be sexually frustrated the Shaper had accomplished the feat and even mastered it. What she had not yet riddled out was whether her yearnings were a part of Brouton's Bind and, thus, the feelings of her host, or whether she, herself, had actually fallen for the A'Shea. It mattered little: she was mad for the woman, and every day, hour, minute or second Vykers managed to ignore her was torture for Arune. If she was ever going to obtain what—and who—she wanted, Arune was going to have to force the issue and manipulate the Reaper.

That, she knew, could be very, very dangerous.

"And that there's your second reason we've had no return traffic from this coast," the Captain said, pointing up at the towering cliffs, topped by an equally forbidding wall. 'Tis madness to even contemplate scaling such heights. How many have died tryin'?"

Vykers stared at the cliffs, brooding, echoing the general mood on board, which had gone from elation at first sight of land to defeat upon closer inspection. "That'll be our last resort, then."

"Which leaves sailing up or down the coast in hopes of finding some more hospitable shoreline."

Vykers turned to the Historian, who'd been standing at his side for the past hour. "You mighta mentioned this," he grumbled.

"And I would have, you can be sure, if that wall had been there last time I visited these shores."

Sometimes, it was easy to forget the Ahklatian was almost nine hundred years old. Vykers returned his attention to the cliffs and wall, now bathed in the pinks and oranges of sunset. It was a pleasant evening, as such things went, but the Reaper was largely unaware of it.

"Question is, was that wall built to keep us out, or the natives in?"

The Captain looked confused. "What difference does that make, 'specially if we ain't gonna bother with it?"

"It matters," the Historian cut in, "because whoever resides behind that wall is more likely to have patrols outside it if it was built to repel rather than contain."

"Just so," Vykers agreed. "Guess we'd better plan for either contingency." He put his back to the rail and surveyed the ship, its passengers and crew. A breeze from the west wafted across the deck and the Reaper took a moment to enjoy the relative peace. Soon, he and his companions would be on the move again. Soon, there would be running, fighting and perhaps even dying.

He couldn't wait.

To everyone's astonishment, it took another week of sailing down the coast to find a suitable landing site without either cliffs or the enormous wall that seemed always to accompany them. Initially, the wall had seemed a curiosity. But as the miles crept by, its impossible size began to weigh heavily on the minds of passengers and crew alike. How could there be so much stone in all the world, or the men to cut, cart and place it? Every so often, its color and texture changed—presumably as one quarry was exhausted and another opened up—and occasionally the style and shape of its blocks changed as well. In the end, it did not end or even turn inland so much as it petered out, as if its builders had run out of money, time or interest. Or maybe they'd forgotten why they built it in the first place, though that didn't strike Vykers as any too likely.

In many ways, the search for a beachhead felt like the longest week of a long, tedious journey. To be so close to land—a new, mysterious land, full of prizes just waiting to be discovered—and yet to be unable to come ashore was agonizing. But at last the day came when the first mate identified the perfect place inside a sheltered bay and the Captain ordered a scouting party to investigate. Of course, the Reaper insisted on going along, and who'd dare to argue? The Frog wanted to go, too, but Aoife put her foot down and insisted he stay aboard until the safety of the beach had been established.

"Let 'em clear away the beasties, bugs 'n brambles first, lad," the Fool chipped in helpfully, "that way, there'll be naught for us to do but rest and relax when we come ashore."

"Don't wanna rest!" the Frog complained, "I wanna find some treasure, or maybe a new pet!"

The strangeness, the excitement of this alien coastline had restored some of the Frog's boyish sense of wonder, Aoife was glad to note. For too long, he'd been forced to put on a brave face. It was comforting to see and hear him acting like a boy again.

As to the landing party, well, Aoife struggled with whether or not she should join them. Being a healer, it made sense, was probably even her duty. A part of her, though, was looking forward to putting a little distance, however briefly, between Vykers and herself. In the Sisterhood, she'd aided other A'Shea in treating addicts from time to time, unfortunates hooked on booze, wild mushrooms or various other substances. She'd witnessed firsthand their awful struggles to escape the grips of these things. She worried she might be beginning to feel that same sort of need for Vykers' company and she resented that—and him. Which, naturally, reinforced her desire to get away from the man, if only for a few hours. With relief, she watched the tender pull away from the ship, carrying the first mate, three sailors, Vykers, the Historian and the two chimeras. She felt a moment's anxiety at the thought she'd never see the Reaper again, but immediately dismissed it as nonsense. Like it or not, he'd be back.

Vykers was sweating, despite the sea breeze in his face.

"Warmer, here," he said to no one in particular.

"We're a good deal further south than you're used to," the Historian replied.

Both chimeras had their mouths open, in the manner of cats smelling another animal's spoor.

"What?" Vykers asked.

"So many new aromas. It's quite...intoxicating," said Three.

"Don't know as I like the idea o' you two bein' intoxicated," Vykers joked lamely. He wasn't nervous, exactly, but neither was he accustomed to entering thoroughly unknown territory.

After nearly a half hour's labor, the sailors managed to row the small boat ashore and lost no time in loading their crossbows. Vykers jumped overboard and landed in the shallows, soaking his boots, but enjoying the sensation, anyway.

Arune spoke up for the first time in days. *If you can wait a few minutes, the Ahklatian and I should be able to learn something of Her Majesty's fate.*

Got your magic back, eh?

It's nice to be back on solid ground.

You can say that again.

Vykers noticed the Historian was staring in his direction, though not looking at him directly. Must've been communicating with Arune, Vykers figured. The chimeras spread out, north and south of the boat, and continued sniffing the breeze. Out of habit, Vykers drew his sword and glided into an ageless, nameless drill of focus and balance while waiting on the two Shapers' findings.

She's alive, Arune said eventually. *That's something, anyway.*

"Alive," Vykers grunted aloud. "But where?"

The Historian responded, "To the southeast, it would seem."

"You've been here," Vykers reminded him, "what's to the southeast?"

"That depends entirely upon how far we have to travel."

"Within two weeks' travel, then," the Reaper said.

"Plains, mountains, the largest lake you've ever seen."

"And beyond?"

"Jungle."

Vykers had never heard the word before. "Jungle..." he said, testing the word.

It's a type of forest, Arune offered. *But I'll wager you won't recognize a single plant or animal we find there.*

Long as a sword kills 'em, I don't give a fuck.

"Let's make camp near that driftwood over there," Vykers told the First Mate. "Spend the rest of the day gettin' our bearings and depart in the morning."

"Yes sir," the First Mate replied. "Just let me take the tender back to the ship and inform the Captain."

The Reaper nodded. All things considered, he felt pretty good. He was back on land, had decent weather and the Queen still lived.

It seemed too good to be true.

Arune, he thought, *any uglies out there we gotta worry about?*

I've been searching. Nothing nearby we can't handle.

Keep looking.

In the Reaper's experience, anything that seemed too good to be true was usually prelude to a shit storm.

Rem, House Hawsey

The plan was simple enough; it was going through with it that demanded more pluck than Rem perhaps possessed, for it required him to seduce and then bed Lady Hawsey. The goal was to get her to reveal the location of the diary, and then to wear her out so thoroughly that she slept through the ensuing search for and retrieval of same. But had Rem the stomach, backbone and other anatomical necessities? He'd never been shy about such things before. Then again, he'd never attempted a creature quite like Her Ladyship.

For one thing, the woman wore more make up than an entire troupe of actors. Rem wasn't sure there was an actual person under all that stuff. In addition, though there was no danger of disease thanks to the house A'Shea's zealous commitment to her job, there was also no guarantee that Her Ladyship's sense of hygiene was within social norms. Finally, she was old—not as old as Her Majesty, but undoubtedly old enough to be Rem's mother, which thought nearly rendered the actor permanently impotent.

Still, he had to have that diary and a second chance at its secrets.

At dinner, the boy who played most of the company's female ingénues began flirting with Lord Hawsey, as planned. After much wine and ribaldry, His Lordship became almost uncontrollably excited, whereupon the boy led him on a merry game of hide and seek. Lady Hawsey watched these proceedings with a gimlet eye, but eventually turned away in evident bitterness; her husband's weaknesses were an old and insoluble conundrum. Enter the dashing actor, Remuel Wratch. How he laid on the charm and flattery! In no time, he had the old wench by the short and curlies. She giggled—a sound not unlike the cry of the common loon—at his every joke. She batted her eyes so often and dramatically, he feared they might fall from their sockets and roll across the dinner table, only to be eaten by a glutton mistaking them for hardboiled eggs. A dew of perspiration formed in the not-so-fine mustache on her upper lip. And Rem was going to make love to her? Madness! Masochism! More wine!

Phase two of Rem's plan involved sneaking away with Her Ladyship during a distraction, caused by the props master "accidentally" setting fire to his end of the table. This would unquestionably result in long-term banishment from His Lordship's dining room, but it was a loss Rem and his comrades felt they must buck up and bear bravely. And, truth be told, it was a rather impressive fire, which was fortunate because the actor and his prey suddenly lacked the physical coordination necessary for a rapid or stealthy retreat. Alcohol, it has oft been observed, does a fine job in reducing one's inhibitions, but is also impairs one's agility.

In a hallway just off the dining room, Her Ladyship bull-rushed the actor and pinned him into a corner, where she started tickling him as if he were a child and breathing heavily onto his neck. Ah, yes, there'd been sardines for dinner, hadn't there? And onions, too. But what accounted for that strange, rotten odor? It didn't bear thinking on.

"Is my boy ticklish?" Rem's assailant crooned. "Come to mama, then, come to mama!"

Rem ducked under her arms and dashed off down the corridor, careful to remain just out of reach but no so far away as to discourage Lady Hawsey's amorous intentions. Funny, Rem mused, that her husband was having an almost identical experience on the opposite side of the estate. As the couple neared the master bedchamber, Her Ladyship pushed past the actor and dismissed the guards. Then, with what he assumed was meant to be a fetching, come-hither look (it was more of a wretching, go-thither look), she beckoned him to follow. He hadn't had quite enough wine, he decided sadly, but perhaps there was more within.

He had barely gotten all the way inside when Lady Hawsey tackled him and knocked Rem to the floor. In seconds, she was upon him, grinding her hips against his thigh and her rubbery lips against his mouth. Impossibly, inexplicably, Rem felt himself rising to the occasion, and he wondered, not for the first time, if he weren't a bit mad. This was not the sort of thing one would regret merely in the morning, but for the rest of one's life.

"Is...there...more wine?" he forced out.

"Oh, silly boy!" Her Ladyship scolded, "Am I not liquor enough?"

Mahnus! The stench of sardines and onions was deadly. "Just a little more, milady. A toast to your beauty!" Somehow, Rem managed to wrestle his way to his feet and locate a half-full decanter near the bed. With no cups in evidence, he drank straight from the vessel itself. "To you!" he said quickly and took a prodigious gulp.

"To me!" the woman said, climbing her way up his legs and lingering near his wedding tackle.

"Uh," Rem sputtered, "Er...will you...will you write this down in your diary, milady?"

She giggled. "Haven't got one." She began unlacing his breeches.

"Indeed?" Rem sounded surprised. "I thought all great people kept diaries!"

"P'raps I will, then..." Her Ladyship said in a deep, throaty voice full of lust, "after this..."

Rem drained the last of the wine and tumbled, just beyond Lady Hawsey's grasping fingers and onto the bed. "I'm sure His Lordship must keep a diary..." he prompted hopefully.

"Oh, he does," his tormentor answered disinterestedly, "But it isn't his. But why should we care for that, my naughty, naughty boy?" And she commenced to strip in what, Rem supposed, was meant to be seductive fashion.

An eternity later, Rem lay on his back, naked and feeling as though he'd been beaten by a mob of angry children. Her Ladyship had pulled his hair, bitten him, raked her nails across his flesh and nearly strangled him to death in her ecstasy. And she had been insatiable, as if she hadn't made love in years. Fortunately, she had also let slip the location of the hidden diary. Rem could barely imagine how he would have coped if he'd gone through all this without acquiring that information. Now, while Lady Hawsey snored blissfully away at his side, he needed to retrieve the diary, exchange it for the forgery he'd created and depart before His Lordship returned—easier said than done, especially given his sore and still-inebriated state. And it was dark in the room, a mixed blessing because it hindered his search for his clothing and the counterfeit diary, but also concealed the parts of Her Ladyship best forgotten.

Luck was with him—for the moment, anyway. He found his trousers, shirt and jacket and rummaged around in its pockets for the false diary. After dressing as quickly as his addled wits would allow, he set about his quest for a chair with a removable back cushion. Since there were only three chairs in the room, it wasn't difficult to find, although he had to admit the cunning nature of the chair's design would have kept the book secret for eternity had he not known where to look. He peered over at Lady Hawsey, was reassured to find her still quite asleep. With the original diary and its twin in hand, Rem crept towards the nearest candle to compare the two. He was quite pleased with his own memory and eye for detail; the books were not flawlessly identical, but they were close enough, especially if, as Rem hoped, Henton had already finished reading his copy and had only hidden it for safekeeping. In that event, the forgery should easily pass any cursory inspection. But even if His Lordship had not finished the book, it was Rem's intent to read it through himself and return it within the next twenty-four hours. Of course, this meant a possible repeat of tonight's grueling gymnastics. Well, no one could say Remuel Wratch had not suffered for the cause. Fast as he dared, Rem made the switch he'd come for and slunk out the door.

There was no one about and the torches and candles burned low. Rem made it about two or three in the morning. He was dying for a long, hot bath with enough soap to scrub the night's sights, sounds and other sensations from his mind. But he needed to get reading.

Long, House Thornton

Long opened his eyes to the familiar—and now welcome—darkness of his cell. Alerted by the faint rattling of the prisoner's chains, the Steward spoke through the blackness.

"Not dead, then. I thought perhaps we'd given you too large a dose of elixir."

Long's tongue felt swollen and his mouth too dry to produce words. He croaked out something unintelligible. To his surprise, a tin cup of water was pressed clumsily against his lips. He opened them and drank. "No torture?"

The Steward laughed. "Oh, there'll be torture. Don't you worry about that. We got a little behind schedule in your interrogation due to the idiot in the next cell over, so we had to go straight to our truth serum. But now that we know who you are, we can afford to take things at a more leisurely pace."

"You know who I am?" Long asked stupidly.

"Captain Peter Fendesst, A.K.A., Long Pete, an operative of her most royal Majesty and erstwhile apple farmer."

Yes, they knew. But maybe Long still had a card to play. "That's me, right enough. But do you know the real identity of your torturer?"

A snort in the darkness. "That's a new one: the double-agent torturer. You'll have no difficulty convincing me he's a bad fellow. That's why we hired him."

Long tried to return the snort with feeble results. Still, he forged ahead, "That's as may be, but he used to work for me, nonetheless."

"For you?" The Captain was somewhat mollified to hear surprise in his captor's voice. "For you, you say? I'm having difficulty deciding if that is the most brilliant lie I've ever heard...or the most idiotic. Tell me, if he worked for you, why didn't he just identify you outright?"

Long had no answer. "I don't know. He seems to have developed amnesia or some damned thing."

"That's rather convenient, wouldn't you say?"

It surely seemed that way, even to Long.

"And it doesn't change anything. You're going to be tortured and most likely killed. That's how it usually goes, at any rate," the Steward concluded cheerfully.

"Then why are you sitting down here in the dark with a dead man?"

The Steward yawned audibly. "Sometimes men break when they finally see what's coming. Sometimes they want to... unburden themselves."

Long thought of his old friend Janks. "Yeah, and sometimes they rise from the fuckin' dead and make your life a nightmare."

For once, it was the other man who could think of nothing to say. Instead, Long heard him get to his feet and shuffle away, almost as if he could see. There followed a brief thumping on this side of the cell door, in response to which it scraped open, admitting just the tiniest amount of torchlight, against which Long was able to make out the Steward's retreating silhouette. The man turned partially and said, "The next time you see me, Captain Fendesst, will be the last time you see me."

Later, alone again in the blackness, Long realized those words offered not one but two different possibilities and took what comfort he could in that knowledge.

Peppers was yammering away again, making enough noise for several men. As usual, there was a faint tissue of sense to it that was utterly obscured in a hurricane of awkward and self-conscious rhymes. At present, the lunatic was furiously attempting to find purchase with the words 'totem' and 'scrotum' and having less luck than a eunuch in a whorehouse. The concept of futility, however, seemed as alien to Peppers as the notion of silence, so he kept at it until Long begged him to stop. Before he forgot why he'd stopped, Long tried to distract him with questions.

"Say, Peppers," he growled, "Why'd they throw you in here, anyhow? Don't tell me it was your poetry."

"Verse, terse, rehearse, nurse, purse, worse. It was my poetry, it was my verse. They want old Peppers to be terse. But I says what I want, I don't have to rehearse, I am no one's wet nurse, therefore put money in thy purse and that's how things go from bad to worse."

If any of that meant something, Long would be damned if he knew what it was. "Peppers, can't you just...talk...like a normal fella? Just for a minute?"

Peppers was quiet a moment and then, softly, furtively whispered "Don't let 'em show you the bleeding eye." In the next breath, he returned to his rhythmic babbling.

The bleeding eye? Long got goose bumps at the sound of it and a cold shiver ran down his spine, rattling his shoulders to and fro. "The bleeding eye?" he asked into the darkness.

The mad poet ignored the question and carried on with his nonsensical mutterings. All hells, why couldn't Long have been imprisoned next to a compulsive singer or chronic snorer? Right: he was in a dungeon. He was supposed to be miserable. Then, in a flash of inspiration, Long understood something.

"Peppers, my friend, did you steal from this house? Is that why they put you in this trap like a mouse?" Not a great effort, certainly, but then, Long didn't make a practice of rhyming.

"Like a mouse? Like an ant. They threw me in this shithole 'cause they didn't like my rant. I made a jape about the master and what a disaster, I took off down an alley but they ran a little faster. Then they brought me here in chains after beating out my brains and my head hurts like a bastard, like a bastard."

"If your head hurts like a bastard," Long began, "you might like a bit o' quiet, you should try it..." He couldn't think of any way to finish, but his more practiced neighbor had no such trouble.

"Can't deny it." His voice grew softer. "I'll apply it." And faded into inaudibility.

Long had learned nothing he hadn't already guessed, except for the best—the only—way to communicate with Peppers. It was a tiny victory, but it beat all hells out of waiting for his own demise.

There had been plenty of times in Yendor's life when he'd belonged to nothing and no one, so that when he milled around aimlessly, it didn't much bother him. Now that he was part of an alleged team, however, he wore his inertia uncomfortably, unable to escape the feeling that so much depended upon him and yet not knowing how to identify it or rectify the situation. He could not, after all, simply do any-old something for the sake of action; he needed to understand how it might advance the mission, such as it was.

He'd discovered his employers had been spying on him. No surprise there, really. Indeed, he'd've been surprised if they hadn't. The thing was, they'd been so careless in letting this fact slip that Yendor didn't know whether they were actually incompetent or merely playing upon his supposed credulity in order to set him up for...well, he couldn't imagine what. The more sober he became, the harder it was to think. He'd have been happier and more productive as a security guard in a distillery. Too late, too late: he was mired in the bowels of House Fyne without the slightest idea how to proceed.

All of this went through is mind as he trudged dutifully along the parapet, atop the Fyne mansion. It was night time, and a summer rain was doing its level best to drown Yendor in his clothing, but he was largely unperturbed by this fact, so lost in his thoughts was he. After much effort, he finally remembered a crucial point: the kind of gossip he needed could only be overheard in the presence of the House elite, the highest of its lords and ladies. They, after all, were the ones who stood most to gain from the Queen's disappearance. Standing in a sodden mess on the roof, though, seemed about as far as Yendor could possibly get from the kinds of rooms and situations in which he might glean what he'd come for. Unless...

He had an accomplice. An unwitting accomplice. Pivoting in a puddle to commence the return leg of his patrol, Yendor contemplated the other men in the bunk house, searching for one sufficiently weak minded and pliable for his purposes. This was especially difficult because he suspected himself of being the single-most weak-minded man in the guard, if not the estate. Ah, but he knew of an equalizer, did Yendor, an old friend that had gotten him out of or through many a worse scrape in the past. With some relief, he was pleased to discover he had the makings of a plan...

"Wondrous poison!" Moult proclaimed. "What is this fell stuff?"

"'S called 'skent!" Yendor beamed, raising his flask in the air as if he were toasting the ceiling.

Moult literally drooled as he looked up at it, for he was an accomplished drunk, a fellow citizen of the mythical land of Inebria. Yendor knew it the moment he'd laid eyes on him, and, with that knowledge, Yendor owned the man, because while skent was highly addictive, it was also relatively unknown in the midlands and, thus, hard to come by. But Yendor had a secret and reliable source. Soon, Moult would be willing to trade anything, do anything for one more bottle, gulp or sip. Yendor would like to have felt pangs of conscience, but, alas, the wondrous poison was doing its work on him, as well. The other guard would become his surrogate in all things dangerous, until such time as he had provided Yendor with something useful or been killed in the attempt. Naturally, if Moult got killed, Yendor would have to disappear quickly.

Vykers, Ashore

It took until nightfall for the entire party and half the ship's crew to come ashore and get situated in the makeshift camp Vykers and the chimeras had created out of driftwood. The fire they'd built was much larger than necessary (or was probably prudent), but as it was their first in weeks, Aoife supposed it did more good than harm, bolstering morale and allowing the men folk to celebrate their escape from the confines of the ship.

Arune, former combat mage to a king, was considerably more wary. *What are you doing?* She demanded of the Reaper.

Havin' a bit o' fun. What's it look like?

What's it look like? She echoed incredulously. *It looks like you've set up a beacon to announce our arrival.*

Like I said, havin' a bit o' fun. Besides, I thought you said there weren't any threats nearby.

They'll be nearby, soon enough, if you keep building that Mahnus-cursed bonfire.

Good. I'm itchin' for a fight.

If it's a distraction you're looking for, I'm sure the A'Shea can provide it.

The Reaper was cannier than he came across, sometimes. *Oh, now you're steering me in her direction? What are you after?*

Arune instantly regretted her choice. She'd been too ham-handed and been caught out. *I just think it's healthier for you to chase after something you'll never get than court an assault by unknown enemies in a foreign land.* She hoped Vykers would respond with something like, "Oh, I'll never get her? Care to wager on that?"

But he didn't. He tossed another log on the fire and stopped communicating entirely. In his experience, when someone said or did something out of character, it meant he had ulterior motives. Vykers didn't like anyone attempting to manipulate him, least of all friends. For weeks, Arune had tried every argument she could think of to steer the Reaper away from the A'Shea; now, Aoife was just the lesser of two evils, the first of which was so common in Vykers' life as to be mundane. His suspicions were further aroused when she interrupted his brooding to apologize.

I'm sorry. Your...personal business is...your business.

Another, larger log flew onto the fire. Vykers had nothing to say, in part because the old 'silent treatment' was how they'd come to punish one another over the years, and in part because he needed time to consider and digest this latest development. He glanced beyond the fire to the rest of his companions, those welcome and those not. The Fool—fool, indeed!—was flirting with Aoife, whilst the Frog interrogated the Historian on some matter or another. A third of the way around the fire circle, the two chimeras, still given a wide berth by most of the sailors, huddled in close conference. Vykers wondered if Three had learned anything new about the smaller chimera and determined to ask at the first opportunity. The Reaper didn't trust the creature. Or the Fool. Or the Historian. Or, sadly, Arune, at the moment. With a fatalistic grin, he realized he couldn't recall a time when he'd ever trusted more than one or two people besides himself.

"Let's have a story!" one of the sailors called out. "We've got a fire; let's have a good story to go with it!"

A number of suggestions were called out, but Vykers cut them off. "I'd like to hear how it is that our homeland and this place have remained unknown to each other." He was gratified to see the Fool frown, as this was clearly outside the man's repertoire. "I'd like to understand how it is, in three thousand years, we ain't interacted, much less conquered each other."

As expected, it was the Historian who spoke up. "The simplest, easiest answer is often the best, and that answer is that the gods have conspired to keep us apart." He had everyone's attention now, but paused in order to allow someone—the Frog, no doubt—to ask the obvious question. To Vykers' surprise, it was Aoife who spoke up.

"But why would they want to do that?" she challenged, the firelight flickering in her eyes. "We're taught that we are their children."

The Historian nodded. "Yes, that is what we have been told, down the years. Several thoughts occur to me: first, why does any parent separate his children? Because they do not, cannot get along? Or because they might plot to overthrow their parents' rule?"

Vykers could tell by the expressions on the faces around the fire that these thoughts were new territory to most in the company; he sympathized.

"There is another, perhaps more disturbing possibility," the Historian went on, "Perhaps we are not the gods' children, as we have been told."

One of the sailors jumped in this time, and the Reaper had

to admit he was impressed with the way the Historian led his audience. "If we ain't their children, then what are we to them?"

Aoife barely managed a feeble "Of course we're their children!" before the Historian cut back in, louder.

"There are few options, and none pleasant. It may be that we are their slaves, or their pets. It may be that we're nothing more than insects to them. Is it not written 'we are as flies to wanton boys; they kill us for their sport'?"

"I will not believe that!" Aoife objected.

"Then you have seen precious little death," the Historian countered.

Much as he was attracted to Aoife, Vykers had to agree with the Ahklatian on this point.

"I've seen enough," the A'Shea said, and then, almost to herself: "Too much."

"Still."

Aoife was taken aback. "I am aware of your own…suffering… Historian," she said sharply. "But you do not have a monopoly on horror."

A cold anger burned in the Ahklatian's black eyes. "I was not referring to myself, Mender, or my people. I am not so self-absorbed as to think my experiences are of interest to anyone present."

A quick look around the circle would have told him otherwise, Vykers thought. There wasn't a sailor amongst them who wasn't curious, fearful or both. Old prejudices die hard.

"But I think whatever you have suffered pales in comparison to what has happened across our land over the three thousand years we do remember. And who's to say what has occurred in this land?"

Vykers grew tired of the bickering between his companions and shifted the dialogue in a different direction. "You've been here before. Tell us about it."

"I thought that's what I was attempting to do."

"Yeah, well, keep attempting."

The Historian stared into the fire and got a far away look in his eyes. "So…many of you know the essentials of my story and that of my people. After our own awakening, each of us went through a seemingly endless period of soul-searching, followed by a longer period of literal searching, looking for answers, any kind of information that might explain what had happened to us and our...progeny."

Arune, listening carefully, was initially struck by that word, progeny. It wasn't hard to see why he'd chosen it, instead of 'children.'

"Inevitably, I searched every acre of our homeland. Every forest, every village, every hole in the ground. Many things I found, but none of them shed the least light on the darkest episode of my people. And so, I had to cross the sea. The journey should have killed me, as it has undoubtedly killed countless others."

"And when was this?" Vykers asked.

The Historian swallowed, smiled grimly. "Best have it out, eh?" he asked. "Some seven hundred years ago."

This was followed by much whispering amongst the ship's crew and a smaller amount between Hoosh and the Frog.

The Historian pretended not to notice. "I spent what you might call a lifetime exploring these lands," he continued, gazing inland. "You cannot imagine what you'll see in the coming days and weeks ahead of us."

"Such as...?" Vykers prompted impatiently.

"People who think and act quite differently from us, beasts unlike any you've known, mountains that dwarf our own, deserts, jungles..."

"Explain 'deserts'."

"Imagine a plain of sand that stretches in every direction for weeks, a vast expanse without shade or water, watched over by a blazing sun. In this plain, experienced men die of thirst every day, others, from the unrelenting heat."

"Sounds like hell."

The Historian laughed. "And so it is! Would you believe some have found a way to live and even thrive there?"

"To what end?" One of the sailors asked. "Who wants to live in a place without water or plants?"

"Those who don't like to be disturbed?" The Historian responded. "I do not claim to understand their motives; I only know they exist."

"And the jungles you mentioned? What of those?" Hoosh asked.

"As hot as the deserts, but full of plants and water. In sooth, the plants in these jungles grow to monstrous proportions, as do the predators. Do you know those biting flies we have at home? Tiny and few in number? In the jungle, they are the size of eggs and number in the millions. Men have been known to die whilst trapped in a swarm of them. And they are not close to the worst insects you'll find in the jungle—leaping spiders the size of small dogs, wasps as big as birds with venom that burns like molten steel, ticks whose bite will make the flesh rot off your bones in mere hours…"

"I think I've heard enough of these horrors," Aoife exclaimed.

The Historian smiled at her. "The best news is, Her Majesty's captors may not be headed in that direction, or, if they are, may not travel that far. Chances are good we'll never see a desert or jungle."

"We'll never see one from the ship, that's certain," one of the sailors said smugly.

Vykers! Arune shouted.

The Historian leapt to his feet.

The night exploded. Mounted figures boiled from the darkness, as if forcing their way en masse through a door too small for their numbers. Shouts of panic and screams of terror erupted from those around the campfire. Magical energies flared up in several spots, and Vykers yelled, "Don't hurt the horses!"—a command that was greeted by a torrent of profanity from Arune. The mysterious enemies were armored in midnight blue steel adorned with golden stars. Their weapons and even their horses' barding were of the same design and material. Vykers hoped to catch a sample of their speech, but he was to be disappointed, for they attacked in utter silence.

Silence was not the Reaper's way. He roared in fury and swung his sword—when had he drawn it?—at the nearest knight and sheared right through the man's upraised weapon, through his armor, and into his shoulder with laughable ease. The man's silence was broken by his cry of pain. Vykers whirled, swept two more knights off their horses. A third tried to smash Vykers in the back of the head with an enormous mace, but the Reaper ducked and, dropping his left hand from the hilt of his sword, used it to pull the fellow from his saddle and into the fire, where he screamed in such fear and agony it gave Vykers goose bumps...of pleasure. Gone were his pain, his issues with Hoosh, his problems with Aoife and any and all of the myriad other annoyances he'd had to put up with since he'd been dragged from his sickbed. He was separating bodies from souls, and he hadn't been happier in ages.

Around him, he sensed the chimeras equally engaged in their bloody work. Busy, too, were the Historian, Arune and Aoife. Even the Fool was fighting. Some of the sailors had joined the fray, a few had already fallen, and a few had fled. Vykers was dimly aware that the Frog ought to be somewhere in all of this, but he hadn't the time to worry about the boy. The surprise attack had nearly overwhelmed the landing party; the present and foreseeable future offered nothing but more of this desperate battle for survival. They could take stock when and if they repelled their assailants. Vykers took a nasty slash across his upper left arm, an event almost unprecedented in his life, but it only served to inflame his already raging anger. On a backswing, he smashed the pommel of his sword against the faceplate of one attacker; on the fore swing, he drove the point above a second man's gorget and just under his visor, almost decapitating him. A red mist filled the air, so furious was the bloodshed. Hysterical, frightened laughter added an eerie element to the goings-on and found its echo over and over again throughout the melee, a sure sign that Hoosh was having his way with the attackers. The night stank of sweat, urine and bile.

"Spare the damned horses!" Vykers yelled again, though he doubted anyone cared at this point.

Fire and lightning rampaged through the enemy's force, taking men from their saddles faster than they could be counted. Yet, more continued to pour from an unseen rent in the darkness. Vykers had never experienced the like, but found it exhilarating nonetheless. Bodies began to pile up around him, making it look as though he stood in a pit. Eventually, he had to climb up the dead just to reach his next target. Then, as suddenly as they had appeared, the remaining knights galloped off at speed.

As his battle-induced adrenalin subsided, Vykers lost his strength and collapsed backwards onto a pile of the slain. In short order, the pain of his wound became too great and he lost consciousness.

When he regained consciousness, he felt ashamed, unmanned by his weakness. Tarmun Vykers never failed. He shook his head to clear his thoughts and saw Aoife standing a few feet away, watching him.

"Are you injured?" she asked.

"No more 'n usual." Vykers got to his feet with difficulty, gritting his teeth at the pain in his side. "Everybody make it through alright?" Aoife didn't answer quickly enough, and Vykers knew there was a problem. "Who's done, then? Not the boy..." he said.

The A'Shea shook her head.

The Reaper was in no mood to play twenty questions. He waded through the corpses, searching left and right, until he came to the body of Number Three, whose head was nowhere to be seen. Vykers fell to his knees and closed his eyes. It couldn't be so. Three had been his most staunch companion, a force of nature, a true warrior. It hadn't occurred to Vykers that Three could be killed...except by his own hand. And Three had never given him reason. It was easy to blame the Queen: if she hadn't been abducted, they'd have never gone on this Mahnus-cursed journey.

But the truth was, it was Vykers' fault. He'd been courting an attack and had proven woefully unprepared when it came. Three was dead because of the Reaper's hubris. Well, the chimera wasn't alone in that regard. Long indeed was the list of friends who'd gone to it because of Tarmun Vykers' arrogance. This loss was especially painful though; this one hurt as badly as the wound in Vykers' side. Without opening his eyes, asked, "There any horses hereabouts?"

Aoife was confused. "Horses? Yes, there seem to be several in the area. I guess their owners are dead."

Arune wanted to weigh in, as well, but deemed it a bad time

to criticize her host. Let him sort this out, let him heal a bit. She needed to understand his thinking.

"We lose anybody else of note?" Vykers wanted to know.

"Most of the sailors. Nobody else."

"What about that other chimera?"

"He's still alive, licking his wounds at the moment."

"Too bad," Vykers muttered. Then, "Where is he?"

"Over by the fire. You're not planning to hurt him, are you?"

And so what if he was? Vykers wondered. What fuckin' business had the A'Shea to question him or intervene? He stood, stared at the pile of dead knights. How'd they get the jump on us? He asked Arune.

They blinked in as a group. I've never seen that before with this many men.

So, you've never tried it?

Not with this many, no. And I didn't notice a Shaper in their number.

Guess I'll have to ask the Historian.

With the toe of his boot, Vykers flipped one of the knights onto his back. Knights in full armor. Some local king's gonna sleep a lot less comfortably tonight, I'll wager.

Arune couldn't help herself. *So, the bonfire was about getting horses?* But she knew he wouldn't respond, and he didn't.

Instead, he strode over to the remaining chimera and grabbed him by the scruff of his neck, in the same way a lioness might carry her cubs. The creature did little to resist. Wordlessly, Vykers dragged the chimera to the body of his fallen brother.

"You know what to do," Vykers rumbled.

The chimera did nothing, clearly confused.

The Reaper cuffed him on the back of the head. "Go on. Do what needs doing. Three would've expected it."

"I do not understand," the chimera confessed.

Vykers was flat out of patience with the new chimera. He extended his claws and ripped into Three's corpse, removing, after some effort, what looked to be a kidney. "Whenever one of the Five fell, the survivors ate him. In that way, they kept him alive, forever a part of their number. You must do the same."

When the new chimera remained inert, Vykers struck him across the face. The Reaper would've been gratified to see the creature react in anger; it did not. "You a coward, then? That why my friend died?" The chimera's eyes wandered to the folks sitting by the fire. It seemed he needed privacy to carry out the ritual.

"Fine," Vykers growled. He stooped, grabbed a hold of Three's leg, and dragged the dead chimera off into the saw grass, a good hundred yards or more from the fire. "Eat," he commanded. Yet again, the chimera resisted. Vykers pondered the kidney for a minute or two, considering the possible consequences, and then bit into it. When he'd eaten the liver of an earlier chimera, he'd had no relationship, no history with the beast. Eating a piece of Three, however, was a great deal more difficult. He forced down a mouthful or two and then turned to the surviving chimera. "See? Do it." He slapped what was left of the kidney into the creature's paw and stalked off towards the fire, hoping the beast could do in solitude what it could not accomplish with witnesses.

"Anybody round up the horses?" Vykers barked, back at the fire.

"They are secure," the Historian answered with equal surliness.

Arune and Aoife each knew better than to ask questions; it was clear what had happened: Vykers had been careless. No one and nothing would be harder on him than the man himself.

"And the ship's crew?"

"Those who survived have gone back to the boat."

"And the Frog?"

"He's alive," Aoife was happy to say. "He's around here, somewhere." Then, she realized "somewhere" was not good enough. Not for her, anyway. She started looking for him.

The Reaper threw himself down in the sand near the flames, though not even their heat and light could penetrate the cold, blackness of his thoughts.

"Perhaps we should move our camp away from these... bodies," Hoosh ventured.

Vykers was unreachable.

With a heavy sigh of resignation, the Fool began dragging bodies away.

A while later, the surviving chimera returned to camp. The Reaper was alert enough to note a complete absence of blood on its face or body. He stood up and walked off to the place he'd left Three's body, only to find a large mound of sand. Certain of what he'd find, he asked Arune, anyway.

There a full body under there?

It wasn't the kind of thing that required a conversation. *Yes,* Arune replied.

Vykers was inclined to kill the chimera and be done with it. But he'd made a mistake, a grievous mistake, in being so cavalier about the bonfire, and his friend Three had paid dearly for it. Well, the Reaper could kill the other chimera in the morning if it still needed doing. He wasn't going to rush this decision.

On his way back to the fire, Vykers passed a growing mound of bodies that the Fool had been building. It seemed the loony fucker was good for something after all. Again, Vykers lay down in the sand. Eventually, the exertion of battle took its toll and he fell into a deep and dreamless sleep.

SEVEN

He felt a cool hand on his shoulder, knew it to be Aoife's. "I can't find the Frog," she whispered urgently.

"Prob'ly just gone off to take a piss," Vykers replied without opening his eyes.

"He's been gone for hours."

Vykers lurched into a sitting position. "What do you mean, 'hours'?"

Aoife looked exhausted. "The last time I recall seeing him was just after you came back to the fire."

Vykers took in his surroundings, noted the sun's position in the sky. "Shit," he said. The boy had been missing for as many as ten hours. The Reaper extended an arm and the A'Shea helped pull him to his feet. His wound was giving him extra grief this morning. *The new chimera still around?* He inquired of Arune.

Aye, said she. *He's fishing in the surf.*

Sure enough, the crazy beast was up to his shoulders in the water. Like that's gonna help him or us. "Have you questioned the Historian or that idiot jester?"

Aoife nodded.

What about you? Vykers asked Arune. *Tell me the lad's still alive.*

Oh, he's alive.

Then where the fuck is he?

You'd best go check on Three's body for the answer to that.

Another one of Arune's games. Vykers made a beeline for Three's remains and found the sand completely scraped away and the body half-eaten. For a long time, he just stood and stared. Then, *Why would he go and do a damn fool thing like that? What in all hells was he thinkin'?*

Trying to please you, maybe?

How the fuck's that s'posed to please me? Vykers demanded, before looking down and seeing his own hands, with claws fully extended. *Aoife's gonna shit.*

I expect so.

The big man turned and walked to the water's edge, where he stopped and whistled at the last chimera. It heard him immediately and waded sheepishly to his side, carrying a couple of good-sized fish in his left hand.

"Yes?"

"I know you didn't eat Number Three, like I told you to."

The creature bowed his head, shrunk into himself almost imperceptibly. "I did not."

"I need a reason not to kill you."

The chimera, having no doubt of the warrior's abilities, answered, "What must I do?"

"You can still hunt, no?"

"I can hunt," said the creature.

"The boy's gone missing. Find him and bring him back. Alive and unhurt."

The expression of relief on the chimera's face was almost comical. "I can do that!" he proclaimed.

"Then get about it. I ain't askin' twice."

The chimera ran off like death was chasing him.

Oh, she was angry, all right. Vykers had never seen her so angry. "I wanted to take him back to Lunessfor, but you knew better!" Aoife thundered at him. "I said travelling with you was too dangerous for him, but did you listen? Have you ever considered anyone's counsel but your own? You are not a god, Tarmun Vykers, however much you may believe the contrary!"

No, he wasn't a god. Neither was he used to being yelled at. By anyone. And for Aoife to go after him like this in front of the Fool and the Historian was more than he could stomach. "You've said your piece. Have done, now."

But the A'Shea was not so easily controlled or appeased.

"Have done? You may've killed the boy! You certainly got your friend Three killed!" She felt justified in thinking such thoughts, but as they spilled off her tongue, she could see she'd gone too far. The look Vykers shot back at her was so full of menace, she felt sure her death was but seconds away. A trickle of sweat ran down the center of her back.

The Reaper looked out to sea, where a longboat had been dispatched from the ship. Without acknowledging Aoife in the slightest, Vykers retrieved his pack from the fire circle, fished something out of its depths, and stalked down the beach to meet the incoming sailors.

All this, Aoife watched with the dread certainty that Vykers was not finished with her.

As for Vykers, the longboat's approach was evidence the shit storm in the aftermath of the previous night's battle continued. He knew exactly how this would go: the Captain would argue that he and his crew had been contracted for transport, not battle, and thus threaten to leave.

There was only one answer for that, and the Reaper was more than ready.

As the Captain drew near, Vykers could see the man was working hard to maintain a take-no-prisoners demeanor. But he was still just a man, with the unenviable job of telling the Reaper how things were going to be.

"Save your breath, Captain," Vykers called and held out a handful of the largest gold nuggets the sailor had ever seen.

"Do you think to buy me, Reaper?" the man asked, his boots crunching in the sand as he climbed from the longboat. "I've lost a good part o' my crew. We'll be hard-pressed to make it home safely, which I mean to attempt this very day."

"You were hired to bring us here and wait 'til we were ready to leave again."

The Captain eyed the gold, still sparkling in Vykers' outstretched hand. "No one said nothing about dying ashore," he said half-heartedly. "Still, that gold would go some ways to compensatin' my crew for damages…"

"And this ain't the half of it!" Vykers laughed. "But I'm willin' to give you this-here, now, and the rest when I come back. And, o' course, you'll get your share of whatever treasures we find inland..."

That was more than good enough for the Captain. Gold in hand and the promise of plenty more to come? He couldn't agree fast enough.

"There's just one other thing," Vykers said...

She wanted to rage; she wanted to *continue* raging, but she feared she'd pushed the big man to the very edge last time. One more slight, she suspected, and he'd snap her neck. "You're leaving me behind?" was the best she could manage.

"That's right," he said scornfully. "'S too dangerous, travelling with me, anyway. Ain't that so?"

"But you need..."

"I need nothing, A'Shea. I got by for decades before we met; I figure I'll do the same once you're gone."

What could she say? He was right, after all.

"The boy shows up, the Historian knows how to bring 'im here. I'm sure you two'll be right comfortable aboard the ship 'til I get back."

A lesser man might have added, "If I get back." But Vykers had no need for such games. Too, he was confident to his marrow that he would succeed in his quest and equally confident that he would return. As furious as she was at him, Aoife couldn't help admiring these qualities.

Arune, on the other hand, was disgusted. Vykers' stunt with the bonfire had resulted in absolute catastrophe, and the Reaper's decision to banish Aoife from the party was far and away the most frustrating experience the Shaper had ever shared with her host. But, with the mood he was in, there was just no way to broach the subject of Aoife's importance to the mission without drawing Vykers' ire. For all her power, Arune felt every bit as trapped as the A'Shea. Even the Fool, Hoosh, enjoyed more freedom than either woman, even though Vykers had vowed to kill the man someday. A great sadness came over the Shaper as she observed Aoife being trundled into the longboat, as if she were part of the Captain's newly acquired treasure. Oh, Arune had no doubt the woman could take care of herself in Vykers' absence. What was less clear to the Shaper was how she would cope with the A'Shea's absence.

And now Vykers was talking to the Historian, like he did any other morning.

"Where'd all the bodies go?"

"I buried them."

"By yourself?"

The Historian made the odd wheezing sound that passed for his laughter. "I am a Shaper, after all."

"Right." Vykers was somewhat embarrassed at having forgotten this rather obvious detail. "What can you tell me about 'em?"

"The knights? Heavily armored, well-trained...and I'd say there were somewhere between thirty-five and forty of them."

"How'd they all...appear...like that, just all at once?"

Now it was the Historian's turn for embarrassment. "Ah, that's hard to say. Fascinating, though, isn't it? I've never seen a group that large in a Shaper's Leap before. And then, of course, there was no Shaper in the group."

"Shaper's Leap," Vykers repeated. "Cute." And then, in vintage Vykers' fashion, he changed the subject entirely. "We kill 'em all, or did anyone have the foresight to take one prisoner?"

The Historian grinned the tight-lipped grimace that passed for his smile. "There, I can be of some help. Yes. We have two."

"And horses?"

"Seven."

"Huh."

"A small observation, if I may," the Historian said. "You don't seem to take much pleasure in good news. Is it possible your forebears were Ahklatian?"

Vykers understood this to be a joke of some kind; it just didn't strike him as funny. He hoped the Historian and the Fool could practice on one another—out of earshot—until one of them developed a sense of humor.

"Let's mount up. We can question the prisoners as we ride, or wait 'til we camp. I wanna get the hells away from this Mahnus-cursed beach."

A man doesn't get nicknamed 'the Reaper,' because of his penchant for sentimentality and mourning. Tarmun Vykers had mourned exactly once in his life and had sworn never to do so again, never to put himself in a position where he might be tempted. He didn't like feeling helpless and lost, adrift. In truth, he didn't like feeling, period, unless it was the euphoria that came from smashing his enemies. The way he looked at it, one could either be pushed around or do the pushing.

And yet, he brooded on Three's death, as well as his own probable culpability in it. He'd assumed his chimeras and Shaper would catch wind of an attack before it happened. He'd even imagined there might be some sort of parley beforehand. But he'd been wrong, terribly wrong, and Three was dead as a result.

Even supposing he could get his mind around that, the Frog had gone missing. Vykers had an idea what had happened there. The evidence suggested something dire and desperate. When and if the kid returned, his...predicament...was likely to put a permanent end to anything good building between the Reaper and the A'Shea.

Finally, all of this weakened his party, at a time when Vykers himself was weakened. He'd never admit it to anyone else, hardly dared think it himself, but if they were beset by another such group, he wasn't sure they'd survive.

Vykers couldn't remember a time since his beloved's death when he'd felt so low, so dispirited.

It made him angry.

Spirk, House D'Escurzy

Lord Titus spent more and more time asleep, leaving Spirk alone in the gloom for longer and longer periods. He would like to have been worried for His Lordship, but the truth was, he was already so frightened for himself that he had little emotion left for the old man. Titus was dying, he knew. And his relatives, like wolves, were surely circling in to gnaw his bones. More than once, Spirk thought he heard whispering in the walls— entirely likely, given the secret door he'd found and the nature of the other D'Escurzys—and he feared falling asleep, lest the wolves take him, too. There must be a lot of unpleasant ways to die, Spirk reflected, but having one's bones gnawed whilst one was still using them had to be amongst the worst. Not that he really believed the D'Escurzy relatives would bite him, with the possible exception of Faenia (the prospect of which he found weirdly arousing, much to his chagrin).

But Spirk was saved one evening when Lord Titus' personal chef came to visit. He was a soft, round little fellow with long, golden-blond hair tied back behind and down his neck, in the fashion of a northerner. He'd explained to Spirk once that he was not, in fact, from that region, but that, in order to ensure his hair did not find its way into his master's food, he'd been commanded to wear a cap or tie it back. As he was almost as proud of his hair as he was of his cooking, he tied it back. If he was talented and slightly vain, he was also kind, and always brought Spirk a little something special—a tart, a biscuit, once even half a pheasant cooked in a wonderful sauce. This particular evening, he'd come to determine the reason for His Lordship's dwindling appetite.

Upon seeing Lord Titus' condition, he turned to Spirk. "I can't leave you alone in here, my friend."

"I'm not alone," Spirk insisted, "His Lordship's here, too."

"If the others get wind o' this, they'll swoop down on this room like vultures, and neither one o' you will be seen alive again," the chef said quietly. "Best call the town Constable."

"The Constable? Don't you mean the Captain of the Guard?"

The chef laughed. "He's been bought and paid for, I'm sure. Nah, nah: Constable's the only way to go." The fellow grew serious. "Can you manage to stay alive for the next hour or so?"

What an alarming question! Spirk was so taken aback he needed a moment to think about it. "Yes, I think so. I hope so."

"Good, then," the chef replied, patting Spirk on the shoulder. "Now, you lock that door behind me when I leave and put something heavy in front of any secret doors you find hereabouts."

"Secret doors! You know about them, too?"

Again, the chef chuckled. "My friend, I've kept myself alive and employed here for more 'n a decade. I know which side of the pancake's hot." Spirk supposed he knew what side of the pancake was hot, as well, but couldn't for the life of him figure out how that came into things. Nevertheless, the instant the chef left the room, Spirk barred the door and began moving tables and chairs into strategic positions along the walls. He soon discovered, however, that this left the floor woefully unprotected. Frantically, he started shifting the room's area rugs into new positions in hopes of defeating an unexpected assault from below.

What was below? Spirk had no idea. Since the day he'd wandered into House D'Escurzy, he'd been in the constant employ and company of His Lordship. He really had no idea what wonders—or horrors—the rest of the estate contained. There might be anything underneath Lord Titus' bedchamber. There might even be tunnels teeming with nasty Svarren. With that thought in mind, Spirk grabbed the fire poker and scrambled onto a table. When the Svarren came, he'd be just that much harder to reach!

On two occasions over the next hour, Spirk thought he heard movement in the walls and even noticed an armoire rattling ever so slightly. The D'Escurzys—or Svarren—were trying to breach his defenses, but had so far had no luck. Spirk was so grateful, he swore he'd kiss the chef when next they met (the prospect of which was also weirdly arousing).

When the chef and Constable finally arrived, Spirk was sound asleep on the table, and it took several minutes of increasingly urgent banging to wake him. Embarrassed, he rushed to the door.

"Who is it?" he asked.

"Who d'you bloody think? It's the bleedin' Constable, isn't it?" a gruff voice responded through the heavy wood.

"I'm here, as well!" the familiar voice of the chef sang out.

Spirk couldn't open the door fast enough. He'd survived the Svarren onslaught! With the door finally flung wide, he saw not two, but one, two, three, four, five men. The Constable barged past without so much as a 'how-do-you-do' and moved to Lord Titus' bedside. Lifting a candle on His Lordship's nightstand, he held it close to the old man's face. With the other hand, he produced a small mirror from his pocket and held it close to Titus' lips.

"Nearly gone," he pronounced. "Will somebody fetch the House A'Shea?"

"Actually," one of the other men interjected, "he left specific instructions to be left alone in this case." The man unfolded a sizeable piece of parchment that he'd had hidden in the sleeves of his robe. "To wit: "No special attempts are to be made to revive me whatsoever. When it is my time, I wish to go with dignity and without..." and these are his words, here, "bullshit."

"Wh...wh...what do we do, then?" Spirk asked, on the verge of tears.

The Constable scowled at the floor. "We wait," was all he said.

"That's it, then."

A younger Spirk might've said "What's what?" or some such. But that was before the End-of-All-Things, before Pellas' sacrifice. Now, Spirk could feel the change in the room and instinctively knew two things: first, the old man was gone, and second, things were about to get a whole lot more challenging. As if through some prearranged signal, the other five men turned silently in his direction.

Here it comes, thought Spirk. They're goin' to punish me for Lord Titus' death.

It was the Constable who spoke first. "You'd better tell 'im, Barnes," he said to the man who'd read from the parchment, earlier.

"I suppose so."

Spirk couldn't stand the suspense. "I'm in trouble now, ain't I?"

The other men laughed, every last man jack of them.

"Oh, aye, you're in trouble, all right," said Barnes. "The D'Escurzys will be coming after your head."

"But...but why?" Spirk mewled pitifully.

"His Lordship's named you his sole heir and inheritor, and we're here to bear witness."

Spirk was nonplussed. "He...I...what?"

The Constable cut in. "You're the new Lord of House D'Escurzy."

And one, apparently, who had issues with incontinence.

Kittins, House Gault

He hadn't even asked her name or determined if she could speak the Queen's tongue. In part, this was because he knew she'd been traumatized and was unquestionably overwhelmed by her predicament and surroundings. But he was also seized by conflicting desires: he didn't want to know anything about her that might make her matter more to him, but he also didn't want to rush the building of trust that might lead to...him mattering more to *her*. *Face it*, he'd told himself, *you've got no face!* What other kind of woman would have anything to do with him? And what in Mahnus' name was it he saw in her, a savage? The gods knew what she had lurking in her family tree—not that Kittins anticipated or even wanted children, especially with a Svarren woman. But he was not so naïve as to think he had complete control over such things. Life, like a Svarren woman, was a wild, untamable creature, a thing of beauty, perhaps, but not remotely tractable.

After rescuing the woman from the Grotto, Kittins had given her his bed, whilst he planned to sleep in the hall outside his door. The Svarra, however, was having none of his mattress and chose, instead, to sleep in a nest of pillows in the corner. After a few days of this and seeing his bed unused and unappreciated, Kittins threw gallantry out the window and reclaimed it. For the first couple of nights, he feigned sleep, listening to the woman's breathing and rustlings. Each time, he eventually fell asleep, despite his best efforts to remain vigilant. Each time, he awoke in the middle of the night, feeling a mild uneasiness or embarrassment at his lapse. He was not afraid of the Svarra, but neither did he wish to become complacent. Accordingly, he stashed a small knife between his mattress and the wall, in a spot only he was likely to find it. Better safe than sorry, after all.

And then the night came when she climbed in beside him.

They were both as tense and taught as bow strings, but Kittins found that as he relaxed, she relaxed. He rolled towards her, to get a better look into her eyes, and she smiled back at him. She gave off an almost-dizzying odor of floral bath oils (thanks to the household staff), over a much more subtle earthy musk. Kittins ran a large, callused hand down her naked back and she made a soft, guttural sound he took to be pleasure.

Their coupling was rough, frantic and spoke of a need Kittins was usually loath to acknowledge. When they were finished, the big man was exhausted and fell into a deep, contented sleep...

Until an intense, stabbing pain blossomed in Kittins' neck—she'd bitten him! Knifepoints of agony exploded across his back and along the right side of his head, where her nails—her claws—anchored into his flesh, granting her teeth better purchase. If he allowed her jaws to close completely, he knew, she could well sever an artery and he'd be done. His vision went red with rage, and he pulled back on her hair hard enough to dislodge her upper teeth from his throat. She hissed like an angry cat and raked her nails down his back, much as she had hours earlier, only with much more lethal intent. Still, Kittins did not let go, but indeed pulled harder and harder, until the Svarren woman's face was a full arm's length from his own. Abruptly, he let go of her hair, and her head naturally snapped forward, where it met his rushing toward it in a furious bash. For a second, her eyes lost focus, and in that moment Kittins flung her off the bed and onto the floor. She scrambled to regain her feet, but the big Captain was too fast, smashing her in the left cheek with a massive, bony fist. Strong as she was, she went down hard and fast. Kittins fell on her, wrapping his hands around her throat, and crushing her windpipe. In less than a minute, the fight was over and she was dead. Kittins' anger, however, was just getting started. Retrieving the knife he'd hidden against the wall, he removed the woman's head. Then, drenched in his own blood and drunk with rage, Kittins staggered from his room and out into the Grotto proper. When its other occupants caught sight of him, they quickly grew silent and slunk away. They'd seen the big man in this humor before and the results had not been pleasant.

Kittins encountered no resistance as he stormed over to the Svarren cells, his lover's head still leaking a trail of blood in his wake. From a post nearby, he fetched the master key that would allow him access to the surviving Svarren. Once inside the first cell, he came face-to-face with a pair of smaller males. He beat them to death with the female's head and headed off to the next cell. Its occupant was a much larger and more aggressive male, but such was Kittins' wrath that he killed it in even less time than the previous two creatures. By now, the Svarren woman's head was a soft and shapeless mass of blood and hair—useless as a weapon, so Kittins again pulled his knife and hacked an arm off his latest victim. It would make a nicer club, anyway.

By the time Kittins reached the final cell, he'd abandoned the arm and simply attacked the three brutes inside with his bare hands. He took some damage this time, but didn't feel a bit of it as he fought.

At last, all the Svarren were dead. As he was about to turn to leave, Kittins heard the cell door slam and its lock engage. Looking up, he saw a host of men at the bars, none more prominent than Lord Darley, who frowned at him in palpable disapproval. At His Lordship's left shoulder was a man who looked like Deda, minus a few teeth and an ear.

"Give us the room," Darley commanded those standing around him, although he wasn't really standing in a room. His meaning was clear.

Kittins exhaled, sat on a corpse.

"You have an anger problem," Darley said.

What the fuck was Kittins supposed to say to that?

"Which means we have a problem. I cannot simply allow you to run around beating or killing whomever you please, whenever you choose." His Lordship said nothing for a moment and then continued. "It appears I was wrong about you." He scanned the area for eavesdroppers. "That is embarrassing." After another lengthy pause, he concluded, "I believe a little time in here will allow you to reflect upon your actions. I need time to think on this, as well."

Kittins listened to His Lordship's heels clicking on the stone floor as he walked away, wondering if he'd finally gone too far and, more, how he'd become what he'd so clearly become. He'd always been a brawler, yes, but in the army he'd had discipline, respect for command, a sense of right and wrong. Now...? He was an animal, little different from the Svarren he'd just killed. He'd come to this an agent of the Queen. Somehow, he'd gotten hopelessly, irrevocably lost.

He was worse than dead.

Long, House Thornton

"And now for the torture you were promised," Janks beamed, selecting a small, sharp knife from a collection of tools he'd laid out for the purpose.

"But you already know who I am and why I came here," Long protested.

Janks nodded. "I'm told you claim to know me, and, as I think on it, I do seem to recall running into you the street recently, when you made the very same assertion. But...I assure you, we've never met?"

"Might be, you're blocking all memory of me," Long offered. He had to try something, after all; he wasn't looking forward to whatever it was Janks had in mind.

"I think we'll peel the skin off your left arm, to begin with, starting at your little finger and progressing outwards and upwards as we go. I like to apply various acids and such to the newly exposed nerves in order to identify what causes the most pain in any given subject. Some people scream in agony at mere salt water, whilst others barely flinch at Dimonian acid. I'll be interested to see which of those extremes is closest to your own nature."

"I'm sure I'll start as soon as you make the first cut."

"You don't want to do that," Janks warned, "You'll wear yourself out before we even get to the good stuff."

Long strove to keep his tone level, without the least hint of panic. "That's as may be, friend, but if you start cuttin', I start screaming."

"And I heard you were a war hero," Janks countered plaintively.

"As were you," said Long, "before I put my sword through your chest." At this, Janks balked, enough that Long picked up on it immediately. "Yep, I reckon you've got a nasty scar on your chest and one on your back, to match."

Faster than Long could track, Janks whipped his hand forward and gently touched the point of his knife against the prisoner's naked eyeball. Blinking was the last thing Long wanted to do.

"Who've you been talkin' to?" Janks demanded. "There's no way you'd know that unless someone's been spying on me."

"Or," Long offered carefully, "you and I have met before..."

Janks was breathing heavily through his mouth now, clearly agitated. "Know what's worse than losing an eye? Bein' forced to eat it afterwards."

The sound of the room's door opening was amongst the sweetest Long had ever heard.

"Hold!" came a voice.

The knife point receded and Janks stepped backwards from Long with surprising haste.

"Your Lordship," Long heard his tormentor say.

Long closed his eyes, gathered himself, waited.

"Is this the fellow?" a new voice asked.

"It is," said the Steward.

"Open your eyes, Captain Fendesst," the new voice ordered.

Long was relieved to see Janks had retreated a good ten to fifteen feet, replaced by the Steward and a man who could only have been the Lord of the House. His Lordship was impeccably dressed in light, summertime colors. His auburn hair and beard were flawlessly trimmed and styled, and the man himself seemed both healthy and fit. His hazel eyes fixed on Long with a combination of concentration and curiosity.

"Had you begun your work?" His Lordship asked Janks.

"No, milord," Janks answered softly.

"That's lucky." His Lordship responded. "Lucky for you, lucky for all of us."

Long was inwardly pleased to see Janks' look of confusion at this last comment.

"And you're positive this is the man, the one-and-only

Captain Peter Fendesst?" His Lordship asked both Janks and the Steward.

"That's what he confessed under the treatment," the Steward replied, "And that's never failed us before."

Janks nodded silently, but vigorously.

His Lordship broke into a broad smile. "Well, it's the damnedest thing that ever I heard, but I think we've stumbled into a most advantageous situation...if we can figure out how to work it."

Janks stepped forward. "Pardon the intrusion, Your Lordship, but what situation is that?"

"You've not heard?" His Lordship asked. "It's all over the city: the Captain here's been named sole heir to the D'Escurzy estates, mansion and fortune. What we've got here is nothing less than the current Lord of House D'Escurzy."

Thunderstruck doesn't even begin to describe Long's feelings at that moment.

Rem, House Hawsey

Henton Hawsey had no penis. Neither did he possess its female counterpart, and since, in most ways, he was more or less obviously male, he'd been named Henton. This was the startling, scandalous revelation His Lordship wished to keep private. In his youth, Gelter Radcliffe had apparently attended at banquet at court. When he excused himself to use the jakes, he inadvertently walked into one already in use by the future Lord Hawsey. Gelter had then seen what he'd seen—or not seen, to be more precise—and bided his time with the knowledge, waiting to see how young Henton would respond. Years went by. At an auction, one day, Gelter was approached by a large, frightening brute who simply whispered, "You speak ill of Lord Hawsey, your death'll be too, too slow for your liking." And that was it. Gelter sat on his secret knowledge, determined to use it, but unable to imagine how he could do so without losing his life.

And now the knowledge was Rem's, too, as well as the quandary about how best to use it. If only there was some way to make Henton's secret public. Possession of the diary, Rem realized, also gave him leverage over Gelter Radcliffe. None of this, of course, was bringing Rem any closer to understanding House Hawsey's potential role in the Queen's disappearance, but if the need for mayhem ever arose, the actor felt sure he could bring it.

What bothered him most in all of this was the fact he now needed to return to Her Ladyship's bed chamber in order to switch the true diary with the counterfeit. That he'd gained insight into Her Ladyship's libidinous behavior helped not all. She would assault him from the moment he appeared, he knew, and pummel him nigh unto death with her insatiability. There would be moments of pleasure, like the way a swimmer feels when cresting a wave, along with moments of terror, as when the wave comes crashing down upon said swimmer. With a hearty sigh, Rem stood up and began the too-short journey towards Her Ladyship's room, wishing himself a better swimmer.

Mardine, On the Trail

It is strange thing that in chasing someone there seems a point at which fatigue gradually gives way to increased health and vigor—provided one has enough to eat and drink. So far, Mardine had, but she knew that could change at any time. Thus, she tended to overeat when the opportunity presented itself, just in case. The fear and anxiety that had driven her for the first week or so had abated to some degree, but her anger remained as potent as ever and manifested itself in countless little ways throughout each day. She tried not to take it out on her companion, Tresa. After all, the woman was helping her. Still, she was a former thrall, like Nelby and Jaddo. Lunessfor had made every effort to rehabilitate these unfortunates, casting them as hapless victims of a fate beyond their ken, and Mardine wanted to believe it, which was why she brought Nelby into her home in the first place. But look where it had gotten the giantess. No, trust would be slow in coming—*was* slow in coming. Entire days went by when Mardine and Tresa spoke less than ten words to one another. So be it. They would never be friends. All that mattered was finding Esmine before anything worse befell her.

Summer was in full flower; the days were warm, and the nights were pleasant. As she trudged along, Mardine worried about her apples and her husband, in interchangeable order. The one represented the financial security and future of her little family; the other, its emotional core. Yes, Long was a good deal smaller than she, but her husband loomed large in her heart and imagination. He was a good man and, dammit, good men truly were hard to find. Would he forgive her, though, if the worst came to pass and she could not find Esmine? Would she ever forgive herself? Could she even live with the guilt? Grimly, she pressed onward.

Every so often, the giantess and her companion encountered someone in a village or passing by on the Queen's highway who claimed to have seen a man matching Jaddo's description. One night, both women even stayed in an inn where Jaddo and Nelby had been spotted by several of the locals. Mardine estimated that she and Tresa were a day to a day-and-a-half behind their quarry. She was not entirely comforted by this, however. The whole chase seemed too easy. She suspected a trap and considered hiring mercenaries, but didn't know how long she'd need them or whether her money would hold out for the duration. And, again, she figured she could handle a goodly number of thralls in a fight, if it came to that. The real question was, could she expect any help from Tresa. Oh, the woman seemed amply angry with Jaddo and Nelby, but could she fight?

What choice did a mother have? Like a bear, Mardine would protect her child to her dying breath, come what may.

Late one evening as the sun began sinking behind the mountains in the west, Mardine and Tresa happened upon a peddler and his wife camped by the side of the road. It was universally understood that there was safety in numbers, and custom held that everyone was welcome 'round the campfire. The peddler and his woman were initially uneasy at the sight of a giant, but, once Mardine introduced herself (and Tresa, who was often taciturn at such moments), the tension dissipated and the mood brightened considerably.

By the time the group had finished supper, Mardine had discovered that the peddler was bound for Lunessfor, to resupply and test the market for his outlands trinkets. The giantess also revealed her own purpose in travelling. To her surprise, the peddler's wife had information in that regard.

"I seen a man leadin' a couple o' women on horseback off the road and up a game trail a ways north o' here."

"When was this, love?" the peddler asked.

"Couple-three hours ago."

"Why din't you say nothin'?"

"Why would I? T'weren't nothing strange about it at the time."

The peddler grimaced. "And now?"

"Well, now, it fits our friend here's story, don't it?"

The peddler could only allow as it did. Still, he cautioned, there had to be lotta folks travelling to and fro near the Queen's Highway on a fine summer's day.

"Two or three hours north, you say?" asked Mardine.

"'Bout that, sure."

The giantess rose, to an audible groan from Tresa.

"You're not thinkin' of..." the thrall woman whined.

"That's exactly what I'm thinking," Mardine retorted. "I know travelling in the dark's dangerous, but so's letting that bastard get any farther away with my daughter." With that, Mardine shouldered her ponderous pack, thanked the peddler and his wife and started hiking up the road.

Tresa sat and seethed for a minute or two and then cursed and scrambled after her huge companion.

"Stay safe!" the peddler called after them into the growing dark.

In fact, the game trail proved to be less than two hours distant, although that may have been due to Mardine's enormous strides and the energy that came from finally approaching a sought-after goal. But it was full dark when she and Tresa arrived, and Mardine took a long moment to ponder her next step. The trail meandered away into the undergrowth and, subsequently, a forest beyond. Anywhere along that trail, Mardine and Tresa might encounter a trap, treacherous terrain,

or, worse, wolves, bears or Svarren. The giantess couldn't
rule out the possibility of running into all of those things, in
countless perverse combinations. She expected misfortune, but
there was no point in compounding her difficulties by courting
it. Sadly, she tossed her pack down near an old fire pit and set
about gathering kindling.

"So," Tresa began irritably, "we rush all this way in the dark
and you decide to camp, anyway?"

Without taking her eyes off her task, Mardine responded,
"Barging into an unknown forest at night's a sure way to get
yourself killed. Whose side are you on, anyhow?"

"My own."

It was a good answer, a smart one. If she'd have said anything
else, Mardine would have been suspicious. It was pretty clear
the thrall woman wanted her measure of vengeance upon Jaddo,
though. Unless she could extract it from the hash Mardine
intended to make of his corpse, however, she was like to be
frustrated.

Once the fire was crackling away to Mardine's satisfaction,
she glanced over and saw her companion fast asleep, her feet just
trailing onto the Queen's Highway. That was probably okay. This
far from anywhere, no one was likely to trip over the woman.
Mardine shifted her attention to the morning's challenge: the
wooded game trail. She felt reasonably sure the threat of predators
would diminish with the sunrise, and the terrain would be much
easier to navigate, too. But there remained the possibility of trap.
The problem was, the giantess didn't know enough about traps
to even begin to prepare for one. If only she could trust Tresa to
scout ahead while Mardine attempted to circle around through
the trees. Circle around to where, though? Jaddo might not be
expecting her, but if he was, he'd have planned for a big, angry
giant to come rushing right at him. Mardine sighed at the futility
of it all. All of this 'planning' was based upon nothing more than
conjecture. The peddler's wife might have been mistaken, or, if
she did see a man and two women, they might not be the ones
she was after. Or this might be the wrong game trail.

Or Esmine could be dead.

Mardine got no sleep that night.

Breakfast was hard cheese, harder bread and nearly unchewable prunes. That didn't stop Tresa from wolfing it down, Mardine noticed. She reckoned the woman's years as a starving thrall had impacted her in more ways than this. And the giantess was no slouch when it came to eating, much to Long Pete's initial dismay.

"What's yer plan?" Tresa asked around a mouthful of bread.

"I guess we go straight in. With you in front, of course."

"Me?" Tresa scowled. "Why me? You're the big 'un."

"Because I'm the big one," said Mardine. "If there's any kind of trap, they'll be expecting my big old bulky self, not your slight little frame. Maybe you'll be able to avoid it completely."

"And if I say no?"

"I thought you had a score to settle with this Jaddo."

"That don't mean I fancy an arrow in my belly."

"It might not be an arrow," Mardine pointed out. "It could be a spear."

Tresa glowered at her. "What's that, giant humor?"

"Something like that. Now, let's get packed and get onto that trail."

"With me in front."

Mardine nodded.

"You still ain't explained how that makes sense for me."

"Look," the giantess answered. "What do you think is more likely? You rescuing me if I'm down, or me coming in and rescuing you?"

Tresa wasn't quite buying it. "Why would you wanna rescue me?"

"You're helping me, aren't you? You think I'd pay you back by abandoning you in your time of need?"

"You don't put me in front, might be I won't have a time o' need."

Mardine looked past the thrall woman and down the path. "I'm even less interested in abandoning Esmine in her time of need. Let's go."

With resignation, Tresa picked up her pitiful bundle of gear and stood at the edge of the trail, waiting on Mardine. It was a fine summer's morning, with little to no dew on the grass and other plants, which meant both women would remain dry, even if they had to push their way through the underbrush at times. There was nothing worse than trudging along for untold hours in wet clothing.

"I'm ready," Mardine told the smaller woman.

"Right," Tresa replied flatly.

As it turned out, there was no trap lurking just inside the tree line. Or a mile up the trail. Or even an hour. At some point, Tresa acquired a limp, which only grew worse over time.

"What's wrong with your leg?" Mardine inquired.

"Got a rock in my boot, I think."

Mardine was dumbfounded. "Well, why didn't you say something? Let's stop and get it out. You come up lame, and I'll have to carry you, which will go badly for the both of us."

Tresa peered up the trail. "Looks like there's a bit of a clearing up ahead. Maybe I can find a rock or stump or somethin' to sit upon."

Sweet Alheria! These former thrall women didn't have the brains to stay out of their own way. Not for the first time, Mardine wondered if they hadn't all been damaged in some fundamental way by the End's sorcery. The giantess watched as Tresa tossed herself down on a tussock of grass and commenced yanking upon her boot. Weirdly, she began giggling to herself and then looked directly at Mardine, smiling merrily. The giantess had no idea what to make of this inexplicable behavior, until she heard a strange whooshing sound behind her. Before she could even register the fact she was under attack, an impossible weight smashed into her and sent her flying through the air and into the clearing. Unable to breathe, Mardine crashed to the ground and prepared to die.

Vykers, in Pursuit

Arune was aware that Vykers thought her temperamental, that she sulked too much. But she had never known him to sulk until now. And she was sick and tired of it. It had been going on for days, and she had had enough.

How long you planning to keep moping?

Fuck off.

You fuck off! Arune shouted back. What could he do to her, anyway? *You're acting like a big baby!*

Vykers didn't respond.

Tarmun Vykers, destroyer of empires! Nobody pouts with such magnificence.

I said fuck off.

Or what?

Bitch.

Bastard!

Vykers couldn't help himself: he laughed. *Is that meant to be an insult? I'm proud o' being a bastard. I work hard at it.*

I don't think you have to work that hard, Arune muttered. *I think it comes naturally.*

Out of nowhere, Vykers blurted, *The thing is, if there'd been a second wave o' those knights, we'd've all been killed, 'cause I was out cold.*

You did pretty well for a man with a hole through his gut.

Pretty well ain't good enough. When I was whole, I coulda taken those fuckers all day. After an extended silence, he added, *But I'll never be whole again. That's the hell of it.*

You don't know that.

And because I'm weaker now, Three got himself killed.

You don't know that, either.

And the Frog? Who in all hells knows what's going on with him. If he ate Three...

Why don't we focus on things we know?

Such as? Vykers asked.

The Queen's alive.

Heh, Vykers grunted, unimpressed.

The Frog's alive.

Is he? That's good.

And you're alive. She could tell the Reaper was feeling better already. *Oh, and, uh, that woman you're so fond of is alive, as well.*

As was his wont, Vykers changed tack again. *We gettin' any closer to Her Majesty?*

She remains at least a week's travel south of us.

Dead south?

More or less.

And again, he changed tack. *You think you'll be able to give me more warning next time those knights show up? Seems like a couple of 'em escaped and I'm bettin' on another visit from an even larger group any time now.*

You don't have to worry on that score. The Historian and I have been erasing our back-trail.

So, nobody following us, then?

I suppose someone could stumble onto us by accident.

That'd by okay by me, Vykers growled. *Only thing makes me happy anymore is puttin' fuckers in the ground.*

Vykers, Vykers! Arune thought to herself. *You are one crazy son-of-a-bitch.*

For all its differences, this mysterious new land had much in common with home, Vykers thought. For instance, they had vultures back home, and they clearly had vultures here, as well.

"That's an ill omen!" Hoosh declared as he spied the birds circling in the distance.

Vykers shot him a look of contempt. "You think there's anyone alive doesn't know that?"

The Fool bit his tongue, for once.

"Then why say it?" Vykers asked.

"Sometimes, it helps dispel anxieties to give them voice."

"Sometimes," the Historian agreed.

Peacemaker, thought Vykers. *Hey, Shaper,* he called to Arune, *got anything to tell me?*

The birds you see in the sky are a fraction of those at work on the ground.

Ain't that always the way? What're they at, anyway?

More of the knights we faced.

And they're dead? Wonder what killed 'em this time.

My guess? They ran afoul of whoever's taken the Queen. Maybe we'll find one of her captors' corpses among the dead.

Vykers brightened. *That'd be nice. I'd like to finally get a look at one of 'em. See what's what.*

They weren't on any road, as such, but riding more or less straight south over rolling grasslands, dotted with occasional clumps of a kind of shrub Vykers had never seen before. The attack had taken place right out in the open, much as it had on the beach where Vykers and his crew had landed. There were dead knights everywhere, but no immediate sign of their adversaries. The Reaper spurred his horse in amongst the corpses in order to disperse the vultures and, it turned out, rats, that had congregated to eat.

"Oof! Such an odor!" Hoosh complained.

"Yeah, I been hoping you'd take a bath for some time now," Vykers said.

"After the last one you gave me?" Hoosh might've risen to the Reaper's bait, but he'd simply turned the jibe aside.

"What is that?" the Historian asked, pointing to a small skirmish between several vultures and something scrabbling along the ground.

"Makes no sense they'd go after a rat, with so much meat lyin' about," Vykers said. Sliding off his mount with a grunt, the Reaper drew his sword and shooed all the birds away. What he saw in the space they'd vacated left him fumbling for comprehension. "What in the countless hells...?"

"It's a hand!" the Fool declared.

"I can bloody well see it's a hand!" Vykers spat. "But why's it still alive?" He pulled back his arm as if he meant to spear it with his blade, but the Historian stopped him.

"One moment!" the man said, with uncharacteristic emotion. "I believe I recognize..."

As he stared more carefully at it, Vykers did, too. "Well, I'll be buggered."

"It's Her Majesty's hand," the Fool confirmed. "I'd know those rings, anywhere."

The Reaper scanned the area. "You see any sign 'o the rest of her?"

She's not here, Arune replied.

Can you tell me why that thing's still moving?

I'm working on that right now.

Vykers was not a squeamish man, nor was he particularly superstitious, but he was surprised when the Historian bent over and gathered the hand into his own, especially since it continued to wriggle and twitch the whole time. For reasons he did not fully understand, the Reaper was more interested in the Historian's reaction to the grisly find than in the hand, itself.

"Well?" Vykers inquired.

The Ahklatian turned the thing over and over in his hands. "It's a clean cut."

"To hells with the cut. Why's it still alive?" Vykers asked for the second time.

The other man turned his black eyes towards the Reaper and held his gaze. "It would appear," he said, "that there is more to Her Majesty than we have been led to believe."

Suddenly, the disembodied hand went rigid, a lone finger pointing in the direction the group had been travelling.

Arune?

Sorry. I don't…I can't figure this one out.

"She wants us to follow her captors," Hoosh offered.

"Just when you think life can't get any fuckin' weirder," Vykers muttered.

Although they hadn't yet reached midsummer, Vykers noticed the sun set earlier than he might have expected back home. The Historian assured him there was a perfectly sensible reason for this, but every time he began to explain it, Vykers lost interest and stopped listening. Days were what they were.

Of more concern to him was the scarcity of game. When it was available, it wasn't as easy to catch without Three's particular talents, so that whenever the Reaper got hungry, he was necessarily reminded of the death of his friend and of his own culpability in that death. And subsequently lost his appetite.

Arune, however, needed Vykers to eat. *Remember the time I summoned that wild pig for you?* she prompted.

*What, back in that cave? O' course, I remember the...You offerin'
to scare us up some supper, then?*

That or Svarren. Take your pick.

They got Svarren over here?

Why wouldn't they?

Huh, Vykers sent, *Well, I'd just as soon eat before any more
fighting.*

Why don't we make camp, so I can search out something suitable?

Now? We got a good two hours o' sunlight left.

It'll be a lot harder for game to find us if we keep moving.

There any fresh water nearby?

Arune searched for a bit. *There's a small stream a couple
hundred paces to the left.*

"This is far enough," Vykers said aloud, for the benefit of the
Fool and the Historian. "Who wants to make a fire?"

"I'll do it, of course," the Historian said dryly.

Anyone lurking out there in the grass, waitin' to ambush us?

No one.

*Where's that chimera got to, and what's taking him so long to bring
the Frog back in?*

*I think...*Arune began. *I think the Frog ate the new chimera.
Killed him and ate him, I mean.*

Vykers was stunned. *What?*

*I said, I think the Frog ate the other chimera. The boy's...presence,
for want of a better word...seems much stronger and more substantial...
and...I'm not sensing the chimera any more.*

Vykers shook his head, called over to the Historian. "What
was that saying about flies and the gods?"

"We are to the gods as flies to wanton boys; they kill us for
their sport."

"Aye, that they do. And sometimes, they just fuck with us."

The Historian regarded him quizzically. "Is this apropos of
anything in particular?"

"I got no idea what you just said. I'm just wondering what's
become of the Frog's all."

"He's out there," the Ahklatian answered, affirming what

Vykers already knew.

"Well, maybe if we can scare up some good grub, he'll come home for dinner."

They did, but he did not. Vykers pushed that worry aside and slept.

In the morning, his hand reached for his sword before he'd even opened his eyes. The ground was trembling—not as it had when the grebbers had attacked, nor even as it might during a stampede. No, this was the deep, rhythmic rumble of an army on the march.

Shaper?

They're miles away. Likely to cross our path but never draw near. And the Historian and I can make sure their shapers never see us.

Can you lift me up again, like you did in battle?

A gentle, almost flirtatious laugh from Arune, and then Vykers was ten feet in the air and rising. At thirty feet, he said, *Good enough,* by which he really meant "stop the fuck right there!"

Sure enough, cutting across his group's intended path at a distance of several miles was the unmistakable shape of an army at march.

I want a closer look.

I was afraid you'd say that, said Arune. Nevertheless, she propelled her host through the air until they were both within a mile of the unknown troops.

So, it's some of the same ones we been fightin', Vykers observed. *Only a helluva lot more. And I've gotta admit I like their ranks and formations. They look well trained.*

And supplied, Arune offered.

They woulda given the End a good challenge, I'll wager. What do you figure, twenty-five, thirty thousand?

I wonder where they're going.

Doesn't matter to me, long as it's away from us.

That doesn't sound like the Vykers I know.

Yeah, Vykers agreed, so softly the Shaper couldn't swear she hadn't imagined it.

EIGHT

Yendor, House Fyne

It was the latest in a series of lousy plans, but it was all Yendor could come up with on his own and under the time constraints he'd set upon himself. He needed to do something—and soon—in order to contribute to his team's mission, even though he hadn't seen any of the other fellows in days and days. Weeks, probably. But his drinking tended to wash away great chunks of his memory, so he was never as confident of the date as he might otherwise have been.

"Mark me, look you," he said in a drunken drawl to his new friend Moult, "On our next roof patrol, which I do think falls on Fiersday—or has it passed already?"

"Nay, friend, 'tis the night after next," Moult offered.

"Just so!" Yendor beamed. And then frowned, confused. "Er, what was I speakin' of?"

"Fiersday."

Yendor giggled himself helpless. "Yes, yes, Fiersday. Fiersday. On our next roof patrol, which, now I do bethink me, falls upon this Fiersday..."

"Ya said that, already," Moult pointed out, "Unless I'm deeper in me cups than I thought."

"Did I now?" Yendor remarked. "And did I perchance essplain the sinifficance of it?"

"O' what, Fiersday?" Moult pulled on his nose, wiped his chin and said, "I can't recall. Can we have it again?"

Yendor wasn't sure if he meant the bottle of Skent or the plan, but he obliged with both, passing the bottle and repeating the plan. "On our rooftop patrol, we'll have occasion to pass the big oak—you know the one?"

Moult nodded. Or he may've had the hiccups.

"A nimble fella might climb hisself into that oak and, from thence, into one o' the other trees, one o' them blossoming ones, that grace His Lordship's private garden."

"Where's the profit in that?" Moult demanded. "Unless you fancy a bushel o' smelly flowers."

"What I fancy is a bushel o' secrets, friend Moult. "Ain't you never heard the very true saying 'knowledge is nobles'?"

"Mmmm. Can't say as I have. What's it mean?"

Yendor groaned at his friend's apparent dimwittedness. "It means that secrets are worth money, to the right person. Great heapin' gobs o' money."

Having finally gotten the drift, Moult broke into a lopsided grin. "I like money, all right."

"Who don't, eh? But there's more in it than mere money, my lad. There's all the Skent you could ever drink."

Moult was skeptical. "Just for climbin' into a tree?"

"Well," Yendor admitted, "there's a bit more to it than that. You'll need to find a sturdy, bushy branch where you won't be seen and spend the night there, so as to catch as many secrets as you may."

"Spend the night?" Moult gasped, incredulously.

"And you'll be taking a bottle o' my very best Skent to keep you warm the whiles."

Again, Moult grinned. "How can I say no to that?"

"The next day, afore sun up, you climb back to the roof and return to our barracks."

"How do I know I won't be caught by the morning shift?"

"Because," Yendor articulated with extra effort, "I'm going to do something so stupid, the guards'll have to deal with me. Which means they won't see you."

"And what's that?"

"I'm planning to take a good, long piss off the roof and into the street."

"Ach!" Moult spat, "They'll dock your pay for that. You might even get flogged."

Yendor put on his most brave face. "It's true, friend, that I've given myself the most dangerous task, but I could hardly ask you to take such a risk, could I?"

Yes, it was an awful plan, exactly the kind of mindless skullduggery that drunks found so brilliant while intoxicated and so shamelessly idiotic upon sobering up. The trick, Yendor knew, was never to sober up.

Aoife, at Sea

Life aboard the cog had gone from difficult to impossible since the onshore battle that had concluded with Vykers' departure and Aoife's accompanying banishment to the ship. A number of the crew were still seething about the unexpected loss of their mates and, without the rest of Vykers' party aboard to protect her, the A'Shea felt more threatened than she had in ages. Added to this was the fact that she was the only woman in Mahnus-knew-how-many leagues, a detail the sailors never failed to bring to her attention in ways both subtle and brazen. Oh, she could defend herself; the point was, she didn't want to be compelled to do so. The captain was on her side, too, but she doubted how long that might last when the days at sea became weeks, and the weeks, months.

She continued to fret and fume about the Frog's absence, as well. She lacked the Shaper's gift of remote sight and vision, but she believed—had to believe—that the boy had rejoined the Reaper's company and was even now travelling south with the man in search of the missing Queen. Anyway, this was the story she told herself to stave off brutal self-recriminations; it was not as convincing or effective as she might have liked.

Worst of all, she could not get the damned Reaper out of her head. It was almost as if something was pulling at her, summoning her, commanding her to come, to follow. Late one night, as she lay in her bed listening to the footsteps of the sailors up and down the deck, fearing their approach, it came to her: Vykers' Shaper was calling her. It could be none other. Why, though? Aoife had always believed Vykers' resident ghost disliked her, hated her, even. Why would she attempt to communicate...unless the Reaper was in danger, or perhaps great pain?

Carefully and with as much calm as possible, Aoife cleared her mind and sank into herself. For reasons she could not articulate if challenged, the A'Shea rarely took advantage of her training and skills on her own behalf, rarely took the time to meditate and alleviate her own grief and anxiety. She did so now and rapidly sensed a growing peace and receptivity she hadn't known in years, since the last of her birthings.

With remarkable ease she formulated a plan: she would tell the captain that she needed to go ashore to gather some herbs for healing and such, and then she would enspell her escort and escape to follow the Reaper and his party. She had been able to fight off would-be assailants in the past, and she felt confident in her ability to follow through on her scheme.

Vykers would be furious with her at first, but she hoped - no, she *knew* - he would be pleased to see her as well. And anyway, she was her own person, beholden to no one and taking orders from none. When it came down to it, she could go where she would and do as she liked. At least she hoped that was the case. Her spirits buoyed by a plan at last, she fell into a restful slumber.

Normally, Aoife had no trouble sticking to a plan, but as Arune continued to pull on the A'Shea with greater and greater insistence Aoife found it more and more difficult to think and act in a deliberate manner. Thus, when she woke around midnight to fetch a drink of water, she impulsively threw herself overboard. Thrashing about in the darkness, she was greeted by a chorus of panicked voices, the voices of the crew who understood that someone had gone over the railing, but not yet determined who or where. Aoife had her own concerns.

Although the water was considerably warmer than Aoife had been used to back home it was nevertheless deep and black and everywhere. The A'Shea felt a moment of fear herself but again extended her senses, applied her powers and was able to calm herself amidst the waves. In doing so she was able to determine the direction of the waves and by extension, the distant shore. The only question in her mind was whether she had the stamina to make the swim in full clothing, but as she had little choice she was forced to attempt it. Behind her the ship's crew used lanterns to search the water around the ship and one or two even threw blazing torches into the salty brine. Their efforts were for naught. In time, Aoife was able to make out the dark silhouette of the distant shore. With simple incantations she extended her strength and kept herself sufficiently warm so that drowning posed no real threat. In the distance she heard the shouting aboard the cog temporarily grow louder as its captain and crew discovered whom they had lost. Eventually, the A'Shea could hear them no more and the sound of surf crashing onshore grew louder and louder. Because she knew they would come looking for her at first light Aoife could not afford to simply drag herself onto the beach; she had to make distance and find a suitable place to hide until she was rested enough to continue her journey. This was easier said than done of course because as she slowly emerged from the surf she was no longer buoyed by the water around her but instead carried it with her in the heavy sodden layers of her clothing. She worried, too, that she had no means of following Vykers party, so that no matter how fast she walked she would fall further and further behind every day, assuming she was even able to follow in the first place. They would not likely leave signs to aid her. But that was a concern for the morrow; now she needed a place to hide and dry herself.

Spirk, House D'Escurzy

He had never felt so alone in his life, but he'd had that feeling so often that he'd begun to believe that loneliness *was* his life. The Constable, the notary, the doctor, and the others had left Spirk only one man as protection-a tall skinny blonde fellow who walked with an obvious limp. Spirk noticed that the other men, particularly the Constable, called this fellow Deathbow, at which appellation the man blushed a furious crimson. When at last the Constable and the others had gone, leaving Spirk alone with his new companion, Spirk said "that's a pretty spooky name you got there."

"Yeah well that ain't my name," the man said defensively. "My real name's Ron."

"Then why did they call you Deathbow?" Spirk asked.

"It's nothing. It's stupid." Said Ron.

Spirk giggled. "I been told I'm an expert at stupid." He said.

"Ain't no big story," Ron shrugged. "We was takin' target practice with crossbows, and I sneezed and shot myself in the foot."

"That must hurt something awful."

Ron regarded Spirk with a look that was a mixture of suspicion and hostility. When it was clear that the other man, this new Lord of House D'Escurzy, was not mocking him, Ron relaxed considerably and a foolish grin came to his face. "You really are as thick as they say, ain't you?"

Now, although Spirk was accustomed to such abuse, it still rankled him. But there was something about this Ron or death blow or Ron deathblow that Spirk could not help but embrace. The fellow was just inherently likable, charismatic.

For his part, Ron seemed to have decided that his new employer was relatively benign, for he continued, "Hurt like a bitch, to be honest. Worst part was, I nailed my foot to the ground and couldn't move or sit down till help arrived to pull the damn thing out. And every one who came by was laughing so hard nobody even tried to help for a good quarter hour. Oh, they brought an A'Shea by at some point and she did some good, but my foot's never been the same. But you know what they say: man can't run, can't run away."

Spirk stared at his own feet awkwardly, uncertain what was expected of him or how to proceed "Don't rightly know how it happened, but it looks like His Lordship has put me in charge of this place."

"Yes," agreed Ron. "They say you're the new Lord D'Escurzy. I think it's probably time you came out of this bedroom, don't you?"

"I *would* like to see some sunlight again," Spirk replied. "But I ain't... I'm not sure what to do first, where to go. I'm not used to being in charge and all."

"There is usually a big room, like a throne room sort of. Like these lords and ladies wish they was Queen. If there is such a room here that's where we should go."

Spirk sighed. "I think I know where there is such a room,

but I've always been too scared to go in there."

"I reckon I'd be scared, too, in your place, but you are the new Lord here: you've got to take control."

Spirk must have been palpably terrified at this prospect for the other man reached out and put a gentle hand on his shoulder. "I'm here to help you Your Lordship," said Ron. "That's my job." As it turned out, the two men had no difficulty in finding the room they sought. The murmuring of agitated voices that came from within could be heard a long ways off. A few minutes walking brought them to their destination, a spacious chamber with an enormous dark wood table at its center, around which sat or stood the largest assembly of D'Escurzys that Spirk had ever seen. He recognized them at once for the features they all shared, low foreheads dark eyes a bit of a pout in the lips. They recognized him, as well; if not by sight, then by demeanor. One or two of Spirk's new family members made as if to stand, but were quickly discouraged from doing so by the rest of the group, which was odd because so many were already on their feet. They seemed as conflicted in how to respond to this unforeseen upheaval in the family fortunes as Spirk was himself. Indeed, Spirk had never seen so many expressions of absolute befuddlement since he had walked through the house of mirrors at a traveling carnival. A long, awkward silence ensued, during which each and every person in the room seemed to be weighing his options and calculating outcomes. Out of the corner of his eye Spirk noticed his new friend Ron had become considerably more tense. Spirk was spared the indignity of having to prove he could not resolve this standoff by the abrupt movement of an old nemesis. In a few short, sharp steps, Faenia propelled herself to within striking distance, and all but dared Spirk to fully enter the chamber.

Again, Spirk could smell her perfume, a heavy, floral aroma that rose from her prominently displayed cleavage. He found it difficult to tear his gaze away from the woman's bosom, especially since her eyes glazed with defiance and resentment. But there was also a dark, seductive mischief to be found there as well, and the new Lord D'Escurzy was afraid.

"It is so kind of your Lordship to join us at last," said

Faenia, over-enunciating her words as if there were some toxic substance on her tongue that she feared to swallow.

"Um...yes." Was the best Spirk could manage.

"Stand aside, cousin," a large, thick-shouldered man said to the woman. He had longer hair than the other men in the room and an extremely impressive mustache, the ends of which trailed right off his block-like jaw. "So, I don't know how you did it, nor do I think it's right, but the city authorities have declared it to be so, and I'll not gainsay the decision. You are the new Lord of the House, the new Head of the Family. A few of us older folk have decided tis meet we recognize your station and celebrate your arrival."

Spirk and Ron exchanged looks of discomfort and disbelief. Neither man trusted the apparent situation but neither man was willing to say so aloud, especially not in this company. Nor had Spirk forgotten the one time many years ago when he had been duped into entertaining brief delusions of grandeur, only to be sorely abused for it shortly thereafter. He would not make that mistake again. He was not a smart man but he was smart enough to know that he was not a smart man.

The D'Escurzy gentleman continued, "Accordingly, we're planning a tremendous feast, as befits someone of your magnificent stature."

That, thought Spirk, sounds like trouble.

Long, House Thornton

His new accommodations were an enormous improvement over the dank cell he had previously occupied. For one thing, he had a window. Yes, it was barred with a steel grating he could never remove, but during the day it nevertheless provided him with enough natural light that he no longer felt like a man in his own grave. He had also been given a mattress of sorts, nothing like a real bed but much better than he had enjoyed for weeks. Naturally, it was infested with vermin of every sort imaginable, but now that he could finally see them, he could either avoid them or attempt to kill them, two options that had been denied him in the dungeons. As if a window and a mattress were not luxury enough, the water he was given was actually clean, and the food had every semblance of actual food. In short, he felt like the wealthiest pauper in the kingdom.

None of this, however, brought Long any closer to understanding the baffling, the maddening circumstances in which he now found himself. In searching for answers to one mystery—that of the Queen's disappearance—he had found only a series of evermore disturbing and perplexing mysteries: how had Janks come back to life? For it was Janks, Long was now convinced. Why did the man not remember him? Why had he become a torturer, a profession so antithetical to his nature? And perhaps most astonishing of all, how in Mahnus' name had Long Pete become the next—or current—Lord D'Escurzy? Or was this simply just another elaborate ploy to break Long's will? If so, it was the most original such attempt he'd ever experienced or encountered. He supposed the Lord of the house would explain himself in time.

In a strange way, Long was grateful for the mass of riddles that had been thrown his way, for they diverted his attention from other issues, other subjects too painful to contemplate. Early in his incarceration his mind sought out Mardine and Esmine the way a ship lost at sea will look for the beacon of a lighthouse, but too much time had passed, and his fear and loneliness threatened to overwhelm him when he thought in their direction. He perceived himself retreating emotionally from any and every thing that might cause him the slightest suffering. He now had some hope, however misguided, that he might achieve the impossible and survive this debacle; steeling himself against his own feelings, his own fears, longings, and desires was, he felt, a necessary step in ensuring his survival.

How then to pass the time? Initially, long made lists of varieties of apples, types of martial weaponry, of brandies he'd enjoyed over the years, of card games he knew, the names of towns he visited, and the names of whorehouses, too. But whorehouses made him think of women; thinking of women made him think of his wife—not a whore but the paragon of her gender. He stopped making lists.

He tried to wrap his mind around the Queen's disappearance,

but there was too much he did not know for him to make any headway in that regard. He then spent some time considering his impressions of the other man in his crew, his old friend Yendor, Rem, Spirk, and Capt. Kittins. If he had to wager on the question, he judged Kittins most likely to achieve success in their common mission. The idiot, Spirk, was the obvious choice to fail most disastrously, but Long felt a right bastard for thinking such a thing, and after all hadn't he himself failed in about as thorough and catastrophic a manner as one could imagine? Who in the Infinite Hells was he to look down his nose at Spirk Nessno?

A key rattled in the lock, the door's handle turned, and the door itself began to push inward. Long climbed to his feet. In a moment, the Lord of House Thornton appeared accompanied by two rather belligerent looking guards. His Lordship stepped forward, about as un-threatened in Long's presence as a bear might feel standing before a rabbit.

"Still with us then, I see. Sometimes boredom is a man's worst enemy."

"Sometimes," Long agreed. "And sometimes it's other men."

Thornton-for that was the only name that Long had as yet been able to attach to His Lordship-gazed back at his prisoner with eyes that betrayed nothing. "You don't care much for the nobility, do you?" He said. "I mean, if you did you'd behave in a much more—what is the word I'm looking for?—deferential manner. You've made a terrible mistake in sneaking into my home, but that doesn't necessarily mean you're stupid. Perhaps you are just desperate, or you underestimated our security." Clasping his hands together behind his back the man began slowly pacing around the room's perimeter, speaking more for his own benefit, his own understanding, than for Long's. "The thing of it is, the information you gave us under interrogation is unquestionably accurate: you were sent here by this Colonel Bailis, an agent of the throne, to spy upon us. I suppose that makes some sense, but all available evidence confirms what I said before, that you are the new Lord of house D'Escurzy, which makes absolutely no sense whatsoever." His Lordship paused a moment to run a hand through his hair in an act of obvious frustration. He looked over at the two guards who had accompanied him as if they had the answers he sought. "How am I to reconcile these disparate realities? Should I have you killed, or attempt to ransom you? If in fact you have been sent here by or as an agent of the throne killing you would seem unwise. On the other hand, ransom is no easier a choice, for the question becomes do I ransom you to this Col. Bailis or do I ransom you to House D'Escurzy? And it's entirely possible that neither party will prove inclined to cooperate." Thornton concluded his pacing directly in front of Captain Long and smiled at the man. "So, you can see my dilemma."

Once again Long was visited by the unpredictable and therefore unreliable wellspring of courage that had somehow gotten him through the last war in spite of the impossible odds and overwhelming evil arrayed against him. Once again, he found the mettle to speak as if he were not afraid and no one's fate hung in the balance.

"Of course, if you're asking me, I prefer to live," said he.

"Without doubt," Thornton replied. "Without doubt. But I'm not concerned with your wishes, and you forfeited the right to an opinion when you snuck into my home uninvited. No, a Lord's first duty is to his house, and I must needs determine what will best benefit House Thornton." His Lordship turned and paced away again.

"I'm certain House D'Escurzy will offer a healthy pile of gold for my return," Long said.

His Lordship spun back to face the prisoner with a most wicked smile upon his lips. "There may be something in this more valuable than gold."

"And that is?"

"Chaos."

Without any further explanation the man nodded to his guards and left the room. As the door slammed shut Long realized he now had something to occupy his time: pondering and dreading the meaning of chaos.

Vykers, in Pursuit

South, South, ever South. The Reaper set a grueling pace. Fortunately, he and his fellows had twice as many horses as they needed, courtesy of the Knights who had ambushed them on the beach, and although they were not A'Shea, the Historian and Arune together were able to extend the horses' health and range. The two shapers also did a fine job of clearing the path ahead, keeping potential threats at bay or misleading them entirely. In truth, the greatest threat the party faced was Vykers' ever growing impatience, his need, which became an almost corporeal force, to close with the Queen's abductors. With every day that passed without sign of his prey the reaper grew increasingly irritable, to the point that both Hoosh and the Historian gave him a wide berth whenever possible.

"Where the fuck are these bastards?" Vykers grumbled to no one in particular.

It was hot, and the sun burned noticeably brighter than it did back home. How this was possible was beyond Vykers' understanding, nor did he care to understand. All he knew was that his discomfort grew with every mile. But what was a little more discomfort on top of what he already felt? Toss it onto the shit heap of grievances he already had with the gods.

The heat and the light were not the only things Vykers noticed. In these warmer, drier climes, the lush, verdant groundcover and underbrush with which he was familiar gave way to sparse, feeble groundcover. The mighty pine trees, the maples, alder and ash, were replaced by groves of oaks and by other trees whose names he did not know or recognize. He wondered what sort of people would choose to live in such a place, how they made do without the plants and animals that everyone depended upon back home. For a man who lived exclusively to do and to be he had a lot of questions. It occurred to him that his curiosity was born of a desire to understand this new land better in the event he chose to come back and claim it for his own. On the whole, he was not particularly covetous of the place, but then he hadn't really had time to explore, so driven was he to rescue her Majesty. And then, of course, there was his gaping wound. Time was, he'd have wondered if he'd ever recover; now, he steered clear of the question altogether.

He grunted. In another hour the sun would set. Vykers would take the longer, cooler summer days of his homeland, any time.

Ever so subtly, the historian led his mount close to the reaper, and after several minutes the two men rode side-by-side.

"Something on your mind?" Asked Vykers.

The Historians movements were so precise and minimal that the Reaper barely noticed the man's nod in response. "The boy, the frog is still out there."

"Glad to hear it."

"Over the last few days he's been working his way closer and closer to our little party."

Vykers' gaze never deviated from the horizon. "Don't tell me the boy's got you worried."

"Worried? No. I believe he'd like to rejoin the group, but he's too afraid or... Ashamed."

"Well," Vykers sighed, "he *did* eat my best friend."

The Historian said nothing in response. And how in Mahnus' name was the Reaper supposed to discuss the Frog without dredging up memories the Ahklatian would as soon leave buried?

Shaper! Where in the countless hells are you?

I am here, Arune responded.

Well, what the fuck are you doing?

Just listening to you step in the shit.

Some friend you are, Vykers complained.

Oh, said Arune. Now we're friends.

Vykers was angry. What a surprise. *Where have you been these last few days?* He demanded.

Where have I been? Are you mocking me? Where have I ever been these past few years but trapped inside you?

So, it's that bad, is it?

Arune knew she had gone too far. *I could be bounded in a nutshell, and count myself a king of infinite space, were it not that I have bad dreams.*

Vykers had no idea how to respond to that, so all he said was, *Bullshit!*

As if he could hear the conversation and had been waiting for applause, the historian interjected, "It may be easier to bring the boy in if we make camp while it's still light, and he can still see and follow our actions."

To everyone's surprise, Vykers agreed. "Yeah, might as well call it a day. I don't suppose an hour or two is gonna make a difference. And I could use someone new to talk to, besides a couple of crazy Shapers and a fool who ain't funny."

With that pronouncement, rough edged as it was, the party members fell into their usual routines: Hoosh would gather wood for a fire, the Historian lit the fire, and Arune attracted game into the camp where it was easily killed. Naturally, the Reaper did the killing. Normally, in a family or a military unit the choicest cuts of meat went, by right, to the head of household or the commander. In this case though, the act of killing was the choice of meat, and Vykers never failed to claim it for himself.

Once everyone had settled by the fire with a meal of his choosing, Vykers cleared his throat and looked over at the historian. "The boy out there now?"

"He is," the Ahklatian responded.

"Huh," Vykers grunted, "he must be using that fey magic he learned, 'cause I don't see him."

The Historian regarded him with renewed respect. "You are correct; he is about 200 strides to the North East."

"I'm going out there to bring him back," the Reaper declared.

I believe he's afraid of your sword, Arune replied.

"Afraid of my sword?" Vykers repeated, astonished. "It ain't my sword that makes me what I am."

That attitude isn't going to make him any more comfortable.

Vykers thought up an immediate retort, but the fact was he missed Arune whenever she went silent too long. He tried a different tack: "so, I'll leave the sword in camp and approach him unarmed."

The sword was none too happy with this turn of events and let Vykers know it in no uncertain terms: it squealed, it whined, it intensified his pain, but the Reaper remained intractable. He didn't like being manipulated. At the same time, he saw this as a test of his own recovery. How long, how far could he go without his sword? Time to find out. Setting it down across a log near the fire, Vykers struck out in the direction the historian had indicated.

He walked what he reckoned to be about halfway to the frog's location, but was still unable to spot the boy. "Okay, then," he said aloud, "think I'll take a seat right here, lad, and whenever you're ready to talk, you can come on in. I'm unarmed, I'm on the ground. Couldn't be less of a threat, unless I was asleep. But that wouldn't make for much of a conversation."

Vykers waited. The sun went down. Back at the campfire, the Fool began singing, softly. Vykers didn't imagine that was for the Historian's benefit; perhaps it was meant to provide further cover for the Frog, or maybe it was meant to soothe the boy's nerves. Whatever the reason, the Reaper found it just a bit harder to hate the old man.

He's working his way closer, Arune's voice whispered (though none but Vykers could hear her) after more than an hour had passed.

He's taking his sweet time.

He's a boy, and he's lost. You will understand when you see him.

The fool continued to sing.

Later, Vykers had nearly fallen asleep when a voice called to him from the dark.

"Reaper?" It was a husky, gravelly voice but strangely vulnerable for all that.

"I'm here, son," said Vykers.

Son? Thought Arune. That's a nice touch. Who would have thought the Reaper had it in the him?

A hulking, muscular shape that was much larger than Vykers had expected emerged from the landscape. "What did I do? What've I done?" it mewled pitifully.

The Reaper wanted to stand, remained sitting. "Nothin' bad, son. Nothin' wrong."

"But I ate...I ate... and now I'm...I'm..."

"You're the Frog, lad. You're my friend, the Frog."

The Frog came to within fifteen feet of Vykers, fully visible now. He'd changed all right. Fully as large as Number Three had been and perhaps bigger, he was an impossible amalgamation of human and animal parts and attributes. The Reaper did not feel pity, but he understood the boy's desolation.

"I ate the other one, too. The smaller one. I didn't mean to, but he kept trying to catch me; he wouldn't leave me alone."

Another soul on Vykers' conscience. He barely felt it. "Why don't you come back to the fire with me?" He asked the boy. "I think there's some game left from dinner; you're welcome to it, and you can warm yourself up."

"You gonna kill me," the frog queried. "Back at camp?"

"No."

"But someday?"

He wasn't going to lie to the kid. "I don't think so. I hope not."

"Me too," the frog said, as he fell in beside the Reaper and they began the journey back to the campfire.

Well done, Vykers. Well done, Arune wanted to say. But it was not her moment, so she stayed out of it.

Mardine, On the Trail

Everyone understood that giants were harder to injure and healed faster than other races; everyone, that is, save Mardine herself, who was having such a difficult time merely breathing in and out that the conventional wisdom seemed offensive and idiotic to her. Harder to injure? Faster healing? She was broken and undeniably so. She could feel the snapped ends of her ribs grating against each other, and every such occurrence caused her pain beyond anything she had previously experienced, including childbirth. From what she could tell she had been struck from behind by an enormous log, possibly weighing several tons. How her attackers had gotten it airborne defied comprehension. Anyway, Mardine had more important things to worry about, like remaining alive and finding her daughter.

If only she could remain conscious.

She was jostled awake sometime later and realized she lay bound in a rustic wagon that trundled along the forest path without a care for her comfort or sanity. It was never especially bright in the forest but now it was growing well and truly dark.

She could make out the sound of horse hooves negotiating the path, the creaking of her wagon and its wheels, and the faint sound of conversation, though she could not tell who was speaking or what was being said. Probably it was that treacherous bitch Nelby and her equally conniving man. Well, she would sort them out, given half a chance.

Come morning, Mardine felt no better but at least she could see. Still in the forest, then. She heard the sound of footsteps shuffling in the rocky soil and waited to see who approached. She might have expected Nelby, but it was Jaddo who rounded the wagon's corner and smirked at her upon making eye contact.

"Thirsty?"

She wanted to squeeze his skull in her hands until she felt his brains oozing out his ears. That would have to wait. "Yes," she managed. Even that single syllable had nearly taxed her to her limit.

Jaddo dipped a ladle into a bucket he'd been carrying and held it to the giantess' lips. "You surely can take a thumping," said he. "But I'm glad you survived; you're worth a lot more alive than dead. Truth to tell, you ain't worth nothing dead."

"My... Daughter?"

"Oh, she's fine, she's fine," the former thrall said in an offhand way. "She's the real prize anyhow. Wouldn't let any harm come to her, no way." He grinned and showed his tobacco-stained teeth.

"Why?"—Not meaning why was she the real prize, but why had Jaddo and Nelby stolen her in the first place.

"Why?" Jaddo cackled. "Didja damage yer brain when ya fell? For the money! Any and everything for the money, always! Your girl's a bit of a freak, and there's a feller up north what collects 'em. Freaks, that is."

If only Mardine had the strength to respond. Her world was naught but a bitter, reddish fog.

Later still, she woke to the sound of giggling. She made it about mid-day, felt no better. And now, on top of her omnipresent thirst, she was also ravenous. Hard to believe, given her injuries, but there it was. How long had it been since she'd... *Oh*, her nose told her, *she'd already done it*, must've happened when she'd been struck. They'd left her to stew in her own filth like an animal.

Craning her neck to one side and turning her head with great difficulty, she sought out the source of the giggling. If there was any room for further pain, she felt it now upon seeing not Nelby, but Tresa in Jaddo's arms, nuzzling him, nibbling upon his neck and otherwise engaging in all manner of shameless foreplay.

"Where's Nelby?" Mardine called out in a voice that was half shout, half-groan.

The lovers approached her wagon, still wrapped around each other. "What do you want with that stupid cow?" Jaddo asked in amazement.

Tresa snorted derisively, "The big oaf's just figured it out, love, she's just now realized it 'twas not Nelby who deceived her, but me!"

Mardine forced a smile, despite the pain.

"What?" Tresa snapped. "You think that's funny, do you?"

Mardine shook her head no. "You just saved me from killing the wrong woman."

Jaddo found this amusing and chuckled at the giantess' pluck. Tresa, on the other hand, was infuriated by the remark and slapped Mardine across the face with a resounding crack.

"You keep talking like that, bitch, and I'll gut you while you lie there!"

The giantess closed her eyes; there was nothing to be gained from prolonging this conversation. Instead, she would bide her time. If she only ever got one chance to escape, to rescue her daughter, to enact her revenge, she wanted to be ready. She was dimly aware that the thrall woman continued to hurl invective her way, but she lacked the energy and desire to make sense of it, and so it became a rapidly fading droning noise in the background of her consciousness. She sank back into sleep.

Jaddo spoon fed her cold stew, which she fairly inhaled without tasting or thanks. She had never been so hungry in her life.

"Always wondered how much you folk et," Jaddo remarked.

Mardine couldn't risk a response. He was feeding her, and

that was all that mattered for the moment. She didn't want to do or say anything that would kill his generosity, whatever his motives might be. And anything good that might come in the future was predicated upon her regaining her health and strength.

"Imagine you might like a little wine to go with this here."

Mardine nodded. Jaddo poured half a bottle of wine down her throat. It wasn't a good vintage; Hells, the giantess wouldn't even use it as a cleaning solution under normal circumstances. Things being as they were, she drank it gladly.

The former thrall had a strange smile on his lips. "Oh, you like that, do you? Might as well finish the bottle, then."

And so she did.

As Jaddo withdrew the bottle at last, his arm not so subtly brushed against Mardine's breasts. Now she understood. It seemed men were the same everywhere, excepting of course her beloved Long. Well, that wasn't exactly true, either. Shortly before they first met, long Pete had made his living as a gigolo. But there were so many qualities her man possessed, or rather came to possess, that this man did not that the comparison was utterly unfair. So, Jaddo was curious, was he?

Mardine felt a brief surge of euphoria: an idea was beginning to take shape in her mind.

Rem, House Hawsey

He'd been acting like a coward, really, and he knew it. The thought of spending even another moment between Her Ladyship's legs was more frightening than anything His Lordship might do to him if the man discovered the forgery. He'd been on the verge of approaching her door numerous times, but lost his nerve. Indeed, Rem had intended to switch the diaries within 24 hours, but 24 had become 48 and then 72 and now almost a week had passed. Funny, he had never been afraid of a woman before. Of course, Her Ladyship was no ordinary woman. How long could he continue to avoid her? Well, he wasn't dead yet, so he figured he could hold out until Lord Hawsey killed him for one reason or another.

What foolishness! This mission was not about him and his petty little fears, but about her Majesty's disappearance. Too, if he never escaped House Hawsey, his acting career and his growing fame would be finished. There was nothing for it but to put on his best doublet, strap on his most dazzling codpiece and sally forth into battle. It could hardly be as bad as he remembered; he must've embellished certain details with his over active imagination. Yes, yes, that had to be it. Just to be on the safe side though, he downed a half bottle of excellent brandy before leaving his chambers and heading off to confront Her Ladyship.

As he approached the door to her bedroom, he couldn't help but notice the two guards stationed outside smirking at him. At least, he thought they were smirking at him. Perhaps they were as drunk as he. If not, he pitied them their station in life.

"Is Her Ladyship in?" said he.

The guards exchanged looks of confusion. "Can't rightly remember," said the man on Rem's left.

"Why don't you knock and see?" said the other.

Rem knew a conspiracy when he saw one, but he'd come this far, the brandy was wearing off, and he felt if he didn't act now, he would lose his resolve forever. His nerves betrayed him, though, and the knock he produced was so feeble as to be almost in audible.

Her Ladyship heard it, nonetheless. She must've been some sort of sorceress. The door creaked open a scant three or four inches, and Her Ladyship's voice rang out accusingly, "Where have you been?" Before Rem had a chance to answer, a hand flew out of the darkness and pulled him violently through the doorway. Another hand—presumably the last remaining one in the room not belonging to the actor—snaked past his head and pushed the door shut behind him.

Too soon, his eyes adjusted to the lack of light, leaving him face to face with the insatiable one. Except, for the moment, she seemed preoccupied. "I must tell you, my love," she began with a husky whisper, "that I now carry your child."

Bollocks! A lie! A bald-faced lie, if ever there was one! If anything frightened Rem more than contracting some horrid venereal disease, it was leaving a trail of bastards in his wake, children who'd weigh him down emotionally and financially as he strove to become the greatest actor in history! A bit overstated, perhaps. But if he was ever to have children, they would be conceived with a woman of his choosing, a witty, comely wench with a good leg for dancing and a strong arm for wielding the wood axe. With that in mind, he'd made a habit of seeking the help of every A'Shea, Shaper, Alchemist and Mountebank he encountered, to ensure he could not, would not ever impregnate a woman against his will. He had a private stash of anti-fertility elixirs that was positively unrivalled in the middle Kingdoms, and so he was, for the nonce, as sterile as an army of eunuchs.

So, yes, a lie. What, then, was Her Ladyship after? If she was truly with child, who was the father? And whom was she protecting with this cover-up, the other man, or herself? If she was not with child, what did she hope to gain by saying so? Rem was stymied.

"Well?" Her Ladyship demanded, pressing herself against the actor until he was pinned to the door.

"You know I live to serve you," Rem heard himself proclaim, "What would you have me say?"

Her Ladyship wrenched him away from the door and spun him towards the bed. "Kill my husband!"

"Whu...w...w...whaaaa?" He'd never stuttered in his life, but he stuttered now like he'd been born to it.

"You must needs kill Lord Hawsey."

Rem could think of nothing intelligent to say. "But why? How?"

Lady Hawsey tackled him and continued whispering urgently into his face. "Because milord is what he lacks; that is, a prick."

Confirmation.

"And thus he cannot get me with child. If I begin to show, he'll have me killed...right after he murders you."

His thoughts were so busy scrambling for purchase that Rem was incapable of formulating any sort of response. Until Her Ladyship bit his lower lip. "Ouch!" he cried.

"You'll do it, won't you, love? For me? For us?"

Damn it all! His Mahnus-cursed privates were not cooperating.

"Mmmmm," Her Ladyship groaned. "I see you will."

He was her toy. And he well knew what happened to most toys, whether their owners were children, dogs or cats. This was Her Ladyship's attempt to seize control of House Hawsey for herself. If she was in truth with child, she could claim it had been Henton's heir and no one could gainsay the matter... except for Gelter Radcliffe, a fact that was clearly unknown to Her Ladyship.

And who and where was this alleged child's real father? Rem would bet any amount of gold the man didn't have long for this world, if he was even still in it. Rem's concentration was broken by a hoarse, carnal grunting, and he realized he had somehow almost-magically disassociated himself from Her Ladyship and whatever it was she was doing to his body. All he knew for certain was that he needed to switch the diaries again and get himself and his company the hells out of House Hawsey before the ceiling came crashing in.

At length, Lady Hawsey wore herself out and passed into blissful slumber. How like a man, Rem thought. Then, if she's the man, what's that make me? Quick as he dared, Rem put Gelter's real diary back where he'd found it and retrieved his forgery. He spied one of Her Ladyship's myriad rings on the bedside table and, without knowing why, slipped into his vest pocket. He was worried about how he'd handle the two guards outside Her Ladyship's chamber, but was relieved to find them gone. They must have departed by prearranged signal from Her Ladyship as soon as the actor had been admitted. Rem didn't doubt those men were in for a rough go of it in the days ahead.

Over the next hour, he sought out each and every member of his company and advised them to prepare for a final performance, followed by a hasty departure.

Always exit the stage with a flourish!

Aoife, In Pursuit

It turned out that Vykers' party hadn't managed to round up all of the dead knights' horses. Aoife happened upon a frightened and exhausted mare that had somehow gotten its reins tangled in a copse of thorny bushes and been unable to extricate itself. By the time Aoife arrived, horse and woman were in equal disarray and, wary though they were of one another, each found hope in the other's presence. The A'Shea consciously radiated calm and well-being as she approached the mare, and it gradually became so docile that it was as if they'd known each other forever. It took Aoife several minutes to unwind the unruly reins; when she'd finished, she gently led the horse to a small pond she'd passed but a short while earlier, and, thus, the adage was proven wrong, for the horse drank both long and deeply. When at last it had finished, it began munching on leafy plants it found at the water's edge. Aoife would not rush the poor beast. Although it was only late afternoon, she thought it best they both got some sleep. Again, she led the horse by its reins to a new destination, a small grove of trees. Here, in the shade, the A'Shea cast a few spells to hide herself and her new companion, removed the horse's saddle and bags and encouraged it to lie down. The mare would have preferred to sleep standing, but Aoife wanted to rest against its reassuring bulk. Apologizing as she did so, the A'Shea cast another spell that caused the horse to cooperate.

Later, as the sun went down, Aoife was glad of her choice. The days were warmer here, it was true, but the nights still had a bit of a chill.

Something touched her face, and Aoife's eyes flew open, momentarily blind in the darkness of deep night. Slowly, she perceived the outline of someone against the night sky, someone standing over her, unmoving. At her back, the mare slept on.

"Who are you, and what do you want?" the A'Shea asked the shadow.

In response, it gave off a faint, violet aura that allowed Aoife to see its face.

"Too-Mai-Ten-La?" But she could see it was not.

The creature inclined its head in an attitude of curiosity and...something else. "How do you know these words?" It asked in a deep, gravelly and heavily accented voice. "You are not of the people." He drew closer.

Aoife could see why she'd mistaken this newcomer for Toomt-La: like her old companion, he, too, was a satyr.

"Not of the people, and yet marked by the people. Who are you that you should merit this honor?"

That last was remarkably hostile. "I am mother-sister of Nar!" she shot back, a little too loudly. "Who asks?"

The satyr drew closer still, until his nose was nearly touching Aoife's. "Mother-sister of Nar?" he repeated contemptuously, "A human female? What madness is this?" Arcane energies began to crackle along his arms and hands.

"I am no mere human," Aoife countered. "Do not think to try me, lest you would wage war against your own kind!"

The satyr appeared to consider this. "It is your kind with whom I would wage war, your kind I would exterminate had I the opportunity."

"You have my pity, then. I wish no such thing upon anyone."

"Then you are a fool!" the satyr sneered. "Humans are a wildfire that will burn the world to the bedrock if given the chance."

By this point, Aoife was glowing with an impressive blue fire of her own. She expected an assault at any moment. It might even be necessary to strike first. "For all your age and experience, you know so little," she quipped.

"We shall see, Mother-sister of Nar. We shall see," the creature growled. "Make one mistake in my land, and even the wind will not lick your bones." Then, as she expected, he faded out of her vision and into the night.

The A'Shea needed every spell, cantrip and meditation in her repertoire to banish the jitters that seized her in the aftermath of the satyr's visit. So, the fey folk of this land were even less enamored of her race than was Toomt-La. She would have to tread carefully, indeed.

Aoife spent the rest of the night watching, through the leaves above her head, the constellations whirl across the heavens. The satyr did not reappear, but the A'Shea's memories of Toomt-La were so strong and plentiful, she could almost feel him beside her. "Toomt-La?" she whispered into the night breeze. She knew, of course, that he would not reply, but it saddened her that he did not, nonetheless. There were times when her loneliness was almost unbearable. After sunrise, the mare was again thirsty and hungry. Aoife found a brush in the beast's saddlebags and curried its coat while it grazed. In less than a day, she had earned that much trust. At last, she re-saddled the mare, adjusted its tack and reins and pulled herself onto its back, murmuring words of peace and comfort all the while. For herself, she found a bit of dried meat and brown bread in one of the saddlebags, which tasted far better than she'd anticipated. Quieting her thoughts, she focused on Vykers and felt the by-now familiar pull of his Shaper. South, then. With a gentle nudge from her heals, the horse set off at a canter, happy as you please.

Vykers, In Pursuit

He hadn't forgotten his two prisoners; he just didn't give a shit about them and couldn't imagine they had anything of value to offer in trade for their lives. After more than a week's hard riding, though, the tedium of the hunt began to wear on him, and, as the party made camp one evening, he wandered over to the stump to which the Historian had bound them and squatted next to the most alert of the pair. The fellow had black hair, two weeks' or more growth of beard and soulful brown eyes. The Ahklatian had been good to the prisoners, fed them, slaked their thirst whenever necessary, bound their wounds. Hells, Hoosh appeared worse off than these two. Vykers extended his claws, reached out a hand, and turned the man's face towards his own. When their eyes met, Vykers flashed his canines. The knight's face became a mask of fear.

"You'll need my help in communicating with him," the Historian noted from the fire.

"I think I've made a fair start," the Reaper responded.

"He fears you, that's certain. But I'll wager he fears the ague, as well. Does that mean they're communicating, too?"

"Very well, Historian, have it your way. Ask him who he serves."

The Historian drew closer, recited a brief incantation and placed a hand on the prisoner's head. "Now, you may ask him yourself. But only for the next hour or so."

I could have done that! Arune objected.

But you didn't offer.

"Who do you serve?"

Whom.

The soldier's eyes widen perceptibly. "What...are...you?"

Vykers struck him across the face. "Whom do you serve?"

By now, the second soldier had roused himself somewhat and regarded the proceedings with a mixture of resentment and horror.

"I serve His Exalted Magnificence, Emperor Mendis Staurachia, the Eleventh."

Vykers' rolled his eyes in disgust. "Not another o' these big titled bastards! It's deeds makes a man, not words."

"Ah," the Historian interjected, "But it's words that record those deeds after a man's death."

The Reaper placed the talon of his forefinger under the man's chin. "And where is the throne of this Emperor? How far away, would you say?"

"A month's ride to the northeast."

"A month?" Vykers was stunned. That can't be true, can it?

He isn't lying, if that's what you're asking.

"And what were you men doing so far from home?"

"This is our territory. We're one of the units assigned to patrol and protect the western quintile."

Gibberish. All Vykers could make of it was that this emperor's domain was enormous. "We passed within a few miles of one o' your armies. What's the story, there? They protectin' your western whatever, too?"

"That," the man breathed, "And putting down some rebellion or other. That's how His Exalted Magnificence stays strong."

"Mmm," Vykers grunted. He understood that.

"How many soldiers does this empire o' yours boast?"

The man looked at his companion, asked a question the Reaper did not understand. The second man repeated the same phrase, shrugged and said a single word. The first man then said "two million."

The Reaper struggled to keep his face emotionless. *That's gotta be a lie!* He said to Arune.

That's what he's been told and led to believe.

Vykers felt something strange, but it was not fear or even awe. It was covetousness, it was envy. *There ain't two million fighters in all of our homeland. I doubt there's two million men of any sort. Two million men was a lot of killin'.* "You asked what I am," he said to the first knight. "I am the Reaper, *destroyer* of Empires."

He was gratified to see the other man return a look of unwavering certainty.

The Reaper was not given to dreaming. He did not know why; it was just something he'd never done much. He didn't miss it, spent no time worry about it. It was what it was.

He dreamed that night, though.

He'd stormed into a huge temple of white marble. The air was hot, dry and smelled of incense he knew he'd never experienced before, yet nevertheless recognized. He and those with him slew wave upon wave of defenders to achieve the building's inner chamber. At last, his forces came face-to-face with a final row of elites that stood between him and the man they guarded, a man on a tall, stone dais.

The man on the dais screamed in fury, "Who dares profane the sanctum of the Emperor, Mendis Staurachia, Third of the Name?"

The Reaper wanted to laugh aloud, "I do. I, Tarmun Vykers!" What he heard himself say instead made no sense: "I, Treamann Wykerrian. It is I who 'profanes' your sanctum, and it is I who will tear it down upon your cowardly head!"

There followed a bloodbath that predictably concluded with Vykers—or Wykerrian—holding the severed head of the Emperor high above his own in triumph, to the thunderous cheers of his fellow warriors.

And then he was himself again, in Heride, getting yelled

at by good old (mean old) Hobnail, his once-upon-a-time Sergeant.

"You act like a child, Vykers. That what you are, a wee one? You want to be suckling your ma's teats, boy?" Hobnail drenched Vykers' face in a haze of spittle. "Or are you a man? 'Cause a man thinks, a boy don't. A man considers before runnin' into a cave, a boy don't."

"I was…"

Hobnail smashed him one, right in the teeth. Vykers could've ducked, but that would only have made matters worse.

"You was nothin', Vyke, you was nothin'. Not without my say-so!"

He was eating a handful of odd fruits called 'olives.' They came in black, brown and green. They were cured in briny vinegar and stored in oil. Vykers had always loved 'em, but… that couldn't be right, 'cause he'd never had one before.

The face of his lost beloved, Hesh-Tu, rose up out of nowhere and, rather than revisit the pain of her loss, Vykers forced himself awake.

The sky was still dark, but no stars could be seen. The Reaper wondered if rain was coming.

Burner? He called to Arune.

Vykers.

You ever hear of someone named Treamann Wykerrian?

No, Arune lied. *Why do you ask?*

I dunno. Just some bullshit dream I had. Wake me when it's sun up, will you?

Before she could even agree, Vykers had fallen back asleep.

In the morning, the Historian approached the Reaper, carrying the Queen's hand. "Her Majesty is no longer moving away from us."

"'Bout damned time. Don't tell me she's dead, though."

The Ahklatian smiled wanly. "No, not dead."

"How long 'til we catch up with her, you reckon?"

"Assuming her captives don't resume their pace? Within a fortnight."

Vykers cursed. "A fortnight? Why is it never a day? Never an hour? The hells blast this Mahnus-forsaken land to oblivion!"

The Historian chuckled. "You've become more eloquent in your old age."

"You're a fine one to be callin' anyone old, Shaper."

The Ahklatian changed the subject. "What are your plans for the prisoners?"

"Haven't decided," Vykers answered. "Right now, they're naught but dead weight. Might be, it's better to finish 'em today and have done with it. Or maybe I should let the Frog eat 'em."

"I would advise against that," the Historian said.

I bet you would, Vykers thought wryly to himself. Time was, he'd have said that out loud. There was nothing to be gained from antagonizing the Historian, though, and the man had dealt fairly with the Reaper thus far, so Vykers said nothing.

The days and leagues went by, and still he could not get the dream out of his head. When he recognized his first olive tree, he became incensed.

Burner! Arune!

Yes?

This Brouton's Bind?

There was a pause. *Is what Brouton's Bind?*

This tree, here. It's an olive tree. Why do I know that?

I've no idea, the Shaper responded defensively.

That wasn't good enough for Vykers. *You're supposed to be the smart one. Figure it out. I feel like my mind is…leaking.*

I'll ask the Historian. Privately, Arune was worried. There had always been parts of the Reaper's mind to which she could not gain access, no matter how hard or how often she tried. What was becoming clear, though, was that her host—and friend—had visited this part of the world before. When that had been and what he'd done here were questions that offered only disturbing possibilities, at a time when seemingly everyone needed the man focused on the task at hand. Even Arune had hopes and ambitions that hinged on the successful rescue of Her Majesty.

Do that, Vykers ordered.

Oh, trust me, Arune thought to herself, *I'll positively grill the bastard.*

Fortunately, an event near midday offered the whole party a bit of distraction.

"I smell somethin'..." the Frog said to Vykers as he rode up alongside.

A sad smile came to Vykers' lips. "Three was always doin' that, too."

The Frog didn't understand.

"Anyway," the Reaper continued, "what are you gettin'?"

"I dunno. I never smelled it afore. It eats meat, though, and it's big."

"What? How can something smell big?"

"Dunno," the Frog shrugged. "It just does."

It's some sort of cat, Arune offered.

Like a lynx?

Sure. A lynx the size of an ox.

Are you shittin' me? Vykers asked.

I wish I were.

"Any idea where this thing is?"

"Off in the trees, to the..." The Frog couldn't quite figure out how to explain.

Northwest, said Arune. *I think he's got his eyes on our two captives—and probably their horses, too.*

Think we could get him to settle for the Fool?

Now, now, the Shaper laughed, *he hasn't been as bad as all that.*

You mean, apart from the fact the man smells like a midden and can't tell a good jest from a boil on his ass?

How do you know there's a boil on his ass?

I heard him singin' about it t'other day. Anyway, how far away's this big cat?

I hate it when you get bored, Arune complained.

Seeing the Shaper was unwilling to oblige him, Vykers asked the Frog. "How far away is this thing, you figure?"

The Frog pointed to a mound of good-sized boulders, from which seven or eight waxen-leafed bushes grew defiantly. "Just there, in the shadows between them rocks."

Vykers didn't see anything.

"He's in there," the Frog confirmed.

What are you going to do? Try to lure it back to camp like you did with the Frog? Arune asked. *Or are you really so desperate for a fight?*

I'm just curious, is all. I just wanna see this thing.

And then?

Haven't decided. Without an ounce of caution, Vykers slid off his horse, slapped its backside, and began walking towards the pile of boulders. He noticed the Historian had turned his horse in Vykers direction, but the Reaper waved him off. As if to reassure the Ahklatian, he drew his sword and held it up for all to see.

And then resumed walking.

When he got within fifteen or twenty paces, he heard a low, warning rumble that gave him pause. Oh, this kitty was bigger than an ox. A damned sight bigger. If only he could sight it. "I'm right here," he told the boulders. To his astonishment, a gigantic shape faded into view at the edge of the shadows, no more than ten feet from his position. It had been moving all this time, and he hadn't heard it, save for its warning growl. The beast was impossibly large—easily the biggest land creature Vykers had ever encountered—with eyeteeth as long as swords. It had a scruff of mane, and its tawny fur was mottled in blacks, greys, and browns that seemed to shift and change with the beast's position in his surroundings, a natural, ever-changing camouflage.

The Reaper was fairly confident he could kill it before it killed him, but ten feet was much closer than he'd planned on getting, and he didn't want to make any obvious adjustments to his stance that might alarm the big cat.

It moved closer.

Vykers could smell it now, too, and found its odor not altogether unappealing. Its giant, shield-sized eyes, like its coat, seemed to change color with every step, now bronze, now green, now yellow. But whatever their color, their expression remained unchanged: an unmistakable mixture of curiosity and naked hostility.

I should prob'ly be afraid, Vykers thought to himself. *Funny thing is, I ain't.* "I am Tarmun Vykers," he said quietly. "The Reaper."

The cat pushed at Vykers' head with its nose, loudly sniffing every inch of him.

I could put its eyes out right now, Vykers thought. *Shaper!* He called to Arune.

Vykers?

Tell the Historian to stake the weakest of our mounts to the ground and lead the rest of our party away.

There was no point in contesting the wisdom of this action, Arune knew. Vykers would do as he chose. *As you say,* she responded.

Man and beast remained nose-to-nose and toe-to-toe whilst the Historian carried out Vykers' order. The big cat was too canny to take its eyes off the warrior; a slight shift in the creature's ears was the only sign it had noticed the Reaper's offering. With a degree of patience Vykers rarely demonstrated in any other area of his life, he withdrew, gradually and in such minute steps that it seemed an hour had passed before he'd gotten out of striking range—whatever that might be for such a monstrous feline. In his peripheral vision, he could see the panicked horse some fifty paces to his right. Although the horse had been staked with its back to the cat, it was clear to all that it could nevertheless sense, perhaps smell, the predator. Just as it started to whinny in terror, a tremendous shadow fell upon it, followed by the sharp snap of bone and, again, a deep, throaty growl of warning.

It took a lot to amaze Tarmun Vykers, but he was amazed at the cat.

Even in retreat, dragging the horse's considerable bulk by the throat, the beast kept its eyes on the Reaper until it had disappeared amongst the rocks again. Only then, did Vykers feel safe in remounting his own horse and leading his companions away.

And what was that all about? Arune demanded.

Vykers chuckled. *If you have to ask, I can't explain it.*

We just lost a good horse.

Good? I asked for the weakest.

And so it was. Still, it served.

And has been served, Vykers snickered. *By the way, whose was it?*

One of the prisoners'.

No matter, then. They can ride double. He paused. *Did they see what happened to their horse?*

How could they fail to?

And the Fool? Was he awake and watching?

Yes, yes, Arune cried in frustration. *We all witnessed your little lesson. If only we understood what you were trying to communicate.*

Oh, those knights understood, Burner. They understood just fine.

NINE

Kittins, House Gault

Despite the rank odor of rotting Svarren corpses, Kittins was famished. It occurred to him that this might be part of his punishment, a test to see how long or even whether he could resist devouring the flesh of the nearby dead. When and if he sank that far, he would know he'd fallen beyond redemption. Fortunately, he still had plenty of water, foul though it was, in the large half-barrel at the rear of the cell. He was about to slake his thirst when he was interrupted.

"Look at you," a familiar voice snarled contemptuously, "An' I thought we was friends."

Kittins had been taunted so much in the past few days, he didn't even bother to look up any more. His latest tormentor was Wrensl Deda. Frankly, he was surprised the man hadn't worked up the courage to come sooner.

"You set me up, and now you're sittin' in a stinkin' Svarren cell."

Apart from his stunning grasp of the obvious, Wrensl had just shown a gift for alliteration that Kittins had not known he possessed. "Alliteration" was one of the last new words the big man had learned before going on his latest killing spree. He hadn't quite understood the concept when he'd read about it, but Deda had unwittingly demonstrated its use to perfection. "Sittin' in a stinkin' Svarren cell." Interesting.

"Man don't like to be ignored when he's talking to someone..." Deda growled.

"I'm not ignoring you. In fact, I'm riveted by your poetry."

Deda looked as if he'd just swallowed something putrescent. "My what? My poetry?"

Kittins wasn't moved to say more.

"Well, fuck you, big man!" Deda shouted. "Fuck you! We'll see how long you last with them bleedin' beastly bodies..."

Kittins started laughing and, when he caught sight of Deda's bewildered expression, laughed harder and harder. Soon, he found he couldn't stop.

Deda hurled every kind of obscenity he could at the prisoner, to no avail. The big man howled with mirth at Deda's expense, and it made the smaller man feel smaller still.

Suddenly, another familiar voice barked out, "Get lost" and Deda slunk away. "What's this, then, some new stage of your madness?" Lord Darley.

Kittins struggled to compose himself, took a deep breath, exhaled. "There's easier ways to kill me," he told His Lordship.

The man stared at him with those piercing eyes. "If killing you had been my goal, you can be sure I would have achieved it by now." Kittins hadn't a lot to say, so he waited. "The first time I laid eyes on you," Darley continued, "I knew you were a weapon, that you'd been born, been made to kill. I can see now the fault for this fiasco," he indicated the corpses behind Kittins, "is mine. I should have realized one cannot keep a weapon of such lethal potential unsheathed and lying about the house."

Metaphor, Kittins thought. Alliteration, metaphor...what next? Iambic pentameter? He thought of Rem and quickly pushed the memory aside. Darley was preparing to pronounce Kittins' fate, and he needed to pay better attention.

"Therefore," His Lordship said, "I am sending you away, on an errand that may be beyond even your considerable talents."

"A suicide mission, then?" Kittins intoned.

A slight shift in Darley's gaze told Kittins he'd hit it, dead on. "But," His Lordship was quick to add, "should you succeed, I'll honor you with land and a title."

"Not that I'm in any position to decline," the prisoner said, "but this land...I'm guessing it's a ways off?"

Darley inclined his head a fraction of an inch: correct. "It seems we may count intuition amongst your gifts. Yes, it's a ways off, as you put it. An island, in fact, off the eastern coast."

"And this errand…you want me to kill someone."

"Of course," Darley replied with more than a trace of condescension in his voice.

"I'm not real stealthy," Kittins said, thinking aloud. "So, this must be a straight-up brawl you're looking for."

"You may have to kill several guards before you reach your target, yes. From what I've seen, that should prove little challenge for you."

Kittins sucked on his teeth. Seemed like his hunger had grown tenfold in the last five minutes. Surely His Lordship would have to feed and equip him before sending him off. "And who is this target?"

"A man named Kendell. Every House has a different name for the role he fulfills, but at House Blackbyrne they call him 'Chief of Security.' That's a job you might've had for me one day…if things had turned out differently."

"I hear House Blackbyrne ain't especially important. Why do you want this fella dead?"

His Lordship swept his eyes across the cell and its disgusting condition and contents. "Does it matter?" He turned to look at Kittins, his gaze unflinching.

"No," Kittins admitted. "Not really."

"Good," said Darley. "I've got some men coming to bring you to a bath and a meal. One of these men is a powerful Shaper. If you give him or any of his companions the slightest bit of difficulty…well, you're a bright fellow. I hardly need to finish that sentence, do I?"

"No, milord."

"You understand the same consequences will follow any attempt to escape into the city once we set you on your path?"

"Yes, milord."

"Excellent. I expect our next meeting will be our last. But in the event you do complete your assignment, you'll be a very wealthy man, indeed."

"On a very distant island."

Darley's smile would've looked more at home on an undertaker. "Just so."

"Some men" turned out to be ten, which told Kittins that Darley was in deadly earnest, but also spoke of His Lordship's regard for the big man's abilities. In an ironic parallel to Kittins' rescue of the Svarren woman, his escort led him to the bath, where he was forced to clean himself in full view of the other men. If they wanted to wink or smirk at one another at Kittins' expense, they were damned subtle about it. The captain took his time scrubbing himself clean; the whole event had the air of ritual about it, a cleansing before battle...or death. When he emerged from the water, one of the men stepped forward and handed him a bundle of black linens. More ritual. In no time, he donned the proffered clothing and was ushered towards the room's far exit. After several minutes of walking, he and his guards arrived in a room Kittins had never seen before. It was neither big nor small and featured only a large, sturdy table upon which sat a suit of armor and various weapons. Long minutes later, His Lordship deigned to make an appearance through a door beyond the table.

"You kept me waiting with your leisurely bath; I thought I'd return the favor," Darley explained.

This was another of those moments when speaking at all seemed counterproductive and possibly dangerous, but Kittins felt it important to acknowledge he'd gotten the message, so he bobbed his head in what he hoped seemed an agreeable manner.

"I have hired, through a third party, a number of ruffians and thugs—brainless to a man—to attack a little used entrance near the back of the Blackbyrne estate. I've engaged another group, less stupid, but also less expensive, to stage a large, rowdy party just outside Blackbyrne's front gate. With these two events happening at roughly the same time, you'll be able to climb and slip over the wall on the opposite side and work your way into House Blackbyrne. Kill as many people as you can find; I have no particular preference as to gender, age or occupation. Sooner or later, Kendell will hear of it and feel compelled to take matters into his own hands. At that point, one of you will die. I hope it's Kendell, but I'll lose no sleep if it's you. I'm sure you understand. And, as I said, should you succeed in this attack and return, I shall honor my pledge to make you a very rich man."

"Far away."

"Yes, yes, far away. We've established that."

Kittins realized Lord Darley was about to bid him farewell. In the moment before that happened, he calculated the odds of getting his hands on any of the weapons before him and successfully killing His Lordship and as many of the other men present as necessary to allow an escape. Vykers might pull it off, he decided, but not himself.

"So," Darley said, "Best of luck, Janks. Make those bastards bleed." With that, His Lordship was gone.

Kittins looked around at the men surrounding him. Wonder which one of you fuckers is the Shaper? "Can I get a little something to eat before I get into this armor?" he asked.

"After," two or three said in unison.

Kittins rolled his shoulders, cracked his neck. "After it is, then."

Rem, House Hawsey

Rem's plan was so creative, he thought, he ought to have been spymaster to the Queen, herself. Except that he enjoyed being seen, recognized and publicly applauded for his work. Apart from those little details, though...

Wratch & Company announced its intention to stage a special play for the coming Fiersday, which turned out to be a holiday of some sort, obliquely related to female fertility. The irony, of course, was not lost on Rem.

So, an unexpected celebration! Another play from Lord Hawsey's resident company! Needless to say, the estate bustled and bubbled with excitement and anticipation. And, in order to ensure maximum turn-out, Rem had chosen the bawdiest comedy in the company's repertoire, Lady Twickenam's Tasty Tarts! The piece had the special added feature of relying heavily upon the use of masks, a fact Rem intended to exploit most cunningly.

When the big day arrived, House Hawsey was practically

exploding with anticipation. Various Hawseys interrupted Rem's work throughout the day, begging for a preview or even the barest detail that might put them one-up on the other members of the family once the play began. Rem responded with a million lies. What does it matter? He asked himself. If I'm not outside the gates by the time the applause dies down, I'll be the next thing that dies, down or otherwise.

One who would not be so easily shuffled off was Her Ladyship. She cornered him in the kitchen and barked at him, "When will you do it?"

"You have my most solemn oath it will be done within the next two sunsets!" Rem exclaimed with great joviality, as if he'd just been commissioned to recite a poem in the market square.

Her Ladyship's face pulled into the most melodramatic pout the actor had ever seen. "Why so long?" She whined.

"Because, my sweet," Rem smiled, making sure that no one else was within earshot, "my declaration of love for you requires a masterpiece, and a masterpiece I shall deliver." He really had no idea what he'd just said, but, damn, it sounded fantastic.

Her Ladyship obviously liked it, too, for all she said in response was, "I can hardly wait!"

Standing backstage, Rem peered through a crack in the scenery and was stunned at the turnout. He'd been expecting a crowd, but every last member of House Hawsey must've been in attendance, up to and including the servants and guards. Well, he reflected, that's what happens when you play to the lowest common denominator.

While Rem and his colleagues made their final preparations, two of the company's more-talented boys went onstage in drag and played a rather lascivious number on a pair of out-size and oddly-shaped flutes, to the unbridled laughter of the audience.

Rem pulled one of his actors aside, an actor who was dressed identically to his boss. "You're sure you can handle this?" He asked Keez.

"Please, Remuel, you wound me!" Keez protested. "Everyone in the company says my Remuel Wratch is even better than the original."

"That's what I wanted to hear," Rem laughed and clapped

the other man on the shoulder. "So, we let them see me take my mask off a few times in Act One, and then you're me 'til I get back from my errand."

Keez nodded. "Yes, got it."

In no time, the lads onstage had finished their japery and the company fiddler began the play's introduction, which was greeted with boisterous applause. On his cue, Rem strode from the wings, did a somersault and ended with his head in lap of a fat woman in the front row...as planned. Rem doffed his mask, allowing one and all to see him, and hastily put it back on for the next bit of foolishness. So it went for the first three scenes of Act One. When Act Two began, Rem escaped out a servants' entrance and was replaced onstage by Keez, who, as promised, offered a most excellent if somewhat effete performance of Remuel Wratch playing the comical Lord Bollocks.

Rem could actually hear the laughter receding behind him as he hired a coach and made for the Fretful Porpentine. Inside the coach, he pulled a small bag from his belt and began altering his appearance with the help of a hand mirror and some stage make-up. He also removed his costume, revealing a completely different set of clothes underneath. As it was dark out, he tossed the pieces of his initial costume out the back of the coach as it careened through the streets. A quarter hour later, when he stepped from the coach, he was another man entirely.

For better or worse, he was unable to locate any of his mission members—no sign of Long, Yendor, Kittins or that fool young man. But improvisation did not threaten him. Assuming a Westies dialect and an awkward demeanor, he approached a card game in progress at a table close-by. Three of the four players looked up at him with varying degrees of haughtiness; the fourth was too preoccupied with his hand to bother.

"Room for another?" Rem asked.

Now, the fourth player did look up and then quickly shot a look to his companions: bumpkin! "Always!" the man said in thoroughly unconvincing magnanimity.

"Grab yerself a chair. Ante's a merchant per hand."

"A whole merchant?" Rem remarked, taking a seat. "You're some serious gamblers, then!"

"We're men," one of the others groused. "Goes without sayin', don't it?"

Within another quarter hour, Rem had lost a week's wages and appeared to have gotten quite drunk. Appeared. A large pile of money sat on the table, the pot for the current hand, and Rem stared at it with wistful yearning.

"Well?" the loudest of the other men growled. "You in, or ain'tcha?"

Rem put on his best pleading look. "I don't have the coin, exactly..."

"Then you're out," one of the others asserted.

"But I do have this fine ring, here." He held up the ring he'd stolen from Her Ladyship and watched it glitter in the light. He noticed it did the same in the eyes of every man at the table.

"Here, now. 'Ow'd someone the likes o' you come by something like that?" said a man Rem had come to think of as Bluffer.

"I just happened to be in the wrong place at the right time," Rem drawled drunkenly. "Came across a couple o' nobles knocking boots —only, o' course, they was barefoot—and as the man in question was unarmed, he couldn't kill me to keep his secret, so he paid me. With this."

Rem's audience didn't know whether to scoff, leer or ask for more details. Finally, the Player broke the silence. "And where was this?"

"Durin' the big festivities on Midsummer's Night. You remember: fireworks was going off, everyone was drinkin' and screwin' in the bushes. I'd had a bit too much, meself, and was lookin' for a private patch o' green to be sick in, and I came across these two in Fishers' Park, down by the river."

If the tale was hard to believe, the ring was not. And Rem gave every indication of being too stupid to have been able to steal it.

"I don't s'pose these nobles had names, did they?" Drinker asked.

"Don't be an idjit," Bluffer scolded. "They got caught makin' the beast wi' two backs. They ain't likely to name themselves, are they?"

"I, uh, did overhear the lady in her passion callin' her lover 'Gelter'," Rem added.

Stinky spat beer all over the cards, the table and the mound of coin at its center. "Gelter fuckin' Radcliffe?"

"No: Gelter fuckin' somebody!" Bluffer joked, to raucous laughter from his mates. "All right, then," he said to Rem. "I want that ring, so you're in. You lose, though, and this is yer last hand."

Of course, Rem lost. "Finish my beer at least?"

"Certainly," Player replied absentmindedly, as he scrutinized the ring. "I know a fence in town can tell me more about this ring."

That was all Rem needed to hear. He drained his beer, looked longingly at the ring one last time and bid his table mates goodbye. "Man's gotta know when to quit!" he said ruefully.

"Ya mean, like, when he's broke?" Bluffer sneered.

"Just like," Rem agreed and headed for the door.

Once outside again, he retrieved his bundled costume, hired another carriage and rushed back to House Hawsey, where he changed into his costume and hid in shadows near the front gate, waiting for the curtain call and ensuing celebrations that would allow him enough cover to sneak back inside. If the guards chanced to question him, he'd claim he'd just left the stage for a little night air and then upbraid them for their inattention whilst on duty.

Soon, very soon, the town's gossip-mongers would begin spreading rumors of an affair between Her Ladyship and Gelter Radcliffe. Gelter would either then attempt to flee, which would only serve to make him look more guilty, or stay put and fiercely deny everything, which wouldn't do anything to mollify Lord Hawsey. And when Her Ladyship began to show...

Rem had only one task left to perform.

As he'd predicted, the post-play party spilled through the main gates and out into the street beyond. In Lunessfor, there was no better status symbol than conspicuous evidence of wildly successful "private" festivities. All the neighbors would now wonder what the occasion of such celebration had been, why they hadn't been invited, and what the secret to such unabashed merriment might be. In this atmosphere of rowdy joviality, Rem had no difficulty regaining the Hawsey courtyard, where, rather fortuitously, he ran into His Lordship. "Your betht work ever!" a drunken Lord Hawsey proclaimed upon seeing the actor.

Best ever? Rem was of two minds about this: on the one hand, such a response boded well for the next phase of his plan; on the other, it pained him personally that he'd been so easily replaced in such an obvious triumph. "Your lordship is most gracious, as ever."

Henton giggled in delight. "Not at all, thir. I thwear thith ithz your betht. I adored the part where Lord Mowbray ithz caught with the piglet!"

Ah, yes. Nothing like lowbrow bestiality jokes to win the day! "Is it the kind of play, do you think, that might bring cheer to her Majesty, the Queen?" There, the seed had been planted.

His Lordship considered the question briefly, before an evil smile came to his lips. "I like it!" he declared. "They'll have to admit you, or rithk the pertheption that her Majethty ith too ill even to lie in bed and enjoy a play. And if they do admit you, you thyould be able to relay the truth of it to me. I like it!" he said again, clearly thinking aloud. "Thith move will help either to curry favor with Her Majethty or, in cathe of the wortht, thpeed her death! We might even be able to thtage a coup from the inthide!" Henton had gotten himself so wound up in his fantasies, he began dancing from toe to toe in excitement. "Make you ready! Prepare your men to depart for the Queenthz cathle."

"At once!" Rem replied, knowing his company had already packed and exulting in the fact that Henton himself had unwittingly agreed to send Wratch & Company out of harm's way before House Hawsey erupted.

Yendor, House Fyne

There was uproar and tumult in House Fyne. One of the guards, a certain 'Moult' by name, had been found dead, face-down on the pavers in His Lordship's garden, having unquestionably fallen from one of the garden's many trees. The assumption was that he'd been attempting to spy on His Lordship and/or other, higher ranking members of the family. But he'd done so in such a bungling manner, it seemed unlikely that spying had been his actual profession. For one thing, he'd been drunk, as evidenced by his odor and by the broken bottle whose fragments the guards had found embedded in his chest. For another, hiding in a tree didn't strike His Lordship as particularly crafty. No, this Moult had to have been a disgruntled employee, seeking redress of some petty grievance by selling Fyne secrets to the other seven Houses. Or, he may have gotten himself into debt, and betraying House Fyne was his only means of earning the gold to extricate himself. Whatever the case, His Lordship and his spymaster would carry out due diligence and question every member of the household, from the mucker to Her Ladyship and everyone in between.

At least this is what Yendor had heard from the other guards, shortly after he'd learned of Moult's death. Yendor had upheld his end of the plan; he'd gotten up at first light with every intention of pissing off the roof. By that time, however, Moult had already gone to it, and Yendor was left wondering how in Mahnus' name he was going to escape before he was questioned and inevitably cracked under pressure, revealing his whole team's mission and condemning himself to torture or worse.

One by one, he saw the other guards summoned to His Lordship's study. One by one, they returned, looking shaken. And they'd been innocent, or innocent of this particular crime, at any rate.

Yendor prayed to the god of lying, in the vain hope there was such an entity and that he or she was disposed to help an old drunk. If not...

Spirk, House D'Escurzy

The feast was, as promised, lavish and spectacular. It was held in a vast room, much brighter and more welcoming than any Spirk had previously seen in House D'Escurzy. The ceiling was so high, it soared above a second-floor balcony that ringed the whole room. Great, tall windows ran along the length of the balcony's southern and western sides, allowing evening sun to flood into the chamber, and although the first floor had many festive torches blazing in decorative sconces, their light was feeble by comparison.

In one corner, a handful of musicians played a lively tune in muted volume, as if they'd been commanded to energize the guests without calling attention to themselves. Across the way, a series of long tables had been set up along the walls in preparation for the banquet. Scores of servants bustled to and fro, placing and filling goblets, setting flatware and otherwise making ready. Around the room itself roamed more D'Escurzys than Spirk had ever imagined, and every last one of them glared at him with angry eyes and happy smiles. He suspected this was not a good sign.

"Begging your pardon, sir, but I think we're fucked," Ron told Spirk out of the side of his mouth.

The new Lord D'Escurzy frowned at his bodyguard.

"What?" Ron asked. "Was it what I said or the way I said it?"

Spirk didn't answer, couldn't. It was all of that, and more. If this group meant him and his companion harm, he doubted there was anything he could do to prevent it. He scanned the crowd, hoping, but found no sign of the Constable, the Mayor or anyone else whose presence might prevent bloodshed. Spirk's anxiety became so powerful a force that he briefly shrieked in terror when the dinner bell was rung, causing everyone in the room to look in his direction with mocking smiles.

Again, the bell rang. This time, a voice came with it. "If your Lordship would care to take your seat, the rest of us can finally attack...this glorious supper!" It was the big-shouldered man Spirk had met a few days earlier, Lord Briedach D'Escurzy. Everyone in the room laughed at his jest—if it was a jest—and began a slow stampede towards the tables. Gods, there were a lot of D'Escurzys and their kin. "Here is your seat, your Lordship," Lord Briedach advised, gesturing to a chair next to his own.

Spirk noticed there was no seat for Ron, as the one that might naturally have gone to his friend was already occupied by...Faenia. "What about my man, here?" Spirk asked.

Briedach offered his most condescending smile. "Servants don't generally dine with their masters. But he can man one of the doorways, if you like."

"But...but..." Spirk protested.

"It's alright," Ron sighed. "I'll put meself in plain sight, your Lordship. You'll be able to see me the whole time."

"But...but..."

"A toast!" Briedach called out. "A toast to our new Head of Family!"

Up and down the tables, goblets were raised in half-hearted salute.

Spirk stared at his own, wondering whether or not it had been poisoned. Briedach, it seemed, could read his mind.

"It's not poisoned, if that's what you're thinking," he said, irritation evident in his voice. "Look." And he took a substantial gulp from Spirk's goblet before plonking it down in front of His Lordship, spilling a bit of its contents onto the tablecloth.

Trembling all the while, Spirk raised the goblet, acknowledged his new family and took a brief sip of wine. When he'd finished and lowered his drink, he again observed the entire assembly staring at him, waiting for instruction. "Er...let's eat," he said.

Now the food came, in wave after wave. Whilst everyone else was preoccupied, Spirk made a careful study of his knife and fork, both of which seemed willfully dull, but also clean. Turning his head discretely left and right, he saw that Faenia and Briedach's utensils were not dull. That worried him. Somehow, though, he was able to sense that almost everything that had been put before him was safe to eat or handle. His plate—a large platter, really—seemed to radiate malicious intent, and he noticed that anything set upon it soon took up the same character. Experimentally, he reached into a nearby breadbasket and brought a thick slice of bread directly before his eyes. Receiving nothing from it but warmth and an enticing odor, he bit off a sizeable hunk. He pretended to make small talk, which, in his case, was very, very small, with Briedach, Faenia and anyone else who might glance his way. At last, he tossed the remainder of his bread onto his platter and had his suspicions confirmed when it, too, went bad (as he thought of it). For the next several minutes, he was able to eat an adequate meal by grabbing things off their serving trays and biting into them before they reached his platter. Eventually, Faenia intervened.

"My lord, it is unseemly for the Head of the Family to snatch his food out of the air. You must wait until you are served. You must be served!"

Unfortunately, Spirk was hypnotized by Faenia's bosom and didn't catch a word of her speech, forcing Briedach to reiterate what his cousin had said.

"You can't be snatching things out of the air, Your Lordship. It's embarrassing. Now, eat off your plate like a civilized man!"

"Uh...I'm full," Spirk proclaimed, as he emerged from his mammary trance.

Briedach laughed a harsh, angry laugh. "You're what? You're *full*? We've just gotten started. We've had cooks working for days on your account."

"Well, I...er...I'm sure I'll want more, later."

"You'll want more *now*," Briedach said through gritted teeth.

In a moment of panic, Spirk looked across the chamber and locked eyes with Ron, who, as promised, was watching the proceedings with grim interest. Suddenly, Ron made a strange gesture with his hands and mouthed something without speaking.

"What?" Spirk asked softly.

"I said you'll eat more now!" Breidach repeated.

Spirk looked over at the man, confused. "Whu...? Huh? I wasn't talking to you, I was..."

Briedach's face turned a dangerous shade of crimson. "I was talking to you, though!"

Except for the musicians, the room had gone quiet. Spirk could hear Briedach breathing heavily, like an ox after pulling the plow on a hot day. As expected, everyone resumed staring in Spirk's direction.

"More wine?" Faenia suggested, extending a jug across Spirk's platter towards her cousin.

"More wine!" Spirk squeaked. "Yes, more wine!" Clumsily, he wrenched the jug out of Faenia's grasp, lost control of it and let it drop onto his platter. Both items broke into shards, spilling wine across the table and down into laps on either side.

Briedach roared in fury, grasped Spirk by the hair, and flung him over the table and out into the middle of the great room's floor. Ron dashed to his master's side, even as the room's other guards moved to block the doors. By the time Spirk was able to sit up, Briedach, Faenia and a host of other D'Escurzys had closed in about him.

"You whoreson idiot! You couldn't go quietly, could you?" Briedach snarled through his spit-sodden moustache.

"Go? O' course I'll go!" Spirk replied.

"I think he means 'die,' milord," Ron whispered in his ear.

"Die?" Spirk squawked, struggling to his feet. His new family had completely encircled him and his companion, leaving no room to maneuver in any direction.

Briedach barked out a harsh laugh. "Yes, die! Lord Titus could level no greater insult to the rest of us than to put a yokel like you in power!"

The room erupted in laughing agreement.

"And I think I'll enjoy killing you with my bare hands!" Briedach reached out towards Spirk's neck, only to be brushed aside by Faenia.

"Please, cuz," she crooned, "there's no need to be so boorish and violent."

Suddenly, Spirk loved the woman.

"No need for violence, I say, when the mere touch of a real woman is enough to make him crumble and blow away like dust!"

More laughter from the crowd. Suddenly, Spirk hated the woman all over again.

"Indeed?" Briedach asked. "One of those, is he?"

Everywhere he looked, Spirk saw sneering piggish or vulpine faces, sniggering at his weakness and impending demise. It was like being surrounded by a bunch of animals that couldn't decide whether to eat or to violate him. Of course, they might do both. To his horror, Faenia continued her advance until her chest brushed against his own.

The room grew quiet, no one so much as breathed, and time

itself seemed to wait upon the moment's outcome.

"Are you wondering, little Shaper, why your magics don't affect me?" Faenia drawled in her most lustful, throaty voice. Her wide eyes directed Spirk's gaze back to her bosom and into her cleavage, where a charm of some sort hung on the slenderest of chains.

Spirk felt his knees begin to wobble something terrible. He had never known such an impossible mixture of desire and fear. Forgotten were His Lordship Briedach, his companion, Ron, or the gawking faces of the extended family D'Escurzy; nothing existed outside the all-consuming hunger he felt for the woman in front of him and the terror he experienced at the thought of giving in to it.

"Nothing to say, milord? Quite chopfallen?" Faenia prodded, in her intimate, husky whisper. Then, louder, "Or do still burn for me, little Shaper?"

To his horror, Spirk felt a hand...down there. Faenia's hand. She giggled in delight. "Ooh!" Raucous laughter reverberated throughout the chamber. "It seems His Lordship *does* burn for me."

He burned for her, all right. Inside and out. A heartbeat later, Faenia's eyes flew open and her mouth pulled into a small 'o' of surprise. And she began to stiffen, to harden. Spirk heard a few murmurings of concern that built into shouts of outright alarm as, little by little, Faenia became translucent. In an instant, Spirk had breathing room and more than so. The crowd that moments ago had been pressing the air right out of his lungs now retreated a good five to ten paces, mortified and transfixed by the spectacle that was unfolding before them. In seconds, Faenia transformed into a crystalline statue of her former self.

"How? What evil is this?" Briedach bellowed, rallying his troops. "What have you done to my cousin, cowardly whelp?"

The tide of D'Escurzys flowed inward again, staring with curiosity at Faenia and rancor at Spirk and his guard. Just as Briedach stepped forward, his fist raised in fury, a loud crack resounded throughout the room. There was a fleeting period of confusion, until someone yelled, "It's Faenia! She's breaking apart!" Another loud crack from the statue confirmed this assertion, and before anyone could decide what to do about it, the woman exploded, blasting the room and everything in it with sparkling, jagged shards of crystal. Briedach went down, his face a mask of absolute confusion. Spirk toppled backwards onto Ron, more out of panic than injury. An unholy symphony of panic and death broke out, comprised of the sounds of people shrieking, yelling, falling to the floor or dropping whatever they held.

In the chaos, Ron spoke forcefully into Spirk's ear. "We have to go, milord. We have to leave, now!"

"Huh?" Spirk moaned in shock.

Grabbing his master under the arms, Ron proceeded to drag him backwards, towards the nearest door. "I say, we must needs go!"

In the hallway, Spirk began to regain his composure. "What happened to the other guards?"

"They're down," said Ron. "Everyone's down. Don't know how we escaped it, frankly. But we can't stay here."

"I know where we can go!" Spirk announced.

Vykers/Arune, In Pursuit

He should have felt the increased burning. For the longest time, Arune told herself that he'd come to expect it as part of her regular scrying, efforts to conceal the group's back-trail, or roust game each evening. But her long-distance manipulation of the A'Shea required a much greater use of magic than she'd had to expend in the past, and, damn it, Vykers should have noticed. Then she told herself that the pain of his wound made him numb to other discomforts, and the extra she added through shaping was negligible by comparison. But that couldn't be true, either.

On top of all this, there were the efforts, large and small, that she'd made to slow Vykers down, so that Aoife might reach him before the coming conflict. The great cat, for example, had come by on her invitation; such creatures could not be compelled. Arune wasn't sure what she expected from the encounter, but it sure as all hells wasn't a five-minute sniff session and a fare-thee-well. Yet, she couldn't risk taking more obvious measures for fear of angering her host.

Thus, with each passing day, it became more evident that Aoife would not catch up with Vykers in time, that the Reaper might well have to face his greatest test since the End-of-All-Things without any additional help or hope of healing.

Arune could only think of one last thing to try. If Vykers found out, it could well be the last thing the Shaper *ever* tried.

Aoife, In Pursuit

The A'Shea had troubles of her own. The desperate scramble after the Reaper had brought her no closer to rejoining or even spotting him, and her mystical and natural resources were fast nearing their limits. Even her horse, despite the A'Shea's constant ministrations, was almost finished.

In a fit of despondency, Aoife led her mount into a small grove of trees, slid from its saddle and threw herself down on a patch of grass. She pulled a water skin from one of her robe's many pockets and shared half its remaining water with the mare, before downing the rest herself in three great swallows. In frustration, she threw the empty container into the dirt.

What was she doing? How, in Alheria's name, had she convinced herself to chase that beast, Tarmun Vykers, halfway across the world, through lands she knew nothing about and from which she might expect no help or mercy? And for what? For Vykers' sake? What was he to her or she to him that this made any sense? Whether he meant to save or to kill the Queen made little difference to the poor and suffering, to whom Aoife ought to have been tending all this while. Surely, Alheria hadn't empowered Aoife with the skills she had for the sole purpose of chasing after a violent brute like the Reaper? To be an instrument of a god was exhausting, aggravating work—especially when the god in question remained so aloof, so remote. What was it Alheria expected of Aoife? How could she best be of service?

Grappling with these conundrums, the A'Shea fell asleep.

Aoife.

???

Aoife. I need to speak with you. Let me in.

Aoife understood she was still asleep, that no one was literally speaking to her. Was this Alheria, then? Had her prayers finally been answered? No. This had a more familiar flavor— the arcane tang of Tarmun Vykers and his...Shaper. *What do you want? Is Tarmun suffering?*

Whether he is or is not, it's become clear you cannot help him.

I most certainly can, Shaper. If I can reach him. Who are you to try and stop me?

This was met by a short, agitated laugh and then, *Stop you? Woman, I have been helping you every step of the way.*

Say you so? Aoife asked, astonished. *And why would you want to do that? Do you think me unaware of your dislike for me?* The Shaper said nothing, so the A'Shea continued. *Do you think I didn't notice your attempts to burn me whenever I touched the Reaper?*

It's true, the Shaper sighed. *I did that. And I am sorry. Things were...different...then.*

And now?

There is a tremendous battle ahead and, despite our combined talents, you cannot get here in time to be of help.

Are you a seer, then? Aoife asked.

Would that I were, the Shaper replied. *No, I cannot see the future, cannot say for certain whether Vykers will triumph or...*

Or die.

Just so.

Without knowing why, Aoife suddenly comprehended the Shaper's predicament. *And if he dies, you die.*

Yes.

Then why were you resistant to my efforts to help him for so long?

Because I thought you an unnecessary distraction.

Aoife's belly began to flutter in anxiety. *A distraction? How a distraction?*

Because he...fancies you. And I was afraid that might get him killed.

It was hard to focus, hard to breathe as deeply as she wanted. *How...how would that get him killed, as you say?*

Aoife, the Shaper said softly, almost lovingly, *Tarmun Vykers was made for one purpose: destruction. It's what he does best, what he enjoys most...at least, that was true until he met you. Whenever you're around, he's...conflicted.*

And if he is, how is this bad?

Tarmun Vykers is poison. He exists only to kill those worse than himself. If he forgets that....if his purpose is diluted with...with love, for instance, he may be vulnerable by being less effective.

Aoife wanted to scoff at the Shaper, reject her arguments with some sort of clever dodge, but she found she could not. *What is your name?*

Arune.

A shock. *A woman's name,* Aoife remarked coldly.

And a woman I once was. But you have nothing to fear from me, A'Shea. Then, *Aoife.*

After a lengthy pause, Aoife asked, *What would you have me do?*

I don't know. I simply do not know. Short of catching up with us, is there anything else you can think of that might prove helpful?

I will....meditate on it.

Do so, Arune responded. *And be well, until fate reunites us all again.*

Is Tarmun well? Aoife called out, *Has his strength held out?*

But the Shaper had gone.

A strange darkness descended upon the A'Shea in her sleep after that, an almost-familiar sense of the Fey folk, the Children of Nar, mingled with energies and emotions beyond her ken. The awkward, nervous fluttering in her gut at the news of Vykers' affection for her became a deeper, more purposeful rustling, a thing dimly remembered but now stark and clear in her mind's eye: Aoife was birthing again.

Kittins, House Blackbyrne

The whole city seemed on edge somehow, like an animal in the hours before an earthquake. Something was coming.

Kittins was going to be a part of that something, he knew,

even if he died in the next hour or so. An assault on one of the Great Eight could not but result in repercussions for the other seven and, by extension, the city and crown.

Lord Darley's map had been impressively detailed and accurate, leading Kittins to the perfect spot to await his cue. As he'd been promised, a noisy collection of revelers accumulated outside the main gate of House Blackbyrne and grew and grew until its numbers became impossible to ignore. Several guards emerged from the estate and tried to encourage the partiers to move along peaceably, but the crowd's continued growth made the task nigh onto impossible. Just when it looked as if the guards might have to adopt more persuasive measures, a small explosion boomed through the night, accompanied by loud shouts of anger and alarm. This was the second, more-threatening diversion Darley had promised.

In the confusion, the black-clad Kittins bolted from the shadows in which he'd been hiding and approached the south wall of the Blackbyrne compound. He challenged himself to be over the wall in less than a minute. With a great heave, he tossed his grappling over up and over and dragged it back until it found purchase, a far trickier proposition than most people assumed. In fact, he was forced to pull it several feet to the left and back again to the right before it finally snagged on something well enough to support his weight.

Someone in Lord Darley's employ must have caught a glimpse of Kittins, because the celebrants at the front gate instantly became alarmingly belligerent, improving the quality and duration of their diversion substantially.

Kittins cracked a grin, flew up the wall as fast as he could. Before reaching the top, he unfurled a small, heavy rug he'd carried with him and laid it over the edge, a precaution against the iron or ceramic shards defenders often placed as deterrents atop such walls. Climbing onto and over the top, Kittins saw no one in sight, which verified that the estate's guards were otherwise engaged. Working quickly, he wrenched the grappling hook free and re-coiled the rope, stashing both behind a nearby potted plant. An oil lamp burned in a sconce not ten feet from Kittins' location. He briefly considered using it to start a fire, perhaps burning the place to the ground, but remembered that the last time he'd tried something along those lines, and thought better of it. Instead, he tossed the lamp into the plant and snuffed it with dirt.

A voice challenged him from behind. He grabbed a handful of potting soil, spun and threw it, even as he drew his sword with his other hand. The house guard before him ducked sideways to avoid the dirt, which might have seemed a clever move in the moment, but which subsequently gave Kittins a much-needed second to close with him. One strong smash with his sword and Kittins beat down the man's parry and ricocheted his weapon up into the defender's face. It was over before it really got started.

There was a breezeway of sorts that followed the south wall westward, towards the back of the estate, and Kittins ran along it, looking for the door shown on Darley's map. But there was no door. So much for accuracy. For whatever reason, the Blackbyrnes had renovated this side of the mansion and eliminated the door. Unless the details of the map outside the estate had been fact-based and those on the inside fabricated, which meant either that His Lordship had purchased a bad map from an unreliable source, or...Darley didn't actually care what occurred once Kittins had gotten inside. Some twenty paces ahead, the wall on his right came to an end, while the outer wall, on his left, continued into the darkness. There was open space ahead, and Kittins thought he heard the sound of voices lowered in close conversation. Whoever it was seemed surprisingly unconcerned about the "attack" on the estate's north side or the riotous gang at the main gates. Kittins slowed, peered around the corner and discovered an ornamental garden. From here, he couldn't make out the least noise of trouble anywhere else. Instead, he heard the gentle tinkling of wind chimes, the splashing of water in fountains, and the rustling of leaves in the breeze. And the unmistakable sounds of desperate, furious sex. Well, that explained a lot.

He also spied, at last, a door on the building's western side. And beyond this building and across a narrow footpath, a second structure. On a hunch, he stayed low and crept towards the far building; it made sense that the family's more-important members would lodge in the estate's innermost dwellings, away from the racket and potential danger of the neighborhood's main streets. The lovers, oblivious to all else, continued their ridiculous cacophony of grunts, groans and gasps in the darkness off to Kittins' left. He had hoped to take a quick peek into the doorway on his right as he approached and passed, just to be sure no one lurked there, but instead encountered two fully armed guards, as shocked at his sudden appearance as he was of theirs. Evidently, they'd been eavesdropping on the lovers. When they caught sight of him, though, the closest man lunged from the doorway in an attempt to knock Kittins off his feet before he could bring his weapon around. The second man grabbed his crossbow off the floor and started cranking it, even as he yelled for help at the top of his voice.

No turning back now, Kittins thought. He spun with the impact of the first guard and flung the man into the bushes, then allowed his momentum to carry him back around towards the second guard, whom he slashed across the belly. Blood spewed from the man's gut, but he continued screaming for aid until Kittins hacked through his neck and pushed his corpse back into the hallway. There was no point in trying to run or hide, now. He could hear armored boots stomping towards him from within the building. No one approached from his left or right, and the lovers had wisely fallen silent behind him. There was nothing for it: he'd been sent here to kill as many of Blackbyrne's family and staff as possible, and he didn't suppose it mattered much which ones he started with. In the back of his mind, he was dimly aware that he was travelling ever further down the road of damnation, a journey he'd begun the first time he entered House Gault. But he didn't—couldn't—see any way back to the man he'd once been, or had at least aspired to be. Now, he lived only in the moment, fought only to live from breath to breath.

Four guards came into view at the end of the hallway, having rounded a corner Kittins couldn't see from his vantage point. Four. Fuck! Their numbers were doubling every time he encountered them. He considered himself a formidable fighter, but he didn't like his chances if this trend continued. In a flash, he grabbed the second guard's discarded crossbow and fired it into the oncoming group, missing the man in front he'd intended to hit and instead picking off one of the three behind him, who went down in a heap. The survivors showed no sign of panic, however, as they fanned out as much as the generous hallway would allow and flatly dared Kittins to attack them. He understood: if they got him inside, he'd be much easier to surround than he was in his current position outdoors.

A scrabbling to his rear alerted Kittins just in time that the man he'd thrown in the bushes had recovered and was preparing to strike. The big man ducked and rotated forty-five degrees to his right; a sword whooshed by his head. He could still make the far building if he ran for it. With a burst of speed, he surged across the footpath, ever closer to his objective. He was probably going to die; he'd already reconciled himself to that. But if that was the case, he wanted to take someone of importance with him, someone that House Blackbyrne found indispensable. He'd been ordered to make certain that person was Kendell, but, in a pinch, he'd take anyone of name or rank. It wasn't as if his shade would be compelled to apologize to Lord Darley if Kittins fucked up.

He reached the new building and ran to the left, on instinct. Darley's map had already failed him once, and he no longer trusted it. Left, though, was a bad choice, as it turned out. Two more guards came running at him from that direction. A quick backward glance revealed that Kittins had no time to retreat: the other four guards were nearly within striking distance. He wasn't panicked: all of these men were smaller, slighter than he. Still, it was frustrating as all hells to be running around in the unfamiliar warren of another estate, not knowing when, where or if he'd find the man he sought. Kittins bull rushed into the two oncoming guards, slapping aside their weapons and sending both men tumbling like children's toys. As he passed through them, he thought, Six behind me, now. Not good. He'd have to start fighting soon, reduce their numbers, or he would find himself in the shit for sure. Ten feet away, he saw what he'd been looking for: a doorway leading inside this second building. Wasting no time, he barreled through the archway and crashed into a large, wooden double door, blasting the half on his right completely off its hinges and knocking it back into the hallway beyond. He wasn't remotely surprised to find more guards, although he wondered who in Mahnus' name they had left to deal with Darley's two diversions. What was it now, ten, eleven guards he'd encountered? Picking up speed, he raced towards the latest threats and engaged them as quickly as possible.

This time, there only three—only! Kittins raised the sword in his right hand and pulled a long knife from his belt with his left. The closest guard wore the most armor and was wielding a mace. Kittins had only contempt for mace-wielding buffoons. With a sword, even a nick could kill if you got lucky. A nick from a mace? A lot harder to accomplish and nowhere near as deadly. But the man was carrying a round shield in his off-hand, which meant he might avoid death long enough for the six at Kittins' back to arrive. Again, Kittins tried to trample over or through his adversaries. The man in front toppled backwards into the two men behind him, knocked them down, but managed to stay on his feet. Kittins came in, swinging. The guard blocked Kittins' sword with his shield and parried Kittins' knife with the haft of his mace, but the bigger man kept driving with his legs, until at last the guard tripped over the men behind him. Kittins chopped at the fellow's mace arm and took it right off, between the shoulder and elbow. The men underneath him struggled to regain their feet, and the big man hacked them both to death within seconds, before bounding over their bodies and charging further into the building.

Somewhere along the line, he'd taken a puncture wound to his upper left thigh and been gashed along his right forearm, just above his gauntlet, but below the cuffs of his chain shirt. He might've worn more armor, but he found the full suit far too cumbersome for his tastes and fighting style. Anyway, the wounds he sustained so far were of nominal importance. So far.

Soon, he came to a stairway that went both up and down from his current level. He chose the former, bounding up the stairs two at a time, harried along by the shouts and bellowing of his pursuers. He ignored the second floor altogether and decided to head for the top, however high that might be. It seemed to

Kittins that the wealthy and powerful favored looking down on cities and, thus, the people who inhabited them from great heights, as if they were raptors looking for prey. Or vultures looking for carrion.

At the third-floor landing, he encountered a nobleman, ignobly trying to run away. Kittins grabbed the fellow by the scruff of his neck and, without so much as a 'by your leave,' tossed him through one of the many windows that adorned the stairwell. The man screamed for longer than seemed possible, given the two-story drop. Below, the racket raised by the House guards subsided suspiciously. Kittins surmised there must be another route to the top floor, and likely his pursuers were looking to head him off or ambush him. With his need to rush reduced, Kittins slowed down, climbed the stairs more carefully, and made a special effort to visually explore all possible avenues of escape or attack.

The stairs concluded at the fourth floor, which was so silent, Kittins was all but certain he was alone. He stopped for a moment, rested, and readjusted his armor and his grip on his weapons. He stood at a tee; the hallway continued off to his right and left. There were doors in both directions, some of which stood open. Of these, some were dark and others glowed with lights that suggested they were either occupied or recently had been. Kittins thought back to the Baby Butcher's house. He'd gone right into trouble when he should have gone left to salvation. Fuck it, he thought, and went right again. He listened at the first closed door and heard nothing. That didn't mean it was empty, however, and he couldn't very well leave it unchecked at his back while he moved on. Carefully, he turned the knob and eased the door open a crack. Then he became disgusted with himself. He was not a skulker and wouldn't act like one. He raised his weapons and kicked the door in. The room stayed dark, was clearly empty. As he turned to explore the next room, he was greeted by the sight of several men standing quietly in the hallway ahead of him. How had they gotten there so stealthily?

"Skulkers!" he spat.

There was laughter behind him. More men.

Kittins dove into the room, rolled across the floor, crashed into a table or some such (it was hard to tell in the dark) and leapt to his feet. He couldn't fight ten or more men in the closed quarters of the hallway, but maybe he could gradually reduce their numbers as they came through the door.

Two men stepped into the door's frame, one high and one low, and fired crossbow bolts into the room. One of the shots went high and wide, hitting the back wall somewhere near the ceiling. The other shot was a good deal closer to Kittins and shattered a ceramic something-or-other that had been on the aforementioned table. The crossbowmen disappeared while they reloaded, and then someone called out to Kittins.

"You must be the most incompetent thief in the kingdom!"

He wouldn't rise to the bait. To do so would reveal his position, and denying that he was a thief would help his opponents in determining what he was.

"Either that, or you're the world's worst assassin," the voice continued.

It occurred to Kittins that maybe he was breathing too loudly, so he struggled to calm himself. Sooner or later, they'd get some light in the room and he'd be dead. Then he heard men coming in through a side door from an adjoining room he hadn't foreseen.

"Fact is, you've gone and got yourself cornered. What kinda idiot runs to the top floor of an enemy's mansion and tries to hide in a corner?"

All this prattle was misguided: Kittins would never give himself away. Might be they knew that, however. Might be, this was just some attempt to stall until…until…the House Shaper showed up.

Kittins exploded from his position and slashed away at the men on his left flank like a man butchering a steer. He rained blows from long knife and sword upon the surprised guards with the full force of his considerable strength. Caught flatfooted, they stumbled backwards, two of them dropping almost immediately. The bolt from a crossbow twanged off his right pauldron and struck one of his opponents in the face. The man didn't even have time to scream.

"Cease firing, dammit!" the voice yelled. "You've hit the wrong man!"

Seeing that the side door was almost within reach, Kittins redoubled his efforts to destroy everyone between him and escape. There were three men, now, and at least one of them seemed completely unmanned by Kittins' ferocity. "I didn't sign up for this shit!" was a phrase the Captain had often heard from cowards in the army, when a particular scrap turned out to be more than they'd expected. Kittins would be doing House Blackbyrne a favor by killing this white-livered nothing. The problem was that the two men between Kittins and the coward were giving him all he could handle, and he feared every second that passed brought the Shaper closer to entering the fray. The big man had no qualms about facing scores of steel-wielding enemies, but he sure as all hells had no interest in being paralyzed, set afire, or frozen like a block of ice.

Finally, he killed the man on his left with a swift uppercut to the groin. The long knife sank in its full foot-and-a-half; Kittins gave it a wrenching twist for good measure—eliciting bloodcurdling screams from his victim—while he fended off the man on his right with his sword. Suddenly, he had both hands, both weapons available to him, and he offered too many blows to be countered. In no time, the last of the brave men went down, leaving no one but the coward between Kittins and the hope of freedom. He was further spurred by the sound of hard, heavy feet tromping into the room behind him. With one bold push, he shoved the coward backwards through the doorway and ran over the man's prone body, breaking something in the process.

This new room had a window, through which moonlight fairly blazed (in comparison to the room he'd just left), and Kittins saw that he only succeeded in buying himself a few extra heartbeats, at best. He still had men at his back and more could come in from the hallway at any moment.

Spirk, House D'Escurzy

The refuge Spirk had in mind, as it happened, was underneath

Lord Titus' bed. Much to Ron's chagrin.

"You can't be serious!" he exclaimed. "We ain't safe here!"

"I know that!" Spirk laughed nervously.

Ron took a deep breath, let it out slowly. "How'd you do that, anyhow?"

"I dunno, really. Might be Pellas' again."

"Pellas? The great wizard?"

"Yeah," Spirk sighed. "We was friends."

Ron rolled onto his side, the better to see Spirk's face. "Truly?"

"Truly."

A faint clamor sounded somewhere off in the house.

"We can't stay here," Ron reminded his master.

"We won't. There's a special door under here that only Titus knew about."

"Only Titus and you," Ron corrected.

Spirk bobbed his head in affirmation and smacked it on the underside of the bed. "Alheria's balls!" he cried, eliciting a chuckle from Ron.

"That's a new one," he said.

When Spirk pivoted towards the head of the bed, he inadvertently kicked his companion in the face, causing Ron to develop a nasty nosebleed. "Alheria's balls!" Ron swore.

"Sorry. Did I hurt you?"

"Long as you don't turn me into no statue, I'll be good."

"I don't think I could do that again if I tried," Spirk answered, fiddling around with the wall near his face.

"That's a comfort," said Ron.

A sudden draft of cool air swept across both men, and Ron realized Spirk had opened the secret door he'd spoken of.

"It ain't real big," Spirk warned. "'Cause Lord Titus wasn't real big. We'll have to shimmy our way along on our bellies."

As he was still struggling to staunch the flow from his nose, Ron didn't have time to object. "Just let's get out of here," he pleaded.

"Here we go!"

It was a very black, very tight crawl, and it seemed to go on longer than was possible, even for an estate the size of House

D'Escurzy. Eventually, the passage widened enough to allow both men to crawl on their hands and knees. Ron supposed it had been designed that way intentionally, to reduce the number of possible pursuers. But he couldn't figure out how it had been created in the first place.

"Oh," said Spirk, "that's Shapers' work."

"Something you could do?" Ron panted, a bit winded from the exertion.

"No, no," Spirk replied dismissively. "I ain't a Shaper, really."

"Tell that to Lady Faenia," Ron said. He'd thought his master might find that amusing, but Spirk said nothing in response.

Without warning, Spirk came to a halt and Ron stumbled right into his backside.

"Wall, here."

"You can open it, right?" Ron asked, a hint of desperation in his voice.

"I hope so."

And then there was a crack of light and a scent of flowers.

The 'door' opened into a little-used alley, a good two hundred or more paces from the eastern wall of the D'Escurzy estate. In the distance, the two men could hear shouting, but it was difficult to tell whether the tone was one of anger or joy.

Terrified of being apprehended, Ron swung his gaze left, right, left, right. "Where do we go now?"

"Do you know the Fretful Porpentine?" Spirk asked.

"That a tavern, is it?"

"And a good 'un."

"Well," Ron said, "we can maybe pass the night there. But we'll need to leave town by sun up. There's no telling what the survivin' D'Escurzys'll do to us if they find us."

"Have you ever been to Teshton?"

Ron thought for a moment. "Teshton? Can't say as I have."

"I know a place we can go."

"Good enough, then. The Fretful Porpentine for tonight, and tomorrow it's Teshton."

TEN

Rem, the Queen's Castle

It took much longer than Rem had anticipated to convince the Queen's functionaries to admit him and the rest of his company, even with the ostentatious and highly perfumed letter Henton had sent along by way of introduction. Yet, the royal staff was distrustful, as was their wont, perhaps, or their charge. After nearly an hour's wrangling, a dour bald man in robes appeared, snapped up the letter and glowered at Rem.

"It is nearly midnight," the man said flatly. "An unusual time of day to present yourself at her Majesty's door."

Rem cleared his throat. "Well, yes, we…er…"

"I understand you are an actor, but let us dispense with the charades for the time being. You were initially employed by one Colonel Bailis, were you not?"

Rem could think of no clever way around the truth in this instance, so he confessed. "Aye."

"Follow me," the bald man commanded.

"With pleasure!" Rem answered gamely.

Kittins, House Blackbyrne

He had come to kill this Kendell fellow and, beyond that, to wreak whatever havoc he might before the Blackbyrnes killed him in turn. Things weren't turning out as he'd planned, though. So far, he'd only managed to kill one scrawny and nameless nobleman and several guards. Oh, and he'd gotten himself pinned down in a moonlit dressing room (from the look of it).

He'd considered starting a fire—another fire—but had thought better of it. Now, he second-guessed himself. A fire might cause the most panic and confusion, allowing him time to evade his pursuers long enough to find Kendell.

He waited for an instant, expecting reinforcements to come storming into this new room from the hallway, but none came. The men at his back kept advancing, however. Kittins slid his knife into his belt, ran for the door and yanked it open. It seemed no attack was forthcoming. Before running into the hall, he glanced backwards and saw two men following him, neither of whom were carrying...

Crossbows fired away at him as soon as he stepped fully outside the room. This time, he wasn't so lucky, as one of the bolts slammed into his right hip. How the other bolt missed him defied comprehension. Rather than running away, Kittins took the initiative and charged the bowmen. He could see the fear in their eyes, as they considered whether or not to take precious seconds to reload or to drop their crossbows and draw their swords. Their indecision, though short lived, cut short their lives. Kittins wasn't fuckin' around. He roared into them, his frustration and, now, his pain giving him strength. He killed one of the bowmen with a backhanded slash from his long sword. He crushed the other man's skull when he brought his sword back around, smashing the pommel into the man's unprotected forehead.

Agony bloomed in his upper back, near his shoulder. He'd been hit by a throwing knife. Kendell! Without bothering to turn and confirm this, Kittins ran/limped back the way he'd originally come, towards the stairs. If he could just get far enough ahead, he might be able to hide and ambush...

Another knife hit him on the same side, this time in the ass. Thank Mahnus for his chain shirt. The knives were penetrating, but not too deeply. Face to face, the other man could probably pick more vulnerable targets. Kittins didn't intend to give him that opportunity. He gained some distance when Kendell and his men stopped to assess the two bowmen. He'd come up these stairs two at a time, but he went down in threes and fours. On the third-floor landing, he found what he was looking for:

a burning lamp. Ripping it off the wall, he tossed it into the first open door he found and continued down the third-floor hallway. He came upon another lamp and did the same at the next open door. Again, Kendell threw a knife at him, but either the distance was too great or the man was distracted by the first lamp Kittins had thrown; in any case, the knife missed. The big man grabbed the next lamp he saw and threw it behind him, in the middle of the hallway floor. He took a second to watch the flaming oil splatter and spread before he moved on. The knives stopped coming and the sound of footsteps faded a bit, so Kittins chanced a look backwards. The fire barrier had stopped his pursuers, but he still needed to kill Kendell. Not because Darley had commanded him to—Kittins didn't give two shits for that anymore—but because it was the greatest challenge within reach and because, he had to admit, he looked forward to the violence of it.

"'Fraid of a little fire, Knife Boy?" he yelled out.

"'Knife Boy?'" Kendell scoffed. "That the best you got, ya stupid bastard?"

Sometimes, trying to goad a person into doing something backfired, and the goader became the goadee. Kittins wasn't having it. "Oh, I'm the stupid one, am I? How many o' your men have I sent to it, and I'm still free, aren't I? Looks to me like you're the idiot, here."

Kittins heard some mumbling, an exchange of orders or some such, and then Kendell dove through the now-roaring flames and scrambled to his feet, coming up with blades in both hands.

"Ah," Kittins smiled. "Good. It's you I came for, anyway."

Kendell seemed nonplussed for a moment and then shrugged. "As you wish. You've only got a couple o' minutes 'til my crew returns with our Shaper, anyway. Best make it good."

Kittins waded in, his sword and long knife in position to deflect anything thrown at him. "Have at you, then!" he roared.

The smaller man did, indeed, get off a couple of knives before his adversary reached him, but neither was able to penetrate the man's defenses. Hand to hand, then. Kendell tried circling to his right, so he wouldn't have the flames at his back. Kittins lunged to his left, to block the move. With astonishing speed, Kendell tossed a blade at the big man's midriff and pulled another. Still spinning from the momentum of his leap, the knife skittered off Kittins' side and thudded, hilt-first, into the wall, opposite. He swept his long knife upwards towards his opponent's face, more to unnerve and unbalance the man than with any hope of actually hitting him. Meantime, he hacked overhand with his sword, aiming to separate the man's shoulder from his neck. Kendell ducked out of the way of the long knife and crossed his own blades to parry the bigger man's sword. Simultaneous with this, he kicked out with his right foot in a bid for Kittins' family jewels. In response, Kittins brought his long knife around and down, swiping at the other man's leg. The kick had been a feint, however, and Kendell launched yet another knife at his assailant—this time, in the direction of the man's face.

This one hit home, piercing through the cheek on the ruined side of Kittins face and jutting out his now bloodied mouth. Kittins made an enormous sweep with his sword, pushing the smaller man away, in order to gain a few seconds to remove the blade.

"Enough o' this bullshit!" Kittins slurred. He tossed his weapons and charged at his enemy.

Hand to hand was one thing; getting into a wrestling match with the big bastard was something else, entirely, and Kendell wanted no part of it. He panicked for the briefest moment, and the big man was on him. Kittins punched him in the face, and Kendell felt something in his jaw crack. The next thing he knew, the brute was grappling for his hands, and, without his hands, Kendell understood he was as good as dead. He tried slashing at the bigger man's hands and forearms in a series of too-quick-to-see blows, but Kittins' gauntlets made it hard to score a satisfying hit. Then Kittins got a hold of Kendell's left wrist and wrenched it as hard as he could in the opposite direction of the joint's natural movement. Kendell heard another snap. In the second that the big man took to bask in his victory, Kendell put a dagger in his left thigh to the hilt. He'd been aiming for the femoral artery and missed; still, he got Kittins' attention.

"You weaselly little shit!" Kittins smashed his body into the smaller man's, pinning him to the wall, knocking the breath out of him. Kittins then bashed his head into Kendell's face, breaking his nose and further damaging his jaw. While the Chief of Security was stunned, Kittins finally got a hold of his right hand and snapped a number of his fingers.

"The fuck?" Kittins gasped. A sharp, blazing pain raged in his gut. He risked a look down and saw that the other man had stabbed him with some sort of spring-loaded blade from the gauntlet of his broken left wrist. It was a serious damned wound, the worst he'd gotten so far. He didn't have time to worry about it, though, because he could just make out the sounds of more men approaching beyond the flames. He spat blood in Kendell's face, pulled his head out from the wall and drove it back again with all the force he could muster. The back of the other man's head collapsed and a flood of bloody fluid gushed out his mouth and nose. Kittins let him slide down the wall, and then he bolted for the nearest open doorway.

As it happened, this room was lit, but unoccupied. It was a small, secondary kitchen with a large cupboard and what appeared to be a garbage chute. Kittins slammed the room's door behind himself and dragged the cupboard over to stall his pursuers even longer. He knew it was unwise to pull arrows, knives and the like without bandaging himself, but he didn't have the time to tend his wounds properly and, anyway, he hoped the blood—his and his enemy's—that now covered him almost completely would serve the purpose he intended. A loud banging erupted on the other side of the door, but Kittins ignored it. Instead, he stripped naked, rubbed the blood over as much of himself as he could and strode towards the garbage chute. Without another thought, he yanked the door open and dove into the dark, rancid space before him. It was, as expected, a terribly tight fit, but untold years' worth of rotting detritus nevertheless greased his passage and, after a few seconds rough passage through the chute, Kittins found himself free-falling through open air. A moment later, he splashed into cold, pervasive darkness, too tired and disoriented even to tread water.

Mardine, Captive

When the bastard came 'round again, Mardine pretended to be grateful for the attention. Men were suckers that way; if you told them they were unusually strong or brave or handsome or special in any way whatsoever, they believed it and started to put on airs. It went straight to their heads. And that meant they could be manipulated.

It was evening, again. Jaddo only came by at that time, perhaps because those with him—and Mardine had discovered there were more than just Nelby and Tresa; she could hear them—were preoccupied with the evening meal, or drinking themselves stupid, or whatever else it was they did to while away the time. Perhaps Nelby was busy cooking, which allowed Jaddo a few minutes for mischief. Whatever the case, he'd found his way to Mardine's wagon once more and managed to "accidentally" grope her twice or thrice before speaking a word.

"I 'magine yer a wild one 'twixt the sheets, bein' a giant and all, eh?"

It was difficult feigning a blush, but, in the gloaming, Mardine pulled it off well enough. "Might be," she breathed, bashfully. "But I've not had much experience of late."

Jaddo ogled her with his yellow eyes. "I 'magine that's as rough for a woman as a man..."

"You've no idea."

"I mean, for a man, you go long enough without and you're like to stick it any-old-wheres."

That's true for dogs and boars and rats, Mardine thought. But some men have more restraint. "It's the same for us women," she lied.

Jaddo grinned, his tobacco-stained teeth jutting out like a row of neglected tombstones. "Might be, we could take care of each other's needs..." He said, letting his voice trail off suggestively.

"Yes?" Mardine asked, trying to sound hopeful, but feeling nauseous at the thought of it.

"I figure we got some time right now, when everyone else is at supper."

She had him. "I'd want to get cleaned up a bit. A woman wants to look and smell right."

"O' course," Jaddo smirked. "We been travelling along the Little Dilber. It's a river. I can lead you down there, get you cleaned up and we can get acquainted, like."

"Oh," Mardine panted, "I can hardly wait."

Jaddo helped her up off the wagon bed and onto her feet, pointing a crossbow at her the whole time. "No tricks, now. I can't kill you with this, but I can make you wish you was dead."

"No, no. No tricks."

Jaddo led her towards the river by a circuitous route that avoided the camp, although once Mardine stood up (on shaky legs), she was able to see the fire. Halfway to the river, she got a good look at her captors and was stunned to see a lot of familiar faces belonging to people who had given her clues—the peddler and his wife, an "innkeeper," and several others. So, it was a conspiracy, then. The whole group had assembled to steal her daughter and deceive Mardine. But why?

"I'm not surprised that Nelby can't satisfy a man like you," Mardine whispered.

"Nelby? That git? I've never 'ad 'er and wouldn't want to. Girl's like a starved chicken!"

"But didn't the two of you plan this whole thing?" Mardine asked as she neared the river.

"Me and Nelby?" Jaddo laughed contemptuously. "Not on your life! Tresa's ten times as clever and fifty as appealing. Still," he said, "man needs something new once in a while, eh?"

Mardine was devastated. She'd falsely accused Nelby of stealing Esmine, when in reality, it appeared to have been Jaddo and Tresa all along. Mardine faced Jaddo. "I can't really undress with my hands shackled behind my back."

"I'll take your skirts and leggin's off," Jaddo said. "Yer dugs don't need cleaning, or, if they do, I'm the one'll be cleaning 'em!" He cackled as he set down his crossbow.

But as Jaddo began unwrapping her skirts, Mardine fell onto him, pinning him to the stones of the river bed with her great weight. He screamed, but the sound was muffled by Mardine's body. She rose enough to allow her crushing momentum and crashed back to the ground. Jaddo tried to time his screams to her risings, but by the third time she fell upon him, he had no strength left with which to complain. Once he lost consciousness, Mardine stomped him to death in seconds, reducing his head to so much jelly.

As long as men were ruled by their pricks, they'd be inferior to thinking women.

Mardine rooted around in Jaddo's foul-smelling, blood drenched clothing until she found the keys to her shackles. It took almost more patience than she possessed, but she managed to free herself.

She'd killed her most obnoxious persecutor, but the most dangerous, possibly, remained alive in the person of Tresa. In addition, there was a host of other folk around the fire that, one way or another, Mardine would have to deal with before she and her daughter were truly free to escape. Giants were big, yes, but capable of remarkable stealth when necessary. With utmost care, Mardine headed for the shadows beneath the trees, just beyond the fire's reach. Sooner or later, someone would come looking for Jaddo; Mardine needed to act before that occurred. Moving more slowly than she could bear, the giantess worked her way around the fire, at one point even dashing across the path, in order to get an accurate assessment of the numbers she faced. Gods, there were at least twelve people and maybe more, if they had someone guarding Esmine. Nelby was nowhere in evidence, which suggested that she might be the one watching Esmine, still a part of the conspiracy. Or she might be dead, killed in the effort to save Esmine. It was all conjecture at this point.

And the wagons? Why hadn't they drawn them up in a circle? And who was watching them? Surely, this group wasn't foolish enough to leave its wagons unattended, which of course, meant there were yet more folks for whom Mardine had to account. Once she'd gotten about three-quarters of the way 'round the fire, she finally spied the wagons, parked in a line along the path, stretching off into the night. Huh, so: her captors were not so bright, after all. Mardine decided to work her way through the trees until she'd reached the farthest wagon and then check them, one by one, 'til she reached the wagon nearest the campfire.

That was her plan, anyway. She failed, as most people would under such circumstances, to consider the possible proximity of wasps, so that when she stepped onto their enormous underground hive, hiding in shadows was no longer an option. As big as she was, they would still kill her if she didn't get away from them and quickly. Recognizing that her choices were limited, Mardine chose to lead them into the party around the fire, making them accidental allies instead of her potential executioners. Although wasps generally don't like to fly after dark, their nest had been attacked, it was a warm evening, and their quarry led them directly to the bright light of a campfire. The smoke, of course, was something of a deterrent, but the plethora of large, sweaty targets proved too much to resist. The wasps followed in Mardine's wake, as, with a tremendous howl, she raced into that light, grabbed a good-sized log off the woodpile and began swinging it at her tormentors—wasp and human alike. Pandemonium ensued. Some of the kidnappers tore off into the dark, some attacked Mardine and some struggled to fight or defend themselves from the angry insects' assault. Mardine felt a flash of pain and turned to see that a wickedly smiling Tresa had stabbed her in the backside. Without wasting a thought, the giantess pushed her one-time companion into the fire and noted with some satisfaction that the smile melted right off her face. The woman shrieked and endeavored to rise, but Mardine pushed her back down with an enormous foot. One of the other kidnappers tried to save Tresa, reached out a hand to the woman even as her entire body was engulfed in flames, but Mardine broke the man's neck with her fire log. Another of the men had somehow drawn the bulk of the wasps' attack and soon he was out-screaming Tresa. Still, a large number of the insects, along with two or three of the kidnappers, continued to battle with Mardine. She was taking a lot of damage, but it wasn't anything she couldn't handle. The important thing was—

Esmine screamed from somewhere amongst the wagons. It was the first time Mardine had heard her daughter's voice in she couldn't say how long, and she choked back a sob at the sound of it. With final, massive sweep of her log, she sent the last of her human opponents tumbling into the night and then ran in the direction of Esmine's voice. She hurried past two or three wagons until she spotted one built like a cage on wheels. Even in the lack of light, she could see Esmine and Nelby inside, their arms locked around one another. Oh, how badly Mardine felt then! She rushed to the cage, smiled at her daughter and began to wrestle the door off its hinges. A strange clicking noise behind her alerted her to a new threat, right before she felt another colossal blow to her back. She staggered. How had they managed to rig up a log trap in the middle of...the biggest arrow she'd ever seen protruded from the wagon just beyond the cage. She could feel blood pounding in her ears, see it in her eyes. She turned. Her daughter's captors had mounted an arbalest on the back of a wagon, and Mardine had stupidly walked right in front of it. She put a hand on her chest, now drenched in a geyser of blood. The arrow had gone right through her. Her knees gave out. She heard Esmine cry out again, not in fear, but in unspeakable sadness. And then Mardine heard no more.

North Hill District, Lunessfor

The hours between sunset and sunrise had been pure bedlam. It was as if the city's wealthiest families had been stricken by a mental illness of some sort. House Blackbyrne had been attacked and caught fire. House Hawsey sent a score of men to House Radcliffe and started a brawl at the front gates that resulted in the death of several men from both houses. The D'Escurzys were claiming a sorcerous attack had killed off the majority of the family's ranking members, and House Fyne vociferously accused the other Houses of spying. The relative quiet at Houses Amberly, Gault and Thorton seemed a guilty silence to the stricken Houses, which responded, predictably, with righteous indignation. How was it, after all, on this night of mayhem and unabashed hysteria that three of the Great Eight had remained unmolested? Why had the other five suffered whilst they alone had not?

A mob of men from the first five Houses determined to even the score with the three unscathed. Standing atop his gates, Lord Darley Gault was quick to deflect the blame for the night's tragedies upon House Amberly, and the credulous throng, overwhelmed by its lust for vengeance, set off to punish the Amberlys first, bombarding their gates with stones, bottles, and flaming offal. Soon, the vandalism and verbal sniping escalated into all-out conflict, with the various Houses staging open raids on one another until the Constable and Lord Mayor were forced to intervene, imposing martial law in the city's wealthier neighborhoods, much to the delight of Lunessfor's less fortunate.

That night marked the beginning of a period the Great Eight would long remember with bitterness and suspicion.

Long, House Thornton

The look on Chade Thornton's face defied description, at least as far as Long was concerned. He'd crossed paths with a few of the wealthy and powerful over the years, and he'd never seen any of them as befuddled as His Lordship seemed to be. Standing before him, Chade had appeared on the brink of making a pronouncement on several occasions, only to reconsider, chew his lips and continue his evident ruminations. Eternity passed and he spoke.

"I'll confess I'm flummoxed. Last night was the worst, most unpredictable in memory. I'd hardly credit the tale if I'd heard it from my own mother, but I witnessed much of the madness with my own eyes. The tension between the Eight finally snapped, like a leather thong pulled to its limit." He sighed. "Where it touches you, Captain Long, is House D'Escurzy has placed a bounty on your head for murder." He had Long's attention now, and no mistake.

"Murder? How am I s'posed to have accomplished this while a prisoner in our House?"

"An excellent question. But no more pressing than that of how you managed to get yourself named heir to the D'Escurzy estate whilst languishing in my dungeons."

What could Long say? Nothing. And nothing is precisely what he offered in response.

"It's not a complete loss, however," Chade remarked. "Before my brother's death, I was studying to become a lawyer and, if I understand such matters correctly, the remaining D'Escurzys can no more place a bounty on the Head of House than they can disown themselves. If they can prove you're guilty of these so-called murders, the matter of your punishment falls to the crown and none other. If they cannot prove your guilt and/or the charges prove false, you'll be allowed to punish your accusers yourself, again, as Head of House."

Long had gotten to his feet when His Lordship and his guards entered; now, he sank back onto to his bed—not out of disrespect, but confusion. "What'll you do with me, then?"

Chade smiled. "I think I'll collect that bounty, maybe take the Constable along with me to see they don't kill you outright."

"No," Long replied.

His Lordship cocked his head at an angle, like a man who'd just been slapped across the face by a small child. "No?" he repeated.

It was happening again. The mysterious wellspring of courage that came on unannounced and always seemed timed to cause Long maximum distress had returned. "Correct. I don't think I'll come willingly unless you sweeten the deal for me."

Both of Chade's guards moved to put Long in his place, but His Lordship reached out and restrained both men. With unmistakable reluctance, they stood down. Chade shook his head in wonderment. "Things just get stranger and stranger. I must say I've never seen a prisoner make demands of his captor before. What is it you think I'll do for you?"

"I want Peppers to come along with me."

"The fool in my dungeon?" Chade laughed heartily. "Gladly! Much joy may he bring you!"

"I have one other condition."

The merriment went out of His Lordship's voice so quickly, it was hard to believe it had ever been there in the first place. "Indeed?"

"I want your torturer, as well."

Chade nodded. "You have a personal grudge with him. I understand. But I must needs remind you that he was only doing my bidding."

Long scowled. "Makes no difference. He and I have unfinished business."

His Lordship took a moment to examine his nails, the polish on his buttons, the links on the chain around his neck. "Done," he said at last. "The three of you will be coming with me and a few of my best men in one hour's time. Shortly thereafter, I will be even wealthier, whilst draining an enemy's coffers, and you will be a new Lord...for however long you can make it last."

Waiting in a dungeon with no hope of hope was one thing; enduring the hour between freedom and captivity, between life and possible death, between the life he'd known and the possible wealth and power of a Head of House was another altogether.

When the time to leave came, Long's body seemed composed of water and naught else. There was no strength in his legs, no resolve in his belly, no stiffness in his spine. He passed out of his room and fell in amongst a large group of armed men. He got a fleeting glance at Peppers and was appalled to see the man entirely naked, save for an old, soiled stocking, hung precariously from his business. It seemed possible that insisting on Peppers' company had been a mistake. Long sought out Janks and found him near the rear of the procession, his face a blank. Was Chade planning to go back on his agreement, or had he simply not informed Janks of his true purpose in coming along? Well, Long thought, I'll find out soon enough.

The whole North Hill District looked like the aftermath of a huge party—or a riot; sometimes it was hard to tell the difference—to which Long hadn't been invited. There was garbage everywhere—bottles, broken crockery, discarded clothing, damaged weapons, loose masonry, rotten produce, excrement and blood, plenty of blood. If there'd been bodies, they'd been removed by the time Chade and his company came through, and, in fact, there were roving groups of menial laborers cleaning the area as fast as they could. They looked strangely happy, but then it occurred to Long that they had reason for it: a mess that needed cleaning meant employment, and a mess in the rich neighborhood meant the wealthy had been introduced to the real world, however briefly. Perhaps it would humanize them.

Or not, Long thought. They'll retreat behind their walls and their piles of gold and lick their wounds. Then he remembered that he, too, was about to retreat behind such walls—assuming he was able to take possession of the estate to which he'd been named heir. There was that little matter of the bounty on his head...

He was so lost in his thoughts, he didn't notice the company had come to a halt until someone yelled down at them from above.

"Who comes to House D'Escurzy with an armed guard? What's your business here?"

"I've come to collect the bounty for the capture and delivery of Long Pete!" Chade replied heartily.

There was a brief pause, and then, "Is that so? I make out the banners of House Thornton. Are you the Lord of the House, then?"

"I am," Chade said without fear or hesitation.

Long wondered at his attitude when he made such an easy target for an arrow or spear, but suspected the last thing anyone in North Hill wanted was another outbreak of violence.

"A moment!" the voice atop D'Escurzys' walls shouted down.

He'd had so many 'final moments' of life, Long didn't even bother to dwell on what might be coming next.

A clattering, banging sound preceded the cautious opening of the estate's massive front gates. Immediately, a small clump of armed men strode through the opening and approached Chade's company.

A short, doughy-faced man in oversized armor stepped to the forefront of the D'Escurzy contingent. "'S a rather large group to come calling with."

"After last night's...festivities...it seemed the prudent thing to do. The streets are not yet safe for any of our families," Chade answered.

"Mmmm," Doughy nodded in agreement. When he scanned Chade's companions, Long noticed the fellow was also a bit wall-eyed. "I don't see Long Pete amongst your number," the man said.

"Curious," said Chade. "He is here, notwithstanding." He waved his left hand slightly and two guards pushed Long forward, somewhat rougher than necessary.

Doughy looked at his fellows and then back to Chade. "That ain't him," he said coldly.

Chade turned to Long, an expression of surprise on his face, and then back to the D'Escurzys. "On the contrary!" he sang out. "This is the one and only Captain Long Peter Fendesst, late of her Majesty's army, under the service of one Colonel Bailis. This has been confirmed under torture and through other means, both magical and mundane."

He was laying it on a bit thick, Long supposed, but the truth was the truth: he'd never met nor heard of another Long Pete in all his days.

"I am telling you," Doughy said, "This is not the man's been living in our House these past few weeks!"

Chade smiled his most winning smile. "That, friend, is not my problem. The bounty specified Long Pete, and Long Pete I would deliver."

"And that ain't him!"

"What's this other Long Pete look like?" Long blurted out. Chade shot him a look of stern disapproval, but he let the question stand.

Again, the D'Escurzys exchanged looks.

"Well," said their leader, "that's the funny part. He…uh…" He turned to his companions, embarrassed, "Help me out, here."

But they could not.

"Do you mean to tell me the man's been living with you for weeks and you can't identify him?"

The men in Chade's company snickered openly, but he waved them silent.

"It's awkward," Doughy whined. "Most o' those who knew him are dead."

"And you've never seen him before?"

"I seen him plenty o' times. I just...can't..."

Chade was done with the fool. He approached another of the D'Escurzys, a tall, gaunt fellow with two days' growth of beard. "You, then. Have you ever seen Long Pete?"

"Two or three times, yes," the man said.

"Describe him."

"I...the thing is..." Then he, too, shook his head in frustration.

"Aha!" Chade cried, triumphantly, "But if you can't describe our man, how can you be certain that my Long Pete—a man I've proven to be the genuine article—is not the one you're looking for?"

"He doesn't look familiar, that's how!" Doughy countered, reasserting himself.

Chade got very close to the D'Escurzy leader and, in conspiratorial tones, said, "Look, we've all had a rough night—and none worse than your House. I can send for this Colonel Bailis, the Constable and the Lord Mayor, or you can save yourselves further embarrassment and pay the bounty."

These particular D'Escurzys, never having been put in positions of authority before, quickly huddled and whispered amongst themselves for several minutes, before Doughy returned to Chade's side and said, "We concede." He pulled an ornately folded document from his belt and handed it to His Lordship. "You'll be able to cash that at her Majesty's bank," he said with a trace of bitterness.

"Don't take it so poorly!" Chade said cheerfully. "I'm including a bonus of two additional men—a mad poet and my personal torturer."

Doughy sneered at the first, but brightened at the second. "Your torturer, eh? Might get some use out 'o him."

Chade's guards escorted Long, Peppers and Janks out of their ranks and up to the D'Escurzy gate. Just as Chade made to depart, he turned back to the unhappy D'Escurzy gang and said, "Oh, and don't think of murdering His Lordship, Long Pete. I've communicated the situation to the crown, through her Majesty's Shaper, and in order to carry out the death sentence you've placed upon him, you'll have to put him on trial, with

her Majesty presiding. And, as I think you know, she's too ill
to do anything for the time being. You can imprison him, of
course, but I gather you've suffered enormous losses in your
House leadership, and you could do worse than tolerate a
decorated military officer as Head of House." With that, Chade
spun on his heel and sauntered off, whistling happily. His men
fell in behind him and, in no time, the Thorntons had receded
from view.

Doughy stared at Long Pete, a sour look on his face.
"Welcome home, *your Lordship.*"

Aoife, Her New Grove

These were not the children she remembered. This brood was
sullen, taciturn. They were different in appearance, as well—
darker, thornier, of dire and dangerous aspect. Looking for
reassurance, Aoife endeavored to engage them in conversation,
but they remained aloof. Only when the strange satyr, the one
who was not Toomt-La, appeared without warning did they
rouse themselves, gurgling and chirruping as he moved near.

"I warned you, human. Did I not?"

The A'Shea would not be intimidated; she was too
disappointed and tired to humor anyone's temper. "You made
some noises. Were those the warning you speak of?"

Without moving, the satyr reappeared within inches of
Aoife, grinning malevolently into her face. She stilled her
breath and inwardly chanted a prayer. "Am I supposed to be
afraid, woodling? I've stood nose-to-nose with the Reaper and
survived."

"Ah," the satyr sighed in a tone full of malice, "the Reaper.
Yes, I have heard of this monster. Another blight, another
abomination that must be dealt with in time."

"Before he deals with you?"

She did not see his hand reach out to her neck, only knew
that it was there and tightening its grip. The A'Shea tried to cast
paralysis upon her foe, but the spell had no effect. She began to
feel lightheaded, but whether that was from choking or some
magic of the satyr's, she couldn't tell. She scorched the creature's

hand with a powerful burst of static electricity. He retaliated by striking her across the face with his other hand.

"Enough!" cried a voice from the shadows.

The satyr took his attention off Aoife for a second, and she desiccated the hand around her throat, provoking a scream of fury from her assailant.

"Enough!" the voice commanded again. Toomt-La stepped into the sunlight. "This must not continue!"

The dark satyr stepped away from the A'Shea, shaking his ruined hand as if he could wriggle it back to health. "You have no authority here!" He spat at Toomt-La.

"Endu-Ro," Toomt-La said calmly, "It is ever the same argument from you. When will you see we are not concerned with a land, but the world entire?"

"And we cannot preserve our world, but one land at a time!"

Toomt-La gestured in Aoife's direction. "This woman is no threat to your land or our world."

"And yet, she has travelled with the Reaper—boasts of it, even!"

"Then tell, me, brother," Toomt-La said, "when has the Reaper ever done battle with our folk? What forests has he burned? What species, eradicated?"

Endu-Ro sneered, "Do you mean to say a man who calls himself the Reaper is as harmless as a shepherd?"

"Oh, he's a danger, brother. To his own kind. To any who oppose him. But he is like the adder: if you leave him alone, he'll do the same to you."

The dark satyr ignored the comment. "I want her to use this grove to return to her land…"

"Why, so I intend," Aoife interjected. "But not today, nor tomorrow. But when I list."

Endu-Ro stared at her, his chest heaving with angry breaths. "I'll take these children, too, and when you've gone, I'll recultivate this place so you cannot return."

Aoife looked at her latest brood and felt no love in or for them. "That's fair," she allowed.

The satyr flashed into the shadows under a tree, becoming all but invisible. "I'll look to see you gone, then. Soon."

"Soon," Aoife agreed.

"And now," said Toomt-La, "you understand another reason for the sea between our lands."

The A'Shea crossed the grove and threw her arms about her old friend, saying nothing for the longest time. Eventually, her curiosity got the better of her. "Was that Endu-Ro truly your brother?"

Toomt-La laughed his strange, croaking laugh. "He is. And many thousands more."

She had birthed Toomt-La, and yet, clearly, she had not. Aoife stepped back in amazement. "You have thousands of brothers?"

Toomt-La nodded.

"And do you know them all by name?"

He nodded again. "I must return to sleep," he said wistfully. "I must sleep."

Aoife had many questions, but her friend had vanished.

Vykers, In Pursuit

After climbing almost imperceptibly for days, the party crested a rise and looked out over a vast plain, far below. Vykers, Hoosh and the Frog were stunned by the altitude they'd achieved without being especially aware, though the Historian (and, of course, Arune) did not seem particularly impressed. The two prisoners, worn ragged by hard travel and constant fear, registered even less response.

"What's that smudge on the horizon?" the Fool asked, pointing a finger to direct everyone's gaze.

"'S an army," Vykers answered. He might have been a bit more sardonic in his reply, but the thought of a battle excited him.

That's not an army, Arune contradicted. *It's a collection of armies.*

Vykers beamed. *Even better.*

"And that bright spot in the middle?" Hoosh wondered.

It was the Frog who replied. "Those are flames."

"You can see that from here?" said the Reaper, astonished. But then he remembered Number Three and recalled the extraordinary vision his friend had possessed. "'Course you can."

"Strange flames, though," said the Frog.

"How so?"

"They climb too high."

What's that mean? Vykers prodded Arune.

It means we've found her Majesty.

They ain't burnin' her at the stake are they?

It doesn't appear so.

What's that mean?

I don't—

Vykers approached the Historian. "The Queen alive?"

The Ahklatian looked at the far away spark. "Yes."

"And?"

"That's all I can tell you."

Vykers grabbed the Historian by his shoulder and spun him so the two men were facing one another. The Historian, in turn, glanced at the Reaper's hand with a rebuking look.

"That's an interesting choice 'o words, that. I got a hunch you know a lot more than you're lettin' on."

The Historian regarded Vykers in silence, his all-black eyes giving nothing away.

"And there's a few things here don't look too good to me."

"For instance?" the Fool prompted.

The Reaper drew his sword from its sheath across his back. He hefted its weight experimentally, felt it quiver in his grip in anticipation of violence. "For instance," he began, "I've been led to the middle o' nowhere, months from home. The only men I've got for help or company were chosen by someone else or," he pointed at the Frog, "came o' their own accord. We finally catch sight of our destination and it's swarming with unknown armies. Tell me this don't look like a trap."

The Fool looked nervously at the sword and responded, "I can see how it might, yes. But I don't think that's the case."

"I ain't tryin' to hurt you," the Frog declared.

Vykers turned his gaze back to the Historian, who said "Do you think I fear death? If you're going to try to kill me, have at it. Otherwise, you'll have to trust me."

The Reaper lowered his sword; that was what passed for an apology in his mind. He would say no more about it. "Let's start working our way down this slope, then."

You waited until now to start suspecting a trap? Arune asked in disbelief.

I always suspect a trap; I'm just lettin' the others know I may have to kill 'em.

I'll bet they found that reassuring.

It took hours to get to down to the plain. At one point, Vykers wheeled his horse in a circle, surveying the landscape in every direction.

"I thought you said there was a giant lake down here somewhere," he said to the Historian.

"I did," the other man agreed. "We're standing in it."

The Fool whistled in amazement.

The Historian shrugged. "A lot can happen in seven hundred years."

"Where'd the water go?" Vykers demanded.

Still smarting from the Reaper's rebuke, the Ahklatian replied, "Does it matter?"

He had a point, Vykers supposed. Whatever his companions' motives might be, he'd come here to find her Majesty. Everything else was irrelevant.

It is the way of things, when travelling great distances over land, that objects on the horizon seem closer than they are, and reaching them takes much, much longer than expected. Since evening arrived before their destination, the party made camp.

"Fuck it," Vykers growled. "I'm tired and hungry. Let's call it a day."

"What of the prisoners?" the Historian inquired.

It wouldn't kill you to make some gesture of trust in the man, Arune pointed out.

"Whatever you think best," Vykers told him.

See? Said Arune. Wasn't that easy?

I only said that to end the conversation. I reckon we'll be doin' some fighting tomorrow, and I wanna get some rest.

You could say one thing about Vykers, Arune thought: he didn't beat around the bush.

Come morning, Vykers surprised himself and everyone else by being the first to rise. Normally, the Frog had that honor, but the Reaper was so excited by the prospect of bloodshed that he couldn't contain himself any longer and rose as the first stars began to fade from the sky. He finished the previous night's game without any concern for the rest of his party and turned his attention to ensuring his weapons and gear were in fighting condition.

"I can now tell you more of what waits, ahead, if you wish," the Historian said, intruding upon Vykers' preparations.

The Reaper was sitting, gingerly, on a pile of saddlebags. He looked up. "Why now?"

"Because we have drawn considerably closer."

"Makes sense," Vykers said, more to himself than the Ahklatian.

"There is, as you've suggested, a collection, a gathering of armies."

As I said, Arune boasted.

"However," the Historian continued, "they are not allied with one another."

"Oh?" Vykers sat up a bit taller.

"No. They appear, instead, to have reached a stalemate or agreement of sorts over their relative positions around that fire our friend spoke of."

The Frog.

I figured. "And what can you tell me about that fire? It's gotta be magic, no?"

"It certainly feels that way. But if it is, it's beyond my ken."

"Huh."

Now, the Frog approached. "Master?" he asked with a degree of meekness that seemed almost laughable in one so fearsome.

"Frog," Vykers said by way of acknowledgement.

"Will we be fighting today?"

"I sure as hell hope so!" Vykers replied cheerfully.

"But..."

"But?" Vykers didn't have a lot of patience, even on a good day, and never before a battle.

"I'm afraid o' what I might do."

"Frog, I can't wait to see what you can do."

"But I might...I might..."

"Good," Vykers said. "Serves the bastards right!" And that was it; he was done chatting. It was time to focus.

Hours passed, and the group found itself surrounded by scores of ruined, discolored pillars, or at least their bases, anyway.

"What's all this?" Vykers wondered aloud.

"Petrified wood," the Ahklatian replied. "It seems there was a forest here, even before the large lake I spoke of. The remains of these trees were preserved by the salt and the lake silt."

"So, how long ago was this?"

"Tens of thousands of years, I shouldn't wonder. Perhaps more."

Tens of thousands of years. How in the infinite hells could he know that? Vykers let it go. The only mystery he cared about at the moment was what had happened to the Queen.

Long, House D'Escurzy

Long Pete didn't waste any time getting settled. He understood that something catastrophic had happened to the D'Escurzys in the last day or so, and those who had somehow survived the mysterious event were so rattled that they barely knew how to handle themselves, much less the affairs of the estate. After seeing to his companions' accommodations, Long plunked himself down in a chair in the first room that seemed large enough to conduct business and commanded the family members that had met him at the gate be sent for. They came at his bidding and were none too happy about it.

"Who are you, pray tell, to order us about?" Doughy sniped petulantly.

"I'm the current Lord o' this House, is who," Long croaked. "Accordin' to Lord Titus' last will and testament, witnessed by the Constable and several others. And it seems I'm the only one 'round here still has his wits about him!" A page standing off to Long's left started to giggle, and Long cut him off with a look of extreme censure. "Now, what in the infinite hells happened to you people the other night?"

A look passed between the three men he'd summoned. Finally, Doughy spoke. "I'm confused as to how you wouldn't know. After all, it was at a banquet in your honor."

Long leaned forward in his chair, glared at the man. "Humor me. What happened?"

Doughy backed down. "Er...some of the family's...um... more important members felt it important to celebrate your... ascension to Head of House from the position of..." he turned to his mates, conferred with them in hushed tones, then turned back to Long. "From the position of manservant to His Lordship."

"And how long had I been in His Lordship's service?"

Again, Doughy consulted his friends. "Several weeks. We not sure of the exact date."

Long did the math in his head; it fit. That, combined with the surviving family's inability to describe the 'Long Pete' who had served Lord Titus confirmed, for Long, that Spirk Nessno had preceded him. But what had become of the young man since?

"Tell me everything you know about this disastrous banquet," he said.

It was an astonishing tale, the conclusion of which demonstrated beyond doubt that Spirk had in fact, as he had always claimed, somehow become a vessel for Pellas' gifts. Most of them, anyway. It was abundantly clear he hadn't acquired the old Shaper's intellectual prowess. After all, he'd chosen Long's name as his alias, and it was never wise to use the name of an actual person, especially one's leader. Had it not been for that gaffe, however, Long would still be languishing in the Thornton's dungeon, or even dead. This gave Long pause. It could be that Spirk was the imbecile he'd always imagined the young man to be, or he might be a genius, a prodigy whose intelligence so far outpaced Long's that the Captain would never understand the fellow's actions.

No. There were miracles, and then there were fairytales. Long had just gotten lucky.

He looked at the three men before him. "How comes it you've all survived this...explosion?"

"Like I said, it was the family's more important members—leastwise, in their view—and many of us weren't invited."

"To your good fortune, I'll warrant."

Doughy nodded. "I'll not gainsay it, though some of us lost a few friends into the bargain."

Long understood: wealthy families were amongst the most dysfunctional, but even within their ranks, love and camaraderie could be found in ample supply. "I am sorry for your loss," he said with evident sincerity.

The men seemed mollified.

"My name's Dendul, your Lordship," Doughy offered.

"And I'm Jasper," the tall one said.

"I'm Tane," said the third.

"Pleased to meet you, good sirs," Long responded. "Though I wish it had been under other circumstances."

"Aye," "Indeed," "That's a fact," the men said.

"But, er, your Lordship..." Dendul said, "the other survivors won't take your title seriously, not bein' an actual D'Escurzy and all."

Long seemed to think about this for a moment and then said, "I've an idea about that. Can you tell me who manages the estate's coin?"

"That'd be Frankus. He's dead." Jasper answered.

"Ah," Long sighed. Then, "Would you be interested in the job?"

Jasper's eyes went wide. "What, me?"

"You, Jasper, or any of you three."

"I can do it," said Jasper, clearly taking to the idea.

"Yeah," Tone agreed. "You'd be good at it."

"Let's consider it done, then," Long instructed. "Now, if you can gain access to the family vaults, I imagine a cash bonus to each surviving D'Escurzy should soothe tempers a bit. Don't get carried away though," he warned. "We'll need funds aplenty to repair the damage done to our House and hire additional guards for increased security."

Dendul, Jasper and Tane nodded right along with Long's

directions, as if acknowledging their wisdom.

"Dendul, my friend," Long continued, placing special emphasis on 'friend,' "Is there a vacant office you fancy?" "And you, Tane?"

"Well," Dendul admitted, "Chief o' Security's dead. That'll need to be filled, an it please you."

"The office is yours, good Dendul."

The man beamed. It's amazing what a little acknowledgement and praise can do for morale.

"I'd like to be the Head Steward. Never did like the way the place was decorated. Looks too much like a damned museum."

"I couldn't agree more!" Long proclaimed. "The office is yours, sir. But now, tell me, whom does the House normally employ to carry messages long distance?"

"There's a company in the city. They got a bunch o' couriers'll go anywhere you please."

"Good, good. Can anyone send for them? I'd like to get word to my wife..."

"I'll go and fetch someone," Tane offered and departed immediately.

"And Jasper, I'd like something done with the fellows I came in with."

"What can I do for you?"

"Well," Long said, "I want the mad poet cleaned up, dressed, fed and confined to his room for the nonce. And I want the torturer moved from the room he currently occupies into a cell, until further notice."

"As you wish," Jasper replied, bowing his head slightly and taking his leave.

"And I'll get on that money issue," Dendul said, leaving as well.

I could get to like this, Long thought.

Rem, the Queen's Castle

The Shaper was about as intimating a fellow as Rem had encountered in some time. There was not a trace of warmth or approval in the man's demeanor as he spoke to the actor, and the last thing Rem wanted was to irritate an all-powerful magician.

"The timing of your arrival," Cindor said, "is rather suspicious, given the chaos that erupted between Houses Hawsey and Radcliffe shortly thereafter."

"I grant you, it looks bad," Rem conceded, struggling to maintain a calm façade.

"Hostilities continue between the families even now, and, in fact, noblemen and women continue to die throughout the city... though I can't see how all of this can be laid at any one person's feet—even those of a shameless narcissist like yourself."

Rem was on the verge of taking offense at the remark when he realized it was probably accurate, and there were certainly worse things one could be. At least the Shaper hadn't questioned his acting ability. "What can I say to reassure you?"

"I imagine the truth's out of the question?" Cindor quipped. "Never mind. Let's try a different tack, shall we? What did you learn during your sojourn at House Hawsey?"

"That's a rather broad topic," Rem pointed out. "Is there a particular subject you're interested in?" He was nearly pissing himself in fear of the wizard's wrath, but he was nothing if not practiced in pretense.

"I wonder," Cindor mused, "if you are interested in the subject of your continued ability to feed yourself without help. I find you overly circumloquacious; that is to say you talk around the issue without ever saying anything of import. You will stop that behavior now or face severe consequences."

"As you say," Rem agreed.

"I know," the Shaper continued in a world-weary manner, "that you were hired by Colonel Bailis of her Majesty's army to investigate the Great Eight's possible involvement in the Queen's disappearance." He paused, gathered himself. "What have you learned in that regard?"

Death by incineration did not seem to be imminent, so Rem said, "My associates and I split up and attempted to infiltrate different Houses. I ended up, as you already know, at the Hawsey estate, in service to His Lordship."

"And?"

"And...while I can see how Henton might prove a dangerous

man, he doesn't seem an exceptionally clever one, certainly not clever enough to have masterminded the abduction of the Queen...if that's what's happened."

"Dangerous word to bandy about, 'if.' Do you have knowledge or suspicions to the contrary?" Cindor asked, his voice a deadly whisper.

"No, no," Rem replied quickly. "Just being...open-minded."

"Enough of this!" said the Shaper, abruptly. Purple-blue lightning flared from his fingertips and rattled the actor in its grip. Rem's body spasmed uncontrollably, his teeth chattered, his lips pulled into a rictus of pain, and his eyes bulged desperately from their sockets. Just as suddenly, the ordeal was over.

Rem slumped to the floor, breathing heavily and battling a bladder and bowels that threatened to betray him.

"For the moment," Cindor said, "I have a kingdom to manage and will not suffer fools gladly. When I ask a question, I expect a direct and immediate answer devoid of equivocation."

Through teeth gritting in lingering pain, Rem said, "You've not known many actors, then."

The Shaper blasted him into unconsciousness.

Vykers, the Lakebed

It took nearly until noon to reach the pickets outside the numerous encampments of the armies arrayed before them. Two short, stocky men in hide armor observed their approach with studied disinterest.

Vykers reined his horse to a stop some twenty paces shy and eyed the Historian, the Ahklatian's signal to speak and translate. The Shaper slid from his mount and walked closer. He made a small, subtle wave of his hand and greeted the soldiers in a language Vykers had never before understood, but now did.

"All praise and honor to your leader," he said.

The two men seemed surprised to hear their tongue spoken by such obvious strangers. "What's your business at the obelisk?"

After a brief hesitation, the Historian replied, "Of the same nature as your and everyone else who has come to visit."

"Where's your army?" the nearest man asked. "Where are your troops?"

"Whom do you represent?" the second man added.

"We come on our own behalf," the Ahklatian said. "And we have no need of additional men."

It was shaping up to be a hot day; Vykers felt sweat running in rivulets down his back as he sat, in diminishing patience, in his special saddle, and waited to hear something that made sense.

"Are you a company of fools, then, that you come to the contest so ill-prepared?"

Vykers tried to respond, but found that he could not form the right sounds. The words he spoke were in his own language. "What contest? Explain this to me." He was forced to wait while the Historian translated.

"What is this contest, and what is the prize?" the Shaper asked in words the Reaper again understood but could not frame by himself.

The soldiers laughed at him. "You claim to come with the same purpose as those behind us, yet you know nothing of the contest? You are fools!" Suddenly, they seemed to notice the Frog for the first time. "And what in Skara's name is that abomination?"

Before Vykers could draw his sword, the Historian put both men to sleep. "No sense in alerting the rest of their army that we're coming," he explained.

The Reaper grudgingly admitted the wisdom in this, much as it pained him, because he knew his chance would come. There was no shortage of foes ahead of him, no shortage of candidates for carnage. The Historian climbed back atop his horse, and Vykers allowed him to lead the group forward. The Ahklatian would be doing the talking, so he might as well be on point.

Several hundred yards later, the group came in sight of a line of tents and yet more pickets. This outer army was not concerned with attack from the north, evidently. As far as Vykers could see, there was little to stop him and his companions from strolling right into the center of the camp. It appeared, from Vykers' perspective, that the bulk of this army's men had gathered on their camp's southern end, where another, sturdier fence had been erected. Beyond that, the Reaper could make out the troops of a different force entirely. Men in dirty crimson armor languished outside their dirty crimson tents; no matter, Vykers would roust them, once he made it through this first army.

A number of men looked up or turned heads as Vykers' crew came within hailing distance, and an older man in more decorative armor than the guards at the pickets had worn ventured near. He called out to the group, but Vykers found that he was only able to understand the man if he stayed close to the Historian.

"I am Penarion. Who or what are you?"

The Historian answered without consulting the Reaper, always a dangerous decision. Still, it saved time, and Vykers had no patience for prattle. "We are emissaries from across the Great Sea. We have reason to believe our Queen is amongst this gathering."

The old man perked up. "Your Queen, is it? There's an old hag stuck to the obelisk, in the heart of yon flame. If that be your Queen, I'm afraid there's little you can do for her."

Vykers turned to the Frog. "You see an old woman in those flames?" he asked.

Like an acrobat, the Frog climbed to his feet atop the saddle, perfectly balanced. "There's someone, aye. A woman? I can't say."

"Anyway," Penarion cut in, "Those closest to the obelisk fought their way in. That's how it is, here. You want a better look, you'll have to defeat every army between me and those flames." Having said this, he laughed. "'Course, with an army of three men, two prisoners and whatever that is," he pointed at the Frog, "I don't think you'll be getting much closer."

"Your sentries told us of a contest. Is this what you mean?"

"Aye," the old man confirmed. "The very same." He turned to go, but the Historian stopped him.

"I offer you gold," the Ahklatian said. "Gold, for information."

"What gold?" Vykers whispered tensely. "Do you barter

with my private stores?"

The Historian looked at him with his dead, black eyes, and then swept his gaze over to the old soldier. He made a conspicuous move to put a hand into one of the external pockets of his robe and withdrew a small, shining ingot. The soldier's eyes widened in surprise and avarice.

"Information?" the man repeated, unable to take his eyes off the Historian's treasure. "I've known men to kill for less gold."

Vykers drew his sword, and it came screeching out of its scabbard. "You're welcome to try," he suggested. "You and your whole army."

The old man didn't understand the individual words Vykers spoke, but he definitely got the gist.

"What is it you want to know?" he asked of the Historian.

"What is the purpose of this gathering before us?"

"Is is said, amongst the armies, that yon obelisk appeared only recently. No man could touch it without being burned alive in an instant. One day, the hag appeared and touched it. It has not consumed her, but neither can she let go of it. Folk of many nations take this as a sign, but of what, they cannot say. The armies you see here jockey for position, for proximity to the obelisk. They wish to be first to witness…"

"First to witness what?"

"Ah," the man laughed. "No one knows."

"And you say these armies have fought to get closer. How is this done?"

"When we first arrived, months ago now, it was a free-for-all. Armies attacking one another on sight, without cause, without quarter, without a plan. It has taken weeks, but we have fallen into a comfortable routine of sorts: when two armies fight, the one furthest from the obelisk offers a challenge, the inner accepts, and a battle is fought. The winner moves inward and earns the right to challenge the next army."

"It would appear your army has not been especially successful, if what you say is true."

"We have not, no."

"But, as you have observed, we have no army. Is it possible to challenge an army's champion instead?"

The old man cocked his head, astounded and intrigued by this idea. "What an interesting thought. I've not seen it done, but it might well save lives. Do you mean, then, to challenge our champion?"

"Yes," Vykers said, though the other man could not understand him.

The Historian translated.

Looking Vykers up and down, the old man said, "I suppose I would be the champion of my army, but I have no interest in fighting with that brute...or the monster, either, for that matter. You may pass right through my army, if you like and challenge the next."

"How many armies are here, would you say?"

"There are representatives of every major power on the continent—eleven, twelve, perhaps, if one counts the Tzuras citystates."

"Is the depth of armies equal all the way 'round the obelisk?"

"No," Penarion replied. "There's nothing 'round the back, but a little lake so salty that naught lives in or near it."

The Historian raised an eyebrow in Vykers' direction. "Now we know what happened to the great lake; it's shrunken and condensed into a poisoned pool."

And magic doesn't travel over any quantity of salt, Arune added.

"Enough of this," Vykers declared. "Let's accept the man's offer and move on to the next army."

Yendor, House Amberly

Yendor awoke on an uncomfortable cot in an unfamiliar room, sandwiched between other cots that held, respectively, an old woman with crackly breathing and a chubby young man with an enormous, filthy bandage atop his head. Ah. He was in an infirmary, a hospital of some sort. His right eye ached something horrible, and when he realized he couldn't see out of it, he nearly screamed in fright. Against his better judgment—if he'd ever had such—he slowly reached up and explored the area with his right hand.

His eye was gone.

Every muscle in his body seemed to go slack at the discovery, and he sank, hopelessly, deeper into his bedding. He'd lost an eye! He'd lost a Mahnus-cursed eye! Damn his liquor-addled brains! He'd always known his drinking would end badly, but this!

He closed his remaining eye and tried to recall how he'd lost its twin. He'd been part of a mob, House Fyne's contribution to the vigilantism of the previous night—or whatever night it had been. Yendor had no way of knowing how long he'd lain here. But he'd seen the other men's fury as his chance to escape the House and disappear into the night, before His Lordship got 'round to questioning him about poor Moult. He remembered throwing rubbish at the gates of House Amberly and dodging the rubbish its members threw back in return. He remembered how the Amberlys had fired arrows, crossbow bolts and slung stones down into the press. And he remembered stabbing one of his comrades in the back, for reasons that now escaped him.

And then he'd woken up in this place.

He felt the warm softness of a gentle hand on his brow, and he opened his eye again. "Whuuu…" he croaked.

The face of a plump A'Shea drifted into view. "Let me help you up, so you can take water more easily."

Yendor allowed himself to be hauled into a more-elevated position and found a ladle placed at his lips. He drank greedily. "Whuu…where…am I?"

"You're in the staff infirmary in House Amberly," the A'Shea said in an unusually mellifluous voice.

Yendor choked on his water, watched the ladle pull away for a moment. "How…?" he asked.

"How did you get here?" The A'Shea's expression grew sad. "I'm told you were involved in the riots yesterday outside the gates."

He'd guessed that much, so he sank back into a more restful position.

"And…"

His body became rigid with suspense. *And?*

"Milord saw you do something he wished to know more about, so he had you brought inside."

"Whuu...what did I do?"

The A'Shea regarded him, wondering whether she'd already said too much. Finally, she explained, "You murdered young Hadreus Fyne, son of Lord Fyne."

Suddenly, the loss of his eye seemed the least of Yendor's problems.

ELEVEN

Vykers, the Lakebed

The crimson armor worn by the next army in was strange stuff. It looked as if it was made of wood, painted and then shellacked with an incredibly hard resin. It wouldn't stand up to Vykers' sword, but he'd no doubt it was lighter on the body and cooler in the hot sun than plate mail or even chain. Underneath, soiled red tunics and trousers kept the armor from chaffing the skin. The little group did not have long to ponder these curiosities, though, before they were met by a larger group of soldiers approaching from all directions. Before violence could break out, the Historian said "We seek a match between champions, that we may earn our passage deeper into the circle."

The soldiers pressed closer, anxious to get a look at these strangers who dared such a challenge. As with Pendarion's folk, however, they pulled back considerably upon getting a better view of Vykers and the Frog.

"There's none will fight you, here," one of the soldiers said. "We're on the outside for a reason."

"Wrong, Voorst!" another of the men snapped. "I will challenge their champion, whatever he may be. We cannot wallow in our own cowardice forever!"

At this, the other soldiers muttered and grumbled demonstratively, but none, Vykers noticed, cared enough to contradict the assertion.

The second man stepped forward and spoke to the Historian, though his eyes were fixed firmly on the Reaper. "I am called Hjuest, Second Finger of the Right Hand."

Vykers jumped from his horse and approached the fellow. Like Pendarion before him, Hjuest was a good head shorter than Vykers. His pale skin was burnt and peeling from too much time in the sun. His paler moustache and beard were gathered into a tight iron ring, just under his chin.

"I don't mind killing you," Vykers said in the Historian's direction, so the Shaper could translate. "But this ain't any kind of a fair fight." He waited until the Historian caught up. "My sword'll cut right through that armor o' yours and you, well, you ain't exactly a giant."

"I'm big on the inside," the man quipped with a fatalistic grin. "And if I'm not, I'm big enough to die."

Vykers decided he liked the man and uncharacteristically decided to disable rather than kill him. He was just about to draw his sword when the smaller man whipped his own to within an inch of the Reaper's nose. To Vykers' amazement, it was also made of wood. The little bugger was fast, give him that. But a wooden sword? He slapped it away with his right hand and put Hjuest on the seat of his pants with a quick left jab to his chin. The other men hadn't wasted any time in forming a tight circle 'round the combatants. Vykers closed on his opponent and, to everyone's surprise, offered him a hand up. Unfortunately, Hjuest attempted to throw sand in the Reaper's eyes as the bigger man reached down to help him up. Vykers spun out of the way and at last drew his sword.

"That'll teach me to be nice," he said to himself.

Hjuest got to his feet under his own power and stared in terror at the Reaper's sword.

"And well you should be afraid, little man," Vykers said. Of course, the Historian had been excluded from the ring, so he wasn't able to translate Vykers' words, but Hjuest understood their meaning well enough.

He feigned a retreat and then leapt at Vykers with his sword extended, hoping to catch the Reaper off-guard. He'd have had better luck making a snowman outside his tent. Vykers anticipated the move and brought his sword smashing down on the smaller man's weapon, obliterating it and Hjuest's hopes in one swing. Vykers then shot his arm all the way out and hit his adversary full in the face with the pommel of his sword. Hjuest crumpled like a year-old cornstalk.

The men surrounding the fight made little sound at their champion's easy defeat.

"He'll live," Vykers said. "But his smile won't ever look the same."

The circle parted to admit the Historian, the Fool and the Frog, along with the two prisoners the group held in tow.

"Tell you what," Vykers said to the nearest soldiers, "I'll trade you my prisoners for this one, here."

The crowd looked from Vykers to his prisoners to the unconscious form of Hjuest. "What do you mean to do with him?" One of them said.

"Teach him the mysteries 'o steel."

The crowd laughed. "Good luck with that, my friend!" another of the men teased. "It's against our religion to handle the stuff."

"And as for your prisoners, we wouldn't dare take them. The Emperor would destroy us!"

"Be that as it may," Vykers rumbled, "I'm taking this one."

Kittins, Adrift

There was nothing in the world but cold, black water, or, if there was, Kittins never achieved consciousness long enough to discover it. He ought to have sunk to the river's bottom or been pulled there by the current, but he'd gotten entangled in the buoys that fishermen set out for their crawfish traps. Eventually, his momentum tore them away from their precious burdens, and he and they floated free down the river.

This might have lasted an age; he had no way to know. Most of the time, he barely remembered his own name. He was freezing, in pain, constantly choking on water splashed in his face. Why was it taking so long to die? Once in a while, he was roused long enough to find fish and other creatures gnawing at his wounds. He hadn't the strength to shoo the bastards away. And if they'd eat him, they must be desperate, indeed. Later, Kittins heard the sounds of an unfamiliar bird cooing and cackling loudly in his ear. Something grasped him by the hair and pulled him through the water.

Time passed. He gradually became aware he was no longer surrounded by or immersed in water. He was dry, warm. A there was a firm surface under his back. He slept. He had a terrible fever. Each time he opened his eyes, he saw nothing, but that the quality of light had changed: it was daytime, it was night, it was afternoon, it was morning. One night, he came well and truly awake.

And found himself flat on his back in a hovel. A fire he could not see cast flickering shadows upon the ceiling above him, revealing a patchwork of sticks, cloth, and dried grasses. He doubted it held up to the rainy season.

An old, withered face with pinprick eyes, a large hooked nose and nearly toothless mouth gazed down on him. Above it all, an unruly mop of white hair, in spikes and snarls and elf knots completed the picture of someone not quite human. Kittins suspected he didn't look quite human, either.

"Awake!" the crone crooned. "Awake, awake, awake at last! Such good care I takes, such good care."

Kittins was surprised to learn he could talk.

"Who are you?"

"Who? Ha ha! Who? No one. Some one. What does it matter? Poor Tom, poor Tom."

She was mad, clearly. Kittins tried to rise, could not.

"Too soon, too soon!" the crone remonstrated. "Dead, you were. Dead and gone, but for Croonbasket!"

If he'd been stronger, in greater possession of his wits, Kittins might have been worried to find himself at the mercy of such a lunatic. His memory currently played at hide and seek with him, but he imagined he was probably deserving of such a turn.

"Drink now!" the hag sang out. "Sip and sip, drink and drink, but slowly, for 'tis hot."

She held a shallow bowl to Kittins' lips and allowed him to slurp at its contents. He'd been expecting something foul, something loathsome. Instead, he was pleased to find the broth's flavor appealing. "What is this?" he asked.

Croonbasket cackled. "No, no you don't! Is my secret, it is. For me to know, for you to drink."

There was magic in it. Of that, Kittins had no doubt, for he began to relax as soon as the liquid ran down his throat. The woman—if she was a woman—was a witch then, a sort of rustic cross between a Shaper and an A'Shea, self-trained and, therefore, utterly unpredictable.

"Why did you save me?" Kittins demanded in a break between gulps.

"Why? Why why why. Always questions. Croonbasket sees worth where others doesn't."

"Don't. Where others don't," Kittins corrected, although he couldn't say why he'd felt the need.

"Doesn't don't can't won't. You're alive."

"Don't know as that's welcome news."

More cackling. "'Course it is! Croonbasket's seen the other side, she has. Foh! 'Tis no place to be!"

Kittins tumbled off to sleep again, hoping it all would make more sense when he awoke again.

Vykers, the Lakebed

The next army attacked Vykers' group the instant it appeared at the makeshift gate. Frankly, he found this refreshing. He was tired of talk, negotiation, and the like. He'd travelled for untold leagues, and all he really wanted was to take his miseries out on someone else, to maim and kill and destroy. To his delight, his newest foes had given him just that opportunity.

The men of this army wore billowing white robes over shining breastplates. Their heads were wrapped in fabric, too, atop which sat small, pointed skullcaps of steel. Their swords were great, curved things. Vykers couldn't wait to get his hand on one, see how it handled in combat.

As the men of this latest army attacked, Vykers turned to the Frog and said, "Do what you have to do, boy. It's them, or it's you."

The Frog didn't need telling twice. He flew into the oncoming mass like a blast of lightning, here, there, everywhere at once.

The Reaper was proud. With the maniacal laugh of a madman, he whipped his sword from its sheath and spurred his horse into the rush of charging hostiles. Some fell back at the sight of his fearsome weapon, others fell down beneath its bite, shorn in half or even multiple pieces. It was good to be back at work!

The other men of this army did not stand idle whilst their fellows engaged Vykers and his crew; scores of them ran to the scene and from all over their camp, carrying the now-familiar curved swords, but also spears and short bows with arrows. In no time, the throng at the gate had grown so large, there was scarcely room for the combatants to swing their weapons, a mistake that favored the Reaper and his friends, who, instead of having to deal with ten or fifteen times their number could focus their efforts on the handful of foes within reach. And, Vykers saw, whenever anyone on his side toppled anyone on the other, the fallen man was immediately replaced by another idiot, equally hemmed in and unable to move. Oh, the attacking force had its moments. Someone had managed to lame the Reaper's horse, and he had to abandon it for fear of being crushed when it went down. He hadn't been especially close to the beast, but it certainly meant more to him than most men he had known. He was angry to see it fall as it had and took his fury out upon his attackers.

There had been no Shaper in evidence in the first two armies Vykers' crew had encountered, but this current force seemed to boast two or three, who stood just beyond the swirling conflict and attempted to conjure and direct deadly energies at the warrior and the chimera in particular. A powerful burning throughout the Reaper's body satisfied him that Arune and, presumably, the Historian were hard at work counteracting the enemy's Shapers. Vykers even heard the telltale hysterical laughter amongst his opponents that was proof of the Fool's handiwork. Yes, it was an impossibly small army Vykers had. But it was capable of astonishing carnage, for all that. He looked up at one point and saw that the other side's Shapers were down and, in one case, on fire. He didn't expect this fight to last much longer. There was only so much damage an army's commander was willing to sustain in order to repel a few trespassers. Better to let them in or through than suffer insurmountable losses.

Vykers watched the bodies pile up for another ten minutes before several horn blasts from within the camp signaled at the very least an end to the army's attack, if not outright retreat or surrender. There followed several moments in which all activity, even breathing, seemed suspended while the attacking force decided how best to extricate itself from the mess it had created. Into this silence walked a tall, dark man dressed like his kinsmen, save that his breastplate was gold rather than the dull silver of steel. His full beard and eyebrows were blue-black. His deep, dark eyes stared at Vykers and his friends in absolute consternation. He did a quarter turn to his left, to survey those injured or killed in the just finished action; he then made the same turn in the opposite direction. Along the way, his eyes swept across those fallen in between the two extremes. He fixed his eyes on Vykers once more and spoke.

His words made no sense.

"Historian?" Vykers asked the Ahklatian.

"A moment."

When the stranger tried again, Vykers understood. "I am not willing to pay the price necessary to subdue you," the man said. "We have paid enough as it is. Say what it is you want."

Vykers addressed the Historian without ever taking his eyes off the stranger. "Tell him we want passage through his camp. And a horse!" the Reaper added, "To replace the one his men killed." He thought of specifying that it be a good horse, but the stranger did not look stupid, or, if he was, he'd been reformed by the beating his men had just received.

The man raised a hand to his lips, whistled. A pair of boys came running at the sound, bowing almost to the sand upon their arrival. The stranger said something too soft to be overheard, and the boys raced off again. The stranger unfastened a water skin from his belt and walked towards Vykers.

"It is not even noon, and it is already too hot. May I offer you drink?"

Vykers squinted, thought it over for an instant and then reached for the water skin. *Arune?*

It's water, she replied. *Safe enough.*

The two men watched each other with interest and suspicion as Vykers unstopped the spout and took an experimental sip. The water tasted of fruit, tart and tangy, a flavor with which he was somehow familiar, despite being unable to name or picture it in his mind. He puzzled briefly over this paradox and took another, deeper swig. Whatever it was, it made the water a good deal more satisfying. He held the skin out towards the Historian. "Know that this is?"

The Shaper sniffed the open mouth of the water skin. "Water. Flavored with lemon, I should think."

"And lemon is?"

"A sour fruit. There's probably a market for these in Ahklat."

So, he'd been right about the fruit in his water. Still, he'd never heard the word 'lemon' before. "I take it they don't grow back home?"

The Historian shook his head. "The climate's too cool in spring and summer."

Now it was Vykers who shook his head. Too cool in summer? Not as far as he was concerned. He drained the skin and handed it back to its owner, behind whom Vykers could just make out the two boys returning with a fresh horse, a sleek, black beast that looked made for running. The other man saw the look in the Reaper's eyes and turned to watch the boys' approach.

"Ah, Shalea. A fine horse. A fast horse. She will make you happy."

"She will not make me unhappy," Vykers corrected.

The Historian translated.

"You are welcome to continue on your journey, then, warrior," the man replied, standing aside and pointing the way forward with a sweep of his hand.

Vykers wouldn't be rushed. He needed to move the saddle Cindor had created for him from his dead mount to the new one, Shalea. Truth be told, he also needed a few moments to compose himself. The wound in his side was hurting him more than he cared to admit, even to himself. Now that the Queen was almost within reach, he could not countenance any weakness of mind or body. He would succeed; he would win, as he always had.

You sure know how to make friends, Arune teased.

I know how to make corpses. Everywhere Vykers looked, he saw expressions of fear, anger and awe. *Good,* he thought. *Good. I'm in familiar territory, now.*

The Historian, the Fool and the Frog seemed largely unscathed by the recent action, though the two prisoners, ragged with travel and exhausted from the heat, appeared almost wall-eyed with panic. The Reaper approached them, stood near the Historian so the Shaper could translate.

"I expect we'll run into some o' your fellows soon. You'd best hope they'll let us buy our way through their force with your lives. If not…"

But the Historian did not translate. Instead, he faced Vykers. "That seems unnecessarily harsh, given everything they've been through these last few weeks."

Vykers stared at the prisoners, who could not muster the courage to meet his gaze. "Never mind, then. I can see they understood me just fine." If he lived to be as old as the Ahklatian, Vykers would never understand the fellow. Sympathy for the prisoners? Hadn't they attacked Vykers and the rest of his party with some sort of bullshit magical 'leap'? Hadn't they killed Three? They'd earned whatever was coming to them. They were already dead men. The only question was whether or not their countrymen valued their dead.

A quarter hour later, Vykers climbed onto his new mount and he and his companions were again ready to move on. The Reaper took in the camp and its strange soldiers one last time and then urged Shalea southward, towards the next encounter.

He was not disappointed. His party came to a trench embedded with sharpened stakes, across which a small, portable bridge had been laid. On the far side, stood two exceedingly tall men in armor of bone, skin and feather, whose complexion was so dark Vykers knew them at once: makers and wielders of the Ntambi club. Sure enough, attached to their belts, each man had a version of the souvenir Vykers had with him even now, stashed with his gear. These men, then, were Ntambi. This was a fight he'd been looking forward to for ages.

Spirk, Ron, in Teshton

Things were slow at Gangrene & Sons, and although the barkeep reported having seen one or two other members of Captain Long's team, he'd no news of Long himself, or Captain Kittins. Spirk volunteered to return to Lunessfor to search for his friends, but the barkeep wouldn't hear of it, going so far as to lay his big mitts on Spirk's shoulders and force him down into a chair by the fire.

"I've orders to keep you all here as you come in," the hulking barkeep said. "City's an angry hornet's nest o' riots, pillaging and the like. You go back into that, you're like to get killed. Or worse."

"What's worse than gettin' kilt?" Spirk asked, confused.

Ron choked on his ale. Some of it even shot out his nose.

The barkeep considered explaining what was worse, but decided against it. If the homely young fellow with the big birthmark couldn't imagine a fate worse than death, he was lucky. Let him remain so. "Never you mind. You're stayin' and that's that. I've got a room in the back you can sleep in and your meals are on me...within reason. I ain't roasting a boar for ya, so don't get any ideas, understand? Now," the man said, "I have to get back to my bar. You get bored, you can see the sights o' Teshton," he laughed.

Spirk grew bored immediately. "Let's go see these sights, eh, Ron?"

Ron hadn't noticed any sights on the way into town. Teshton was one of those places in which a sow giving birth was worthy of a weeklong celebration. But his master and new friend had been unusually restless since the banquet at the D'Escurzy estate, so Ron supposed a little stretch of the legs might do the man good. He followed Spirk out of the tavern and into the muggy afternoon sun. The air smelled of cow dung, and without the slightest trace of a breeze to alleviate the humidity or the stench, Ron was sorely tempted to run back indoors and lie down. Summer could sod off, for all he cared. He'd been made for autumn and winter. Well, mostly autumn. Fact was, he didn't care for extremes in weather. Give him cool weather year 'round, and he'd be a happy man, indeed.

Suddenly, Ron realized Spirk had been talking to him. "I'm sorry?" he said.

"I said I didn't mean to kill anyone, 'specially Faenia."

How much of this conversation had Ron missed? "I don't believe you did, sir," he stammered.

"I did, Ron. O' course, I did! I misused Pellas' legacy and now he'll never forgive me!" Spirk protested, in as agitated a state as Ron had ever seen him.

"But...forgive me, sir, but Pellas is dead. They say he died in an explosion of stars in the battle against the End."

Spirk turned to his friend, tears in his eyes. "He exploded, right enough. I was there, remember. But I won't b'lieve he's dead."

Ron stopped walking, faced his friend. "I'll not gainsay it. But even if you did use Pellas' legacy, don't you think that's what he would have wanted? I mean, he chose you, right?"

"I kilt a whole room full o' people, though," Spirk cried. "And wounded a bunch more. That don't seem like old D'Kem to me."

Ron didn't understand half of the things Spirk rambled on about. But he did understand that his friend was in torment. Not knowing what else to do, he embraced him...and Spirk began sobbing. Ron had never heard such pain in another man's voice, and he almost broke down himself. Over Spirk's shoulder, he saw a couple of farmers staring at him, but Ron ignored them. What did he care if the locals talked?

Vykers, the Lakebed

Vykers jumped from his horse, felt a twinge in his side, didn't give two shits. "Let's see what you're made of, you big bastards." The men facing him might have thwarted his charge by kicking the footbridge into the trench below, but they did not, suggesting they weren't overly concerned with Vykers or his companions. Which further enflamed the Reaper's hunger for violence. He didn't like to be taken lightly. He stormed across the bridge in three prodigious strides and brought his sword swooping in from the enemies' left. They deftly dodged backwards, as he knew they would, allowing him enough room to get off the bridge and back onto solid ground. Both sentries exchanged looks of amused disbelief and pulled the clubs from their belts, nearly in unison. From there, they assumed defensive stances, which made perfect sense, from Vykers' perspective. With his back to the trench, all *they* had to do was gain a few feet in order to push him over the brink and onto the stakes below. It seemed an entirely reasonable plan, except for the fact the foe they faced was as far from entirely reasonable as anyone could possibly be. The Reaper fleetingly took in his adversaries' exotic faces and then launched a withering series of blows no mortal man could hope to parry. The pair on the receiving end did marvelously well...for a time. They were lithe, strong and agile, and possessed far better reflexes and instincts than anyone else Vykers had faced on the old lake bed. Under other circumstances, he might have made an effort to learn more about them and their martial philosophies; as it was, he was in a hurry, burning to complete the task he'd been saddled with lo these many weeks. He pressed the attack, occasionally ducking or batting aside one or the other of the men's Ntambi clubs— they were imposing weapons, but he held a magic sword. The contest lasted nowhere near as long as Vykers had hoped. In the end, he was actually able to kill both men with the same blow, decapitating the first man and shearing deep into the shoulder and chest of the second. With aggressive contempt, he swept their bodies into the trench behind him and turned to face whoever might step into the space they'd vacated. No one came.

Vykers paused to gather his breath and focus his senses on the camp ahead of him. A wall of men stood watching him, their faces, inscrutable. At his back, Vykers heard the sound of his comrades' feet on the bridge, but no horses. He chose not to examine this curiosity, given the force before him.

"Who commands this army?" he challenged.

The wall parted and the largest, broadest Ntambi Vykers had seen stepped through the gap. The fellow had a tremendously large, bald head with an ornate tattoo in white upon its crown.

His teeth were lacquered in an alternating pattern of black and red, so that he appeared to be missing half of them, while the others seemed drenched in blood. Vykers observed that this man's club had two sharp, bladelike projections on either side that made the thing look even more vicious than the usual variety. He thought it would make an excellent keepsake.

"Who dares attack my soldiers?" the man asked.

Without turning, Vykers understood the Historian had to be right behind him, or he would never have understood the Ntambi leader's question.

"I do. I am Tarmun Vykers, the Reaper. I mean to get to the obelisk by sundown, and I'll kill any and every man who stands in my way."

The Ntambi leader said nothing for a good length of time and then broke into a great, broad smile. "I love a good fight!" he proclaimed. "Come, engage me. For the courage you've shown, I promise not to kill you."

You can't both be right, Arune opined uninvited.

You know who's right, Vykers answered.

The Ntambi leader walked fearlessly right up to Vykers and prepared to swing his club. Vykers slapped him on the right ear so hard he burst the man's eardrum and sent him to his knees, howling in pain. When his head came within a couple feet of the ground, the Reaper kicked him full force in the jaw, launching him onto his back not five paces from the rest of his men. Vykers brought his sword around and waited for the larger man to rise.

Not bad, for openers.

Vykers ignored her.

From his backside, the Ntambi leader let loose a thunderous belly laugh and rocked himself into a seated position. He shook his head violently to clear the fog and stumbled to his feet.

"Good, good!" he bellowed. "And now, my turn!"

It was surprising how fast he could move, given his bulk; it was all Vykers could do to get out of his way as he stampeded past without even raising his weapon. The Reaper adjusted his footing and circled to his right just enough to keep the other man directly in front of him. Now, the ebony-skinned warrior did bring his club into an attitude of attack, but it could also be turned to deflect an attack, as well, should Vykers decide to move first. He did not, though. It was up to the Ntambi warrior to land a blow now, if he could. That the other men in this camp did not rush to his defense suggested they viewed this fight as sacred, the only thing needed to resolve the conflict between their attacker, Vykers, and themselves. And this was something the Reaper could respect, for he'd have done the same himself—had, in fact, done the same himself—to spare the other members of his party. He moved his sword into a sort of hanging parry, a challenge to his opponent, presenting a possible opening...or a trap. The other man grinned at him and started dancing on his toes. The half circle of men at Vykers' back began chanting something unintelligible. He thought to ask the Historian what it was, but decided against it. Unless it was magic, it wouldn't have much impact on the outcome of the duel; if it was magic, Arune would have to deal with it. With a sudden roar, the Ntambi warrior leapt at Vykers and swung his club in a lethal arc aimed at the Reaper's head. The man must have known Vykers would parry, so this was a test of strength. If the attacker proved stronger, he'd smash through Vykers' defense and crush his skull. The Reaper considered a moment: accept this test or dodge aside and leave his opponent off-balance and bewildered? He took the warrior's blow and the considerable weight behind it and let the fellow grind his club against Vykers' sword. The Ntambi leader grimaced at him over the locked weapons, sweat now streaming down his face. The man tried to buckle Vykers' knee with a kick, but the Reaper made the smallest adjustment to his stance and the blow missed. In the next breath, the fellow ducked, attempting to bring the lower end of his club under Vykers' sword and score a strike to the face. Vykers somersaulted backwards and sprang to his feet several paces away, causing the Ntambi leader to tumble onto his face in the dirt. Again, the Reaper might have closed for the kill but declined. He relished unfamiliar opponents and unknown fighting styles and wanted to see what else his adversary might try. Too, he felt that only total domination of the Ntambi leader would keep the other warriors at bay. Yet, it was also important to preserve the leader's dignity. Vykers would not toy with him; he would simply prolong the skirmish enough to learn what he wished to know.

But when the other man got to his feet, Vykers could tell by the look on his face that it was perhaps too late to preserve his dignity. In addition, the surrounding warriors had altered their chant, which seemed to infuriate the man even further. With a scream that was equal parts rage and humiliation, the Ntambi leader barged up to the Reaper and lambasted his defenses with a jaw-dropping series of powerful combinations meant to crush all resistance. Vykers danced, as he always did, and nearly escaped the worst of it when he caught a knee in his belt, right over the spot where its two cones plugged his wound. The pain was excruciating and drove Vykers to his haunches, barely able to breathe. Just when it seemed the other man might land a killing blow, a curious thing occurred: the Reaper's mouth filled with the taste of honey, and strength returned to his limbs. With no time to spare, he spun sideways, evading a blow that would surely have pulverized his neck. Before he'd travelled completely out of reach, he lashed out with his sword and sliced through the tendons on the back of his rival's feet, causing the larger man to dive forward in an agony of his own. Vykers rolled, gathered himself and worked his way to a standing position. His enemy thrashed about in the dust, in such pain that nothing outside his body even existed.

"Why don't they send in an A'Shea?" Vykers called over to the Historian.

"According to their chanting, they now view him as an embarrassment. He'd be better off dead."

The Reaper shrugged. Dead it was, then. He walked over to the still writhing form of his former foe and shoved his great sword between the man's shoulder blades and into the dirt beneath, destroying his heart in an instant. Then, he wrenched his sword free and took the man's head off with one mighty swing. He might have spared the man, but with the rest of the Ntambi army watching his every move, he believed any show of mercy would only invite further conflict. Without taking his eyes off the Ntambi, he strolled back across the footbridge to his horse, fetched a cloth from his pack, and wiped his blade clean.

That done, he walked back again and stood facing the half circle of warriors who'd witnessed his victory, waiting for someone to step forward and speak with him. He was pleased to discover that the Frog, the Fool and the Historian had joined him.

"So," he began, allowing the Historian to translate, "Will anyone else challenge my right to pass, or will you step aside and allow my companions and me to go?"

Now, someone stepped forward. This new speaker was shorter than his brothers, with the grizzled look of middle age, an amazing thing in a warrior. "It is customary amongst our people to feast with the victor of such a challenge," the man said.

"Come to think of it," Vykers responded, "a little meat and drink would be welcome about now." He took a moment to gaze into the midday sky...and blacked out.

He awoke briefly whilst the Frog carried him into a nearby tent, but was unable to sustain consciousness. The next thing he knew, he was lying on his back, gazing up into a lattice-work of tree branches.

"Tarmun?" a familiar voice inquired.

The A'Shea's sudden appearance and the presence of her hands upon his face felt so wonderful he almost roared for joy. And then he remembered himself: he was the Reaper. He had come to this Mahnus-forsaken land to find and rescue Her Majesty. Everything else was of secondary importance. But when his eyes found Aoife, he ceased to care about his mission.

"Where am I?"

"You're in my grove...a grove, north of...wherever it is you've been," Aoife replied.

"How'd I get here?"

How did you get here? Arune interjected sarcastically.

Ah. "Never mind," Vykers told the A'Shea. "A better question is why you're not still at sea." Aoife looked bewitchingly beautiful, and Vykers wondered if he wasn't under some sort of spell. He felt sure Arune and his sword would never allow it, and yet...

"I was...worried for you...you and the rest of the party, that is. No one should travel into a potential ambush without an A'Shea."

"I gave you an order," said Vykers, sternly.

"I remember," said Aoife, not ungently. "But I answer to a higher power."

"Ha!" Vykers scoffed. "And this 'higher power' compels you to follow me into the countless hells, does it?"

"Will you never stop arguing?" Aoife said in a raised voice. Impulsively, she kissed him, long and hard.

Gods! Vykers thought, *You haven't lived 'til you've been kissed by a beautiful A'Shea.* He felt all the usual energy, elation and lust, but there was also a profound sense of well-being and renewed vigor that astonished him. When at last Aoife tried to pull away, Vykers gripped her hair, softly but firmly, and continued to kiss her.

Arune's soul sang in its own euphoria, not for Vykers, but for herself, for the sheer, unadulterated wonder of intimate contact with the A'Shea. She experienced everything Vykers did, but there was somehow something extra, a sense of having finally found herself after a lifetime and more of searching.

Eventually, the Reaper needed to come up for air. Reluctantly, he released his captor/captive and relaxed onto the grass beneath his back. In seconds, he was asleep.

"What happened to me?" he asked Aoife after he'd awoken. He'd managed to negotiate himself into a sitting position, and the A'Shea sat by his side, holding his right hand, gazing at his fingers as if she'd never seen such things before.

"It's considerably warmer here than at home. Too much exertion in this sun and not enough water can be fatal. In addition, your wound continues to drain your energies. You've got to slow, or you'll kill yourself."

"Seems I'm the only one who can," Vykers joked.

Aoife didn't laugh. "We could leave, you and I."

He looked at her, was again amazed at her magnificence. "Would that were so," he said. "But I committed to this, and I gotta see it through. That's just how it is."

"There will be other Queens," Aoife retorted in frustration. "Other kings. But you..."

"Yes?" Vykers grinned.

She punched him in the shoulder. "Oh, it's hopeless. I'm an

A'Shea; you're the Reaper. I've never heard of a more ridiculous and inappropriate pairing in my life!"

Vykers sat up even straighter. "You said we could leave...? I'm guessing you didn't mean by horseback."

"No," Aoife confided, confused.

"So, you got some means of moving us, like a Shaper?"

"Not exactly like a Shaper, no. But I can get us home in a heartbeat. Because of this," she indicated the grove around them.

"Huh. I'm not even gonna pretend to understand. What I wanna know, though, is can you get us all home?"

"All?"

"The rest of the party—the Frog, the Historian, the Queen, even that idiot Fool."

Aoife sighed. She could see where this was going and didn't like it. Still, she wouldn't lie to the Reaper. "Yes. I would have to take several trips, but I could do it."

Vykers stood, radiating a sense of urgency. "I need to get back to that lake bed. Did you patch me up well enough?"

"Would it stop you if I said no?"

"You know it wouldn't!" Vykers laughed. *Arune! Whatever you did, do it again. I got to finish this.*

The Shaper was not happy. *Sometimes, you're too stubborn to get out of your own damn way!*

"I'll be back," Vykers told Aoife. "And you know why?"

"Why?" Aoife asked, afraid to hope for a favorable answer.

"'Cause you're worth living for, Aoife."

Before she could even break into a smile, Vykers disappeared, a faint pop the only sign of his passing.

Long, House D'Escurzy

"So, when does the torture start? When do you begin to exact our revenge?" Janks asked demanded.

Long ignored the question. "Do you know the, uh, recipe for that elixir of yours, that truth-telling stuff?"

Janks took a second to consider the question and then responded, "If you mean to try it on me, I can save you the time and expense and simply answer your questions, your lordship."

"You don't drop the sarcasm, old friend, I may bring the hot poker after all..."

"As you say."

"But I'm willing to try it your way, as long as your answers satisfy."

Janks walked to the cell door, smiled at Long through the bars. "I'll do my best."

"Good. Then you know what I want to know."

"You say we're old friends," Janks agreed. "I got some old scars only you can explain."

"Go on."

"But I've got no memory o' you."

Long pondered this a while, then, "What do you remember? Can you tell me, say, what you were doin' four years ago?"

Janks dropped his eyes to the floor, seemed to search its stones for an answer. "I've been wracking my brains about that for some time," he confessed. "I can't recall anything beyond the last two years."

"Which means you can't disprove my claim, then, eh?" Long prodded.

"But you said you'd killed me. Do I look dead to you?" Janks countered.

It was a conundrum, all right.

At that moment, a guard approached, accompanied by someone whose patina of sweat and dust suggested he'd just come from the road.

"Your lordship?" said the guard. "Messenger here wants a word, and it please you."

Long gestured with his chin, indicating the two arrivals should follow him down the corridor, as it didn't seem wise to receive this mysterious message in Janks' hearing. "Well?" he asked.

The messenger looked unhappy with the news he was about to deliver, and Long felt a pang of prescience. "I went to the town you mentioned and sought out the apple orchard, as instructed. There was no one at home."

Long was about to dismiss the significance of that news

when something in the messenger's manner stopped him. The man continued, "I questioned the neighbors, and no one has seen your wife and child in weeks. They say..."

But Long was off and running, racing for the room in which he conducted business with all speed. After what seemed the longest run of his life, he arrived and yelled to the nearest guard, "Bring me Tane, Dendul and Jasper. Now, fast as you can!" The man departed without so much as a "Yes, your Lordship."

While he waited, Long panicked. It seemed the thing to do, given the circumstances and dearth of information. Funny that threats of torture and death had less impact than the possibility that something had befallen his wife and daughter.

The three D'Escurzys arrived almost simultaneously, and Long was gratified to see they were short of breath. He'd called, and they had come as quickly as possible.

"Your Lordship?" Jasper asked, his chest still heaving as it fought for more air.

"I need to leave for an unknown period of time. One of you will have to rule the House in my stead."

Dendul, Jasper and Tane eyed one another skeptically. None of them volunteered for the job.

"Come on, now, men. It is your House, after all, and I've no time to waste."

"But Your Lordship," Dendul protested, "It hasn't been so peaceful 'round here since Lord Titus was young—there's no bickering, no jealousy, no discord of any kind."

"That's because half of you are dead, and the other half are still stunned from that event," Long responded.

"That's as may be," Tane replied, "But it's still a lot more pleasant around the House without a D'Escurzy in charge."

"Look, men," Long cut in, "I need one of you to take over for a bit. I am leaving within the hour!"

Something unspoken passed between the D'Escurzys and Dendul spoke up again. "We respectfully decline."

Long was nearly apoplectic. "You *decline*?" he shouted. "How in the infinite hells can you decline? It's your Mahnus-be-damned House!" If he'd expected his outburst to change the men's minds, he was sorely disappointed. They stood their

ground and said nothing. Long groaned in exasperation. "Very
well!" he said. "You have forced my hand. Don't blame me for
what follows." He spun to the guard who'd fetched the three
men and said, "Bring me the mad poet."

"The mad poet?" Dendul repeated.

"The mad poet," Long echoed. "Until such time as I return,
Peppers is acting Lord of House D'Escurzy."

"Well," said Tane, "It won't be the first time we been ruled
by a lunatic."

Vykers, the Lakebed

Hoosh nearly shat himself when Vykers reappeared directly
behind him in the tent, a fact that would have made the
unplanned excursion entirely worthwhile even had there been
no other benefits. But, of course, there had been. The Reaper
felt rejuvenated and ready to continue his trek towards the
obelisk. And he was strangely hopeful now, too, eager to be
done with this business so he could return to Aoife's side.

It was the Frog who voiced the obvious question, "Where'd
you go?"

Vykers stretched, smiled. "I had a few words with our
A'Shea…"

The Historian raised an eyebrow at this.

"And she tells me she's got a way to get us all home as soon
as we're done with this little errand."

"That doesn't seem likely," the Historian said.

"Lot o' things don't seem likely, but I'd expect an eight-
hundred-year-old man'd know better."

"Point taken."

"Maybe we should talk about what we're going to do when
we leave this tent…" Hoosh ventured. Vykers winked at him
and strode through the flaps into the afternoon sun.

"Where's this feast we were promised?" he called jovially.

"You're in rare spirits," the Historian observed, hard on his
heels.

"And why not? There's a good chance we'll reach her
Majesty and whatever's going on with that obelisk before

nightfall. I want to finish this and go home."

At the sound of his voice, the Ntambi warriors emerged from their own tents and, in short order, arranged a great meal in the larger tent of their former leader. Vykers ate and drank his fill, feeling better than he had in days and amused himself watching his awkward companions try to negotiate the subtleties of the occasion. It wasn't quite the sort of fare that the Ahklatian or the Frog favored, and though the Fool would eat anything, he seemed terribly out of place amongst the ebon-skinned warriors.

Hoosh, not unaware of Vykers' amusement, attempted to turn the tables. "What are ye planning t'do with all o' your captives?"

The Reaper brushed the question off. "One of 'em's half dead and the other two ain't worth much."

"But what of the three new ones?"

That was news. "Three new ones?"

"Yes. Apparently, it's the custom here that the youngest or weakest member of each army is sent along with the victor in each conflict, in order to learn…well, Mahnus knows what you have to teach, but they're supposed to learn from you!"

Vykers extended his claws and gripped the Fool's wrist. "Keep goading me, chuckles. See where it gets you." He then turned to the Historian and asked, "Is this true?"

"Only too. Every army we've passed through has sent someone along, except for the red knights. You'd already taken a man, and they're content you should have him."

"Even these fellows, here?"

"Yes. The boy they've given us is out by the horses, with the other captives."

Vykers set down the slab of goat he'd been gnawing at and sighed. "I can't be draggin' prisoners across the hells and back. And I can't ask Aoife to bring them home with us."

None of the Reaper's companions missed his use of the A'Shea's name instead of her title. They'd have shared knowing looks if they thought they could get away with it.

"Still," said the Historian, "They are yours now. It is up to you what you do with them. Before you rush out and slaughter them, however, I would urge you to spare them. They possess knowledge of these lands and their peoples that no one back home can equal."

"Fine. We'll keep 'em," Vykers muttered dismissively. "But I'll leave it to you," he said and then indicated the Fool, "And the motley menace, there, to tend to 'em."

"Motley menace?" Hoosh giggled. "Tis a wonderful thing when an ass breaks wind of a jest!"

Wordplay. How Vykers hated it. "Let's just finish this meal, thank our hosts and move on. Lotta fighting still to do before moonrise."

Back outside the dead leader's pavilion, the Reaper surveyed his new trophies—along with the original two he'd captured on the beach—and shook his head. What a strange assortment they were!

Climbing into the saddle of his new horse, Shalea, he got a better view of what lay ahead. "We're getting closer, but we've a ways to go, yet." Then, to Arune, *Anything else you can tell me?*

You've got eight more armies to get through.

Normally, Vykers would have greeted such news with excitement. Now, he was itching to be done with the task and get back to Aoife and home. Secretly, Arune shared his impatience.

I assume these fights are gonna get harder.

Oh, you can count on that.

What is it, Shapers, A'Shea and all that?

And a few…beings…I don't even recognize. Who knows? One of them may even be the Tarmun Vykers of this land!

Good. Then I'll enjoy killing him. "Let's go!" Vykers yelled to his comrades and spurred his horse forward to the next line of fortifications.

At the next gate, Vykers encountered the first of those 'beings' Arune had mentioned. It was roughly man-shaped and man-sized, but looked like it had been cobbled together out of disparate parts, like the chimeras had been, only in a much clumsier, cruder manner. And some of the parts looked human—here an arm, there an eye, etc. Vykers was about ask for the Frog's thoughts when his friend burst from the little group and sprang upon the opposing creature, which began squealing like a stuck pig. Soon, the two creatures were rolling across ground together, kicking up dust devils and making it difficult for bystanders to determine which was winning. In addition, both were so alien in shape and nature, it was hard to tell a scream of rage from a cry of pain. There was no mistaking the significance of blood, though, which soon dampened the lake bed floor and reduced the amount of dust in the air. With a loud cry, the Frog catapulted, spiraling, through the air and landed on his side several yards from his foe. Without missing a beat, he leapt up and bounded back into the fray, snarling like an entire pack of wolves. There was a great thud as the two monsters met again, straining and grappling for purchase and dominance. Just when Vykers was beginning to think he ought to get involved, there was a horrendous ripping noise and the Frog hoisted his enemy's head high into the air, sans body. The latest army, members of which had gathered on the gate's far side to witness the battle, faded backwards into their encampment, shaken by what they'd seen. The Frog ignored them, opting instead to sniff the corpse of his victim. Shortly thereafter, he began to eat in earnest and everyone on Vykers' side backed away as well. It was not a spectacle most men could endure without losing the contents of their stomachs.

After a good half hour had passed, a heavily armored man appeared on the gate's other side and demanded...something. The Historian was too far away for the stranger's language to make much sense, but Vykers suspected it was the same old "Who dares attack the camp of the mighty so-and-so" drivel he'd heard his whole life. Who dares? The Reaper.

Again, Vykers slid off his horse, drew his sword and walked towards the bellowing stranger. As he got closer, Vykers could see the man held a military flail in his left hand. He couldn't remember the last time he'd seen—much less faced—one of those in combat. They were powerful weapons, capable of enormous damage. But they were also unwieldy and lacked the speed and mobility of a good sword. And Vykers' was an excellent sword, an unparalleled sword.

Vykers waited for the Historian and his arcane aura to catch up before bellowing back at the man. "My men and I are going to pass through your camp. You can either step aside and allow it, or die trying to prevent it. The choice is yours."

As expected, the other man chose the latter, which was often the case when belligerent shouting was met in kind. The Reaper stalked to within a sword's length of his latest adversary and sneered at him; if the man meant to attack, let him do so. He appeared a canny veteran, however, and would not be so easily goaded into action. Instead, the fellow sneered back at Vykers, making a careful study of the Reaper's stance, his build, and his weapon. The man could study 'til doomsday for all Vykers cared. He raised his sword, hoping to compel a response. The other man—'Flail,' as Vykers came to think of him—came on with the animus of a hurricane and proved a far bigger challenge than the Reaper had anticipated.

Flail aimed most of his blows at Vykers' legs, attempting to lame or perhaps topple him altogether. It was almost as if Vykers didn't exist above the waist, and he was certainly not accustomed to expending most of his energy protecting his knees and ankles. It was an interesting strategy, but the Reaper had no interest in letting it play out. He began leaping over Flail's efforts and counter-attacking with blows aimed at the man's head, hoping to force him to raise his weapon into a more manageable posture. The first time he did, Vykers returned the favor and struck at his legs. Flail was not amused. He tottered backwards a few steps and reset his stance. Vykers could tell he was frustrated, but savvy enough to remain calm. A younger, less experienced opponent would have attempted to bring this dance to a hasty conclusion by sheer force of will, and, in doing so, ensured his own demise. This man was no fool. Still, Vykers began to grow bored of the encounter; he'd seen what Flail had to offer and wanted to move on to the next engagement. He put all of his energy into a feigned lunge at the fellow's head, and when Flail raised his weapon to ward off the expected attack, Vykers sheared him in half at the waist, right through armor and bone as if they were no different from flesh. The Reaper's sword exulted.

If Vykers expected Flail's countrymen to surrender, he was

mistaken. A bolt of pinkish light exploded in the air directly in front of the warrior's chest, and he felt a familiar burning throughout his body.

Arune?

Busy, she snapped.

Eerie tendrils of darkness crept past the Reaper from the direction of the Historian and wound their way into the enemy encampment, evoking screams of pain and terror wherever they went.

Vykers advanced into the gap at the gate, lately occupied by Flail, and swept his sword back and forth as a deterrent to anyone foolish enough to consider approaching. Someone shouldered past him in a rush; the Frog had evidently recovered from his meal and was looking for more.

And where's the Fool? Vykers wondered.

Back with the prisoners, Arune answered.

I thought you were busy.

I was. We killed the enemy's Shaper.

Ah, Vykers replied. *And how's the Fool think he's gonna handle all them captives?*

Arune laughed. *You'd be surprised.*

What did not surprise the Reaper was the enemy had finally decided they'd had enough. After losing their monster, their basher and their Shaper—along with who-knew-how-many others, they'd decided to accede to Vykers' wishes. Looking around the camp, he saw that every man in their force had gone down on one knee, the left knee, and bowed his head in submission.

"What a beautiful sight!" Vykers exclaimed.

Beautiful? Arune asked. *I never thought to hear you utter that word.*

Shows how much you know, the Reaper joked. *There's plenty o' things I find beautiful.*

And I can name one of them, Arune thought to herself. *I only pray we live to see her again.*

Vykers turned and looked back the way he and his party had come. They'd nearly reached the middle of the mass of armies abutting the obelisk and the salt marsh beyond, and yet, for all that, there remained as much or more to come, with ever stronger foes into the bargain. Vykers wiped his blade on the sleeve of Flail's corpse and slid it back into the scabbard across his back. Then, he bent over and retrieved the actual flail, giving it an experimental swing or two. "Damned fool weapon," he rumbled. "Good against savages and peasants, no doubt. Not so good today." That said, he tossed the thing back into the dirt, next to its master.

The Historian appeared at his side. "Shall we proceed?"

"Let's."

Kittins, the Witch's Hut

He sat up. It may have been the greatest accomplishment of his life to date, what with the stiffness of his joints and muscles and the close-to-unbearable pain of his numerous wounds. The old witch had said they were healing, but they hurt worse now than when he'd received 'em. The fact was, he probably shouldn't be sitting up at all, but his savior had disappeared, and Kittins wanted to take a leak on his own for once. He was also curious just where it was that he'd washed ashore. He was more familiar with the countryside upriver of Lunessfor than down, but he hoped to see something, some landmark or other, that might provide enlightenment.

Because he was planning to return to the city and kill His Lordship, Darley Gault. Why? His head was too muddled to provide him with concrete answers; all he knew was that he liked the idea—more than liked it, really: it burned like a hunger within him. So. He would return to House Gault, pretend to come calling for his promised reward, and then strangle the fucker with his bare hands. Darley looked a strong fellow, but, to Kittins way of thinking, he had nothing to lose in the attempt. He'd already died once. More than once, really, if you counted the essentially decent man he'd been before arriving at House Gault. Oh, he'd been a hard man, but he hadn't been a bad one. Now, he had some acts, some murders in his ledger he'd never get erased. But it seemed the gods, fickle as they were, hadn't finished with him, yet.

From his pallet, he lurched to his feet, stifling the resultant scream of pain that would have brought Croonsbasket running to see what the matter was. When he reached his full height, he was overcome with dizziness and nausea and almost fell right back onto his face. He'd been soldier, once, and a good one, too. His training kicked in, his iron-hard discipline, and he stood stock still until the queasiness passed.

In time, he examined himself. He was naked, save for a primitive skirt around his waist that hung to mid-thigh. His skin was a quilt work of stitches running off in odd directions. Apparently, he'd sustained more wounds than he remembered, and perhaps even a few further during his brief career as flotsam. Most of his wounds were mildly puffy and itchy, but none were warm to the touch—a good sign they'd not gone septic. Still, he couldn't exactly saunter into town in his current condition and expect to avoid attention.

He looked around the witch's shanty and found little of immediate use or value. She'd a single metal pot which she kept full of soup that was probably older than Kittins; at least, he was sure that was true of some of its ingredients. There were also some earthenware bowls, one or two of which were so cracked as to be nigh onto useless. Hung from the ceiling's very low rafters were dried odds and ends, pieces of once-living things Kittins recognized, and others he pretended he did not. None of it seemed the slightest bit helpful.

He remembered he had to piss and hobbled his way towards the hovel's entrance. He was hoping the air smelled better outside than in, but it only smelled bad in a different way. Inside, the hut smelled of burnt herbs, grasses, sweat and Croonbasket's soup. Outside, the air had a pungent, swampy quality with a hint of sulphur. It was late afternoon, and Kittins could see no sign of the witch or anyone else. He wandered a short distance until he found what he took to be a tributary of the river and lifted his skirt to relieve himself in its waters.

"Out fer a stroll, are you, Poor Tom?" the witch giggled behind his back.

Kittins let out a long breath. He'd hoped he wouldn't run into her again. Without turning around, he said, "Time was,

I'd've thanked you for what you did. I'm not so sure it's a mercy now, though."

"And still, the dead envy us sumpin' awful."

Finished, Kittins turned his head and regarded the little woman with skepticism. "Do they," he said wryly.

"They do and does, Tom."

"You understand my name's not Tom."

"'Tis Tom to me!" Croonbasket replied blithely.

"How do I get out o' this swamp?"

"Ya canna go, now! Yer not ready."

Kittins wondered what she meant by 'ready,' but decided that, whatever her intent, he had to go. "I don't suppose you've got any coin or a weapon to lend me?" He wondered what he meant by 'lend,' knowing full well he had no intention of ever returning.

The old witch reached into the neck of her gauze-like shift and pulled something out from between whatever remained of her breasts. "Just this." She held the object out and up, so Kittins might see it better in the late afternoon/early evening light. It was some sort of handmade totem on a leather thong, an assemblage of little bones and twine, adorned with a small but truly fine opal at its center. "Take."

"Why?" Kittins asked uncertainly.

"You need it, Tom, if ever a man did."

"I've got nothing to give you in return."

The little witch smiled a tiny, private smile and chuckled.

A more hopeful man might have been paranoid, worried about the consequences of accepting such a thing; Kittins had simply stopped caring. Gently (and when was the last time he'd been gentle?), he took the proffered necklace and slipped it over his head and around his neck.

"Can you at least point me in the direction of Lunessfor?"

She winked her eyes at him and extended a hand to her right. "Might be, you'll find a raft up'n'down the shore, hard by."

Kittins regarded the old woman awkwardly for a final few seconds. He'd no idea how to conclude this conversation and so, in the end, he just turned and walked away.

Rem, the Queen's Castle

Kittins was not the only member of Long's team who was having difficulty getting to his feet. Rem dreamed he was sitting in a cold mud puddle, and, when he woke up, discovered he'd soiled himself as a result of the Shaper's…assault—what else could one call it? To make matters worse, he'd been left where he'd fallen, in the middle of the floor. The complete absence of guards made him realize the Shaper and others of the Queen's staff did not view him as any kind of threat; indeed, it was difficult to say if they viewed him as any kind of *anything*, which was quite a blow to his self-image. He'd believed himself the greatest actor in the land and a spy of no mean ability, as well. He now understood two things: one, the Queen's staff cared not one whit for his acting ability or reputation, and, two, they had even less regard for his skills as a spy.

He was hungry, cold and filthy and had been completely robbed of any dignity he'd once possessed. Luckily for him, he'd been in similar straights before and felt fairly sure he'd recover. He was nothing if not resilient.

But why had the Shaper dealt so harshly with him? Hadn't Rem done what he'd been hired to do and more, in fact? Hadn't he taken tremendous risks and endured unspeakable sacrifices in order to obtain the requested information? And was he then expected to spill everything he knew or suspected without the slightest compliment or gratitude? Gods, the upper classes were worse than peasants!

Unable to endure his own aroma any longer, Rem at last got to his feet and walked, as carefully as possible, towards the door. It opened without impediment and swung noiselessly inward. He peeked around it, looking for guards, and saw none. Was he really so laughably feeble they'd let him wander the halls unattended? The notion was hard to credit. There had to be someone, somewhere, alert to his presence.

He walked down the hallway for several doors in one direction, and finding none that were unlocked, turned and walked the other way. After several minutes, he chanced upon an older man just leaving his room.

"Greetings!" Rem called out, as cheerfully as possible. "Would you be so kind as to direct me to the baths?"

The other man looked him up and down and offered a look of such distaste it was all Rem could do to prevent himself from blushing in shame. "I think you want the servants' baths," the man said snidely.

"Good enough," Rem shrugged. "How do I get there from here?"

"A better question would be how you got here from there..."

"Ah, yes, well, I was a guest of Her Majesty's Shaper, and I gather I failed to amuse him."

"Ha!" the older man scoffed. "I do not doubt it, sir. We've little use for fops in the castle, and even less for incontinent fops." Rem was about to object, but the other man continued, "Continue down this hallway. When it comes to a tee, go left and walk until the new hallway turns right. Take the stairs you'll find there to the bottom, and ask someone who lives down there. I've never been and, if the place will accommodate someone like you, never intend to visit. Good day, sir." The man took a deep breath and ducked past Rem as quickly as possible, only bothering to exhale when he'd gotten well out of reach. Rem heard him muttering something as he faded into the distance.

Following the old man's directions, he eventually made his way to the servants' level, where he found considerably friendlier company. It was true, his breeches were stained fore and aft, but the cut of them and the material they were made of was far finer than most of the servants had ever owned. If they mistook him for a young nobleman recovering from a night of drinking and debauchery, he'd not correct the impression. It was about damned time someone in the castle treated him with a little respect. Thus, he landed in the baths without any further abuse, physical or verbal, whilst an obsequious chambermaid took his clothing for cleaning. Rem was so long in the water, the maid was able to finish the job and return before the actor had even dried off. In this task, too, she seemed eager to please, though she was somewhat less happy to see Rem fully clothed again. Ah, but it was good to be handsome! In recompense for her efforts on his behalf, Rem gave the maid a quick peck on the cheek and returned to the stairs he'd used earlier.

It was time to find his company and leave the castle.

If the Mahnus-cursed Shaper would allow it.

When he reached the top of the stairs, he got his answer. He'd been staring at the steps beneath him instead of watching the path ahead and come face-to-face with the man in question.

"Well, you smell better, at any rate," Cindor said.

Caught off guard, Rem found himself uncharacteristically at a loss for words. "Uh, yes, er...about that..."

"You'd better be about to tell me you're prepared to cooperate fully, with none of your foolery. I have precious little tolerance for evasiveness and word games."

Rem had a hard time meeting the wizard's glare. "I don't understand why you've used me as you have. Have I not done what I was hired to do?"

"I understand you're an actor of some sort," Cindor responded, apropos of nothing.

Rem stood up straighter, met the Shaper's eyes. "Of some sort? You won't have to look long to find many who'll say I'm the best in the kingdom."

Cindor smirked. "Indeed? Then you understand the importance of sticking to the script, of following directions."

So, this was a conversation about his attempts to set Houses Hawsey and Radcliffe at odds. "I do. I know, too, that sometimes a little improvisation is necessary in order to...advance the plot."

"And sometimes 'advancing the plot' results in disaster. Henton Hawsey is dead, as is his Ladywife, along with Gelter Radcliffe and several other members of the Radcliffe family."

Rem felt as if he'd been punched in the gut. "Wh...what? How?"

The Shaper's eyes seemed to bore into Rem's; the actor could almost feel his brain heating up. "How? Rumors were spread, supported by circumstantial evidence and bolstered by the testimony of a witness or two who can't be found. Hawsey launched a series of assaults on Radcliffe, Radcliffe retaliated in ways Hawsey wasn't expecting. Quite the bloodbath, actually."

If he'd had anything in his stomach, Rem might have thrown

up. "But…I was given to understand Her Ladyship was with child…"

"Not anymore."

Rem fell against the wall, overwhelmed with guilt.

"Come, now. You must have expected something of the sort."

"Why? I'd never heard of open conflict between any of the Eight. Enmity, yes. But bloodshed?"

"Don't pretend you rue their loss," Cindor said dismissively. "You're not that good an actor."

"You should write for the town's daily news. You sound like every other critic I've ever heard," Rem chuckled sadly. "Anyway, I'd like to take my company and go now, if you don't mind terribly much."

"Alas," Cindor sighed, not untheatrically, "I told them you were dead, and the whole group's disbanded."

"What???" Rem screamed. "Why?"

"Because you certainly looked dead to me."

"You knew I wasn't dead!" Rem yelled accusingly. "Otherwise, you'd have had me taken away. But you left me where I fell!"

Cindor smiled a ghastly smile. "Yes, but look on the bright side: I didn't kill you after all."

"What am I supposed to do now?" Rem asked, more to himself than Cindor.

"As it happens, we have an opening for…a spy. And you fancy yourself a spy, so it would seem our interests intersect."

"A spy," Rem repeated without intonation.

"Well, after all, Remuel Wratch is dead, so you can't very well go on being him."

TWELVE

Vykers, the Lakebed

Try as he might, he could not completely overcome his wound. Even with help from Aoife, Arune, his sword, and Cindor's belt, Vykers felt himself less than half the man he'd been before meeting the End-of-All-Things. He'd struggled in every duel he'd fought on the lake bed, though none knew it but himself. His parries were a touch too slow, his attacks lacked their customary strength, his overall ability to anticipate was sluggish. If he couldn't function at his best...

But it wasn't in Vykers to finish that thought. He would do whatever he must; he would kill anyone who dared stand in his way.

As the afternoon waned, he felt frustrated at how much distance remained between himself and his goal. He'd bashed his way through several more champions since he'd killed Flail, and still the obelisk and the Queen were not within reach.

I remember my old sergeant, Hobnail, was fond o' saying 'I'm gettin' too old for this shit.' Vykers told Arune. *I never understood him until now.*

That's your wound talking.

You're telling me? I killed that bastard sorcerer too quickly. I shoulda taken years, decades to finish him.

You did what you had to do and probably saved fifty thousand men or more in doing it.

Right, Vykers thought crabbily. *'S been a while since any o' you have given me any news about those magic fires, the obelisk or the Queen.*

Okay. Here's what I know: the obelisk radiates magic…

Surprise, surprise!

And the Queen is…stuck to it.

Stuck to it? You mean, chained or some such?

No: stuck to it, not bound by physical means.

Missing a hand probably makes it hard to escape, I'd wager.

I'm not sure she could extricate herself even then.

So, how'd she get stuck?

You'll have to ask her.

She's still alive.

She's alive, alright, and angry as a hornet's nest.

Vykers started laughing and didn't stop until the pain in his gut silenced him. *Now she knows how I feel,* he said to Arune.

Vykers, Arune whispered, *I don't think we're going to get to her before nightfall. I know that isn't something you wanted to hear, but…*

"Historian!" the Reaper called out. "Tell our hosts we're staying the night, and we'd like a couple of tents."

You took that easier than I expected.

I'm bone weary, Burner. Bone weary.

It wasn't what the Shaper wanted to hear, but she'd been expecting it for some time nonetheless. No one could maintain Vykers' pace for long, and many could never match it to begin with.

He was awakened by the sound of weeping, furtive weeping, and anything furtive was cause for concern. Vykers sat up in the dark, silently as a shadow and allowed himself a moment to remember where he was. The previous day, he'd beaten a series of champions, and the last had offered to host him and his party for the night. Huh. The legend of Tarmun Vykers grew, even when he was fixated on other things.

The weeping stopped.

"Frog?" Vykers whispered. "Let's get some air." Without waiting for a response, the Reaper stood, pushed aside the tent flap and stepped outside. He had an abiding fascination for stars and could sometimes spend hours looking at them; he looked up now and inhaled deeply, as if he could take all of the heavens into his lungs. He felt a presence at his side. "What's bothering you?"

"Bellyache."

"Huh. I thought you guys could eat anything."

The Frog hunkered down, seemed to sink further into himself. "Me, too. But that thing I ate today...didn't taste good. Didn't feel right. Not like...Three did. And that other chimera."

"I don't think the fella you ate was made in the same way."

Neither spoke for a while, and then Vykers said, "Anything else on your mind?"

"I'm a monster," the Frog said.

And a boy, Vykers thought.

"I'm a monster, and I don't think I'll ever be normal again."

What could he say to the lad to console him? Would the Frog care that many considered Vykers a monster? No, because, for all his violence, he still looked like a man. Should he lie to the boy and suggest that a cure might be found? No. A painful truth was better than an obvious lie. The Frog might even take such an attempt as an insult. "I ain't had a lot o' friends in my life," Vykers confessed. "And old Number Three was one o' the best. I still can't figure out how they managed to kill him on that beach. I've never known a better fighter."

"You're a better fighter," the Frog said.

"Lotta good that did Three on that beach, huh?"

"Well, but you got that famous wound, slows you down a bit."

Vykers gently slapped himself on the belt. "I do," he agreed. And then an idea came to him. "I do, Frog, but I guess I don't regret gettin' it."

The Frog turned his homely, misshapen head towards Vykers, uncertain if he'd really heard what he thought he'd heard. "But...why?"

"'Cause I wouldn't be standing here with you, for one thing." He clapped a hand on the Frog's shoulder. "I wouldn't have come to this land, seen the things I've seen, including this mass o' strange stars. You ever seen the like, Frog?"

The Frog allowed as he hadn't.

"And I s'pose there'd be a lot fewer men in the Queen's realm right now if I hadn'ta faced the End. I tell ya, it was a pleasure puttin' that bastard in the dirt." Vykers gazed at the

Frog, made sure the boy noticed. "So, I guess what I'm sayin' is, you can't take back the bad things without losing the good that came after. Over the years, I've lost some people and things that meant a great deal to me…and I've found new ones that come to mean just as much to me." In his peripheral vision, he saw the Frog nodding. Vykers changed the subject. "Big day, tomorrow, lad. We crack a few heads, save the Queen and go the hells back home. Let's get some sleep."

As before, Vykers didn't wait for an answer, but reentered the tent and returned to his bedroll. He'd either done some good, or he hadn't. Story of his fuckin' life.

From horseback, the Reaper had a clear view of the obelisk and Her Majesty's predicament. What he couldn't yet figure was how she'd managed to survive. Had to be the obelisk, and if it was, maybe the thing might be of some use to Vykers.

He arrived at the next official gateway between armies, with a small army of his own now at his back, an army composed of his original companions, the slaves he'd won or been awarded in combat, and curious onlookers of higher rank from the armies he'd passed through. There was an energy in Vykers' mob, a feeling of being witness or party to destiny, an excitement that impacted all five senses and hinted at the existence of others. Something unimaginable was in the offing; everyone knew it, but no one knew how.

With the Historian at his side, Vykers asked the lightly armored man who stood in his way "I've had no trouble getting this far. You really wanna waste your life tryin' to stop my passage?"

The Historian translated, and then the latest champion spoke. "We are born to die, stranger—some sooner, some later, but no one escapes it. I pray you, reveal my fate so I may understand."

The Reaper dismounted, pulled his sword again—an action he now did without thinking—and studied the man before him. His opponents in the lake bed had run the gamut from heavily armored to practically naked, from pale as snow to dark as obsidian, from short and stocky to tall and lithe. This man wore a mail shirt of bone and metal, with gauntlets and greaves of the same materials. His long black hair was braided down his back and oiled with a substance whose fragrance Vykers recognized but could not name. His bronzed arms and legs were wiry, with knotted ropes of muscle and numerous scars. In his hands, he held a steel pole, with a blade on one end and an apple-sized knob on the other.

"And if your fate is to die in these next few moments?"

"Then I will have done so at the hands of a worthy champion."

Vykers attacked. His target slipped backwards, ducking out of the path of the Reaper's first swing and bringing the knob end of his pole swooping around towards Vykers' head. But Vykers' opening move had been a feint; he abruptly chopped sideways with his blade, in order to intercept and perhaps break the other man's weapon. And missed. The champion's counterattack had been a feint, too. And so it went, as the combatants measured one another: back and forth, feint, attack, retreat, engage, and disengage. Just when Vykers was certain he had the upper hand, his opponent stepped back and, with a sharp click, pulled his pole apart into three sections, joined through their centers by a flexible chain. When he advanced again, he was able to whip either end at the Reaper like the tail of a scorpion. Vykers was not amused and decided to end the encounter. He was conscious of a sea of eyes on his every move and well understood the importance, the necessity of a decisive victory. His sword quivered in anticipation of what was to come. His foe charged again, pinwheeling his weapon with dizzying speed to the oohs and ahs of the onlookers. Faster still was Vykers, who lashed out in an instant and sheered through the other man's weapon, his armor, and his life. The only sound on the lake bed was that of the pole-fighter's corpse tumbling in two separate directions onto the dirt. Nothing happened for several breaths, and then Vykers heard whispering on all sides. And his gut ached. He looked around, found his horse, and crossed over to it. He pretended to be retrieving his water skin, but in truth he needed something to lean against or he'd fall down and possibly lose the benefits of his recent victory.

Two more, warrior, two more, Arune told him.

Vykers misunderstood. *Where?*

I mean, two more armies, and we've broken through.

And none too soon. This fucking heat, on top o' the hole in my belly, is really taking it out of me.

You hide it well.

Vykers took in the waves of spectators. *'S not like I gotta choice. These fuckers'll come crashing in on us if they get the slightest whiff o' weakness.* The Reaper found a rag in his saddlebags and wiped the blood from his blade. "Anybody else fancy dyin' today?" he yelled out loud. He leaned harder into his horse while the Historian translated.

Nobody stepped forward.

Long, His Farm

He'd ridden so hard and fast that he fell off his horse when he finally reached the orchard. There were apples on the trees— not ready for harvesting, yet, but the last time he'd been home, he'd seen only blossoms. He shouldn't have had the strength to crawl, much less walk, towards his front door, but fear and desperation drove him. He turned the knob without knocking and stumbled into the room with such velocity, he tottered across the floor and collided with the wall, opposite. He then tumbled into a nearby chair to recuperate.

If he'd been expecting someone to come and investigate, he was sorely disappointed.

"Em?" Long called out, knowing he'd get no response, but hoping otherwise. "Em? Esmine?" Still, no response. Long closed his eyes and breathed in the aroma of home; it was stale and faint. Besides himself, the only thing present was absence; it hung in the air like smoke.

When he recovered his strength somewhat, Long pulled himself to his feet and walked through the cottage, paradoxically smaller now without Mardine's massive form lumbering from room to room. How was that possible, Long wondered. How could any place be made smaller by removing its occupants? He suspected he knew the answer but balked at revealing it to himself for fear of falling apart.

Looking through his wife's possessions, it was clear she'd taken her travelling gear and little else. She'd rushed out the door and...?

"Long Peter?" a small voice called from the doorway. Long poked his head back into the front room. When he laid eyes on Leetsa, he nearly choked up with emotion. He rushed to welcome her into his home and then offered her a chair. "Leetsa, I'm so happy to see you!" he said, on the verge of tears. "Can you...can you tell me anything about my ladywife and daughter?"

Leetsa bowed her head in affirmation, but shyly, too, as if she were afraid of sharing what he wanted to know. "Aye, Peter, somewhat."

He didn't want to rush the sweet old woman, but Long needed to act, and in order to act, he needed information. "And?"

"She came by the farm some time ago..."

"How long ago?"

"Days and days, it must be."

"A fortnight?"

"Aye," Leetsa nodded sadly. "And then some."

"What did she say?"

The old woman could scarce meet Long's gaze. "That your babe had been kidnapped by your thrall and her...man, I guess you'd call 'im."

Long was too agitated to stand still, now, and began pacing in circles around the little room. "Did she know the man's name?"

Leetsa shook her head, no.

"But the thrall...she must've have had a name, yes?"

"Nelby," Leetsa replied.

"Nelby," Long repeated. He needed to remember that name, and worried, too, that he'd never forget it. "And why," Long asked, "did Mardine come to you instead of the constable?"

"Ooh, she did, by and by. But she needed someone to look after your apples. That was most important, she said."

Of course, she did. That was so like his wife: even in times of chaos and confusion, she kept her head about her.

"Cargon's been over every day. Sometimes, he hires a boy or two to help out. Only..."

"Only?"

"Mardine promised the lot to my husband, if he'd keep the orchard in shape 'til you returned."

How could he be angry? Long would have done the same in Mardine's position. The important thing was finding their daughter. "And then Mardine went looking for this Nelby, I'm guessing?"

"Ooh, indeed she did! She went into town and gave 'em all hells is what I hear. Even killed a thrall."

"Did she?" Long asked, astonished. "Had he been involved?"

"There's no tellin'," said Leetsa. "Most think he was just in the wrong place at the wrong time."

"And then what happened?"

"You'll have to ask the shopkeeper, Myx, or the Constable. I know she went roarin' out o' town, but I don't know the whys and wherefores of it."

For reasons he didn't quite understand, Long gave the old woman a quick kiss on the forehead and said, "A thousand thanks, Leetsa. I reckon I'm off to find Myx." And then, impulsively, "And tell old Cargon, if I'm not back by harvest time, the orchard's his for good and all."

Before Leetsa could begin to protest (as she surely would), Long was halfway across the orchard.

Yendor, House Amberly

Yendor had been transferred to a private room—a turn of events that was perhaps not as fortuitous as it seemed, given the horrifying revelations of the previous day...or whenever it had been. His mind remained too muddled to maintain an accurate sense of time or it might have been he'd suffered too much trauma. The one thing he felt fairly sure of was that being sober was not demonstrably better than being drunk. He may have done foolish, even horrible things whilst intoxicated, but he only seemed to suffer from his actions once he'd sobered up, therefore, it stood to reason...

The door to his room swung open on hinges that needed oiling. An alarmingly tall man in ring mail came in, followed by a younger fellow of normal height. The tall man walked to within striking distance, but the second man remained just inside the room. It was he who spoke first.

"Good morning."

Was it morning? "Morning," Yendor mumbled sullenly.

"How's the eye?"

"Gone."

"Still," the man said, "you've got the one, haven't you?"

This small talk was equal parts maddening and frightening. "I'm 'fraid you got me at a disadvantage."

The other man grinned. "By the short and curlies, I believe the saying goes."

Yendor didn't like the sound of that.

"My name is Lennard. I'm Lord of House Amberly," the man said. "And you are Yendor Plotz, decorated war hero and infamous drunk." Yendor must have gone pale or something, because Lord Lennard hastened to add, "You babble in your sleep. Did you know that? Normally, I'd wager that's an unhealthy habit, but as it saved us the trouble of having to torture the information out of you, it appears to have served you this time."

Yendor rolled slowly onto his side, so he could get a better view of his latest tormentor. Lennard was remarkably young to be Lord of a House. Sooth to say, it was doubtful the young man could grow a beard given a year's time. Yendor was about to comment on this when the door opened again, and a sheepish look came to His Lordship's eyes.

"Middiks!" an imperious female voice called out, "Leave us."

The bruiser immediately turned and walked from Yendor's bedside and exited the room. There followed a moment of near silence, quiet, save for the clicking of heels on the floor, and then His Lordship was joined by a sturdy woman of middle years and opulent taste in clothing.

"Can't a man have a little fun?" His Lordship asked the newcomer.

"Men do not have fun," the woman retorted sourly. "At least real men don't. Fun is the province of rascals and fools, the sort of fellows who dither away their time in fruitless pastimes whilst their families starve."

"We're hardly starving, mother," Lennard observed.

"And you may thank your late father for that, and his before him. If it's fun you're after, you should have been born a Gault or an D'Escurzy. As it is, you're an Amberly, and you will behave like one or find your fortunes very much reversed."

Yendor heard rather than saw most of this exchange, having only the one eye, and that diverted so as to allow his visitors as much privacy as possible for their awkward exchange. Sadly, he was pulled into the fray just the same.

"You! Cyclops!" the woman shouted.

Yendor rolled his eye her way.

"What has the boy told you?"

"Nothin', milady, save that he's Lord of the House."

"Lord, but not ruler," the woman scoffed. "And if he's not more careful," she warned, "he never will rule."

Nothing was worse than being caught in the middle of a family spat, Yendor reflected, unless it was being caught in a family spat without access to spirits.

"You have my leave to go," Lennard's mother informed him. "I will represent our House in this business from here on out."

This business? That had an unsavory quality to it.

Lennard pursed his lips, clasped his hands behind his back and departed, flushed and breathing heavier than the circumstances seemed to merit.

"Now then," the woman began, "I am Raisa, the young fool's mother—much to my frequent embarrassment—and true ruler of House Amberly."

"Pleased to make your acquaintance," Yendor said, as gallantly as possible.

"I doubt it. Your name, as I have been informed, is Yendor Plotz…"

Gods, did he have to go through all this again?

"A ridiculous name for an assassin, but there you have it."

Ah, yes, he was supposed to have killed someone.

"Let me get to the point, assassin: I am not the sort of woman who goes for torture, truth serums or painful magics. I prefer the direct approach: you will tell me what I wish to know, or I will take your other eye with these very nails."

They were, according to Yendor's admittedly cursory inspection, more than long and sharp enough for the job. "I'll tell you whatever you wanna know!" he cried bravely.

"I rather thought you might."

Yendor dared a closer look at his newest tormentor. She wore the whiteface that had lately come into fashion amongst Lunessfor's wealthiest women (and more than a few men), with rouged checks, blood red lips and garishly painted eyebrows. Her hair was pulled back into a net that appeared, from Yendor's limited vantage point, to be studded with pearls. An ornate and heavily starched lace collar spread out under her chin, making it look almost as if her head were on a fanciful platter. Her dress was of red so deep it was but a half-step from black, and it, too, held more than its share of pearls. He would have continued to stare, but Her Ladyship cut in.

"What I wish to know is who hired you to kill young Fyne."

"Nobody," Yendor replied quickly. It was the truth, and he hoped she could see that.

"Nobody. Was there some animosity between you? Had you known him previously?"

"No, neither." He realized a moment too late that he ought to have added, "Your Ladyship" or some such, but she didn't react, so he counted himself lucky.

"Had he done something to you during the riots?"

"No."

"Did you know who he was when you killed him."

"No."

"Tell me you remember killing him?"

Yendor nodded. "I do. More or less."

"Why did you kill him?"

"I don't know."

Raisa scowled, looked down at her lap. When she looked up again, she said, "You seem a rather weak-minded fellow. Perhaps you were ensorcelled. But that begs the question of who has the power to do such things..."

"A Shaper?" Yendor offered.

Her Ladyship nearly spat in contempt. "Of course a Shaper, you clodpoll! I've heard it's not easy to manipulate humans, but if they're stupid enough..."

"Stupid?" Yendor objected. "I was smart enough to survive the last war."

"And so did countless thousands of rats," Raisa countered. "Still, even if you're nothing but a pawn in this affair, you're still a pawn. Someone's pawn. I wonder who'll come calling if we leave you dangling out there in the middle of the board without protection..."

"Your Ladyship?"

"I'm setting you free, one-eye."

"But...Fyne's people may come after me."

"Mmmm," Raisa agreed. "They might. Doubtless will. And how will you handle *that*?"

Vykers, the Lakebed

The next champion in line was about Vykers' age, decked out in armor that must once have been magnificent, but had seen a few too many skirmishes. His grey-blonde hair was pulled back in a topknot, and he sported a long mustache that trailed off either side of his bare chin. The most interesting thing about him, though, were the tattoos of tears that ran from the outer corners of his eyes and down his cheeks to his jaw line. He watched Vykers' approach with an expression of ineffable sadness, a fact the Reaper found more than unsettling, as no one had ever regarded him thusly before.

"If you would not fight me, your army must have others who'll take up the challenge," Vykers told the knight.

As usual, the Historian translated. Within his aura, however, the other man's words were easily understood.

"Alas, it is my duty," he said flatly. "And more, it is my curse."

"And I am the Reaper," Vykers said.

"So I have been told," the knight responded.

Vykers raised his sword. "Let us see whose curse is greater."

Always aware he was being studied by the surrounding throng, Vykers again varied his tactics. This time, he planted the tip of his sword in the ground at his feet and rested his hands on its pommel. The tattooed knight raised his shield and sword and calmly walked within reach of Vykers' blade. Without haste or tension, he assumed a defensive stance and waited.

And waited.

And waited some more.

The sun crept across the lake bed; many in the crowd sat, others laid down. Just when it seemed the two adversaries had turned to stone, the tattooed knight leapt at Vykers, testing every part of the Reaper's defenses with a dazzling array of blows from every conceivable angle. It seemed impossible that anyone mortal could withstand such an assault, and yet... Vykers did, without returning fire. Eventually, the knight stepped back out of range, tossed his shield aside and leaned on his own sword. He looked down at Vykers' feet, studied his ankles and knees, considered the orientation of his hips and shoulders, and attacked again, in a barrage of blows that was even more spectacular than the last. Now and again, Vykers clearly winced in pain, but he never gave an inch of ground or went on the offensive. The knight came soaring in with another combination, whirling his sword in great, looping figure-eights, and then reversing his grip in the blink of an eye, spinning completely and chopping at Vykers' left shoulder. Which was no longer where it was supposed to be, so the knight found nothing but air. Undeterred by this development, he faked, feinted, tried to goad his challenger into making a mistake, or overconfidence. None of it worked. Again, the tattooed knight stepped back. There was no sign of panic on his face or in his posture; instead, he looked merely perplexed.

When the Reaper finally came at him, the knight was almost surprised. Vykers was like a violent wind, everywhere and nowhere. Impossible to block, impossible to hit. But the knight acquitted himself well, proving himself Vykers' far greatest opponent to date and worthy of the title of champion. At one point, the knight even achieved the unthinkable: a palpable hit on the Reaper's upper chest, carving a shallow trench from shoulder to shoulder. Vykers got angry and bashed away at the knight's defenses, smashing his parries down or aside until the beleaguered fellow could barely stand. Vykers was moments from victory.

And then a funny thing happened: the knight began to laugh. And it was not the lunatic laugh of a warrior in full blood lust, no. It was a laugh of joy, the laugh of a man relieved of a longstanding, crushing burden. The laugh of a man set free after years of cruel durance.

Irritated at this unexpected response, Vykers disengaged. "Why do you laugh?" He demanded. "You're spent and could die at any moment."

The Historian explained Vykers' comments to the knight, who regained his composure enough to reduce his laugher to a broad smile.

"I laugh, my friend," the knight answered, "because I am the Weeping Knight." He indicated his tattoos. "That is my name, because I have never been beaten in arms and thus am destined to kill any man who faces me. It has been my curse to see untold hundreds—thousands, even—fall under my blade. That makes me weep in sooth. And often, I know the outcome before the first blow is struck. But you..." His voice trailed off, thick with emotion. "You, I cannot kill! Your death will never be laid at my feet!"

Vykers considered the man's words for a long time and finally decreed, "And you, I will not kill. Will you accept defeat and allow me to pass?"

"I must," the Weeping Knight said. "And am honored to do so."

The mass of soldiers and warriors around Vykers' crew cheered heartily, as if a holiday had been declared, and followed the Reaper's every step towards the next and final gate. From there, even at ground level, Vykers could see the obelisk sat atop a small hill, perhaps twice the height of a man. He could also see Her Majesty leaning against the stone, still alive, against all logic. Behind the hill, the land sank away into the promised salt lake.

One more challenge, and Vykers could go home.

Kittins, House Gault

Kittins had to frighten and bully a few peasants, travelers and even a merchant or two along his trip back to Lunessfor in order to secure the clothing and food he needed, but he told himself these little acts of evil were as nothing compared to what he'd already done and was in fact still planning to do when he reached the city. What were a few more petty crimes to a man like him?

And, really, the important thing was vengeance. He would punish Lord Darley for his role in transforming Kittins into a monster, and if that wouldn't satisfy Mahnus and Alheria, then perhaps they'd accept Darley's death as payment for His Lordship's cruelty to others. Kittins could only imagine how many folks the callus bastard had damaged or killed. Well, now it was his turn.

When he arrived at the gates of Lunessfor, he was dressed in pauper's rags and carried nothing with him except for the charm Croonbasket had given him. The guards were reluctant to allow him into the city, but as he wasn't armed, they supposed him incapable of causing much harm.

They were mistaken.

Kittins walked right past the Fretful Porpentine and nearly went in, for old time's sake, but reckoned he no longer fit in with the team, if he ever had. Its members were bumbling but well-meaning, whereas he was neither.

It was late afternoon when Kittins reached the Gault estate. A couple of greenhorns he had never seen before stood outside the gates, fidgeting nervously with their weapons. The former Captain of the Guards walked right up and saluted them; they simply stared at him in return.

"What are you about then?" the one on the left asked belligerently.

Kittins punched him in the face so hard that the man flew backwards, collided with the wall and crumpled to the ground, unconscious, or worse. The other guard saw this and immediately lost all pretense of courage or competence.

"Wh...wh...what do you want?" He whined.

"Tell His Lordship that Captain Janks has returned and is here to collect the promised reward." Kittins didn't care three Shims for the reward, but he wanted to confirm his suspicions about Darley.

"Yessir, right away, sir," the guard stammered. He then rapped out a particular sequence on this side of the gate and waited for a response. When it came, he rapped out another sequence and the doors opened.

That was new, Kittins thought, as he watched the man slip inside. He might've forced his way in himself, but he had no interest in killing anyone other than His Lordship. Of course, he'd probably die, too, in the effort, but Kittins was at peace with the possibility. You can't be a bastard forever and expect there to be no consequences. Unless you were Tarmun Vykers.

The door creaked open again and Lord Darley appeared in the gap, backed by a number of heavily armed men. "You do have a disastrous effect on my guards," His Lordship remarked sardonically. "I understand you've come for a reward of some sort?"

Suspicions confirmed. "Just the one you promised for eliminating a certain...target."

His Lordship pulled a melodramatic expression of surprise. "Oh? But you failed, you know. Haven't you heard?"

He'd failed? Kendell had survived? He was about to dismiss the notion when he realized that he, himself, was proof of the impossible. "So, Kendell's alive?"

Suddenly, it dawned on Darley that this probably wasn't a conversation to be had outside the walls of House Gault, so he stepped aside and beckoned Kittins to enter. "This is, perhaps, best discussed in private," he said.

Ambushes were also best conducted in private, Kittins knew, but he went inside, anyway. He made eye contact with every one of His Lordship's bodyguards, to let them know he was watching and prepared for anything they might attempt. The door swept closed behind him, and Darley's men barred the gates.

"You look like you've been on a tour of the infinite hells. I'll wager you could use a drink, eh?"

"I wouldn't refuse one," Kittins replied.

Darley was a bold son-of-a-whore; he fell in right beside Kittins and continued chatting as they walked along. "How did you manage to escape the Radcliffes?" he asked.

"Turns out, they're not great lovers of fire."

"Aha!" Darley chuckled. "I'd forgotten about that. Yes, you may've failed in killing old Kendell, but you certainly damaged the Radcliffe fortunes. I'm told they lost half their buildings that night."

"And a goodly number of their guards."

They arrived at a room that was more elegant than any Kittins had seen in House Gault.

"Have a seat, Captain Janks," His Lordship urged. "What'll you have? Red? White? An ale, perhaps?"

Out of the corner of his eye, Kittins noticed Darley's bodyguard—all six of them—had taken up positions around the room. "I'll have whatever's closest to hand."

"Ever the pragmatist!" Darley exclaimed. "Here you go: it's a red Penser, a favorite of mine, actually."

Kittins accepted the goblet and waited until His Lordship had poured one for himself. The question was, would he drink it? Seeing that his former Captain of the Guard hadn't yet tasted his wine, Darley knocked his own back with relish.

"You see? No poison. And, really, what reason have you to suspect treachery from me? After all I've put up with, all I've done for you?"

After all you've done to me, Kittins thought. "Old habits," he said by way of apology, before draining his own wine.

"You look terrible," Darley said.

"Yes, well, your map wasn't entirely accurate, was it? I probably skirmished with half of Radcliffe House. And then I died, of course. That can be hard on anyone."

Lord Darley perked up at that last bit, looked around at his bodyguards to be sure he'd heard correctly. "You say you... died?"

"So I hear. But now, you tell me Kendell isn't dead. I smashed his brains out and felt 'em running down my arm."

"And yet, everyone says he's still alive."

"Has anyone seen him alive?"

Darley said nothing.

"'S what I thought. And anyway, you said yourself I damaged the—how'd you put it?—Radcliffe fortunes. I'd say I'm due."

His Lordship's jaw muscles twitched in irritation. "Do you know why I chose to meet with you in this room?"

"Don't really care, to be honest."

"Because this room belongs to my Aunt Dorshia. She's meddlesome, presumptuous and, as you can see, has rather poor taste in décor." His Lordship slid a dagger out of his sleeve. "I can't think of a better place to spill blood, frankly."

In unison, the bodyguards took a step closer to their master.

"What were you just saying about treachery? I reckoned right about you," Kittins said.

Darley smirked. "Did you now?"

"But you've vastly underestimated me, even after everything you seen."

His Lordship stopped smirking. "I'll allow you did well at Radcliffe, but there you were armed and armored. Here, you're facing six of my best men and myself, barehanded. Who do you think you are, the Reaper?"

Kittins was on him so fast, His Lordship barely had time to raise his dagger before the Captain grabbed him by the throat and dragged his body between himself and the guards, effectively blunting their attack. Once he got over the shock, Darley did plunge his dagger into Kittins' side...to no avail. The big man never so much as flinched in response, and no blood came from the wound. His Lordship found it increasingly hard to breath, so he focused his jabs at Kittins' head. The Captain released his right hand temporarily and punched Darley in the face as hard as he could, stunning His Lordship and stalling his attack. One of the guards tried to sneak past on Darley's left, so Kittins placed his hand back on Darley's throat and wrenched his body towards the oncoming guard, who, not wanting to injure his master, wisely backed off. Now, His Lordship began to turn an awful shade of purple, and his deep-set eyes, to bulge from their sockets. Kittins squeezed harder. The guards were yelling something at him—threats or the like—but it was all white noise. The only thing Kittins was fully aware of was his unspeakable rancor for the man he held between his fists. Darley regained his wits and again tried to stab at Kittins' face, missing instead and scoring a deep gouge on his assailant's arm. Along with his dagger strikes, Darley kicked at the bigger man's legs over and over, hoping, somehow, to force the man off him. Kittins had had enough. He put every last bit of strength he possessed into crushing His Lordship's windpipe and was gratified to feel a gruesome but welcome collapsing sensation under his fingers. He stared into Darley's eyes and saw that the man knew he was dying, knew Kittins had killed him. There was such rage in His Lordship's expression, such impotent rage, that Kittins was almost overcome with laughter. It was a surprisingly slow death, and Kittins took it all in, despite the efforts of Darley's men to punish him. He felt blows to his back, shoulders and even head, but none managed to pry his attention of His Lordship's final moments.

Only when Darley had finally expired did Kittins wonder why the other men in the room had abandoned their attack. When he looked up, they were gone—not for reinforcements, he suspected, but because they'd hated the old bastard as much as he. Well, he'd done the Gaults a favor, then. He wasn't sure how he felt about that.

He examined the wounds he'd sustained in the fight and saw for the first time that they weren't bleeding; moreover, there were far more than he remembered receiving. Darley's men had hacked away while his back was turned, and still there was no blood. The hair on Kittins arms and the nape of his neck stood on end, and a terrible dread came over him. He lifted the witch's charm off his chest, intending to tear it from its leather thong and cast it away, but found he could not. He was not afraid to die; rather, he was afraid what he'd learn if he tried to let death take him. Nonsense! He told himself. Superstition! And yet he could not remove the charm.

He stood, considered his options. If the witch's charm was protecting him in some way, Darley's bodyguard had probably gone to fetch the House Shaper. Kittins didn't want to be around for that. He pondered inflicting more damage on the House but decided against it. If he was going to leave under his own power, he needed to do so now. His time spent in service to the estate served him well, though, and he was able to recall a servants' entrance not too far off that would likely have lighter security than the front gate. There were other ways out of House Gault, but most involved travelling through areas where Kittins was sure to attract too much attention. Best to head for the servants' entrance and hope for the best. No, fuck the best. Kittins was leaving and anyone who stood in his way was worm's meat.

As it turned out, there were a few guards stationed at the door after all, including Wrensl Deda. The instant he set eyes on Kittins, he dropped his sword and bolted outside, obligingly-if-inadvertently clearing a path for the Captain. Kittins walked right past the other guards and out of the House. Wrensl was nowhere to be seen.

For a minute or so, Kittins was at a loss as to where he should go next, what he should do. Then he realized he needed to know more about the charm he wore. If he had no future, he'd as soon learn that now as later.

Vykers, the Lakebed

"Figured I'd see these bastards again," Vykers said.

The final army standing between him and his goal was one of those belonging to his Exalted Magnificence, Emperor Mendis Staurachia, the Eleventh. Resplendent in their midnight blue armor with stars, they looked better rested, better fed and much better trained than any of the other armies Vykers had passed through on his way to the obelisk. This army's spokesman was not a soldier but a Shaper.

"I see you have two of our own in your retinue. They are captives, no?"

"Trophies," said Vykers.

The Historian translated, as always, and the foreign Shaper frowned disapprovingly in response.

"And who are you, that you dare take prisoners from the armies of his Exalted Magnificence?"

"I'm the fuckin' Reaper. Now, stop asking idiot questions

and send me your champion. I mean to reach that obelisk within the hour."

The Shaper's face assumed an extremely snide expression. "The who? The Reaper? I don't believe we've ever heard of any reaper."

"Well, pay attention, asshole. You're gonna wanna tell my story to your grandchildren...if anyone's stupid enough to share a bed with you."

It's a fair bet the Shaper had never been spoken to like that in his life; nevertheless, he continued to act as if he held the upper hand in dealing with Vykers. "I've no doubt," he warbled, "you made quite an impression on the rabble back there." He pointed to the outlying armies. "But we in the blue serve his Exalted Magnificence, for whom nothing but perfection will serve. Let us see, warrior, how you fare against the juggernaut."

The what? Vykers looked over at the Historian, whose face was a mask of concern. Great.

"You'd better hope I lose," Vykers said to the enemy Shaper, "'Cause if I don't, I'm takin' you for my slave." He was gratified to see the wizard's smirk disappear.

What am I dealin' with, here? The Reaper asked Arune.

It's...it's...

A loud thudding sound came from within the enemy's ranks.

Hard to describe, Arune answered.

Vykers was about to say "try," but figured he'd see soon enough. When he finally did, he wasn't immediately impressed. *It's a giant in a suit of armor,* he told Arune.

No, she corrected. *It's a living, solid mass of steel that's been shaped to look like a suit of armor.*

Oh. His face must have betrayed him, because the enemy Shaper was smirking again.

The juggernaut stomped in Vykers' direction. It carried a huge mace in its right hand, but its left was empty—a mistake, to Vykers' way of thinking, but he wasn't about to point that out. *If there's nothin' but more steel inside that shell, then how'm I s'posed to kill it?*

I'm not sure you can, Arune confessed.

Thanks. And I imagine it won't get tired, either, huh?

Probably not.

What's makin' it move, though?

Shapers. Not this one here, though I suspect he's got some influence on it.

Fuckin' Shapers, Vykers spat, completely aware of the irony.

Well, Arune replied, ignoring the insult, *we already knew the Emperor's Shapers were powerful, based on their ability to jump entire groups of knights.*

Fuck the Emperor, too. Vykers pulled his sword and stalked towards the juggernaut. Normally, his weapon would have been howling for blood; now, it was curiously agitated in a way Vykers had never experienced before.

"All right, you big metal bastard, let's see what you've got!"

Enter the King

Eoman Harkin Hainin was a king, though most of his subjects didn't know it until he told them so. And this was because, at the time of the Awakening, his kinfolk fled humankind as if men had been infected with a plague, which, for all Eoman knew, they had. Thus, giants disappeared into the wild places, the mountains, the forests, the swamps and the canyons, wherever humans were not. The king's job, then, was to travel the world and to find his people, to remind them of who they were and who'd they'd been, in hopes of one day reuniting them. At least, that was how Eoman viewed things.

When he came upon the arm, he knew it at once it was the arm of a giantess, and anger bloomed within his chest. As he moved across the clearing, he found other parts, all savagely hacked from their owner, and his anger grew. This was not the work of Svarren, but of men, men with blades and fire. At last, he found the head belonging to the murdered giantess. Despite his fury, he wept. Her hair had been red, and he had known her once, when she'd been but a child: Mardine.

Eoman tore a small tree out of the ground at the clearing's

edge and beat the ground with it, over and over, until he exhausted himself. His rage reduced to a more-manageable degree, he returned to Mardine's head and gently lifted it into his arms. He then gathered the rest of her body into a pile and set about digging a great hole at the base of a suitable tree. Once this was done, he put the giantess' remains in the ground and refilled the hole. Next, he drew his axe and topped the tree at eye level, which for Eoman was about fourteen feet. He stripped the bark from the stump, and into the fresh wood underneath he carved the runes of grieving, adding also a few lines about Mardine's beauty, and Eoman's oath of vengeance. Finally, he carefully scorched the trunk, from the top of the roots to the cut. This was the practice of his people, and their king observed it when and wherever necessary, though it never alleviated his sorrow, never brought him peace.

He did not know why these unknown men had killed Mardine, nor did he care. They had committed an atrocity against his people and must now be put down like mad dogs. He scoured the clearing and surrounding woods and found the shallow graves of several humans. One, he unearthed in order to learn what he could of the men he was looking for, the rest he desecrated with urine.

There was a large fire pit near one edge of the clearing, and Eoman examined it for a good, long while, trying to determine how many had gathered there and how long ago that had been. He also saw ruts made by wagon wheels; these ran from the south to the northwest. He deemed it likely his quarry were fleeing civilization in the south—perhaps they'd been outlaws or some such—so northwest was the direction in which they'd gone.

He would follow them and make them suffer.

Vykers, the Lakebed

The thing was, as Vykers suspected, immune to damage, fatigue and even intimidation. It pursued him around the enemy's camp like a dog chasing a rat, whilst the Reaper struggled to figure out how he could destroy it.

He tried to out-quick the juggernaut, but it was just as fast. He tried to beguile it with agility it could never match, but it was every bit as agile. He knew he couldn't overpower it, and the juggernaut proved it almost from the start. Even his magic sword scarcely left a scratch on the thing's surface. The Reaper wasn't prone to despair, but he was rapidly coming to the conclusion he could not win.

He danced across the lake bed, kicking up dust, parrying the juggernaut's every mighty blow. *Can't you and the Historian attack their Shapers and rob this thing of its magic?* He asked Arune.

It doesn't work like that, Vykers. They brought it to life—some time ago, I believe—and...it's just alive.

That's helpful, Vykers snorted, as he fended off another thunderous blow.

Are you worried?

Hell yes, I'm worried!

The Emperor's troops were a civilized lot; still, they whistled their approval whenever the juggernaut managed a solid hit on Vykers' sword or struck the man off balance. The Reaper's ever-growing entourage was silent, troubled and wondering how their man could possibly prevail. Vykers was wondering the same, himself. For a time, he thought perhaps the answer lay in the juggernaut's joints. Surely, they were thinner, weaker than the usual torso or mid-limb targets. But they were not.

And the worst part was, Vykers' wound was giving him grief and he was tiring fast.

Kittins, with Croonbasket

"What have you done to me, witch?" Kittins demanded without preamble.

Croonbasket didn't seem remotely surprised by the Captain's sudden appearance or his angry demeanor. "I knew what you was thinkin', poor Tom. You had killin' on yer mind, and I knew, too, that ye wouldn't survive 'out a little help from old Croonbasket."

"At what cost?"

Now, she lowered her eyes, turned partially away, embarrassed or ashamed.

"What are you hiding, you Mahnus-cursed hag? What's the price for my survival?"

"You can't never remove that charm, Tom," the witch admitted.

"I bloody well can!" Kittins countered.

"Not if ye don't wanna die on the spot."

Kittins was silent.

Croonbasket went on. "Every wound you've ta'en since ye put that on will start to bleed and throb somethin' awful. And then you'll die in truth."

"But if I don't take this off..." Kittins responded, following the logic.

"Yer enemies can stab you all they like; it'll all be for naught."

"And these wounds I've got now, they'll heal?"

"They have done!" the witch giggled. "They are! Look, see!"

She was right: the gash in his arm, the horrible rent in his side, the chunks taken out of his back were all rapidly closing. The tension bled out of Kittins' face and body, and he realized he was hungry. Ravenous, in fact. "What have you got to eat?" He asked the witch. "Some of that infernal stew?"

"Ah!" She laughed. "Poor Tom loves my cookin', he does! Yes, yes, I've got stew. Stew and black bread for ye."

"I've no doubt it's black," Kittins retorted. "Black as your heart."

"And yours," Croonbasket quipped. "And yours."

And there was truth in that. Kittins had become an evil bastard, full of spleen over the last several weeks. He'd *wanted* to become an educated man, but the only things he'd learned had been new ways to hurt people. Now, he saw that his new condition allowed him to continue doing it. And the world was full of people who needed hurting in the worst possible way, beginning with Colonel Bailis.

Vykers, the Lakebed

He was down on one knee, where he'd fallen when the juggernaut had shoved him away with its free hand. Not so stupid, after all. Vykers took the occasion to breath; soon, his adversary would be on him again.

"Longest fuckin' fight o' my life," Vykers muttered to no one in particular. He raised his sword to parry the juggernaut's latest strike without a second to spare. The sword screamed in frustration. "You think you're frustrated?" He grumbled. Over the grappling weapons, Vykers studied the juggernaut's face, which was remarkably lifelike. At the moment, it was sneering at him. "A man with an army o' these could conquer the world ten times over," Vykers whispered.

Experimentally, he ducked under the juggernaut's next blow and came up behind it, where he jumped into the air and struck it atop its head with the pommel of his sword. The thing spun around and tried to take out Vykers' head with its mace.

The Reaper continued his dialogue with himself. "Great. That doesn't work, either." He looked down and noticed that his wound was weeping from underneath his belt. For the first time. "Shit." He dove at the juggernaut's legs, hoping to trip it and send it crashing to the ground, but its mass was too much to be budged by such an effort. "Fuck am I s'posed to do, here?"

The juggernaut lashed out with its mace, backhanded, and grazed Vykers' shoulder, sending him sprawling into the dust.

"It shant be long now!" the enemy's Shaper called out.

For once in his life, Vykers wondered if it might not be true. The juggernaut stormed over to where Vykers lay, but the Reaper rolled out of the way and used the momentum to reach his feet. He was moving slower and slower, with less and less grace, but he was still moving. To his right, the sun glinted off the salt lake, and Vykers thought that if he couldn't drink the stuff, then at least he could cool his skin off. He began a strategic retreat towards the water.

Long, in the Village

"Mardine thought they mighta taken the river, but Tresa convinced her to head north," Myx offered.

"But they could have been long gone if they'd taken the

river," Long protested. "Takin' the road north don't make any sense."

"Aye. That's what Mardine thought, too, I'm guessing."

"Might be," the Constable interrupted, "that yer daughter's kidnappers took the north road because it seemed such a foolish idea."

"Well," said Long, "I've gotta go after them. Mardine and this Tresa, anyways. If I can find them, we can all go after Esmine together."

"You need any help?" Myx asked, clearly hoping Long would decline the offer.

"I do," Long admitted. "And I know where I can find it, too. Before I go, though, I'm gonna need a new horse. Mine's blown, I'm afraid. Anybody here able to sell me one?"

"Sell you one?" Myx repeated. "I can do better'n that. I've got one I'll give you for nothin'. 'S the least I can do."

Long nearly wept at the man's gesture. "I appreciate it, Myx. I truly do."

A quarter hour later, Long was galloping southeast, on his way to Teshton.

Vykers, the Lakebed

The damned thing was relentless, a term Vykers had often heard applied to himself, but that now seemed to take on a whole new level of meaning. It rained blows on him with such frequency and force, Vykers began to feel the unfamiliar sensation of despair creeping into his bosom. If only he could just reach that water, cool himself off enough to think what to do.

He feinted going left and dodged to his right, using a last burst of speed to reach the water's edge. There, the few rocks along the shore were crusted with a thick layer of salt, reminding Vykers of winters back home. Looking up, he saw the juggernaut rapidly approaching, so he sheathed his sword and jumped into the shallows...only to find them not so shallow. There was two to three feet of water, and the same again of mud. The juggernaut was almost upon him again, so Vykers thrashed violently and propelled himself out of the mud and into deeper waters. It was not as cool as he'd hoped and the extra salt burnt like the countless hells on his wound and various cuts and scrapes, but Vykers found he was also more buoyant than normal.

He heard a tremendous splash, and his gut tightened at the sight of the juggernaut pursuing him into the lake. And then it began to sink.

Vykers laughed for joy. Of course! The accursed thing was made of steel, solid steel, and couldn't swim no matter how hard it tried. Indeed, the further it pushed into the lake, the deeper it sank. Vykers came closer, taunted it to follow and then took a few strokes farther away. He could see the thing battling to reach him, but all in vain. Its every move sucked it deeper and deeper into the mud. Vykers wondered whether the juggernaut understood that it had lost. It didn't matter. Vykers was alive and forever beyond his opponent's reach.

As he swam to shore, the Reaper was greeted by the cheers of an adoring throng—even the Emperor's knights seemed appreciative of his victory. The only holdout was the Emperor's Shaper.

"I should blast you where you stand!" the man snarled.

Vykers drew his sword. "Try it," he said flatly. The Historian didn't need to translate, and the Shaper stepped back, patently alarmed.

One of the Emperor's knights, a man in armor slightly different from the rest, stepped forward and removed his helmet. He was an older man, balding on top and possessed of a carefully sculpted beard. "You have defeated our champion, which means you have defeated all others before him. You have earned the right to approach the captive at the obelisk. But I should warn you of two things: one, she is very dangerous, and two, the Emperor will not forget today's events, which he will certainly view as a loss of face."

The Reaper was in no mood for diplomacy. "If he doesn't like it, he can come and find me." With that, he pushed through the crowd and advanced on the obelisk. "Son-of-a-whore! We've got her at last!"

Fifty feet away, inside a narrow column of flames that rose

into the heavens, Her Majesty glared back at Vykers with a look of profound impatience. "What in all hells took you so long?" she demanded.

Long's Crew, Gangrene & Sons, Teshton

The first to show up had been Rem, but a greatly transformed Rem. Gone were his flowing locks, his fancy clothes, and his cocky, boyish charm and enthusiasm. The man who remained was gaunt, with three days growth of beard and a wary look in his eyes. But if Rem's appearance had worried Spirk, Yendor's shocked him. The man had lost an eye and was stone cold sober for perhaps the first time in Spirk's memory. Try as he might, Spirk was unable to get his companions to unburden themselves of their obviously painful experiences in Lunessfor, but he hoped, when and if the Captains Long or Kittins showed up, that everyone's mood would improve.

Was he ever wrong about that!

Long arrived first, days after Yendor, frantic and out of breath.

"Ah, lads, you're here!" He exclaimed in apparent relief. "I was afraid…well, no sense in going into it, is there? Any sign of Kittins?"

Everyone shook his head, including Ron, who had yet to be introduced to the group.

"How long you all been here?" Long asked.

"Days," Yendor said.

"Days and days," Rem corrected.

"I been here maybe a week," Spirk concluded.

"I'm sorry about that, making you wait so long," Long said. "I got sidetracked and, well, my daughter's been kidnapped and my wife's gone missing in search of her."

The whole group leapt to its feet.

"She's what?" Spirk cried in disbelief.

"I need your help, lads. I need your help like I never did before."

That's when the door burst open and Colonel Bailis came tumbling through, only to land face-first on the tavern floor.

Behind him, a frighteningly changed Captain Kittins materialized. "Ah, you're all here. Good," he said.

The group remained on its feet at this latest spectacle and even the tavern's massive barkeep came closer.

"Ere now," the man said, "what's all this about?"

"What's it about?" Kittins smiled humorlessly. "It's about treachery. It about being played for fools."

Long stepped closer to Bailis, who remained in a heap on the floor, panting desperately. He hardly looked like the same man without armor and after the beating he'd evidently been given. No, what he looked was old, tired and afraid.

Having been on the verge of enlisting his old crew to help in finding his wife and daughter, Long was not disposed to humor the other captain, whom he had never especially liked from the get-go. "Explain."

Kittins kicked Bailis. "Tell them," he commanded.

In a halting, fragile voice, Bailis said, "As I understand it, Cindor..."

"That's the Queen's Shaper," Kittins clarified.

Bailis nodded. "Yes. Cindor's real aim in sending you into the Great Eight was to create as much chaos as possible..."

Long laughed, bitterly. "I'd say he succeeded on that score."

The other men agreed in a chorus of "aye"s and "that he did"s.

"Go on," Kittins prodded Bailis.

"What else is there to say?" the Colonel asked of his tormentor. "I suspect Cindor never believed in your ability to discover anything of the Queen's whereabouts or the manner of her abduction..."

"Which suggests he already knew something, himself," Kittins added.

"You all were sent in to keep the Eight occupied."

"Tell them the rest."

"The Eight have been...destabilized. I'm told your actions precipitated the recent riots and murders amongst the families. The result is, predictably, none of the great Houses will pose any threat to Her Majesty for some time."

"So?" Yendor asked after a long silence.

"So?" Kittins echoed in disbelief.

"Our lives were in danger, either way, and we was paid, right?

"Maybe I don't like being used and deceived."

"What do you propose we do about it?" Rem inquired.

"I propose," Kittins snarled, "that we find this Cindor and set him straight."

"Now hold on, there," the barkeep interjected. "I work for Cindor."

There was almost a whooshing sound in the room as all heads turned in the barkeep's direction. Rather than looking sheepish, as one might expect, he looked ornery. "Who'd you think I worked for? Alheria's cousin Ninnia? Anyway, we're gonna have problems, you folks 'n me, if you're thinkin' of making trouble for my boss."

During his abduction of Colonel Bailis, Kittins had acquired some decent chainmail and a fearsome-looking sword. He drew it now. "As it happens, I love trouble."

"Whoa, whoa, whoa!" Long shouted. "Wait a minute! I don't know as we're all in agreement here."

Kittins stared irritably at his fellow captain. "You're fine with letting this Shaper walk all over you?"

Long shook his head. "I didn't say that, but I ain't sure more violence is the answer. And, anyway, we got other problems just now."

"Like what?"

"Long's wife and daughter have gone missing," Rem answered.

"Fine," Kittins growled through clenched teeth. "You all go take care of that, and I'll deal with the Shaper on my own."

"You'll have to get past me, first!" the barkeep shouted.

Kittins grinned his ugliest grin. "I was hoping you'd say that."

Vykers, the Obelisk

Vykers walked to within inches of the arcane fire burning around the Queen and obelisk. The flames gave off no heat, but a strange, crackling energy. At his back, the amassed armies watched in absolute silence. "Took me longer to get here and find you than I planned. You're still alive, though, so you ain't got much to complain about."

"There's always something to complain about."

"What I don't get is why you're still alive," Vykers replied, ignoring the Queen's comment. "You lost a hand. You've been standing next to that rock there, for what I'm guessing is days and days. No food, no water, no shelter. What's keeping you going, that obelisk?"

"This obelisk is a trap."

"A trap? And you're the one caught in it." He stared down at his boots, linking the facts in the story together into a coherent chain.

"Yes, well," the Queen continued in obvious exasperation, "it was meant for me."

The Reaper looked at her in feigned surprise. "Was it, now?"

"Oh, stop being so coy, Reaper. It doesn't suit you. You obviously think I've withheld information from you, and I'll happily answer all your questions once you've released me."

This is a dangerous game, Arune cautioned.

There any other kind worth playing?

She had nothing to say to that. Vykers looked down at his boots again, as if they held all the mysteries of life.

"What are you dawdling for?" the Queen demanded.

"I ain't forgotten how you schooled me in all those games we played when I was bed-ridden."

"And?"

"I'm not lettin' you do it again. Not here. Not now."

"You think this a game?" Her Majesty roared. "Trade places with me and see how amusing you find it."

"I'm afraid I'll want more 'n answers in exchange for settin' you free."

"Men!" the Queen snapped. "I'll never know why the gods created you."

"Why don't you pray to Alheria and ask her," Vykers quipped. He thought it a fairly witty remark, but was not prepared for what came next.

"Pray to Alheria, you witless brute? I AM ALHERIA!" This

was said so loudly that every last man on the lake bed could not help but hear it.

I warned you, Arune whispered in the back of Vykers' mind.

You coulda been a little more specific! He snapped back.

On the surface, Vykers pretended to be unshaken and unconvinced. "If you're Alheria, where's Mahnus? Why doesn't he save you?"

The Queen lowered her voice again, spoke in more intimate tones. "Because I had a fling with a mortal, the old fool became insanely jealous, and I had to kill him."

Vykers digested this. Or tried to. "You're sayin' you killed Mahnus."

"Are you deaf as well as dim-witted? Yes, I killed Mahnus. And I'd do it again if the big oaf were nearby."

"Huh." Vykers turned away, studied the collection of armies before him.

"Release me!" the Queen barked.

"Why me?"

"Self-pity, Vykers?"

"Not at all. I mean, why's it gotta be me in particular who releases you? Why couldn't any o' these men do it?"

"None of those men possess your sword."

"Oh," Vykers said, the light dawning, "so, I could hand my sword to the least o' these soldiers and he could free you in my stead?"

"Perhaps," the Queen responded. "But then, he'd get the reward I intended for you."

Vykers brushed this off. "Tell me about my sword."

"You are taxing my patience!"

"Am I? You been standing here for how long, and a few minutes' chat with me is taxing your patience? I'd've expected more from a god. Goddess. Whatever."

Alheria couldn't argue the Reaper's logic. "Your sword," she said, "was forged by the same god who made this obelisk. Your sword is the only thing that can destroy it."

"Right. And this other god would be Mahnus?"

"Yes," said Alheria.

"And he's dead, and you killed him..."

"We've been over this!"

"I'm still gettin' used to the idea. Now, tell me, how is it you fell for a trap set by a god who's dead?"

The goddess thought for a while and then answered, "The obelisk only forced its way to the surface recently. Until then, I was unaware of its presence. When I...felt it, I was afraid Mahnus had found a way to cheat death, so I came down here to investigate."

"That explains why we never found any trace of your abductors: they never existed."

"Correct."

"And your hand. How'd you lose that?"

"I cut it off myself, to help you find me easier," Alheria said. "But I would like it back once you've released me."

"And this trap, how's it work?"

"Since when have you shown an interest in anything other than killing?"

"So, you're not going to answer my question?"

"You may be the most annoying human who ever lived."

"I'm honored you think so."

Alheria sighed. "A small quantity of my blood must have been used in the construction of this obelisk; it is bound to me, and I cannot escape its grip unless it is destroyed."

"Won't that hurt you in some way?"

"Probably. What do you care? Are you going to free me or must I stand here until you die of old age?"

"If you're Alheria, I imagine you can heal me."

"I can," the Queen admitted, somewhat reluctantly.

"Then do it now!" Vykers answers.

"I cannot heal you whilst bound to this stone. I could not heal myself, if it came to that."

"But you will heal me, if I free you..."

"Yes, yes, you accursed oaf! I'll heal you; I have given my word!"

Well, Vykers told Arune, *here goes nothing*. He raised his sword, strode into the uncanny flames, and struck at the obelisk.

Long's Crew, Gangrene & Sons, Teshton

The interior of Gangrene and Sons was a disaster-in-progress. The hulking barkeep hadn't had time to retrieve a suitable weapon, so he was forced to make do with the tavern's tables and chairs, sweeping them off the floor as if they weighed nothing and throwing them in Kittins' path. The captain, meanwhile, waded through the wreckage like a child running through piles of dead leaves. The chaos, the violence seemed to delight him.

Long's crew had run to all points of the room's perimeter, not yet ready to flee, nor willing to raise a hand on either side of the fray.

Rem, for example, was terribly torn. On the one hand, he resented Cindor with the kind of passion only a great actor (or an especially deluded one) can muster. He hated the Shaper for disbanding his acting company and making a glorified slave of him. On the other hand, if Rem stepped in on Kittins' side and the captain failed to kill Cindor, Rem would surely suffer for it. It was the kind of quandary only a stage manager could solve.

Spirk, naturally, hated to see either of the combatants hurt; he just wished they'd sit down and talk out their differences over a mug of…something. Ron stood helplessly nearby, still hoping that someone would introduce him to the rest of the group and tell him which side he was supposed to be rooting for.

Yendor didn't particularly care one way or the other, as long as he didn't lose his remaining eye.

Long seemed to be the only one still thinking. The moment the barkeep moved on Kittins, Long dodged over to Bailis and dragged the poor man into a corner. A few seconds' examination told him that none of the colonel's wounds were fatal, though some unquestionably required an A'Shea's attention. The only thing Long could think to do was to act as a shield for the colonel until the brawl ended and either the barkeep or Kittins had been killed. Of course, there was no guarantee that the survivor would be satisfied with the one death—he might well come after the rest of Long's crew out of sheer spite.

"Can you crawl?" Long whispered to Bailis.

The man groaned. "If needs must."

"Needs fucking must," Long said. "Unless you fancy dying today." The next closest man was Yendor. Long called out to him over the noise of battle. "Follow me and tell Rem to do likewise."

"Follow?" Yendor seemed slightly disoriented, but eventually turned and shouted the same directions to Rem.

Long didn't wait around to see whether Rem understood or had passed the instructions on to Spirk and his companion. Kittins and the barkeep were making such a racket, it was like to make Mahnus himself deaf, so there'd never be a better time to sneak away. "Come!" He barked at Bailis.

The colonel coagulated into a coherent heap and dragged himself in Long's wake. As Long crawled along, ducking detritus as he went, he marveled at the duration of the fight, was surprised that neither man had thus far managed to end it. Before he knew it, he'd escaped through the door. Once outside, he helped Bailis to his feet and the two men moved off another hundred paces.

"We'll want a head start if one o' those crazy bastards decides to come after us," Long explained.

In short order, Yendor, Rem, Spirk and his nameless companion emerged from the tavern as well and wisely decided to join the captain and colonel at their safer distance.

"Now what?" Rem asked. "We wait and see who wins?"

Long shook his head. "What's the point? No matter who wins, we'll always be on the other side, no?"

"So...what should we do?" said Spirk.

"I still need your help, friends. I still gotta find my wife and daughter."

"Findin's better 'n killin'," Yendor observed.

"But what about captain Kittins?"

"You saw the man, saw what he's become. I don't know what he was like when you first met him, but he's barely human now. More of a monster, really. And if he wants to go chasing some wild conspiracy all the way up to Her Majesty, well, you really wanna be part o' that?" Long had addressed the question to Spirk, but he made sure he looked at each of the other men, in turn.

"Seems to me the safety of your child is more important, right now," Rem said.

Long could see the other men agreed. "I can't thank you enough, lads."

"Well," Yendor drawled, "you could try."

THIRTEEN

Vykers, the Obelisk

Those closest to the blast were catapulted twenty-to-thirty feet away, with the lucky ones landing in the lake. Those farthest away were merely knocked off their feet. Close or far, though, injuries abounded, and two or three unfortunates died.

Vykers survived, oblivious as he was for a while to that fact. When the thunderstorm in his head subsided, he perceived that he was on his back, with his arms and legs splayed in all directions. And yet, he felt surprisingly well. Taking a brief inventory, he was momentarily shocked to see that his massive belt had broken open and the two ends had fallen on either side of his body. When he understood the significance of what he was seeing, he whooped for joy and scrambled to his feet as fast as he could.

He was whole again! The Queen—Alheria—had healed him at last! The evil, sucking wound that had plagued his every breath since he'd received it was gone. In its absence, Vykers became aware of the Shaper's burning of Arune at work. But either he'd gotten used to the sensation after all these years, or she was expending less energy. Whatever the case, the Reaper was truly, finally himself again, and the rest of the world had better take notice. He certainly wanted the assembled armies to take notice, but, at the moment, they were preoccupied, recovering from the blast.

"So, you see, I keep my promises."

Alheria. She stood atop the tiny hill, as if she'd never moved. But even in spite of that and everything else he'd just experienced, it was hard to see the old crone as a goddess. "I suppose it's a fair trade," Vykers admitted. "Have you seen my sword about?"

"Ah," Alheria sighed. "Your sword. It's gone. Your sword and the obelisk destroyed each other, which is, ultimately, what set me free."

Gone? He'd had the sword for more than three years. He'd been through the countless hells to acquire it, had some memorable battles with it—it had even helped keep him alive in the early days of his illness. And now it was gone? Unthinkable. "That's all you wanted from me then, is it?"

"Don't pout, Reaper. No one but you could have wielded it. That must count for something. And, anyway, what does the great and newly-recovered Tarmun Vykers need with a magic sword? Time was, you had disdain for such things."

"Time was, it was just me against the world. Now, I get called upon to save it every few years."

"Well, you'll have to do so without your sword next time around."

Vykers squinted at the Queen. "Now what? Back to your throne room?"

"For a while," Alheria said. "Hoosh!" She yelled. "Where's my Fool?"

"Here, Highness!" came the too-jovial voice of the Fool.

"Have you got my hand?"

"But o' course!" the Fool said, extending the object in question with a flourish.

To Vykers' amazement, the old Queen took the hand and reattached it to her wrist, as if it were merely a bracelet that had fallen off. When she caught the Reaper's look of astonishment, she said "I am a goddess, after all. What were you expecting?" As he was unable to articulate his thoughts, Alheria changed the subject. "Fool, it is time for you and me to leave!"

"Just the Fool? Why? What about the rest of us?" Vykers demanded.

"I have shared too much with you, Vykers. A fact I'm sure to regret sooner or later. But if, after a good, long trip home, you insist on further answers, you know where to find me."

With that, Alheria extended her left arm to Hoosh, wrapped it around his shoulders and disappeared in a flash of light.

"That bitch!" Vykers roared.

"For once, I agree with you," the Historian said as he sidled up. "It is a perilously long way back to the boat, even for someone of my experience.

Then Vykers remember Aoife, and his mood brightened again. "No sense in hanging around this damned place. Let's grab the Frog and start home."

"And what of your prisoners?"

"Can't we just…leave 'em here?"

"They would most likely be killed. No, if we try to leave them, they will follow. They are yours now, for no one in this land will have any mercy upon them."

The Reaper dropped his head back, pointed his chin at the sky and exhaled forcefully, clearly aggravated with this turn of events. "Baggage!" said he. "Very well, then, let us bring the baggage and depart."

The armies gave Vykers a hero's send-off; even the Emperor's men cheered lustily as the Reaper rode through their ranks and back the way he had come. He had bested their champions and conversed with a god. His actions and appearance resonated in the memories of the spectators, arousing things only dimly remembered…

Kittins, Gangrene & Sons, Teshton

They'd all slunk off like rats. It figured, really. He'd never thought much of that Long Pete fellow, and this confirmed his suspicions. They left him to his fate with that mountain of a barkeep, and Kittins had survived nonetheless. Of course, if he hadn't been in possession of Croonbasket's charm, that might not have been the case. The barkeep had broken Kittins' jaw, a number of his ribs and his left arm. The captain must have stabbed and slashed the big fella thirty times or more before he finally succumbed. He'd have made a good basher, sure. Maybe a great one. Hells, for all Kittins knew, he'd been a great basher in somebody else's unit and they'd never really sized one another up until today. And now the barkeep was dead.

What to do, though, about Long's boys?

Kittins limped around the bar, poured himself a huge flagon of something and drank deeply. It hurt like the hells, with his jaw the way it was, but he didn't give a damn. He scrounged around a bit and found some cheese and sausage that went well with his drink, though he had to chew with only one side of his mouth. The way he felt, he was lucky to get anything past his lips.

But he knew he would heal, and heal much faster than he'd any right to.

Two flagons later, he ransacked the barkeep's strongbox, took every shim he could find—might as well make man's death look like the result of a robbery instead of a murder—and lurched out the front door, wheezing faintly.

He reckoned he'd have to deal with Long and his crew when he'd finished with Cindor. They'd heard him speak against the Shaper and knew what he intended; therefore, they were as good as witnesses to the attempt. If he did want Her Majesty after him one day, he'd have to make sure of Long and the others.

The bigger, more immediate question was how he'd handle Cindor. It was one thing to decide to kill him, but another entirely to actually pull it off. Getting close to the wizard would be nigh onto impossible; sticking a sword in his belly might well prove beyond impossible. Well, Kittins had no other mission in life. Whatever he'd once wanted to be or accomplish had gone by the wayside. All that mattered now was revenge. If pressed, he probably couldn't even articulate why he wanted it; he only knew that he did. Various people had helped, intentionally or otherwise, to shape him into the villain he'd so clearly become. Kittins only wanted to show them what they'd accomplished for their efforts.

Vykers, On the Road Home

Often, the journey home seems shorter than the journey away, but it didn't feel that way to Vykers. Not this time. With every passing league, he thought more and more on Aoife, wondered

whether there was any chance of a future with her, worried she
might have gone home without him.

He wanted her to see him whole again, to feel his strength
and his passion, to know him free of pain. Most of all, he wanted
her.

Both the Historian and the Frog had tried to initiate
conversations with Vykers, but he couldn't remember a thing
they'd said—or anything he might've said in return. At some
point, he looked back and saw them chatting with one another,
riding side-by-side, but at the head of the pack of slaves. At
first, Vykers had wanted the slaves bound, but matters stood
as the Historian suggested they might: the slaves were now
men without a country, no longer welcome in their homelands.
But that was the way of things in war; Vykers wasn't about to
apologize for defeating them, nor did he feel any particular
obligation towards them. When he got back home, he'd keep
them or sell them. He might even free them. It was all one to
him.

Days passed. They felt like years. Decades. Vykers endured,
as he always did. Behind him, the Historian and the Frog
quietly continued to manage the larger group. Occasionally, at
the evening's fire, Vykers thought he spied a hungry, dangerous
look in the Frog's eyes as the former boy studied the slaves.
But the Reaper had never known the other chimeras to covet
human flesh, and he couldn't believe the Frog did, either. And it
didn't make sense that the Frog would try anything in Vykers'
presence. Anyway, he told himself, Aoife would straighten the
kid out, if anyone could.

Thinking of Aoife naturally caused all other issues to fade
into the background. It had been too long since Vykers had been
with a woman and even longer since he'd been with one he
cared for. Fleetingly, he wondered why Arune hadn't weighed
in on his feeling for the A'Shea, the revelation that the Queen
was Alheria, or the still-astonishing fact that she'd healed him
of his seemingly eternal wound.

Hey, Burn, He said.

Yes? Arune responded after a lengthy silence.

What's going on with you? All kinds of amazing shit happening, and you got nothin' to say? That ain't like you.

I think we'll be able to go our separate ways, soon...if you're still willing.

Willing? You're damn right I'm still willing, He said a little too quickly.

It'll take a great deal of gold...

Ha! The Reaper laughed. *I got more gold stashed away than you've ever seen before!*

It is...strange, not having to struggle constantly to keep your wound from worsening.

I'll bet it's a relief. I know I'm relieved. I could almost have kissed that old bitch.

Now, it was Arune's turn to chuckle. *Old, yes. Much, much older than we imagined, eh?*

And it don't make sense, to be honest. What's a god—or goddess—want with a mortal throne? What's Lunessfor to her? She oughta give it over to me, is what she oughta do.

Of course, Reaper. It is all about you, after all.

What, Vykers asked, *are you feelin' left out? I'll make you my personal Shaper!*

Do you think you're truly the ruling sort? Seems to me, you're better at destroying.

She had a point. Still, he didn't like her tone. *You tryin' to pick a fight with me? What's this all about, anyway?*

Nothing, Reaper, nothing, Arune answered. *I'm sorry I said anything.*

Whichever of the gods it was who had first decided to make women Shapers must have been mad, Vykers thought. Separately, the two were almost impossible to deal with; combined, they made up without question the most irrational force in the world.

Hang on, Shaper. I meant to ask you: what did you think of Alheria's story about killin' Mahnus? D'you really figure he's dead?

But Arune had retreated to wherever it was she went when her feelings were hurt. Fortunately for Vykers, he had plenty of other things to occupy his mind while he waited her out.

One afternoon around mid-day, the Frog spotted the A'Shea's grove, her oasis, on the horizon. Vykers took off like a shot, spurring Shalea into a full gallop, completely unconcerned for the horse's health. Fortunately, Shalea was, as promised, an exceptional beast, and a lengthy bolt for the trees was nothing to her.

Aoife heard the sound of Vykers' mount and came to the edge of the tree line to await his arrival. When he finally reached her, he was taken aback by her appearance. She looked like she hadn't slept in weeks.

Vykers jumped from Shalea's back and strode to Aoife's side. "Aoife," he said, "are you unwell?"

The A'Shea smiled self-consciously. "It's the grove. I don't think these trees care for me." Before Vykers could comment, Aoife continued. "But you! Look at you, Tarmun! You're healed!"

In an instant, they were in each other's arms, laughing and savoring the intimacy.

"Yes," Vykers replied. "Amazing, ain't it?" And then he paused. "You'd better brace yourself, Aoife," he warned.

A look of profound concern came to her face.

"I know Alheria means a lot to you A'Shea…" Vykers began. "Well, I just saved her life, I guess you'd say."

"What?"

"The Queen, Her Majesty…she's Alheria."

Aoife stared at him as if he'd just sprouted a second head.

"It's the truth!" He declared. "Ask the Frog. Ask the Historian."

"I…believe you," Aoife said quietly. "But how…how can Alheria have been living amongst us whilst my sisters and I failed to notice?"

"Who knows what the gods are about? Here, now, I'm worried about you. Are you sure you're well?"

Aoife beamed, looking up at Vykers. "I am now."

Vykers pulled her close, whispered to her. "I want some time alone with you. But the men'll be here any minute, and I gotta get them settled."

The A'Shea blushed, lowered her eyes. She wanted time alone with Vykers, too, but how could she ever admit such a thing? "I'll help in any way I can, of course. Tomorrow, I believe, I can get all of us home safely."

"Can you?" She'd surprised Vykers, and he discovered that he liked the feeling. "You'll have to tell me more, later," he grinned. He felt like a schoolboy around the A'Shea…and yet, he reveled in the sensation.

It took some time to get everyone settled in the grove, because the slaves and their horses were exhausted, and most wanted nothing more than to sleep where they stood. The Frog, Vykers saw, behaved oddly around Aoife, and the warrior wondered whether the boy wasn't a bit taken with the woman as well. It was true, the Frog was too young to feel the same sort of desire a man felt, but he didn't doubt the boy was enthralled by her beauty and grateful for her kindness.

Once Vykers and the Historian had gotten everyone settled and started a small fire—with Aoife's blessing—to warm a bit of food, the Frog was free to go hunting, and the Reaper, to relax. He couldn't recall the last time he'd been able to stretch out, sit back and rest his weary limbs without the constant pain of his wound to distract him. He luxuriated in the absence of that pain, he basked in his health and feelings of well-being. And he felt better still when the A'Shea came to his side voluntarily and joined him by the fire.

"Forgive me for asking, Tarmun, but…who are these men you've brought with you?"

"These?" He said lightheartedly. "These are my gifts, I suppose you'd say. The place where we found Her Majesty—Alheria—was surrounded by armies. I had to fight the champion of each one in order to gain right of passage. And when I did, they each gave me one of their own as a prize."

"But what will you do with them?"

Again, Vykers smiled. Coming from anyone else, the question would have annoyed him no end; from Aoife, it was endlessly charming. "I dunno. What do you recommend?"

"Can't you free them?"

"Well," Vykers sighed, "that's the thing: their own countries won't have 'em, now. They're little more than chattel."

Aoife thought on this a while and then said, "But in our

land, they might find work as soldiers, guards—even map-makers. I'm sure they could tell us things about this place that would take us decades to find out on our own."

"Good point," said Vykers, impressed with her thinking. "They may, at that. But now, there's something else you should know."

The A'Shea was secretly amused—flattered, even—to observe that Vykers' speech was much more refined in her presence than it was when he spoke to others, or even when they'd first met. "And what is that?"

"Alheria claims to have killed Mahnus."

Aoife was silent for so long that, for a while, Vykers thought she hadn't heard him. "What I wouldn't give to talk to the Mother Superior right now. I feel so lost when you tell me these things," she said finally.

"Yeah," Vykers agreed. "You and me, both. But she did heal me with a thought, and an army o' Shapers and A'Shea hadn't been able to do that with three years o' tryin'."

They talked in close conference right through dinner, sunset and into the night. Eventually, Aoife put her head on Vykers' shoulder and huddled closer to him for warmth. It was the greatest, most momentous little gesture he'd experienced in all his life. It meant everything to him. And, when everyone else had fallen asleep, the Reaper and the A'Shea crept off into the denser foliage and at last acknowledged their need for one another.

But they were not alone.

Long's Crew, On the Trail

Elsewhere in the night, a group of friends was gathered around another fire, sharing their fears, venting their frustrations and searching for comfort in one another.

"I'm haunted by Kittins' story," Long confessed.

Yendor pulled his cloak tighter around himself. "I hear you, Long. Much as the captain scares the piss outta me, there's that in his tale troubles me."

Long bobbed his head in agreement. "I was a fool to think I

had any business spyin' on the Great Eight. I'm a soldier, and a middling one at that."

"So, what happened to you?" Yendor asked, voicing the question that was clearly on everyone's mind.

Long stared off into the darkness for a heartbeat or two and then said, "I managed to get into House Fyne, they caught me, and then I was thrown into their dungeons. I was just about to be tortured—by Esmun Janks, I tell you!—when His Lordship informed me I'd been named heir to House D'Escurzy."

"Oh!" Spirk cried out. "That was my fault. Sorry!"

The group had a good laugh at that, and then Long said, "But how did that come about?"

So, Spirk told him. It took a long time, and Spirk had to go back and correct himself on several occasions, but he eventually got the story out. It was only when he got to the banquet that he faltered, still too disturbed by his memories to continue. Fortunately, Ron took up the slack and told the tale from Faenia's death to Spirk's and his escape through a secret passage. Yendor, Rem and Long had a thousand questions, and Ron patiently answered them all as best he could until everyone was satisfied.

"And what about you?" Long asked his friend, Yendor. "What is your story?"

Yendor's story, with embellishments, took nearly an hour to relate, but the group found it every bit as improbable and fulfilling as Spirk's tale. When he was done, the group turned silently and expectantly to Rem.

He scratched the top of his head and said "I don't know, lads..."

Which was greeted with great, exaggerated umbrage and uproar. They'd all told their stories, after all. How could he withhold his own? And being an actor, no less? After much entreaty, they finally prevailed upon Rem to share his own adventure. He performed it with such gusto, he was again reminded how much he'd lost in losing his acting troop. He'd been made for the stage, not this spying business. But he dared not defy the Queen's Shaper. One nasty jolt of arcane lightning was quite enough for one lifetime.

"So," Long said when Rem had finished his tale, "we,

all of us, walk away from the Eight changed men, scarred, disillusioned, but alive."

"Though it sounds like we left a few dead in our wake," Yendor added.

"And what's that you said about Esmun Janks?" Rem asked.

Long studied the faces of his friends around the fire. "Oh, yes, I didn't get to that, did I? Well, Janks is alive. Sure as I'm sittin' here. And I can't figure out how or why."

The others prodded Long for details until, one by one, they nodded off to sleep, changed men, indeed. Each and every one.

Vykers & Aoife, Aoife's Grove

They were not alone, because Arune was with them, as always. Now that Vykers was healed, though, she knew the time was fast approaching when she'd have her own body again, at last, and she understood that her vicarious sampling of Vykers' intimacy and elation with Aoife was nearing an end. From that point onward, she and the Reaper would be rivals for the A'Shea's attention and adoration. From that point onward, what was good for the Reaper was decidedly not so for her. She wondered if Brouton's Bind had turned her into an echo of the man she'd inhabited for so long, wondered, if she could escape, what sort of person she'd become when free.

So great was Vykers' ecstasy, it swept the Shaper's concerns aside as if they were dust motes in a hurricane.

They were not alone, because the Frog had seen them sneak away and had followed them, as stealthily as his considerable skills allowed. Cloaked in the forest—a trick he'd learned from the fey folk—he watched in fascination, and then envy, and finally bitterness as the man he idolized made love to the woman he revered. And a dark, desperate hunger came upon him, bringing with it thoughts and images of things his boy's mind was unequipped to handle, but which his eldritch, chimera's body silently screamed for.

They were not alone, because Endu-Ro watched, seething,

from the shadows, all but impotent in his rage. He loathed the A'Shea, despised her for her presumption, but he could not defeat her head-on, especially if that meddling Toomt'-La came at her aid. If Endu-Ro could only catch her unawares, as now...The man with her, however, radiated power like a sacred artifact. No, the satyr could never best these two together.

In the shadows, he sensed another, equally unhappy figure. Perhaps this one could be bent to Endu-Ro's will...

In the morning, Aoife explained how she planned to transport everyone home.

"It is called the 'Here-There,' she said. "I can take you from this grove to another in our homeland simply by stepping from one to the next. But I cannot take you all at once. We'll start with Tarmun and that red knight, there. Tadpole...Frog, would you be kind enough to wait 'til the end, so I know things will be safe on this side?"

The Frog lowered his hooded eyes in apparent assent.

"Good, then!" the A'Shea said brightly. "This shouldn't take long at all, then."

The Historian stepped up and placed a hand on Aoife's shoulder. "I won't be returning with you," he said.

"No?" Vykers asked, surprised.

"Much has changed since I was here last, and I would understand the magnitude and the reasons for it. And besides," he added, "someone has to return to the ship we arrived on and tell its captain he's free to go."

"I'd clean forgot about him!" Vykers laughed.

"So I gathered."

"He'll be expecting more gold."

"I believe I can satisfy him on that point," the Historian said cryptically. "But as for you, Reaper..."

"Yes?"

"I will not say our partnership has been pleasant, but you've taught me things of great value. In return...I suggest you seek out the Sholdorn..."

"The Sholdorn? I hate those fuckers."

The Historian made a sour face, as if he'd just smelled

something putrid. "Nevertheless, there remains a great deal you do not yet see."

"Such as what," the Reaper challenged, his dander up.

"I cannot explain. Visit the Sholdorn, hear what they have to say."

This answer was clearly unsatisfactory to Vykers, but he could see the Historian was anxious to get on his way, so he let the matter drop. "Farewell, then, Historian. I thank you for your help in finding my sword and also in finding Her Majesty."

"Alheria," the Shaper said.

"Just so," Vykers replied. He stared deeply into the other man's all-black eyes a final time, looking for some sign, any sign, of a soul. Finding none, he turned away and faced the A'Shea.

"Now, I can take everyone home, eventually, but none of these horses," Aoife said.

That was a shame. The Reaper rather liked Shalea. The thought of her running free across the hills of this land gave him some comfort. He wasn't worried about predators, either. Not with this horse. So be it, then: she would be free.

When the time came, Aoife clasped hands with the Reaper and the red knight. Suddenly, they were in another grove, a place of cooler shade and more familiar trees. And Vykers was not ill from the journey.

"That's a damned sight better'n that Shaper's trick." In the back of his mind, he heard Arune snort.

"Mmm," Aoife agreed, "though I can only travel to and from groves I've...*visited*...before." She'd almost shared more truth than she was ready for, but it didn't seem Vykers had noticed.

He knew they were home—he could smell it and taste it in the breeze. "Where are we?"

"Northeast of Lunessfor."

"A long ways northeast, I'll wager."

But I can get you there from here, Arune reminded him. *Now that we're back across the sea.*

I think we'll camp here for a day or so. I gotta figure out what I'm gonna do next.

You will go to Lunessfor soon, though, no?

O' course I will. I just wanna know what I'm doin' when I get there.

"Will you be alright if I leave to fetch the others?" Aoife asked Vykers.

He embraced her in a sideways hug, kissing the side of her head. "You know I will." He looked over at the red knight, who was idly examining the leaves of a nearby birch. "I'd better try to talk with this fellow…"

Aoife had gone.

I can help you communicate. I learned a few things from the Historian, as well.

Arune's burning intensified for a moment, and then Vykers tried to speak with the man. "What manner of man fights a duel with a wooden sword?"

The knight looked up abruptly, shocked at hearing his own language after so long a time. "What manner of man competes in a challenge of honor with a steel sword?"

"That was what that was, a challenge of honor?" Vykers asked. "No wonder you fellas were so far away from the obelisk."

The knight seemed to deflate, dropping his arms to his sides and his gaze to the ground. "Yes, no one respects the old ways, any more."

"I fight to win."

The knight looked up again, "Ah, but are winning and bloodshed one and the same? In my country, the first man to touch the other with his sword is champion. No one ever need die."

"Well," the Reaper shrugged, "I touched you first."

"Yes," the knight answered, dubiously.

For the better part of an hour, Aoife shuttled Vykers' slaves from the grove in their distant homeland to the grove in his homeland, from there to here. Then, she went back a final time to retrieve the Frog and was gone for a long, long time.

Long's Crew, On the Trail

Long Pete and his friends wandered for miles on either side of the north road, looking for anyone who might have seen

Mardine travelling through, or any physical sign of her passing. Days and days went by, and Long began to despair. Gradually, those days got shorter, the nights got colder and autumn settled into the landscape. Long feared if he didn't find evidence of Mardine's trail soon, the falling leaves would obscure her path forever. And so, the group talked to farmers, peddlers, vagrants, any and every one they encountered. They received just enough fragments of information and dim recollections to prevent them from giving up.

One evening about sunset, Spirk happened to spot a game trail or goat track that the rest of the party had overlooked. Long wanted to skip it, but Spirk said he had a funny feeling and wanted to investigate. Long continued to resist, but they compromised and made camp on the side of the road, agreeing to follow the trail in the morning.

It was the last peaceful night of sleep Long would ever know.

Come sun up, Spirk hustled off up the trail, his friend Ron limping along behind him, whilst everyone else struggled to keep up. A ways into the forest, Rem spotted an enormous footprint, which galvanized Long. He charged ahead, possessed by a frantic energy none of the others could match. Thus, he was alone, well ahead of the others, when he came to the clearing and found The Tree. He knew what it was on the instant, though he couldn't have said how or why he knew. Impossibly, unfathomably, he was able to read the runes carved into its scorched trunk.

When the rest of the crew showed up, they found Long curled up at its base, sobbing the deep, wrenching wails of a soul in torment.

They had found Mardine.

Not wanting to disturb Long in his agony, Rem turned to Yendor and whispered, "How does he know it's her?"

"It's her," Spirk cut in, somberly.

"How do you know? What if it's not?"

"It's her," Spirk repeated.

Rem stood by a good while and then added, "Well, even if it is—and I hope to Mahnus it isn't—we still haven't found the girl."

At this, Long stopped crying and sat up, shaken by the notion he'd forgotten about his daughter. "That's right: we ain't." Yendor offered a hand and Long pulled himself to his feet, wiping his nose with his sleeve and the back of his hand. "Sorry you had to see that, lads," he croaked, his voice still raw and more broken than usual.

Yendor missed half the words, but he got the gist. "You got every right to feel poorly." Poorly? Yendor rebuked himself. I bet poorly don't come half near it.

Long stepped back and inspected the tree stump. "It's a fine monument for her, though, and a fitting. Wish I knew who made it."

"'Nother giant, looks like," said Yendor, pointing to the mess of footprints around the tree trunk. "No reg'lar man coulda made this thing."

"Another giant," Long said quietly.

"Let's see if we can figure out what happened here," Rem suggested. "Then maybe we'll know which way to head next."

The effort seemed to focus Long's thoughts, for after an extensive search of the clearing, he declared, "Way I see it, Em came into these woods along that game trail and ran into this back road, here," he indicated with a wave of his hand. "Looks like there was wagons camped here for a spell. And it's certain there was some kind o' fight all around that old fire pit."

Yendor dreaded saying it, but needed to know. "So, whoever Mardine ran into killed her?"

Long's silence was confirmation enough.

"Then," Yendor continued, "She musta happened on them as stole your Esmine."

"Let's search the trees for graves. If we find 'em, I wanna know who's in 'em," Long rasped.

A few short minutes later, they were digging up corpses.

Vykers, Back Home

Vykers was beyond agitated. When Aoife hadn't returned within a reasonable time frame, he became restless, began to worry. What was he to do if something went wrong on the other side? He was weeks and weeks away at best by conventional means. And he found it excruciating to consider the possibility that he'd finally won the A'Shea's heart, only to lose her again through some unforeseen catastrophe. But no, he told himself, Aoife was a strong woman. It had to be the case that something had befallen the Frog, and the A'Shea had gone to help him. When he tried to consult Arune on the matter, he found her every bit as bedeviled by the situation and, thus, of no comfort whatsoever.

After three more days, Vykers was nearly homicidal with anxiety, and his slaves took special care to stay out of his reach and avoid his gaze. Just as the Reaper was about to snap, Aoife reappeared, stumbling out of the nothing between two trees, disheveled, dirty, scratched and frightened. Vykers rushed to her side.

"What's happened?"

"What's happened?" Aoife spat back at him, anger evident in her voice and manner. "What's happened? *You* happened, Reaper. You happened."

He would like to have believed she was joking, that her strange behavior was a jest of some sort, but the fury in her eyes was all too real. "What does that mean?" He demanded, his nerves frayed from worry and his teeth on edge from having been yelled at so unexpectedly, from such an unexpected source.

"Tadpole...the Frog...assaulted me...tried to..."

"I'll kill him!" Vykers growled in white hot rage.

"You already have," Aoife replied coldly.

So, it was back to this argument again. Was there any point in trying to explain himself while the A'Shea was so angry? Was there any point while *he* was so angry? In the end, he stared at her until she stalked away.

"This will never work for us, Tarmun. I heal and you destroy. We're like summer and winter."

"And what is the one without the other?" He challenged.

Aoife stood up straighter, raised her jaw just so. "I lived many productive years before I ever laid eyes on you, Reaper."

"Productive," he said. "But I did not hear the word 'happy'."

She actually laughed at him. "What do you know of

happiness? You, whose greatest delight is in killing others?"

Oh, there were things he might have said, any number of things. But he felt her slipping from his grasp like sand through his fingers, and it bewildered him to the point of stupefaction.

"Lunessfor is, as I said, to the southwest. You have your men with you; I'm sure you'll be safe on your voyage."

"And you?" He finally managed.

"Will not be joining you." Her voice still quivered with rage, but there was pain in it, too, sadness, a brittle quality like the thinnest of glass.

"And where are you going?"

"I don't know," she said curtly. "Far away from here."

Brave, he was, and strong, but neither brave nor strong enough to swallow his damned pride. He watched her go without a word. She stepped into the space between trees and was gone. He would not admit as much to himself, but the wound he'd received from the End was nothing to the one he'd just gotten from the A'Shea. And she was a healer!

Arune could not help herself; this turn of events was just what she'd hoped for.

Kittins, Wandering

Although he'd recently learned to read, he didn't need to: the crude sketch was obviously meant to be him, and even an illiterate bumpkin could make out the sum of money offered for his capture. Kittins was a wanted man—not perhaps in the manner that most men wish to be wanted, but wanted nevertheless. He cracked an ugly grin at the irony.

He stopped grinning when he heard the clink of steel at his back. He spun from the wall on which the poster hung, hoping to catch his would-be captor napping, only to find himself facing a good-sized semicircle of men. They must have been trailing him since he wandered into this shithole of a town, and he'd been so preoccupied with his plans for vengeance that he hadn't noticed.

"Easy, mate, easy," a scraggly bearded man with a nervous tic cautioned.

"Or what?" Kittins asked. He thought they'd see their own superior numbers and laugh at him, like he was touched. They did not.

"A scrap, I'd guess," the man responded. "You're a bigg'un and I reckon a bunch of us'll go to it tryin' to bring you down, but bring you down we will."

There were seven of them, with more coming. Kittins didn't like the situation and turned to run, only to find several more men at his back. "Won't be much of a reward with all these men," he told the crowd. "You'd better hope I reduce your numbers."

He struck. What else could he do? Surrender was as foreign to him as courtly dancing. And, yes, he did manage to kill a number of his assailants. But this time there were too, too many, rendering the result a foregone conclusion.

Kittins felt a crushing blow to the back of his head and blacked out.

When he came to, he was bound in enough rope to double his weight...and he was paralyzed.

"I believe he's awake," said the voice of an elderly woman. "Tilt him up so I can get a better look at him."

Kittins' feet plunged downward as his head whooshed into an upright position. He surmised that he was on a table of some fashion, designed to rotate up, down and around if its minders so desired. When his head cleared, he found himself in a large, stone chamber with a surprising amount of natural light. Not a dungeon, then. A figure crossed into view—Her Majesty— followed by another, Bailis, and a third, the Queen's Shaper.

"An ugly thing, isn't he? That little charm about his neck...is that what makes him so resilient?" the Queen inquired.

"That is correct, your Highness. But if you remove it..."

"I have no intention of removing it."

"You are aware that he expressed a desire, an intention to kill me."

The Queen turned to her Shaper and patted him condescendingly on the shoulder. "There, there, Cindor. I won't allow him to do any such thing."

Kittins wasn't sure, but he thought he detected a trace of irritation in the Shaper's visage.

"Why let him live?" Cindor asked. "Why keep him?"

Her Majesty turned towards her advisor. "If you found a new poison, my old friend, would you discard it immediately, or would you not rather squirrel it away somewhere, against a possible future need?"

"I believe this one's too dangerous for that," the Shaper responded.

"Ah," the Queen said, "But he'll find there's nothing in the world more dangerous than me."

There was something in her voice that made the statement unsettlingly credible.

Long's Team, at the Grave

Lots of dead humans; one, even, that was more a pile of mush than a corpse. But no Esmine. There, at least, was something to be hopeful about.

"That all o' them? Anyone find any more?" Long asked.

"That's all of them," said Rem. And thank Mahnus, he thought.

"What now?" said Spirk.

It was Yendor who answered. "We follow them tracks, o' course. Whoever survived this fight obviously took the girl along."

Long closed his eyes, focused on breathing. More searching, more endless travel. If Esmine weren't alive at the end of it... He'd drive himself mad if he kept thinking that way. Best to get moving. Move. Do. "Alright, lads. We follow."

At other times, in other places, and under other circumstances, there would have been grumbling, whining. Not here, not now. The other men dusted the grave dirt off their clothing, rinsed their hands in the same stream in which Jaddo had died, and climbed wearily back onto their equally weary mounts.

Time was, Spirk would've broken into song to wile away the miles. But that time was as dead as Mardine.

FOURTEEN

Vykers, Lunessfor

Vykers didn't remember much about the slog to Lunessfor. He'd been lost in his final conversation with Aoife, wondering how it went wrong and what he might've done differently. If he'd been a different man.

He expected to be turned away at the gate, but was not. That made no sense to him, unless, again, he was walking into a trap. He didn't care. Once inside, he emptied his pack and distributed the last of his money to his slaves.

"Now get the fuck away from me. You're all free!"

His slaves looked stricken. What had they done to be cast away like this? A few looked hurt, one or two looked lost. The red knight looked angry.

"What?" Vykers yelled at them. "You're free. Go away or I'll plant ya!" He waved his arms threateningly at them until they got the message.

The lone black man amongst the group seemed particularly aggrieved. What was he to do in a land where he was the only one of his kind and appeared, on the surface, so different from virtually everyone else? How might he explain himself, not knowing the language or customs? Vykers was indifferent. Last to go was the red knight, who simply shook his head in disapproval before walking away.

As soon as the slaves dispersed, a young boy, an urchin, approached and spoke to Vykers.

"I'll do whatever needs doin' for a few shim!" he proclaimed.

"Ha!" Vykers scoffed. "You're askin' the wrong man. I just gave all my coin away."

The boy squinted at him. "Say, you're the Reaper, ain'tcha?"

"And?"

"Can I take you anywheres? Steal you anything?"

After a moment's thought, Vykers responded, "You know the vintner's on Fage Street?"

"There's three o' them on Fage, Reaper."

"Well, I never been. Show me."

The boy was quick as a mouse dashing through the floorboards, but Vykers kept up. It was amazing what finally being healthy could do for a man. A quarter hour later, the boy pulled up outside a seedy looking business with a sign so weathered as to be almost unreadable.

Vykers poked his head in the door, eyed the man behind the counter and said to his guide, "This ain't it."

"This way, then," the boy replied happily.

Vykers wondered if the Frog had ever been to Lunessfor, and his mood darkened. Boy or not, if the Reaper ever got ahold of the Frog again, he'd...

"Here y'are," the boy said.

A much cleaner and better maintained business, this was. My luck, this won't be it, Vykers thought. And I'll have to trudge on to the last. But it was the place he was looking for. A quick peek through the door revealed a man Vykers knew well but hadn't seen in years.

"Two minutes, and I'll have some coin for you," he told the boy.

Inside the shop, the Reaper walked directly to the counter and stood patiently before a fat man in a small cap who was busily reading a large book. Incredibly, it took the merchant more than a minute to recognize Vykers' presence. When he did, he was sorry he'd been so long about it.

"Tarmun Vykers!" he giggled nervously.

"Quinsh," the Reaper replied, his voice dancing a fine line between humor and hostility.

"Come for a bottle of wine, have you?"

"You know I ain't. Where's my money?"

The vintner's nervous laugh became markedly more pronounced. "Your...ah...money. Yes, well, that's the thing..."

Vykers grabbed the fellow by his shirt collar and slowly, inexorably, dragged him up and over the counter.

"Last I heard, you were on your deathbed!" the vintner protested.

"Funny," Vykers said, "'Cause you're seconds from being on your own. Where's my money?"

"It's invested! I invested it! Much safer than hiding it somewhere!" The vintner was no longer laughing.

"Not for you, it ain't. I'll take everything you've got on hand, and I'll be back in a few days for the rest," said Vykers. "And don't try sneakin' off on me. It'd make me too happy to have to kill you."

He let go of Quinsh, who fell to the floor.

"I can get you a few thousand nobles right now," the man said. "And more next week."

"Get those nobles, and we'll see if you live 'til next week."

The vintner scrambled to his feet, dashed behind his counter and disappeared into the back room. It occurred to Vykers that Quinsh might attempt to escape out the back of the shop, but then he realized that not even Quinsh was that stupid. At last, the man emerged from the back room, holding a small wooden chest and looking much put out.

"I'll have a hard go of it until next week," he complained.

"You don't know shit about hardship," Vykers sneered as he grabbed at the proffered chest. Popping the lid, he saw the vintner had made good on his promise. "It's a start, fat man."

"Yes," Quinsh answered morosely.

"See you in a few days," Vykers said over his shoulder as he headed out into the street.

"Yes," Quinsh repeated with even greater sadness.

The boy was right where Vykers had left him; he tossed the kid a noble. "I reckon that's more money 'n you've seen in a month."

"Two!" The boy laughed.

"You can go celebrate now," Vykers suggested. "I won't be needin' your services anymore."

The boy looked a little crestfallen, but the gleam of the coin in his hand cheered him up again quickly. "Thanks, Reaper," he said. "You ain't as bad as they say."

"Insult me like that again, boy," Vykers joked, "And I'll rip yer arms off."

The boy ran off, chuckling.

Arune.

Vykers?

This enough coin to get you your own body?

It'll do.

What do we do next?

She told him.

Long's Crew, In Pursuit

The wagons that he believed were bearing Esmine headed north, a true and constant north. Long hoped he and his friends overtook their quarry before autumn was out; his history with snow had not been good, and he didn't relish the idea of battling through the cold of the wild north in winter.

He ruminated with some bitterness on the unfulfilled promises of the past spring, of a carefree time spent tending his apples and playing amongst the wildflowers with his wife and daughter, of the happy anticipation of an ample harvest in the fall and the comfort and security that would bring—all lost.

Long looked at the weathered and weary faces of his comrades, wondering which of them would survive this latest quest. As much as he loved his friends, he knew that the loss of any or all of them would be bearable if only he rescued his beloved Esmine. He supposed he ought to feel guilty for thinking this way, but his friends had been through a lot—together and apart—and they understood the risks in such an undertaking. Long loved them all the more for it, too.

On the horizon, the daunting silhouette of the Maestarul Mountains slowly rose into view.

What a horrible, lonely place to die, Long thought.

Vykers, Lunessfor

"I wanna see Her Majesty," was all he'd had to say at the gates of
the castle in order to gain admittance, which suggested Alheria
was expecting him. She was a goddess, after all.

After a lengthy walk, Vykers arrived outside the throne
room and was again ushered inside without much concern or
delay. The instant he walked through the doors, Alheria's voice
rang out.

"Well, well, well: here we are, again." This time, Her Majesty
sat in the great throne, making no pretense at being unable to
climb all the stairs leading up to it. Lurking in the shadows at its
base, the Queen's Shaper was just where he'd been the last time
the Reaper had visited this room.

"I see you're feelin' better," Vykers commented.

"I am, thank you," Alheria said. "And you seem healthier,
too."

Vykers unabashedly counted the guards around the room.
"What's a god need with so many swords and a Shaper?"

"These are dangerous times, Reaper. One can never be too
careful."

"Uh-huh."

"Was there something particular you wanted?" Alheria
inquired.

"I been thinkin' about how all o' this turned out."

"Ah. Thinking. There's your first mistake."

Was she goading him? Vykers couldn't tell. "And I think you
still owe me."

"Do you?" the Queen asked, in a way that suggested she
wasn't at all surprised by the statement.

"You healed me for settin' you free," Vykers went on, "but
you coulda healed me three years ago. Instead, you kept me
prisoner for all o' that time, even after I saved your kingdom
from the End. And before that, you had my hands and feet cut
off. Seems to me I've lost damn sight more 'n you over these last
few years and got little to show for it, whereas you still got your
throne."

"It's funny you should mention your hands and feet," Alheria responded, "because I've been working on a little surprise for you in that regard."

"Oh?" Vykers said, doing his best to feign disinterest. The Queen clapped her hands and four of the guards stepped closer to the dais on which her throne sat.

"I planted those little seeds of yours, and look what I've grown!"

She clapped her hands again and the guards raised their visors. All of them wore Vykers' face. At a third clap, each assumed a defensive stance.

"As a warrior, you may be without peer, Tarmun Vykers. But even you cannot defeat four of yourself."

Vykers—the original Vykers—didn't move. Not a muscle, not a hair. "You plannin' to sic these on me?"

"Not if you don't give me cause."

Fuckin' gods! "You mighta found some way to copy my body, but these boys ain't got my brains or experience."

Alheria leaned forward on the throne. "Would you care to test that?"

Common sense unexpectedly paid Vykers and visit, and he said nothing.

"Very well, then. I shall allow you to leave my castle—and my kingdom—unharmed, so long as you do leave and quickly."

Vykers didn't like letting the old windbag have the last word, but perhaps departing in silence would seem more ominous. He wasn't done with her, not by a longshot. With a final scowl in the Queen's direction, he turned on his heel and left the room.

I was afraid you might be tempted to attack those other Vykers, Arune interjected

There are *no other Vykers.*

No, I suppose not. Still, I'm glad you kept your head back there.

Sometimes, keepin' yer head is the only way to keep yer head.

Arune laughed. Philosophy, Vykers?

Call it whatever you want. We've got one last piece o' business…

Vykers lay on a cot, beside a second one which held the covered body of newly dead young woman. She'd apparently died of exposure overnight, and her body had still been warm when an A'Shea had been sent for. No one could bring her back, but…

There were two other people in the small, private room: a Shaper and an elderly A'Shea. Both walked in a circle around the two cots, chanting softly, though not in unison, towards Vykers and the covered body. It was a complicated arrangement, and one, Vykers felt, Arune must've have been working on for some time.

Hey, Burn, when'd you set all o' this up?

While you were lying in bed in the castle, a couple of years ago, it must be.

That long? Huh.

You have to let go, Vykers, Arune urged. *You have to consciously let go of me.*

Believe me, he replied, *this can't happen fast enough for me.*

Arune laughed. *You're going to miss me, Reaper, and you know it. We've done some great things together.*

Vykers grunted. *A few. That battle in Morden's Cairn was something, eh? When you blasted those dead bastards…*

You weren't half bad, yourself.

No.

And what about our fight with the End-of-All-Things?

Don't tell me you didn't love every second of it.

Well, Vykers admitted, *that was pretty damned fine.*

'Cept maybe the flyin' part.

Do you remember the look on the End's face, though, when you rose up to meet him?

It was Vykers' turn to chuckle. *He about shit a porcupine!*

Nice image, that.

You Shapers, always so sensitive.

But that work you did back on that lake bed, against all those other champions? That might have been your best work.

Mighta, Vykers agreed.

Shaper and warrior fell silent a moment, and then…

You will miss me, Vykers.

Maybe, he allowed. *Probably.*

That was as good as she'd get. *You'll feel drowsy*, she warned. *But none o' your burning and twitching, right?*

A warm lethargy overcame him. It was difficult to think what he should say next, difficult to care about it. Perhaps a brief rest...

Something was wrong, horribly, catastrophically wrong. Arune had gotten her own body at last, but...it was *Vykers'* body. The Reaper, with whom she'd shared it for years, was no longer in evidence, which could only mean he'd been sent to the other body, the one intended for the Shaper. It had to be the result of Brouton's Bind. Initially, this realization filled Arune with panic, but as she took the time to consider the situation, she began to see how it might work in her favor. Yes, Vykers had been a friend. Yes, they'd saved one another's lives. But a healthy and whole Vykers stood in the way of her ever attaining Aoife's affection. Unless *she* was Vykers. It was unthinkable, and yet... in the guise of the Reaper, she might just be able to insinuate herself into the A'Shea's good graces long enough to seduce the woman, long enough to ensure and cement an emotional and physical bond that might withstand whatever followed. No question, it was a despicable and desperate plan, and if Arune did not like to think of herself as despicable, she was certainly desperate. *Not my fault*, she told herself. *It's Brouton's Bind, which I wouldn't be suffering in the first place but for my efforts to keep Vykers alive*. Part of her—perhaps even the greater part—knew this to be a dodge, yet she couldn't help feeling this selfish impulse was also a result of Brouton's Bind, that it was behavior she'd learned from the Reaper and not something she'd come to on her own.

For a moment, she feared Vykers' wrath, but it seemed beyond unlikely the new Vykers could catch and punish her. She was the Reaper, and he was...an adolescent girl.

Once more, she weighed her options. Once more she concluded that her need for Aoife overruled all other considerations. She would either have what she wanted, or she would have nothing.

Vykers thrashed about on his cot, bedeviled with ague and fever dreams, often approaching but never quite achieving consciousness. Eventually, he shivered himself awake and saw that he was alone in the room. He also understood in an instant that something—everything—was wrong. His body was weak, sickly, light as a feather and...female.

He leapt for the door, found it locked.

"Open this fuckin' door right now!" he shrieked in a voice he didn't recognize, a voice too small, too frail to serve his great anger. In a white-hot rage, he flung himself against the door, intending to smash it open, but the door rebuffed him and seemed to laugh at his new, slighter frame. Again, he threw his shoulder into the door; again, it proved uninterested in his desires. What's more, his efforts left Vykers's new body throbbing in pain. It was clear the world would no longer respond to him as it once had. He could no longer subdue threats and overcome obstacles with physical might. "Arune!" he screamed. "Arune, damn you! Open this door!"

Arune did not come, nor did anyone else.

Vykers returned to the cot and lay down. He rolled onto his back and stared up at the ceiling, attempting to calm himself, as he'd used to do in the Queen's castle. He held a delicate hand in front of his face and examined it. If he hadn't been so angry, so tired, he might have laughed at that absurdity of it all. He was a Mahnus-be-damned woman! What in the infinite hells was he supposed to do now?

As he lay there, pondering this disaster, he fell asleep. When he awoke, he noticed the door was slightly ajar. Accepting that his new body would not allow him bull rush his way out of the building, he got quietly to his feet and crept towards the exit, expecting at any moment to see it slam shut again. When it did not, he eased the aperture wider and poked his head into the hallway beyond. It seemed he was quite alone.

Had this been a set up from the get-go? It was hard to believe Arune was capable of such a thing, but what else could it be? And if the Shaper had betrayed him...

He wanted to find someone, anyone, and punish that person for the treachery he'd just endured. He wanted to slaughter, to paint the walls, floors and ceiling with the blood and entrails of those who'd betrayed him. But while he knew his usual body could handle any number of opponents and sustain massive amounts of damage without faltering, he doubted his current form could withstand the attentions of a single assailant. In short, he was more vulnerable than he'd ever been. If this body died…

Finally, Vykers made his way out of the building and into the light of an autumn afternoon, a few hours shy of sundown. It was the first time he'd gotten a really good look at himself. Or herself. He was a tiny slip of a thing, little more than fifteen or sixteen years of age, wearing a homespun shift that provided scant cover and less warmth. Vykers felt he might blow away on the next breeze.

Well, he thought, there's no rush to leave town now, is there? It was not as if Her Majesty or any of her attendants would recognize the Reaper anymore, anyway. And he still had quite a bit of gold coming from the vintner later in the week. True, the little girl he'd become would have to collect it on the Reaper's behalf, but he didn't think even Quinsh was stupid enough to refuse Vykers' messenger. And with that gold, he could secure food, shelter, better clothing, perhaps even information about where Arune had gone.

Oh, he would find the Shaper, and no mistake.

Struggling to make sense of his predicament, the Reaper wandered back and forth across the city and, ultimately, out onto the Tronsbridge. He watched the sun set over the south fork of the Aumbre, just outside the gates of Lunessfor. It struck him that in the last month or so he'd lost what few friends he'd had, his woman, his Shaper, his magic sword, and even his body. His body, for Mahnus' sake! He still had his spirit, though, his soul. And an endless supply of rage.

He had never been more dangerous.

Appendix A

Cast of Characters

Tarmun Vykers, A.K.A, "the Reaper"—a legendary warrior
Aoife (pronounced EE-FUH)—An A'Shea or "Mender"
Cindor—The Queen's Shaper
Hoosh Bindy—The Queen's Fool
Three—A chimera and friend of Vykers
The Historian, A.K.A, "the Ahklatian"—An ancient sage and Shaper
Tadpole, A.K.A. "the Frog"—a boy under Aoife's care
Long, A.K.A, Long Pete, A.K.A. "Captain Peter Fendesst"—a retired soldier and husband to Mardine
Mardine—A giantess, wife to Long and mother to Esmine.
Esmine—Their daughter
Nelby—Their thrall servant
Jaddo—Nelby's lover
Tresa—A former thrall
Captain Kittins—A Captain in Her Majesty's Army
Yendor Plotz—A drunk and friend to Long
Spirk Nessno—An idiot and friend to Long
Remuel Wratch, A.K.A. "Rem,"—a famous actor
Keez—An actor in Rem's company
Lord Darley Gault—Patriarch of House Gault
Lord Henton Hawsey—Patriarch of House Hawsey
Lady Hawsey—His oversexed wife
Colonel Bailis—An officer in Her Majesty's Army and Kittins' Commanding Officer
Gelter Radcliffe—A member of House Radcliffe, author of a particular book

Esmun Janks—One-time friend to Long Pete and employee of House Thornton

Chade (Pronounced SHADE) Thornton—Patriarch of House Thornton

Lord Titus D'Escurzy—Patriarch of House D'Escurzy

Faenia D'Escurzy—Niece to Lord Titus

Briedach D'Escurzy—Cousin of Lord Titus

Peppers—A prisoner in the dungeons of House Thornton

Moult—Yendor's drinking companion

Kendell—Chief of Security at House Blackbyrne

Cargon—An old farmer

Leetsa—His wife

Endu-Ro—A satyr

Toomt-La—Another satyr

The Great Eight:

House Fyne (Infiltrated by Yendor)

Moult, a guard

House Thornton (Infiltrated by Long)

Chade Thornton—Patriarch of House Thornton

House Gault (Infiltrated by Kittins)

Lord Darley Gault—Patriarch of House Gault

Wrensl Deda—a guard

House Blackbyrne (Attacked by Kittins)

Kendell—Chief of Security at House Blackbyrne

House Hawsey (Infiltrated by Rem)

Lord Henton Hawsey—Patriarch of House Hawsey

Lady Hawsey—His oversexed wife

House Radcliffe (Infiltrated by Rem)

Gelter Radcliffe—A member of House Radcliffe

House D'Escurzy (Infiltrated by Spirk)

Lord Titus D'Escurzy—Patriarch of House D'Escurzy

Faenia D'Escurzy—Niece to Lord Titus

Briedach D'Escurzy—Cousin of Lord Titus

Ron "Death Bow"—a guard

House Amberly (Damaged by Yendor)

Appendix B

A Guide to Character Name Pronunciation

Author's note:

If you've read this far, these are your characters as much as mine. You may imagine their names however you'd like. This list is really for the sticklers amongst us.

Tarmun Vykers = Tahr-muhn Vahy-kurz
Aoife = Ee-fuh
Arune = Uh-roon
Mardine = Mahr-deen
Omeyo = Oh-mey-oh
Mahnus = Mahn-us
Alheria = Uh-lair-ee-uh
Eoman = Ay-mun
Karrakan = Care-i-cun
Innoman = Inn-o-mun
Eyatu = Ay-ah-too
Ahklatian = Uh-kley-shuhn

Curious about other Crossroad Press books?
Stop by our site:
http://store.crossroadpress.com
We offer quality writing
in digital, audio, and print formats.

Enter the code FIRSTBOOK
to get 20% off your first order from our store!
Stop by today!

www.ingramcontent.com/pod-product-compliance
Lightning Source LLC
Chambersburg PA
CBHW070614260626
47161CB00007B/2434